A GENTLE OCCUPATION

A
GENTLE
OCCUPATION

by DIRK BOGARDE

Alfred A. Knopf 🐇 *New York 1980*

THIS IS A BORZOI BOOK

PUBLISHED BY ALFRED A. KNOPF, INC.

Copyright © 1980 by Labofilms S.A.
All rights reserved under International and
Pan-American Copyright Conventions.
Published in the United States by Alfred A. Knopf, Inc., New York.
Distributed by Random House, Inc., New York.
Originally published in Great Britain by Chatto & Windus, London.

The poem 'The 'Eathen' by Rudyard Kipling, from which the extract is quoted on page 247, is published by Macmillan & Co. The excerpt from the poem 'Renouncement' on page 183 by Alice Meynell is published by the Bodley Head.

The song 'Our Love Affair' quoted on page 78 is from the film *Strike Up the Band* (words and music by Arthur Freed and Rodger Edens, published by Leo Feist, Inc., New York). 'As Time Goes By,' the song quoted on pages 134–35, comes from the film *Casablanca* (words and music by Herman Hupfeld, © 1931 Warner Bros. Inc. Copyright renewed. All rights reserved. Used by permission).

Library of Congress Cataloging in Publication Data
Bogarde, Dirk [date]
A gentle occupation.   I. Title.
PZ4.B6743Ge   1980   [PR6052.O3]   823'.9'14   79-3617
ISBN 0-394-51121-2

Manufactured in the United States of America
First American Edition

*This book is for
Norah Smallwood,
who said, 'Try . . .'*

Author's Note

This is strictly a work of fiction based on one real fact. In 1945, a few weeks after the official ending of the War, some units of the British and Indian armies, counting the days to their repatriation, found themselves involved in trying 'to hold the ring' in the crumbling Dutch Empire in South-East Asia, and suffered heavy casualties in killed, wounded and missing.

None of us knew quite what to expect in this extraordinary peace-time-war which lasted for a little over a year, but we did know, as someone else has said, that we were engaged in 'a mission of mercy in an appalling mess'.

The bravery and courage of those units, and also of the Dutch civilians, is not, I think, much remembered today nearly thirty-five years later.

However, the Island of this book and its inhabitants, the Division and its personnel, are all entirely imaginary and exist, or existed, only in my mind.

Any resemblance to any single person, alive or dead, is quite coincidental; they are all my own inventions.

I am greatly indebted to Peter Cochrane DSO, MC for vetting the manuscript and offering invaluable advice on a number of points, and to Mrs Sally Betts, who has bravely struggled through my errors and corrections for fourteen long months.

D.v.d.B.

A Map of the City

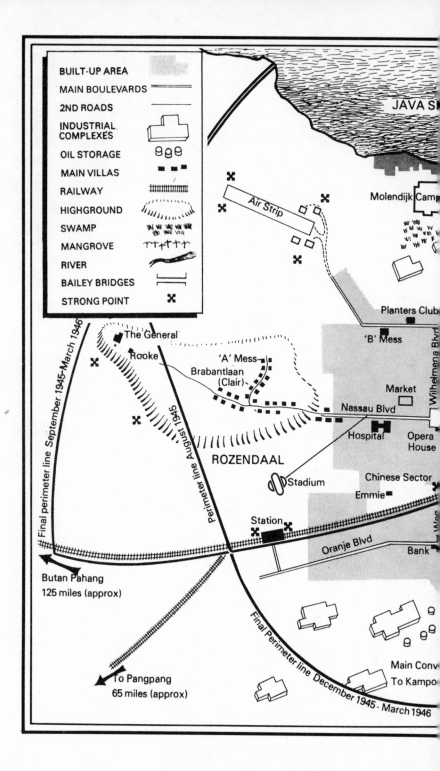

BUILT-UP AREA
MAIN BOULEVARDS
2ND ROADS
INDUSTRIAL COMPLEXES
OIL STORAGE
MAIN VILLAS
RAILWAY
HIGHGROUND
SWAMP
MANGROVE
RIVER
BAILEY BRIDGES
STRONG POINT

JAVA S[ ]

Molendijk Cam[ ]

Air Strip

Planters Club

'B' Mess

Final perimeter line September, 1945–March 1946

The General

Rooke

'A' Mess

Brabantlaan (Clair)

Nassau Blvd

Market

Wilhelmena Blvd

Perimeter line August 1945

Hospital

Opera House

ROZENDAAL

Stadium

Chinese Sector

Emmie

Station

Oranje Blvd

Bank

Butan Pahang
125 miles (approx)

To Pangpang
65 miles (approx)

Final Perimeter line December 1945 - March 1946

Main Conv[ ]

To Kampo[ ]

A Map of the City

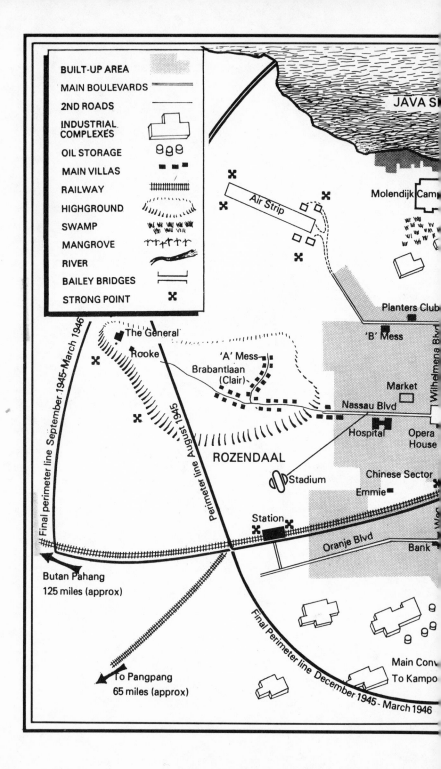

BUILT-UP AREA

MAIN BOULEVARDS

2ND ROADS

INDUSTRIAL COMPLEXES

OIL STORAGE

MAIN VILLAS

RAILWAY

HIGHGROUND

SWAMP

MANGROVE

RIVER

BAILEY BRIDGES

STRONG POINT

JAVA S

Air Strip

Molendijk Cam

Planters Club

'B' Mess

The General

Rooke

'A' Mess

Brabantlaan (Clair)

Market

Nassau Blvd

Hospital

Opera House

ROZENDAAL

Stadium

Chinese Sector

Emmie

Final perimeter line September 1945–March 1946

Perimeter line August 1945

Station

Oranje Blvd

Bank

Butan Pahang
125 miles (approx)

To Pangpang
65 miles (approx)

Final Perimeter line December 1945 – March 1946

Main Conv

To Kampo

Wilhelmena Blvd

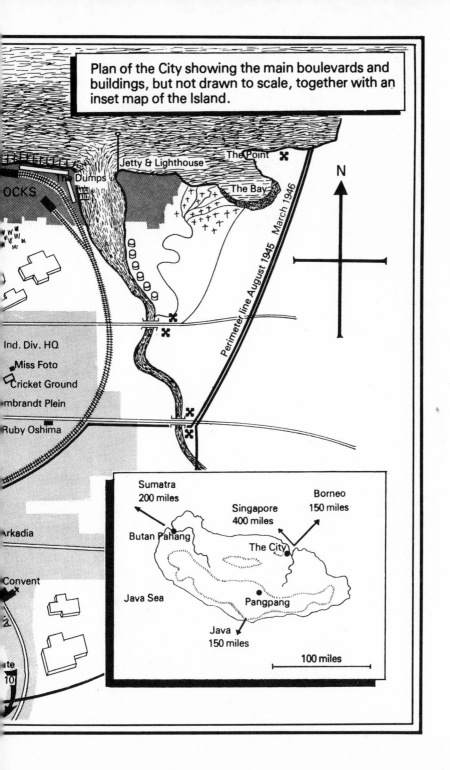

Plan of the City showing the main boulevards and buildings, but not drawn to scale, together with an inset map of the Island.

The Point

Jetty & Lighthouse

The Dumps

The Bay

OCKS

Perimeter line August 1945   March 1946

N

Ind. Div. HQ

Miss Foto

Cricket Ground

mbrandt Plein

Ruby Oshima

Sumatra
200 miles

Borneo
150 miles

Singapore
400 miles

Butan Pahang

The City

rkadia

Java Sea

Convent

Pangpang

te
10

Java
150 miles

100 miles

A GENTLE OCCUPATION

CHAPTER ONE

The engines had stopped half an hour ago while he was strapping up his bed-roll, and the ending of the comforting throb and shudder had brought a sudden astonishing silence. He had stuck a finger in his ear, cracked his jaw, shaken his head. The ship had died. A heart-beat stilled. Then feet thudded along the steel deck above, water lapped and swirled, someone came clattering hurriedly down a companionway calling indistinct orders, a metal door slammed and killed the voice. He humped the bed-roll onto the narrow bunk which Weathersby had vacated at first light. One thing he was glad about the trip ending was no more Weathersby. He hadn't liked him from the moment they had picked him up, halfway down the coast, at Penang. Pasty-faced, small, veined hands, issue-glasses, nervous, dull. He had hardly ever spoken on the rest of the voyage, lost in *Forever Amber,* until last night when he had left the wardroom with a whispered 'Goodnight, going to pack . . .' and they'd all sighed with relief. Someone said he was like an albatross — but they at least had dignity.

Rooke reached up, took his washing-bag and drew the string tight. Above his head ropes hissed and rasped and, as the ship swung gently against the dock, nudging it softly like a flirt, a column of sunlight sprang through the porthole, raking the bulkhead with glittering ripples of reflected water, probing across the rusting bolts and hasty welding of the steel plates; an oval spotlight in a provincial pantomime looking for the Demon King.

He stuffed the wash-bag, his diary and a full tin of State Express cigarettes into his hold-all, buttoned it firmly and slung it over a shoulder. The ship lurched suddenly as it struck the wooden dockside, and juddered to a final stop. Slowly he traced his finger across the stencilled name faded into the canvas bed-roll. How new it had all looked six years ago in the Army & Navy Stores in Victoria. Now soiled and rain-stained, the leather straps scuffed, buckles dulled; a loyal, welcoming companion from Arromanches to Cox's Bazar. The once bold figures of his rank, name and number fading into the worn buff canvas. Capt. B. A. Rooke. 269237.

'You must call him Benjamin, promise me?' his mother had said.

'As you like, darling'—his father, kind, worried.

'After my brother . . .'

'And Andrew after my father . . . keep the family line.'

'Benjamin Andrew . . . that's all right. Promise?'

'I promise.'

'You are good to me. I'm sorry I've been so tiresome . . .'

'You haven't, you haven't, my love.'

'He was rather a struggle for me.'

'I know . . . I know, but it's all over.'

'All over. I'm so dreadfully tired, you see . . .'

And she had died early in the evening. But his father had kept the promise and so there he was now, tracing the name, Benjamin, Andrew, Rooke-with-an-E.

Tip-toeing feet, the door swung open and Weathersby's hatted head, the sunlight from the spotlight glittering on the blank discs of his steel glasses. He looked blind. 'We're in, you know.' He crossed the tiny cabin and started fumbling about on his cluttered bunk hopelessly. 'I think I left my hanky somewhere here . . .' He heaved the bed-roll onto the deck, found the crumpled bit of red-checked cotton, wiped his neck carefully. 'It's hot already up there. Can I give you a hand with your stuff? The rest of mine's all up top.'

The deck of the LST was crowded with suddenly hurrying people, ropes looped, crates and sacks, men stepping over a wide scurry of rice which had spilled and scattered into the scuppers.

'Whose fucking gear is this then?' someone yelled and kicked a suitcase under a lifeboat.

Weathersby gave a little scream and hurried aft, holding his glasses as he ran. 'It's mine! It's mine!'

From the rail Rooke looked down onto the dockside. Barrels and boxes, wandering Indonesians, scraps of cloth round their heads, flapping shorts, jeeps and trucks, a long line of godowns, roofs gaping, windows scorched with fans of soot, iron girders twisted into rusty, buckled loops. To the left a great column of smoke, black and oily, rising slowly into the still, blue morning sky, a slow-growing cauliflower of immense height, the highest billows lethargically drifting and loitering as they caught the

2

offshore air and veiled out over the distant spires and roofs of the city shimmering in the sun. To the right cranes, railway trucks rusted, a half-demolished building with a metal sign 'Rotterdam Lloyd' tilted squint like a fallen brooch.

Pushing his way through the milling half-naked Indonesians with the aid of a neat little swagger cane with which he lightly cracked every obtrusive body in his path, came a British officer crisp in starched Jungle Greens and a bright crimson lanyard. He stopped at the side of the LST and shouted up, waving a piece of paper which he then used to shield his eyes from the glare of the sun.

'Hi there! Anyone on board? Captain Rooke and, or, a Lieutenant Weathersby? I'm from 95 Indian Div. Come to collect them.'

'I'm Rooke . . . Weathersby's somewhere about. I think he's lost a suitcase.'

'Oh bugger it. You got a lot of gear? I've only brought a jeep, I'm afraid.'

'Bed-roll, tin trunk for me . . . same I suppose for Weathersby. I'll go and find him.'

He was still aft by the lifeboat fumbling with his luggage, his cap off. 'They've gone and bust the lock. Rotten sods. No feeling for people's things.'

He grabbed his cap and stuck it back on and humped the suitcase down the deck. 'I'll have to get a bit of string or something . . . can't trust it on one lock.'

'Haven't time for that now.' Rooke was mild. 'There's a chap from the Division here to collect us . . . do it when we get ashore.'

'But everything I have is in here! Books, music, my chess set . . .'

'Oh for God's sake get a move on, he's waiting.'

But he had come aboard, swagger stick tapping the iron rail, hand stroking a small eager moustache. 'There you are then. Had a bit of trouble?'

Weathersby shrugged, 'Someone kicked it about. Broke a lock, I think. I need a bit of string or something . . . you haven't seen a bit, have you, anywhere?' He peered about the crowded, rice-strewn deck, his glasses misting with anger and heat.

The officer with the stick put out his hand. 'Pullen,' he said

3

brightly. 'We'll have it fixed when you get to your billet . . . got to dash now . . . I'll get some Japs to bundle this stuff down for you and then we really must be off.' He yelled down orders to someone on the cobbles below, and with Rooke and Weathersby following made his way down the gangplank and set off for his jeep. A chattering group of Japanese POW's hurried past them, naked save for baggy white loin cloths, enormous rubber-soled boots and long-peaked khaki caps which gave them the immediate appearance of a flock of panicking ducks.

With Weathersby clutching his bursting suitcase and miserably squashed in the back of the jeep alongside the bed-rolls and tin trunks they bounced over the railway tracks, and headed away from the ship. Rooke looked sharply back wondering how long it would be before he would be returning. It looked extremely small and frail. He felt a sudden surge of panic at its loss. A severance with something he knew, felt was secure, safe. The future, as he sat beside the cheerful but harassed Pullen steering through the seething masses of Asia and the buckled railway lines of the Dutch East Indies Company, seemed filled with the gravest uncertainties.

'Where are we bound for?' He tried to keep his voice flat and disinterested although he had to raise it above the blaring of the horn and the noise of the crowds about them.

'Well, fact is, I'm taking Lieutenant What'sisname up to "B" Mess till they sort him out . . . they're putting you in "A" Mess for the time being because there's more room, but I can't take you there, I'm afraid . . . dropping you off at the Planters' Club in town. Major Nettles says he'll give you a lift . . . he's GI and he's up in "A" Mess, you see. It's all a bit confusing really, but we only got the bumph that you were arriving a day or so ago and there's been a bit of a flap on here, as you probably know. No one expected you, I'm afraid, the same old Army Fuck Up of course . . . but what with a nasty flare up on the perimeter last night — that smoke over there is from the rubber dump they hit — AND the Dakota business. I'm afraid it's all a bit of a rumble bumble.'

They had left the dock area now and were driving along a dead straight road, full of potholes and rickshaws. Rooke was not sure which were more dangerous. 'What's the Dakota business?' he asked, clutching the side of the jeep and trying to hold himself out of the seat as they crashed into a foot-deep hole.

Pullen looked at him swiftly. 'Haven't heard? Oh . . . well, one of our Dakotas, we only have three in operation anyway for the moment, made a forced landing on Tuesday just outside the city. Beyond the perimeter. Coming up from Pangpang with twenty refugees, women and children. All Dutch. No one was actually hurt, we gather, landed neatly in paddy fields . . . but the bloody extremists got there before we could get the convoy out and massacred the lot. Chopped them all to bits; twenty women and children, eight of our blokes and the crew. We finally got through yesterday morning; all buried in a mass grave in a banana plantation near a kampong called Kutt. Appropriately. We forced an old woman to tell us . . . she had seen the whole thing. Senseless. Bloody senseless. All this in the name of Freedom. I ask you. You'll see the signs everywhere. A damn great dagger clutched in a fist. All painted in crimson with drops of blood and *"Merdeka"* written underneath. On every wall, all over the shop. Freedom. God! I thought we'd finished with the war, our lot that is, after Imphal . . . but this is a bloody sight worse. A civil war. We can't shoot until they shoot first, we're sort of bloody Civil Servants in a civil war getting the Dutch out of the prison camps and back to Singapore or Holland . . . like armed Red Cross. We aren't soldiers at all.'

He swerved, and cursed, to avoid two colliding bicyclists and drove faster along the dead straight road. On either side the land was flat, marshy; mangrove and swamp with rubbish tips and crumbled buildings long abandoned. Tall chimney-stacks poked into the brilliant sky but flew no pennants of smoke; speckled brown hawk-like birds swooped and dipped over the stinking heaps of rubbish, power lines trailed and sagged into the boggy land; army lorries rumbled among the rickshaws and cyclists in a constant stream from city to docks; runty-backed dogs with saffron eyes padded through the traffic; and thin laughing girls dressed in tattered white cotton shifts ran to and fro dragging wailing children trailing kites. It was all hazed with the acrid, black fumes from the burning rubber dump across the city. A kind of oriental Munch landscape. Rooke felt a numbing despair and unease.

The jeep bucketed and bounced over the potholes. Pullen was driving too fast in reflex anger.

'How many planes, I mean apart from the three, I mean *two*, Dakotas have we got here?' Rooke had to raise his voice again because they had reached the beginning of a built-up area and the shouts and cries and ringing of rickshaw bells and horns blowing made normal conversation impossible. Pullen started to slow down among the jostling crowds and carts.

'How many what? Planes? Oh none. None at all . . . just the Dakotas. I mean no bombers, fighters, that kind of thing . . . no airfield proper either yet, a grass landing strip that's all. Nearest RAF crowd are up at Seletar on Singapore Island. We're just an Evacuation centre, got the Dakotas from our generous American cousins; this should have been their bloody area but after the Surrender they handed it all over to us, said it was our area really on account of Malaya being British . . . they're busy looking after the Philippines and colonizing bloody Japan with Coca Cola and chewing gum. Why do you ask?'

Rooke shifted in his bucket seat and thrust his hands under his buttocks to cushion the blows from the potholes. 'That's my job. Air Photographic Interpreter . . . attached to the RAF all through the war.'

Pullen laughed shortly, slowed down and made signs that he was turning right at a busy crossroads. 'Lost your job, chum. Nothing like that for you to do here . . . no planes, no bugger all. Just a few clapped out Dakotas and happy bands of Freedom-loving nig-nogs armed with pangas and grenades. You'd better think up some new qualifications.'

The right turn at the crossroads had brought them into the European part of the city. Shops along the broad street, trees, two- and three-storey buildings, plaster cracked, red tiles chipped, some windows boarded, signs in Dutch, Urdu, Chinese and Malay. There were few Europeans on the pavements, soldiers for the most part, walking in twos, one blonde woman moving easily, hair blowing, skirt flapping, a large straw basket in her hand full of green fruit; ahead of them, on the right, a shimmer of palm trees, a frangipani; above them a tall white pole from which drooped in the morning air a red and yellow flag with a coiled snake in white. The jeep turned in between two tall pillars. A roughly printed sign on one. 'Officers' Club.

6

95 Ind. Div.' It was a white concrete 1930-Mussolini-Modern building, marble steps from the tired gravel forecourt, two urns of battered sansevieria, a torn awning.

As they crunched to a stop, Weathersby thrust a clenched fist between them. His voice was hoarse with fury and dust. 'A black bishop. You see? *Whole* suitcase has come apart . . . chessmen all over the place, and my books . . . all that bouncing about . . . no consideration. I'll have to repack the lot now. Got to collect the things . . .'

Pullen swung out of his seat as an Indian corporal came hurrying down the steps and cried out orders for the luggage to be unloaded. Rooke climbed out stiffly, joining Pullen on the marble flight. Weathersby was still grovelling about as the tin trunks were slid off and the bed-rolls manhandled down. Pullen called out to him to wait where he was. 'Just for a tick. I'll see that Captain Rooke is taken care of and then we'll be off. Won't be a jiffy.' He ran a finger over his eager little moustache. Weathersby, a hand full of pawns and knights, didn't look up.

The hall was long, lofty, cool, floored with wide black and white tiles. Their boots clacked between the little rush mats set here and there along its length. To right and left tall open double doors, with shadowy rooms beyond, fans turning gently in the high ceilings. Ahead a staircase leading up in a curve to the broad gallery which overhung the hallway supported by ugly, functional, concrete brackets. Up the stairs, clinging close to the curving wall, a short centipede of young women in bright floral dresses, mostly Chinese as far as Rooke could tell, chittering and whispering, patting short black hair, poking in a flower here and there or a pink celluloid comb. They watched the two men curiously as they passed them in sudden falls of silence. At the top Pullen stopped.

'I think he must still be interviewing by the look of things. Nettles, I mean. You nip down and wait in the Bar . . . have a cold beer. I'll tell him you're here. I really *must* get back to the Mess.' He hurried along to the head of the queue, tapped on a door, waited a moment and then went in, closing it firmly in the face of a Chinese girl who laughed and stuck out her tongue. The others tittered behind quickly-raised hands and then fell silent, watching Rooke as he started down past them to the hall. Near the bottom something slipped and clattered onto the tiled

7

steps. To avoid tripping he grabbed at the iron railing and stepped over a musical instrument. It lay there rocking slightly.

'I'm sorry. It's mine.' A cool, clear voice, a long slender arm which retrieved it swiftly. She was taller than the other girls and not Chinese. Long dark hair to her shoulders, wide well-spaced brown eyes, straight brow, pleasant mouth unsmiling. In the crook of her other arm, thrust from a boy's white shirt, a battered music-case. She held the two possessions close to her as if he might possibly request them. He smiled.

'A banjo?'

'A mandolin.'

'Ah. You speak English?'

'Just a little.'

'Noël Coward always said that was never quite enough.'

A flat, long look. Quite blank.

'An English actor.'

'So.'

'Playwright too . . .'

'I see.'

He reached out suddenly and touched one of the strings. It twanged softly.

'Can you play this?'

The arm with the music-case moved swiftly and the hand thrust a strand of dark hair over her shoulder. When she spoke her voice was light, accentless almost, dismissive.

'No. I cook in it.'

The Chinese girl beside her suddenly squealed, cramming two fists quickly to her mouth to smother the sound. No one spoke. He removed his cap.

'I'm looking for the Bar actually . . . anyone know where it is?'

The girl who had squealed removed her fists and pointed down the stairs. 'In big doors there. Left. Many chairs and tables. You go there.'

He thanked her gravely. The girl with the mandolin had turned away; he went down slowly.

A dim room, tables scattered, cane and bamboo chairs in shabby, faded cretonnes. Brass pots with still, spiky palms. A Turkey carpet worn to holes. A long bar with a brass rail and a clutter of bashed leather-topped stools empty at its side. In the

8

ceiling six ugly glass cubist lighting fixtures hung like pink and amber stalactites. Someone had fired a gun at one of them which swung mournfully between the slowly revolving fans, starred with jagged black holes. The place smelled of stale beer and old carpet. An Indian barman in a tired white jacket and a pale blue muslin turban poured him a pint of beer and he carried it to one of the little tables and sat in a cane chair, which sagged. Among the cigarette burns on his table and an ash-tray full of last night's butts, a crumpled double paged news-sheet; the print smudged and blurred. *The Daily Cobra*. 95th Indian Division. No. 36. 'Dakota Passengers Massacred.' A crossword puzzle, small news items from agencies; in the centre, a grey speckled photograph of Henley Bridge. 'In England's Green and Pleasant Land.'

He pushed it from him and drank half the beer in one gulp. Pullen came hurriedly into the empty room, signalled the blue-turbaned Indian, slumped into the cretonne-covered chair opposite him, and laid his cap and swagger-stick on the news-sheet.

'He'll be down in a jiffy. Christ!' he fanned himself with a neat hand. 'Gin Sling. Much ice. Interviewing women. I ask you. We're bloody Civil Servants, told you that. Secretaries for a fighting Division, what next, I ask? The Chindwin, Kohima, Imphal . . . now we're dealing with lost Mums and Dads, mis-laid children, looted property, rights of way, forged papers, indents for everything from shit-house paper to bully beef; didn't tell us this at Sandhurst. No one prepared, no one armed, not enough small-arms, and the petrol's a bloody problem. We're a lot of squalid Quartermasters: until they shoot up the bloody perimeter.' He sat upright in the cane chair, indigna-tion and, to a certain degree, helplessness forcing his hand to shake as he stirred the knobbly ice cubes in his glass. He took a long pull, wiped his moustache and smiled suddenly. His eyes crinkled at the sides in lines of weariness. 'Sorry. Getting it off my chest . . . most boring of me. You'll settle down soon enough . . .'

Rooke took out his cigarette case, offered it across the cluttered table.

'No. Have a pipe when I want a smoke, thanks all the same, can't stay long . . . better get that chap What'sisname up to the

9

Mess. He's a bit of a pill, what? All that chess stuff, the suit-case . . . sooner he's bunged off the better, I've a feeling, although God knows what they'll do with him down at Pang-pang or wherever they send him. What did he do? Never thought to ask. Intelligence, I wouldn't wonder.'

'So was I.'

'So is Nettles . . . brilliant too. Takes all kinds.' He finished the half of his drink and collected his cap and cane. 'Must go.' He rose, pulled down his bush jacket, patted his pockets. 'Forgot you were Air Photographic. Not a chance here, old boy, you'll have to re-think your qualifications, as I said. This is not really a fighting war and we haven't a bloody air force. See you around, I hope? I'll get What'sisname up to the Mess. Nettles will take care of you after he's interviewed his ruddy girls . . .' He crossed hurriedly to the door, turned suddenly and called to the barman. 'Chitty, Pram . . . on me the drinks, tikh hai?' and with a vague laugh he called, 'Good luck!' and left the bar.

The fans click-clacked mournfully but caused so little dis-turbance in the still air that the smoke from his cigarette meandered gently about his head.

'Diplomatic perhaps? Would you like that? Interesting job.' His father straight-backed on the horse beside him.

'No qualifications, Pa.'

'Oh, I don't know . . . French and German . . . bit of Latin. Got the presence. Got that from your mother. Good manners, good school, discretion . . .'

'Not awfully keen. Politics: not my area really.' He tapped his thigh with his crop.

'Be a war in a couple of years, you know; you'd just have time, I know a couple of strings I could pull if you liked?'

'No, not Diplomatic really.'

'Well what then? University? Cambridge perhaps . . .'

'An actor as a matter of fact.'

His father leant forward suddenly and patted the piebald neck before him.

'Sweet God! What for?'

'It's what I want to do, I think.'

'But do you *know*? I mean, when? How?'

10

'Oh you remember. You saw me. *Much Ado, The Merchant, Coriolanus.*'

'My dearest boy! School plays, for God's sake!'

'I was good.'

'Splendid . . . but not for a lifetime.'

'I think so.'

'It'd be such a frightful waste. Your education, background . . .'

'Actors need those too, you know.'

'Bobby Howes, Sonny Hale, Jack Hulbert, that sort of thing?'

'No. John Gielgud, Stephen Haggard, Laurence Olivier.'

'Oh. Don't know 'em. "Not knowing can't tell", as Nanny would say . . . I think you've got a touch of the sun perhaps?' he laughed uneasily.

'No . . . really not. I'm *sure* you know, truly. Sorry.'

The piebald stamped and swished its tail, arching its neck in irritation.

'Horse flies, bloody brutes.' His father turned swiftly in his saddle. 'Talk about this at dinner, shall we? Race you to the brook . . .'

He watched him canter down the slope, the wind billowing in the back of his shirt as a tall, elegant figure in jungle-green paused in the open doors. He rose instantly to meet him thinking him to resemble, facially at any rate, a splendid horse. Or was it just that he had been thinking of horses? A long face, long nose, high brow and when he smiled, as he did now, long white teeth. The hand, when he took it in greeting, was also long, strong: supple fingers, a firm pressure. The grey eyes which appraised him swiftly, were good, clear, deep-set.

'You must think me wildly dilatory. I'm frightfully sorry . . . *such* a wait for you . . .' They moved to the untidy table, the barman already there, hands clasped, a golden smile flashing, head bobbing at familiar pleasure. 'Another beer, was it? And my usual, Pram, steady with the Worcester Sauce. Do sit . . . too exhausting this morning.' He crossed long thin legs and placed his cap on the table where Pullen's had been. 'Geoffrey Nettles. And you're Rook with an "E". Am I right? I've got all your bumph here somewhere . . .' He patted a neat black leather case and flicked the locks open, rummaging about in a scurry of papers. Unable to find what he wanted he snapped the case shut, placed it on the floor, folded his arms and smiled the white-toothed smile. 'Too boring. Can't find it all now . . . we'll sort it out later. Oh! I *die* for my Bloody Mary, I really do. You've come from Calcutta, I gather?'

'Sort of. Via Cox's Bazar and every other port down the coast.'

'Too boring . . . Oh!' He reached up with long blunt fingers for his drink, raised it briefly in a toast, and sipped. 'How delicious! I'm totally drained.' He set the glass carefully on the table and fished for a cigarette in his pocket, accepting one from Rooke who had anticipated the thought. 'Thank you . . . the whole morning interviewing *the* most idiotic girls. All Chinese and all swearing blind that they can speak, type and write English perfectly. None of them can, all nice and willing but *utterly* peasant. Did you see them? Legs like Indian Clubs and frightfully hairy arms.'

Rooke nodded. 'Saw them when we arrived. I wondered who they were.'

Nettles examined his cigarette with care. 'Secretaries. For a civil war. Pullen told you, I suppose? The whole Island is in ferment. We've landed in a kind of hornets' nest. Maddening really. Those damned Americans gave us Java, Borneo, Sumatra and this Paradise Island in a sort of job-lot. No one was prepared for any of it, least of all us, as usual. What we really need are some nice bright Dutch ladies to help out, they all speak English and write it. But . . .' he sighed sadly and took up his glass.

'Won't they help?' Rooke carefully poured his second beer.

'Most of the poor dears are still locked up in the camps at Pangpang or up north at Butan Pahang. Can't get them out. The ones in the city here, which we control, thank God, won't work for us because we are the enemy, they think. Too idiotic. We spend all the time trying to get them out of the camps and back to Singapore or Holland or wherever they want to go and they hurl abuse at us because we aren't fighting the bloody extremists and they feel we are just handing the islands over to the Indonesians without a by-your-leave. Which,' he said with a blinding white smile, '. . . which, of course, we are. Indepen-

12

dence. Freedom from Colonial Rule. Not our affair. Frightfully British really . . . we're just about to lose *our* Empire so why should the Dutch have theirs? Tit for tat really. Or logic. In any case it is all most frightfully tiresome, dangerous and anti-social. Absolutely no fun at all. What do you think of our little journal?' He picked up the crumpled sheet and read the head-line aloud. ' "Dakota Passengers Massacred". Perfectly frightful. Kill anything white that moves. And that old goat with a spinning wheel in India bleating, "Quit India"! Does he even dare to *think* what *they'll* all do to each other if we do? The world is mad.'

'And in the middle of it all,' said Rooke wryly, 'what's going to happen to me?'

Nettles looked at him thoughtfully over his half-raised glass. 'What indeed?' he sighed.

'I was Air Photographic, you know . . .'

'I do, I do . . . it's all here,' he patted the little black case at his side, 'and Pullen told me briefly but, you know'—he spread one elegant hand wide in a helpless gesture—'no air force . . . no planes . . . nothing for you here. I'm rather afraid to tell you but you're a replacement, I believe.'

'Replacement? For what?'

Nettles uncrossed his legs slowly. 'The term is better applied as "for whom". We've had a terrific amount of casualties, you know, in the battalions . . . Company Commanders. Especially down at Pangpang where the fighting has been quite horrid. I rather think you'll go trotting off down there to help out, so to speak. To 14 Brigade.'

Rooke sat white with shock.

'But I'm not Infantry . . . Intelligence . . . I don't know any-thing about Field Work . . . I've never fired a shot in anger in my whole career. I wouldn't know what the hell to do and especially with Indian Troops, I can't speak Urdu even . . . I mean, for God's sake, it's impossible!'

Nettles finished his drink slowly and placed his glass on the table signalling for a refill over Rooke's head.

'The British Army,' he said gently, 'has been founded and staffed by impossibilities; you will be no exception.' And seeing Rooke's ashen face, he added, 'I'm awfully sorry, really, not my decision, you and the other chap were sent down here as replacements . . . six more of you expected next week. It's not my fault! One chap copped it and the other is due for Repat in a week unless he cops it too. I mean, really . . . that's how it goes. The fact is that you are surplus and they need an extra body.' He stopped suddenly and placed his hand to his mouth. 'I'm most awfully sorry. That was *frightfully* bad taste. I do apologize.'

Rooke shrugged resignedly and took his glass. 'I think . . . I'd better get pissed.'

'Not too pissed . . . it's early yet,' said Nettles. 'I'll take you up to the Mess shortly, there's a spare room for you, and you can have a glorious glass of real champagne. Looted by courtesy of the Japanese ex-Commander. What did you do before the war, University I expect?'

'No. Actor.'

'Oh! Really? What fun . . . were you good?'

'Goodish . . . only had a couple of years at it before this job.'

'What did you do? "Who's for tennis" and the handsome juvenile in boots and breeches, that sort of thing?'

'And Shaw . . . Wilde . . . Shakespeare too. Rather catholic really. Repertory stuff.'

'Romeo and Dorian Gray!' Nettles laughed happily, rubbing his long nose with a long finger.

'Mercutio and Ernest actually.'

'I don't suppose that you'll believe me, or perhaps you will alas, but I was in Publishing. Educational books. Anything from Virgil and Herodotus to that boasting bore Catullus: rather good at my Latin and Greek, stuffed into a cellar off Russell Square breathing the dust of ancient wisdom, burrowing about in a sea of quite dire translations and the Chairman's old galoshes. Too frightful. I was damned glad that I joined up when I did.'

He paused and looked musingly into the dim, table-scattered room. 'More scope too,' he said, and smiled.

'Scope for what? I mean exactly . . . languages, promotion, you mean?'

Nettles drained his glass and clinked the melting ice cubes. He shook his head, still smiling to himself. 'No. Not particularly. Let's just say . . . umm . . . this and that, shall we? I say . . . finish that off and we'll get you up to the Mess, I expect you'd

14

like a shower and a change, wouldn't you?' He got up and took his case and cap and walked across to the Bar to sign his chit. Rooke collected his hold-all and cap and went over to the doors thoughtfully. Replacement. Company Commander. Christ almighty! He felt slightly drunk on two pints of Tiger beer. It had, he considered calmly, been a bitch of a morning. Surplus was perhaps the worst part of it all. He shrugged to himself and turned to watch Nettles cross the room towards him with his light, neat steps.

'Thanks for the beer,' he said. 'I'm afraid I left you to deal with them . . . Pullen did the other. I'm becoming a scrounger already.'

Nettles patted him kindly on the shoulder. 'Absolutely not. You're the guest today. It gives us great pleasure, I can assure you. I say: those shorts of yours,' he tucked his little black case tightly under his arm, '. . . not exactly Regulation, are they? At a guess I would say they were the shortest shorts in the Division!' He laughed lightly to indicate that there was no overt criticism in his remark. Rooke looked down at himself worriedly. 'Oh God. Too short? Can't stand those frightful bloomers flapping about . . . so hot. Tailor in Calcutta.'

'Quite right too.' Nettles settled his cap firmly on neatly clipped auburn curls. 'You can always tell the real Regular by his shorts, sort of khaki kilts, too awful. I imagine the Old Man will have a bit of a fit, our General . . . he's fearfully Regular Army, or likes to think so. Actually up from the Ranks, transferred with his commission to the Indian Army, now very 'Pindi and Poona, all that sort of nonsense: desperate to be part of the Establishment but hasn't quite managed to deal with the vowel sounds yet. He'll make some comment, you wait and see . . . bound to. But after all,' he pushed his crimson lanyard deeper into his left breast pocket, 'you were an actor once, and everybody expects actors to be vain and, I must confess, if pressed, that you have every excuse.'

Rooke followed him out into the bright sunlight. 'I'll change as soon as we get to wherever we're going,' he said.

Nettles ran lightly down the steps, 'You'll want a cool shower, I'm sure . . . but don't worry too much; after all, I don't suppose you'll be with us for all that long, the way things stand, at least. This all your gear?'

The city lay, a compact grid-iron, in the plain halfway between the sea and the mountains. No curves, no crescents: each street at right angles to the other and the whole neat agglomeration quartered by two wide thoroughfares, Wilhelmina Boulevard running north and south, and Nassau Boulevard, running east and west. These intersected in the centre of the city at Rembrandt Plein, a vast, ruined, scabby grass square in the middle of which stood a bronze shell-pocked statue of the painter himself, beret and palette, shoulders mantled with the droppings of gulls and pigeons. The streets were wide, tree-shaded, running into distant vistas of brilliant sky or, to the south, the vague blur of mountains. Villas, shops, banks, small stalls; here and there a church with tin or tiled spire; a not unpleasing mixture of Dutch-Colonial-Gothic and Folkestone-Edwardian. As they went swiftly round the Plein heading west to Nassau Boulevard, Rooke was mildly surprised to see an Opera House proud with crumbling portico and four Doric pillars from which the plaster had fallen long ago revealing bright pink bricks. One entire wall of the building was covered with a giant, crudely painted sign. A clenched fist holding a ripple-bladed dagger, drops of blood spilling, the legend *Merdeka!* in high letters above. Just as Pullen had said. He saw the sign constantly as they drove; on walls, the sides of gutted villas, a burned-out bus, the shutters of abandoned shops.

Away from the city centre the traffic grew less, the gardens larger, the villas grander and the feeling of desolation greater and greater. Here there was no traffic, a 'cycle or two, once a lone rickshaw. Here the lawns and hedges had reverted to jungle: weeds sprung luxuriantly from cracked pavements, trusses of rampant Dorothy Perkins tumbled, tossing blobs of cheap toothpaste—pink among the neglected casuarinas and palms; gates hung ajar, rusting on broken hinges, roofs lacked tiles, windows were either shuttered or gazed blankly through their fringes of vine and bougainvillaea. Looted, empty for the most part, secret and silent in their wilderness gardens. Kites wheeled and swooped in the still blue morning sky.

Rooke's beers had lost their impact and lay sour in his gut. His mouth was stale, he was uncomfortable hunched in his seat and wanted to pee. He cursed himself for not having thought of

16

it before he left the Club. The cloak of depression which Nettles had folded about him smothered any real attempt at conversation. Glumly he sat, arms folded, legs braced against the metal of the jeep and the strain of his bladder.

'Frightfully quiet,' said Nettles suddenly. 'You feeling all right?'

'Yes, fine. I want to pee, actually.'

'Well, hop out here in the gardens, no one will see you.'

'No, I'll hang on. Is it much further?'

'Up the road a bit, not far. Tell me,' he added, to change the topic, 'Public School, weren't you? Wellington?'

'Wilmington . . . not quite the same.'

'Still, not bad. Odd for an actor, isn't it?'

'No . . . we're not all from the lower orders.'

'Sorry. How rude. And an ADC too, I gather. From your papers.'

' '41 to '43. Brigadier Wade, North Grampians. Quite irregular, I'm afraid.'

'Ah! Another Brigadier with ideas above his station, what? Not at all unusual. Did you enjoy it?'

'Yes. Very much. Why?'

'Oh, no reason. I was just thinking, that's all. Funny job. Splendid, I imagine, for an actor however . . . quite at home. Our ADC, Tim Roberts, is dreadfully dull. Very nice, very efficient too, I know . . . but, you know what I mean? Dull. No fun, no sort of . . .' he spread his long fingers flat across the steering wheel, 'no kind of jollity. He goes on Repatriation next month, lucky devil . . . I say! Do cheer up! You look most frightfully depressed, you know.'

'Your fault.' Rooke smiled wanly and scratched a knee. 'I mean that word "replacement" followed by "surplus" rather did it. Nasty ring of finality to them. After five years of loyal service it came as a bit of a belly-blow. And all this . . .' he waved his arm wide across the deserted Boulevard and the silent jungly gardens, 'all this is a bit depressing; let's face it.'

Nettles accelerated suddenly, setting up little spirals of tumbling dust. 'Oh really! It's not as bad as all that. It's really quite jolly, you know. And all suburbs are pretty vile, aren't they? From Pinner to Penang. Terribly dreary . . . but there is really quite a lot of life going on here which you can't actually

17

see yet. Give it time. It's really very amusing here, right up to curfew . . . and *after* that if you know the right places to go.'

Rooke shook his head doubtfully. 'I really can't believe it's gay . . .'

Nettles cleared his throat swiftly and signalled to the empty street that he was turning right. 'Very . . . I honestly don't think it'll take you long to find that out, and this is "home", the big villa up on the left there, 12 Brabantlaan, but don't put it on your next PC to Auntie . . . as soon as you've had a shower and settled in you'll have your brimming glass of champagne. I'm Mess President this month, lucky old you, and after that you'll be as bright as a bee!'

'Or gay as a lark,' said Rooke ruefully.

'That,' said Nettles as he turned sharply into the overgrown gravel drive of the villa, 'would be divine.'

He rubbed his head affectionately against the wall, two or three times, with a gentle stroking movement much as he might have done against the neck of a favourite horse. He liked the wall. Solid, secure, safe. His wall. The wall of his room. Good wall. Kind wall. Save me wall. He leant away and ran his hand gently over the smooth pattern: roses and something. Ribbons. Good, sweet, roses. In the centre of the room his bed ready waiting under the draped mosquito net. Trunk and bed-roll neat in a corner. Small wooden card table. One chair in the wide bay window, apart, stiff, nervous, like visitors in a hospital. What a silly thing to think. Red-tiled floor, scratched white paint: over the empty fireplace, fitted with an electric plug, portrait of a man with tall, fluted glass, winking knowingly. Drinking. Along the floor of the wall against which he was so securely leaning, craving comfort, a twelve foot stuffed crocodile, jaws agape, claws spread, glass eyes dulled with dust. He kicked it gently and bent to stroke the wrinkled hide. But it hurt his head to do so. Slowly he straightened up and looked at the winking man over the fireplace. Drinking. He'd been drinking himself all day. He'd admit that. Very happily. I've been drinking all bloody day. Only thing to do. He sat down carefully on the crocodile's back and rested his head on his knees. Recount. Two, or was it three beers at the Club place? Not

18

more. Then the champagne as promised. 'Brimming glass.' Brimming glasses. Nettles said a whole bottle to himself. Wine at lunch too. Don't forget that. Let's not forget wine at lunch. Lunch was fun. If you like End-Of-The-Pier-Humour. Who's next for the hangman? Penny in the slot, the doors open jerkily, the priest staggers out, the trap door falls. Nettles is the priest. The trap door is just under these red tiles. Below this beautiful crocodile. No wonder they didn't loot *him*. Oh shit.

But lunch had been fun . . . had been very civilized and pleasant. Odd food, rather hot, and lots and lots and lots of iced beer as well. Too much. Everyone had been very kind and cheerful. 'Most kind. Too kind of you all.' Very welcoming especially when you consider he was only a surplus replacement Captain. But of course they'd all been very jolly and cheerful because someone had just got their Repat papers, the freedom sign. 'Merdeka' in English was really Repatriation. Simple. The wine and iced beer at lunch might, I only say 'might' mind you, have been a mistake. He hadn't felt drunk then. But now he did. He sat back and rolled his head gently against the roses and the, what were they? Ribbons. Or some such thing. Everything rolled a bit. Not much. A bit. He stroked the glass eyes of the crocodile. They suddenly gleamed bright, huge yellow orbs. He'd had a pee first, that's right; as soon as they reached the place he'd found the lavatory and that was much better. And then refilled on the promised 'brimming glass'. And someone had shown him to his room, this room, ground floor of the house. 'Mind you don't get a jolly old terrorist johnny through the windows!' someone had said. 'Advise you to lock up all your shutters before you go to bed, they are inclined to chuck grenades all over the place at night-time.' Grenades at night-time. Remembering, he got up slowly and crossed, unevenly, to the windows to shut himself in. But the bearer, or someone, had done that already. The bolts were run home. He was quite secure. Jolly kind of someone. Or the bearer. Or someone. He leant against the low sill. After the champagne and the pee, then what, Oh! yes! To change. The shorts, so as not to shock the vicar. General. Who didn't even turn up. But everyone else did. Couldn't remember the faces. But pleasant, smiling, because of the birthday party or the Repat or whatever it was. Not because of his arrival, but it seemed like it at the time. Most

19

kind. Gaunt was, anyway. Very pleasant man, Gaunt, intro-
duced himself straightaway, no fiddle-faddle. 'Major Gaunt.
B.M.' Handsome all right, bloody cold. Eyes like blue flints.
Very much the military man, Regular Army, Bannou Horse,
North-West Frontier. Very upright. A lot of talk about horses,
polo, the Gymkhana he was determined to try and organize.
Had his own little silver tankard, won it for something. Very
proud of it, had had it years. Drank from it slowly in little
measured sips. Very careful man, watching everyone intently.
    'You've got a name?' Odd remark.
    'Of course I've got a name. Rooke.'
    'Got another?'
    'Got two actually.'
    'One'll do.'
    'Benjamin.'
    'Christ!'
    'Ben?'
    'Better. Mine's David. Been out long?'
    He hadn't really listened, looked about the room over his
clutched silver tankard through the flinty eyes. Thin lips. Rather
a cruel sign, wasn't it? Thin mouth, thin-lipped smile: when he
did the eyes didn't. What age? Oh, about thirty something.
One or two. Not more. Good figure, straight back, muscular;
very fair hair very short, strong wrists and very white teeth,
rather small and neat and together like a cat's. Dressed for
riding. Bush jacket, stock, boots and spurs. Something about
him. Didn't like him but did. Don't know. Contradictions. I'll
take off my boots. He moved and sat down on the single visiting
chair and started to unlace them. Not so easy on the head. He
lifted one foot gently on to his knee. Better. And then the
gaiters. They clattered to the red-tiled floor one after the other.
    'Got everything you need? They made you comfortable?
What'll you be doing here?' He hadn't been interested really,
was still looking at everyone else in the ante-room.
    'I'm not actually doing anything here. Just a visitor. I'm a
surplus replacement, you see.'
    Gaunt had given him a sudden look, wiped a thin finger over
thin lips, clasped the silver tankard to his chest and smiled. The
thin smile with the white cat's teeth. 'It happens to us all.
Unserviceable. Never mind. Have a pleasant stay . . . they

aren't bad in this Mess. Anything you need . . .' He waved the tankard vaguely across his chest and started to wander away. In the middle of the room he turned back. 'If you want a mount I can always fix you up . . . collared about a dozen from the bloody Japs . . . some of them quite good. Give me a buzz.' Then he had gone.

He unbuckled his webbing belt, laid his revolver carefully on the table. They had all been armed at lunch in the Mess. Couldn't be sure in this city.

'There's a pretty wide perimeter now.' A fat Lieutenant stirring his coffee into a whirlpool. 'Managed to shove 'em back to the river in the east, the railway in the south, and Rozendaal in the west; that's a suburb but we hold it nearly all now with the Gurkhas: and of course,' he rattled his spoon against the saucer, 'we have the sea on the north so we're pretty well protected really. But it is a bit of a bugger; claustrophobic in a way . . . all stuck together, and the curfew is rather a bind. Can't move anywhere outside the perimeter unless you are in convoy and the lights go out at twenty-two hundred. Difficult. Parties have to go on all night! Just doss down where you are.' He grinned over his coffee cup. 'Lots of pretty ladies about. Not everyone boycotts us. It's not all durance vile, you know.'

'Can you play it?'

'No. I cook in it.'

Where did *she* go to, he wondered, unbuttoning his bush jacket, slinging it onto his scattered boots. She wasn't what you might call a pretty lady. Well. Yes. Pretty. You could give her that. Beautiful probably. Cold and beautiful. But rude, so damned rude. 'I cook in it.' Why that? Why not just, 'Yes, I do.' Or 'I try to' or 'I'm the champion banjo player of the Java Bloody Seas.' Even that. Only it's a mandolin. M-A-N-D-O-L-I-N spells mandolin. Dismissive. Rude. In front of all those sniggering Chinese girls. He undid his slacks and let them concertina slowly down his legs as he hobbled across to the corner and the little white wash-bowl. And the big can of fresh water. Nothing in the taps of course because the terrorists had buggered up the hydroelectric thingummytites. Splashed water into the bowl, scooped some up in the bar-glass which he had taken from the Mess after dinner. Long after dinner. Singing. Slept from lunch till dinner almost. The sleep of the dead.

21

Drunk. Dead drunk. In the ante-room he'd read some old magazines and two copies of *The Daily Cobra*. Half in Urdu or something for the Indian troops. Tatty little sheet. He squeezed paste on to his brush and dropped the tube back into his wash-bag. Rinsed his mouth slowly and spat it all out. Into the bowl of clean water. Clot. Emptied it and filled it up again, doused his face and head, rubbed them dry and neatly stepped out of his wrinkled slacks which he threw over the back of the crocodile.

And-then-what-did-you-do-in-the-war, daddy? Well: some-one came up and offered me a drink and that started it all up again. But I never saw the bloody old General. He's got a house of his own somewhere. Doesn't come to the Mess. Lives in comfort as befits a Ranker General. He pulled the plug and watched the water swirl away and then peered at his reflection in the spotted mirror behind his bar-glass and shaving brush. He smiled, scowled, grinned, stuck out his tongue. You are twenty-four, blond and beautiful, you ride a horse quite well, shoot not badly, and you interpreted bloody, bloody well . . . let's face that, and now you are surplus and a replacement for some idiotic Company Commander, and no one wants you except to get your arse shot off in Pingpong or Bangbang or wherever the hell they said. And you are as pissed as a fart, my boyo. Pissed. He looked away, sadly shaking his head, and with his hands resting on his hips peed into the bowl. Nothing came out of the taps when he turned them. Only dust and rust. He sighed. If you are really miserable the only thing to do is to get absolutely stinking. And if you are frightened as well get *doubly* stinking. Nettles said, at some part of the evening, it was the best thing in the world for despair: a good skin-full. He'd been very kind. He'd understood how bloody it felt. So spruce and neat, ready for his dinner. Combed and showered, smelling of something rather sweet but quite pleasant. 'Sandalwood,' he had said. 'Chinese in the market has a shop the size of Guer-lain's, full of delicious bottles and odours and oils. You know Guerlain's in Paris?' No. Black mark. 'Marvellous shop. Used to spend ages there before the war. Good for morale to smell pleasant in this heat . . . don't you think?' Think? Yes, he thought so. And drink? Yes, he'd love another; I'm beginning to feel high and delirious now. The hell with Pingpong or

Bifbat and cooking in a mandolin; what an absurd thing to say. Absurd. He suddenly ripped off his briefs and slung them with a wide dramatic gesture to follow the slacks. His arm stayed high in mid-flight, elegant, poised, a gesture of defiance, splendour, grace. The briefs arc'd across the room and fell over the crocodile's clawed foot. He swivelled, arm still outstretched, on his heel in a half-circle until his graceful gesture struck the folds of his mosquito net. To bed! To bed! To sleep! Out, out you damned Pingpong. Who would have thought the young man to have had so much booze in him? Carefully, so as not to let the bugs creep in, he slid under his net onto the old familiar, faithful, camp bed from the Army & Navy Stores, Victoria. Was it only this morning? Christ. So much in so short a time. On his pillow, neatly folded, his blue-checked sarong. Too hot for sheets. So a sarong. Which you tucked thus, and thus, and thus. Exhausting. He lay back and stared up into the veils of net. Not quite so pissed suddenly. Not pleasant: mouth foul, but everything steady. Not happy. Not that. It's all gone, the forgetting. The caring. The fright. No. The fright is still there. A fist in the throat. I wish I wasn't here. I wish it had never happened that I had to come here. I want to go home. Anywhere. Not here. I wish I was drunk again and not going to be a replacement. Oh shit. Come on, you're grown up now. A big boy. Maudlin only because of booze all day. He reached up and snapped off the tiny low wattage electric bulb someone had considerately fixed on the pole inside his net. Closed his eyes. Head swung a little. 'Now I lay me down to sleep.'

'Said your prayers?' Nanny Jarvis, folding his dressing-gown.
'Yes. Done them.'
'What did you pray for tonight then?'
'It's unlucky to tell.'
'Nonsense. Stuff and nonsense. Praying isn't wishing, Ben.'
'Well . . . I prayed for you.'
'Thank you, I'm sure.'
'And Father and Aunt Alice and Uncle Harry.'
'And?'
'Oh. To-make-me-a-good-boy-amen.'
'And then what?'
'And a new saddle for Sweetbriar.'

'Poor Jesus! You are greedy.'

She had laughed and tugged his head kindly.

Tug my head kindly now. What a lot of bunk. How idiotic. All that rubbish to get you through a life like this. The hell with Sweetbriar and his saddle and make-me-a-good-boy-amen. Who for? What for? What about a nice fast Dakota to get me out of this shitty mess? A nice *slow* Dakota would do. I'll settle for that. Anything really. Funny, though, how things stick. Remembering. *How* you remember. A sort of habit. I'll remember this sodding day until the day I die: which could be in an hour's time, tomorrow, or about tea-time next Tuesday. Oh hell and high water. Don't think of that in the dark. He turned slowly on his side and slept.

A muffled sound of something slithering; a stifled voice. Silence. He was at once awake, eyes wide in the dark. The sound of breathing. Revolver. Christ! On the table. Stiff with fright, the darkness faded, slivers of moonlight slid through the shutters. A slow, weaving, black figure through the net. He moved upright, grabbed for the light switch, a weak halo of low wattage. A tall figure looming beyond the milky folds.

'It's all right. It's me. Geoffrey.'

'What the hell's the matter, what do you want?'

'Nothing the matter. Don't speak so loudly, you'll wake the house.'

His heart still thudding, he raised the net. Nettles was rubbing his foot, standing on one leg like a crane, in a short black kimono.

'Tripped over something, nearly broke my foot.'

'What the hell do you want?'

'What did I trip over?'

'God knows . . . the crocodile perhaps. There by the door . . .'

'Bloody silly place to have it. A crocodile.'

'What is it, Geoffrey? It's two in the bloody morning.'

'Thought you might be . . . lonely. That's all. Strange room, strange house. You know.'

'Well, I'm not. I was asleep, for God's sake!'

Nettles squatted gently beside the low bed. 'I've been awake for some time. Thinking.'

'What about?'

'You.'

'Me. What about me?'

'So sad and depressed. Absolutely stinking at dinner, you know. About your posting.'

'Oh that. Yes, I know I was. Still am really. But it's all better now. Got over it. Really. Thanks all the same.'

Nettles was examining his foot carefully.

'Stubbed my toe. You told Gaunt and me that you would sell your soul to the Devil to avoid going . . . really.'

'Too many drinks. In vino . . .'

'Ah yes . . . veritas . . . Well, I've come shopping.'

'Don't be dotty. I feel awful.'

'You don't have to go, you know. Worked it all out.'

A rising scent of sandalwood. He placed his hand on Rooke's knee. 'No need at all to go down to the Brigade.'

'I don't follow.'

The hand pressed gently. 'Been thinking all night. Clever old me. Bright as a bee. I could fix it all.' The hand slipped up the thigh, smoothing the cotton sarong. Rooke struck it hard and swiftly.

'Bugger off. None of that.'

'Hoity toity. But it's an amazing thought . . .'

'I don't know what the hell you mean.'

'Course you do. *All* about it.'

'About what? What's wrong with you? What do I know all about?'

'Oh come! Public School. Actor. My dear; come on now.'

'You come on now and piss off.'

'Is it gay? You asked in the jeep . . . is it really gay? I mean. Well.'

'Well what? I was asking you. Fun, living, enjoyable, jolly . . .'

'Gay is gay. You know quite well.'

'I bloody don't. Didn't. Don't. I know Pouf. Queer.'

'Ten out of ten.'

'Gather you're both.'

'Quick as a flash we are. So?'

'So bugger off.'

Nettles leant forward, his elbows on the bed-edge. 'I prefer gay.'

'Good. Well, I'm absolutely normal. Sorry.'

'No one is absolutely normal in abnormal times.'

'Don't make the times an excuse for your abnormalities, for Christ's sake.'

'As good an excuse, if excuse were needed, as any. And true.'

'Nothing to do with Public School and actors. What's that all about?'

'Tolerance? Sympathy? Broadness of mind . . .'

'Oh hell, do clear off. My head's splitting.'

'So it should be. You're shocked?'

'No, not shocked. Bored rigid.'

'And those shorts. Vanity? Sartorial pleasure? Come off it. Who's teasing whom?'

Rooke pulled his sarong tighter round his waist. 'Not me teasing you, chum.'

Nettles placed his hands together as if in a quiet prayer. 'I know you loathe the word "replacement". But we do need one here, at HQ. Our ADC. Remember? Timmy Roberts. Surprise! Surprise! I never thought of it at the time. The General also wants his little newspaper tarted up for morale . . . Came to me in a blinding flash! "The boy we need is up in the gallery, the boy we need is waiting there for me." Got it? You'd be quite, quite *mad* to refuse.'

'For pete's sake. It's after two. I'm dead.'

'I could fix it all. Snap! Like that. "Got your replacement, Sir, frightful bit of luck. Ex-ADC himself, most presentable, a *Gentleman* too, Wilmington, splendid with newspapers." He'd bite right away. Longs to have Gentlemen about him. Didn't care for poor Timmy because he was a golfing pro. from Epsom.'

'You're soliciting.'

'Prefer shopping. Isn't it fun?'

Nettles leaned back slowly and pulled the net a little wider apart.

Rooke turned his head away. 'Do pack it in.'

The scent of sandalwood was closer.

'Scouts' honour? Really? You truthfully want to go down to the Brigade. To Pangpang? With that half-wit who came in with you and is now driving them all mad in "B" Mess. Lost his

26

chess set and asked if there was a Church Parade on Sunday. You want that?'

Rooke closed his eyes in misery, head splitting. 'No . . . no . . . I don't know . . .'

'Well then?'

'I can't. I just can't, that's all. It doesn't work . . . I can't do that.'

'You wouldn't have to *do* anything. I'm not suggesting rape. Just a . . . well, a laying on of hands? Is that better? Companionship? Mutual comfort . . .'

'Oh for God's sake!'

'No. Yours. That's the whole point.'

'I can't. Pack it in please. It's no good; I like ladies.'

'So do I. Adorable sometimes. But think of it. ADC: with your name in lights.'

Rooke covered aching eyes with his wrists. 'Don't go on, don't go on. It's bloody blackmail . . .'

'Utterly muddled and middle-class remark. All's fair in love and war, to coin an appropriate cliché. However, I suppose if you *admit* it's blackmail, it is a start. Don't you think?'

Rooke lay quite still, his fist clenched, wrists crossed over his eyes. 'Just get out . . . piss off. I'm half-drunk, you know that . . . I've got to sleep.'

Nettles watched him for a moment, sighed and slowly rose to his feet pulling the short kimono tightly about his lean frame. 'A blunder. Ah well. Forget all about it. Good try, I thought. Nothing ventured, nothing gained, don't they say? Picked up the wrong clues apparently. Let my baser instincts get the better of me. A blunder. Very silly indeed. My humble apologies.' He turned and went across the shadowy room, neatly stepping over the stuffed crocodile. 'Really ought to move this beast. Frightfully dangerous.' At the door he looked back. 'So you can leave here without a stain on your conscience: and play chess all over Pangpang with your chum. Between mortar attacks. I've been very stupid. Tasteless blunder. Very, very sorry.'

Rooke opened his eyes blearily, rolled on to his side, leaned up on one elbow. 'It's all right. Don't worry. It wasn't the first time.'

'I can imagine.'

'But it just wouldn't work out, you know.' He ran a weary

27

hand through his hair. 'It wouldn't work . . . I mean, well, you know . . . it's never happened to me. I just wouldn't know what to do . . .'

Nettles was quite still, then dropped his hand from the key and moved one step into the dim circle of light.

'You could remove that absurd little table-cloth of yours,' he said, 'to start with.'

CHAPTER TWO

She stood before its sleek, shining virginity, motionless with a
kind of awe; reverence almost. 'Thou shalt not worship false
gods.' Oh, but I do! Her hands slid gently, caressingly, along its
smooth metal flanks, across the neat chromium strip banding its
top, round the cool glittering handle which, when she tenta-
tively pulled, swung wide the heavy door to reveal a cavern of
bright metal, shining racks, neatly fitted boxes and containers.
EGGS said one, BUTTER another. Kneeling to seek further
delights, she found them in the gilt letters CRISPATOR. New.
Unused. Hers. Her symbol. Freedom. Normality. Life. Rising to
her feet slowly, swinging the door closed all in one graceful
movement, she pressed her body close to the smooth metal,
tracing with a finger, the raised golden letters before her.
FRIGIDAIRE. Laid her cheek hard against them, felt them bite
into the flesh like a cold branding iron and the years of unshed
tears spill hot and stinging from tightly closed lids. She wept.
And in this act of submission astonished herself. Tears, burning
tears. The first in three and a half years. Tears for a
refrigerator.

But let them go, don't be ashamed, no one can see you, heal
yourself; a good cry, they say, is beneficial. Release the strain,
the pain. Above all the unspoken pain. Tears for the agonies
of the swift surrender. Smooth Japanese faces suddenly there
at the top of the stairs among the ashen astonishment of the
dancers. 'Please. The General asks that you continue your
dance until midnight. There will be no National Anthem.'
Singapore had fallen, Borneo, the Philippines, Java and now
the Island. Tears for Pieter's last blown kiss, a frail movement
among the three thousand European males herded together
under the blazing sun in Rembrandt Plein, then he had turned
and gone from her, leaving her with Wim alone. Can you be
alone in a crowd of fifteen hundred women and children? Oh
yes. You can. And were. Shuffling through the silent watching
crowds of Chinese, Indonesians, Malays to the slum quarter of
the City which was to be the camp. Tears for Wim's slim arm,
ripped from wrist to shoulder by jagged glass, as she sewed it

29

up with carpet thread and a darning needle. Tears for the years of desolation, the filth, the crowds, the confinement. For the secret kindness of old servants, creeping to the wire, smuggling her fruit, an egg; once cloth for the bandages. For the squalor, the fighting, the frayed nerves, the fear, lack of privacy, of food, of water, the desperation not to give in, to comb one's hair, to wash, to barter for food for Wim, to keep the last and only pretty cotton dress for the day which must arrive, and did. Three and a half years later.

A scoundrel dawn as it proved. No laughing soldiers opening wide the high gates, instead, screaming extremists herding them back, brandishing guns and grenades, spitting at them, throwing dirt and rotten fruit through the wire. No Union Jack, streaming in the summer breeze from the sea, no Stars and Stripes; no joyful liberation under the fluttering Red Flag with its ill-drawn hammer and sickle. 'Death to the Colonists!' and, carried on banners through the jeering crowds, 'Freedom or Bloodshed!' New banners in the wind of change. Tears then for that; but also for the day the new flag *did* arrive. Modest but bravely held. A coiled white snake on red and yellow silk, scrubbed white faces, beaming dark ones from Bombay, Delhi and God knew where else. The Union Jack on the little four-wheeled truck, the tall, very crisp officer who offered his hand and the apology: 'Sorry we're late, but we're here. Had rather a job to get through, but better late than never, what?' Ah yes. Better late than never. Better by far. Tears then for all that. Tears which were never shed and which now had made her nose run and had swollen her eyes. Wiping them with her elbow, pushing the fallen blonde hair from wet cheeks she looked ruefully at her shining steel symbol. You broke me. You: the proof of my survival. She heard wheels crunching on the gravel driveway outside, voices and a familiar laugh. But she was unable to move, sitting slumped back against the door of her freedom.

'Clair! My dear Clair! What happened?'

Pullen's voice filled with sudden worry, his kind face creased with dismay. Swiftly he knelt beside her, taking a hand.

'Are you all right? You aren't ill?'

She shook her head, and taking the hand which held hers so tightly, aided it to brush the hair from her forehead, the tears

30

from her cheeks. 'No, no. I'm well. I'm truly well. Happiness, can you believe?' His consternation made her laugh. Roughly she thrust the hair back from her face. 'It must seem very silly. Happiness. You sent this?'

He smiled gently and helped her to her feet. 'Couldn't resist it. Whole godown crammed with them. All new. Unpacked even.'

'A truck arrived an hour ago. Some Japanese and a nice smiling Indian.'

'Have to have a refrigerator, don't you? Essential in this heat. The requisition orders stated Basic Essentials, I seem to remember, eh?'

She took his hand and held it close to her side. 'You are so good to me. So kind. Feel my heart beating! Such happiness you can't imagine.'

'Well . . . funny way to show it. Crying on the floor. Gave me a frightful shock . . . thought you'd got tummy ache, you know —something. Funny creatures, you women. Anyway, that's all over. Brought you a present, as it happens.'

'Another one!'

'Presents, plural, as a matter of fact.'

Two tins of bacon, a bag of flour, a can of pineapple chunks. He laid them all carefully on the table, stuck the haversack under his arm, and from it, like a conjuror, produced two bars of chocolate.

'For Wim. He about?'

'In the garden, I think.' Her voice was quiet; recovered. She stroked the can of fruit with wonder. 'But where is this from?'

'Hawaii or Florida or somewhere. I don't know. It's all Yankee stuff.'

'No . . . all of it. Where did you get it?'

'LST came in this morning from Calcutta, we call it "Cash and Carry". Had to go down and meet a couple of chaps; replacements I think for 14 Brigade. I know an officer, good bloke, always brings me a bit of stuff. Got this too; at a price, I'll tell you!' He pulled a bottle from the haversack proudly. 'Real White Horse, the pukka stuff. None of that Jap muck. Thought we might celebrate your return to your old house after all the years. Quite a good reason, I'd say.'

'Christmas in September! Oh my dear, you are so kind; but

you keep the whisky, we have so much now. Bacon, flour, pineapple . . .'

Pullen raised his closed fist and pushed it gently towards her smiling face, head to one side, little beads of sweat on the neat moustache, pleasure in his eyes.

'What is it? Show me.'

'Hand out and say please, my girl!'

'Please, sir, unless it's a spider. Oh Nigel! No . . .'

He dropped a small metal tube into her uncertain hands. 'Probably the wrong colour, took what he gave me, I fear . . . maybe too red?'

She held the lipstick cupped in her hands like a spilling of emeralds. 'Even if it is royal blue I cannot thank you . . .' the tears held back.

'Oh Lor'. I say. I mean, don't blub again. What a day! Just a lipstick, the boys use them as currency in the docks. You know what I mean, the ummm, Ladies of the Town. They won't take guilders or something . . . I'm rather bumbling on, I'm afraid . . .' He had suddenly embarrassed himself by his gift. She could have been offended, oh Lor'. But she wasn't listening to him, had unscrewed the little top and touched her wrist with the sticky tip.

'Pink! You see! Clever you. Even if it had been black . . . oh! I could cover myself all over with it. What do you think?'

'Awful waste of you . . . if you take my point.'

'Awful waste of "Dew Rose". Go through to the verandah, Nigel. I'll get you a drink, the sun is just over your yard arm, isn't it?'

He wandered into the hall and through the dim, still-shuttered sitting-room. He noted with a wry smile that she had already furnished her house with the stuff they had got from the godowns at the docks. Sparse, but enough. He heard her singing and a spoon fall to the tiled kitchen floor. On the verandah, overlooking the wilderness garden, tall yellow grasses, a straggle of giant sunflowers, crickets singing, a battered tin table, some odd glasses, a small bowl of orchid things, five deck-chairs. She came out with a tray, jug, bottle and a packet of ration biscuits.

'I think that these were ours,' she said with a nod at the chairs. 'I can't be sure. Wim is. Certain. He says he remembers them

32

clearly. I suppose at twelve you can remember better than at thirty-two. I don't know. Found them in the garage with some bits and pieces of fishing rods. Pieter's perhaps. They could have been anyone's really. I'm sure the table wasn't ours, but it doesn't matter, half the things I now have weren't ours anyway. I followed the Requisition Form very correctly. Didn't take more than we need for basic use, and there were some things still left here.' She had poured the drinks and handed him a tall glass. 'Sit down! You look so formal there!'

He laughed and took off his cap. 'Not sure I can trust those deck-chairs of yours . . . after so long the canvas might be rotten. I distrust deck-chairs infinitely. Beastly things, always jamming one's fingers.' He raised his glass towards her. 'My goodness, I could do with this.' They drank together and then he lowered himself cautiously into one of the chairs, and they both laughed with relief that he remained steady and secured.

'You see, you didn't trust me. I tested them all. Wim too.'

'Very thoughtful woman. Well,' he looked about the tidy, shaded verandah, 'this is all very pleasant. You really have worked hard. Done wonders . . .'

'But everyone has been so kind. Trucks to bring the things, that nice smiling Indian carried boxes and mattresses. I suppose I could have gone mad in that place at the docks. Grand pianos, cocktail cabinets, grandfather clocks, crystal and porcelain, everything. The loot of the city. All very Burger, Dutch and heavy. We had, I remember, a very pretty little Biedermeier desk, very slender, walnut and ebony, it stood just where . . .' She stopped, smiled and shrugged. 'Doesn't matter where it stood, or when, or where it is now. It's today. A day of such happiness. You must realize that after such a silly exhibition just now.'

'Of course I do. Jolly nice to see.'

'Will you eat with us?'

'Very good of you. There's enough? Sure? I'm Duty Officer tonight so I won't stay late . . . but it would be very agreeable.'

'You could even have a shower if you like. I filled the bath quite full.'

'No, no, very kind, must get back to the Mess. The driver's still outside, I hope?'

33

'He was. Don't move. I'll give him a drink, that would be all right, yes?'

'Excellent. Not beer, remember . . . he's a Moslem. Lime juice, something.'

He heard her feet clacking across the sitting-room, a door open and shut; slowly he raised his glass. Funny woman. They all were really. Weeping just because of a refrigerator. Probably reminded her of something in the past. You could never tell. They don't give much away. All bottled up still. Early days of course, early days. Being back in her own house must be a bit of a shock too; hadn't really thought of that. So many changes in the years, everything carted off . . . stripped. Husband dead. Or missing. Worse really. Missing. One still hopes. Bloody war, bloody Japs, bloody Indonesians, bloody everything. Still, she's better off than the others still in the camps; poor buggers, how the Hell we'll get them out . . .' He fumbled about slowly in his pocket and brought out his pipe, and from the haversack, his tobacco pouch, and saw the boy walking up through the high grasses towards him. Like her. Hair the colour of straw. Very brown of course from the years in the sun, but thin — really awfully thin — and that frightful scar down his arm.

'Hullo there! Where have you been to, young man?' Oh Lor', patronizing idiot.

Wim shielded his eyes from the sun and squinted through his fingers. 'Is it Nigel? Major Pullen? Is it?'

'The very one.'

'Ah. So.' He came on up the steps pulling a tatter of coloured papers behind him. 'Good evening, sir,' a formal handshake, a neat bow, indicating respect.

'What have you got there, Wim? A fancy costume or something?'

'No. A kite. I made a kite.'

'Did you, indeed.' Not awfully good at this kind of conversation.

'But not enough wind, or I don't know. Something.' He dropped it listlessly to the floor.

'Managed to get you a couple of chocolate bars this morning. Off a ship.'

'Chocolate bars!'

'Yes. They're in the kitchen, I think.'

34

'American ones with the nuts inside?'

'I rather think so. Very fattening. Just what you need, old man.'

Wim laughed; a wide gleeful spread of even white teeth. 'I *need* many boxes of chocolate bars, I think. Is right? In the kitchen?'

'That's it. In the kitchen. By the way, your mother has a new refrigerator, she's very happy.'

'A refrigerator! Does it work already?'

'Not yet. When the power comes on. We'll have it fixed soon.'

'So much we have now. Beds! Chairs! Everything!' he clapped his hands and ran into the house.

Pullen heard his voice calling out in Dutch and Clair's voice replying in English. 'Here, look. Isn't it fine? So fine. And new, Wim . . . quite new.' He looked at his watch, scratched his arm, looked at his pipe. Decided not to smoke. He was putting it back in his pocket when she came out onto the verandah.

'You won't?'

'No. I'll have it later. Ought to be running along. Matter of fact, I'm getting a bit low on tobacco. The Yanks have every blessed thing from bombs to baked beans but no 'baccy. I say! You do look pretty.'

'You see? And it's not too red, it is just perfect. How can I thank you?'

'Oh nonsense. Clair dear.'

'Restoring a woman's confidence is not nonsense.'

'No, quite. It really does that? A bit of pink on your lips?'

'Really. A bit of pink.'

'I must keep one for myself next time. God knows, I could use it. Don't suppose it works for a chap though, does it?' He was smiling gently. 'Been a brute of a day today. This is the first pleasant moment I've had. Here with you.'

'Even the tears and sobbing?'

'Even that. Because of that somehow. Funny —'

'Well this evening we will have a celebration. My first guests in my own house for, oh, such a time. And a lipstick and a refrigerator.'

'Which doesn't work yet.'

'But which will. And Emmie is coming also, you remember her?'

He wrinkled his forehead and pressed worried fingers into his scalp. 'Emmie. Ah. Yes. The van Hoorst girl. Tall, dark, good English?'

'Exactly. Did you see her today? She had an appointment; you arranged it.'

He looked lost for a second, slipped the tobacco pouch into the haversack and started to strap it up. 'Do you know, I can't remember. Yes, I think she went along. I had these two chaps to cart about . . . I was in the Planters this morning, there were quite a lot of girls there. Nettles' lot. So I imagine she must have been. Can't be sure . . . anyway, I must be off, dear Clair. Bless you for the drink.' He got to his feet, took up his cap, his swagger-cane, patted his pockets and looked vaguely around. 'I always seem to leave things behind me these days. You'd never believe I was a quite efficient Staff officer not so long ago. In battle, that is. Not much good as a Nanny trying to settle all you women; what a business!'

She took his hand, and leaning upwards kissed him gently on his cheek. She thought that he had blushed, but his grasp was firm.

'You could do that again if you cared to,' he said.

She kissed him again, not smiling, and pulled slowly away, eyes bright. With her free hand she lightly traced his lips. 'I won't what you called "blub", don't be afraid. I don't do it very often, sometimes even not for years. And now, because of you, perhaps never again. I'm quite restored, you see. You have given it all back to me: self-respect.'

'With a little lipstick.'

'Not just that—that and all the other things, my house, my son, my job, my life. In these last few, strange weeks all the past has gone.'

'All?'

'Well . . . almost all. Not Pieter, sure. Not him, never him, you know? But all the rest . . .' She broke away, and leant over the wooden rail, hunching her shoulders and looking out into the suddenly darkening garden. 'And when I know about him, for sure, because deep inside I have known for sure instinctively . . . you will have given me the courage to face even that. You can't imagine what you have given me. I could never manage to explain.'

36

'Oh, it's really not important you know, my dear. I think I do understand.'

'I wonder if you do?' She turned and was smiling, leaning back against the rail, her hands crossed in front of her. 'You know so much about me, I so little about you. You never speak, I mean about yourself. Just the little things, but I don't know you at all, do I?'

He settled his cap neatly on his smooth head, tucked the haversack under his arm, tapped gently with his little stick on the tin-topped table. The glasses jumped. 'Good Lor'. Nothing much to know, honestly. Run of the mill . . .'

'I don't think so. Very English, very correct, insular perhaps?' She was smiling.

'Oh no. Not that. Insular. Very unattractive, I think.'

'Then just reticent. Is that the word?'

'Could be. Mustn't be a bore, you know. Fearful thing to be. Voltaire said, "The art of boring someone is to tell them everything".'

'Did he?'

'Something like that. Yes.' He picked up his glass and finished off the last of his drink; replaced it carefully. Smiled at her suddenly. 'Don't want to use up everything I have to say to you in the first few weeks, do I? What would we have to do in the long winter evenings?'

Wim's voice cut through the falling light, high with pleasure. 'There are nuts inside. Inside both.'

Pullen gave her a neat, mock salute, tipping his cap with his cane. 'A figure of speech. Nothing more. About half past eightish all right?'

She nodded and watched him cross the verandah, back straight, haversack under his arm, steps very sure. He called out to the boy, and she heard his laughing answer smothered by the starting of the jeep and the tyres crunching on the gravel. Heard it turn and swing out onto the street as the dimmed-out headlights streaked through the tall rank grasses, and lit up the motionless leaves of the giant datura. And then it had gone and the darkness swept across the verandah. From the house a candle glimmered. Wim in the kitchen. She clinked bottle and jug onto the tray and her glass. Taking Pullen's carefully she examined it closely, holding it up towards the soft, distant candle gleam, and then deliberately almost as an act of acceptance, she pressed it lightly to her lips.

To have had absolutely everything in life you ever wanted, except perhaps blonde hair, Emmie thought ruefully, cycling along Nassau Boulevard in the fading dusk, and then have it all removed in one fell swoop, was a very salutary thing indeed. It was perhaps a pity that it had to come to her so late in life. And twenty was late, she thought. The awareness of small pleasures, the value of trivial things, of rare and treasured possessions had taken her by surprise. A shirt, a spoon, a bed, even this dangerous bicycle which once, in the happier days long past, she had only ridden to someone's tennis match, to go swimming at the beach, to ride up into the hills. She now rode desperately, if professionally, as a life-line. Take my bicycle from me now and I am ruined, my life would be in a tumble of rubble and dust. I would no longer exist. Which is ridiculous, because I could and I did before, but it would make life practically impossible. And life is very good. That has taken me a long time to discover. I must have been a very spoiled and irritating child. I know that I was. And a very arrogant young woman. I know that people said so. And I was because I thought that arrogance might protect me. From what? From whom? It protected me from nothing; now I find out. Why all this self-revelation cycling to dinner with Clair? Why now, on the long deserted length of Nassau Boulevard? Why not years before? In the camp, in the broom-cupboard at the Convent. Before that in the really very bad days. Why not then? Because then I was looking so hard for hope that I had no time even for myself. It was enough to just exist. But now I have the hope. It is all here about me. Today, for the first time, I am quite reborn. I start again. With nothing but faith and this hope I have suddenly discovered for myself.

She turned right into Brabantlaan just as a jeep turned out of Clair's driveway. She watched its rear lights winking red going up the street. Clair's Protector, the British Officer. The British, she thought, pushing the bicycle up to the wide front verandah, are almost as dull as the Dutch. She unstrapped the bashed music case from the back, and with infinite care dis-

38

engaged the mandolin from the basket in the front, with cautious fingers opened the door of her little oil lamp, smothered the flickering wick with a pinch of her fingers, and went up the steps. A light glimmered somewhere from one of the windows. She walked along in the darkness, feeling her way with one free hand, until she reached the light and tapped at the glass.

Inside the room the light moved suddenly. Wim appeared among a host of stretching shadows, a candle held high above his corn-silk head. He turned and called back into the house.

'All right. It's only Emmie.'

'Only Emmie. Thank you. Who did you expect, Saint Nicholas?'

'He's been already. Chocolate bars and a new refrigerator for Mamma, now!'

'Marvellous.' She followed him across the hall. 'From the British Saint Nicholas, I suppose?'

'Major Pullen? Yes. No; it is just that you might have been a Jap.'

'Not any longer.'

'Ah yes, Emmie, they are still about. Deserters and the extremists, even now. Mamma has a gun.'

'From the Major?'

'I suppose so. She knows how to work it, she practises shooting at bottles.'

'But this is all the British area, Brabantlaan. The big Mess is up the street.'

'The der Elst's old house, yes. And the Indians patrol at night but it is all a bit funny still, you know.'

In the kitchen Clair was busy at the cooker in a sparkle of candles.

'It looks like a crèche, Clair. Why the candles?'

'Why not?'

'Well, the power's on again, I think. It was in Rembrandt Plein—'

Wim pressed a switch, the ceiling lamp glowed a dull orange, they laughed and Clair wiped her hands on her trousers.

'Save them, Wim . . . the candles. I just supposed it was off. I seem to accept so willingly these days.'

Emmie placed her music case and the mandolin on the table.

'Flour! Tins of bacon. My God, such riches. It pays to collaborate.'

'Emmie!' A warning in the voice.

'A joke. I'm a collaborator myself. Since this morning.'

'Ah good! They took you on?'

'They took me on. Wim, this is for you. It's a mandolin.'

He took it in some surprise. 'For me?'

'It was just lying on the street; it's not broken.'

'Can you play it?'

She pursed her lips thoughtfully. 'I've been asked that already today.'

'But can you?'

'No.' She laughed suddenly and shook her head in disbelief. 'I said that I cooked in it!'

Clair looked up at her from the stove where she was opening a tin. 'Emmie dear! Are you mad?'

'Oh you know, I was so angry, a British officer, so rude, you know. A perfect stranger, very sure of himself. I just snapped back; that put him in his place, I can tell you. Everyone laughed at him. Serve him right. No, Wim. There it was, in the street, belonging to no one. I just took it. After three years of having nothing I refuse nothing.'

Clair poured the tin into a casserole. 'I got a lipstick this evening. Look!' She smiled a wide, advertising-smile, dead eyes, white teeth. Emmie looked at her critically and sat down on a stool by the table.

'Very pink.'

'Very nice. Like you, after three years of nothing I refuse nothing too. Anyway I feel marvellous. In electric light at least. You don't think so, really?'

'Well: it's pink.' Emmie opened the music-case, scattered her belongings across the table. A folded shirt, a small purse, her battered box of Tarot cards, a Dutch–English dictionary, some hairpins and a copy of *The Daily Cobra*. Wim was plunking ineptly at the mandolin.

'All my worldly possessions. You know about the Dakota? Women from Ledaweg Camp. All dead.'

Clair was stirring slowly. 'Yes. I know. Is there news of the road convoy yet?'

'No. They killed the Commander and some soldiers.

They've sent soldiers out to escort it in, maybe tomorrow at Rozendaal.'

Clair put the lid on the casserole, looked at the tin clock. 'We'll eat about nine. Not too late? Nigel, Pullen, you know . . . is coming in, he's on late duty. I thought we would have a little celebration. He had this sent up today. Brand new. I was so stupid, behaving like a school girl. Crying. Do you believe it! I haven't got used to things yet. The house. My house again. But so strange. I don't recognize anything . . . nothing . . .'

Emmie folded the paper carefully. 'They didn't leave you much to remember, did they?' Her voice was dry, almost amused.

'No. But all the charcoal! Can you believe it? They looted everything from sheets to the lavatory brushes but left all the charcoal we bought in at the start of the war and hid in the inspection well in the garage! So now I am really rich. And five deck-chairs. And we have beds. One for you. You'll stay tonight, anyway. The curfew is too early. I have said so . . . but it stays. For a little while longer.'

Emmie cupped her chin in her hands, her elbows wide on the table. 'Who is Noah Coward?'

'I don't know. Who?'

'Someone called Noah Howard, Coward. English.'

'Clearly. I don't know. Ask Nigel.'

Emmie pulled a strand of hair across her face, sucked it thoughtfully. 'Oh it doesn't matter. Wim, I think that was a mistake. You make an awful noise. Plink, plank, plonk. I suppose we speak English at dinner. Pullen.'

'Of course. And useful practice. You said you have a job with them?'

'I had my interview. So formal! About fifty Chinese and Eurasians. Not one single Dutch girl. They are so silly really. They should help. There was a strange officer, very tall and thin, long fingers. An El Greco angel. Very polite, but he was so formal. Asked me to read something aloud. We did dictation, and shorthand, and he asked me about typing and I pointed out that the Dutch machines had a different keyboard from the English: which surprised him of course. They are so Imperial. Everything has to be English. And when I told him I'd been in Eastbourne for two years he was more surprised and said I would do "very nicely".' She laughed and shook her long hair about her shoulders. 'So now I have a job. I think,' she indicated the folded newspaper, 'something to do with this.'

'My dear Emmie! A reporter!' Clair laughed and started to set the tray with plates and cutlery.

'No, no, a secretary. They don't have reporters. And when I told him that my father had the biggest paper on the Island he was very interested indeed. I am to start on Monday next. But they will pay me from tomorrow. So I am rich too. A rich little collaborator. It's not *my* name for it you know, Clair, the Dutch call it that. Collaborating with the enemy. Just because the British aren't fighting the extremists and won't protect the Island.'

Clair carried the tray across the hall. 'Wim, come and help. Put on the light, please. The British are here to repatriate the internees. Nothing else. Everyone knows that.' She slid the tray carefully onto the rather ugly oak sideboard she had chosen the day before. 'No one expected the Japanese to capitulate to the Indonesians! Everything happened so quickly after the bombs on Japan. No one was sure what would happen after that. After all, no one had ever dropped those things on people before.'

The dining-room was cool, dim, sparsely furnished. Emmie stood leaning against the door. 'You didn't take much. No pictures. I remember two portraits. I always used to think they were watching me eat at table, disapproving of my table manners.'

'Pieter's grandmother and grandfather. Oh yes! Very grim. Very Colonial. They went . . . with all the rest. No; I didn't take pictures, pictures are such personal things. I couldn't have taken them. That would have seemed like stealing. Only Basic Essentials, it said on the form. So that's all I took, and odd plates,' she said, laying them round the oval table. 'I am a Navy wife, remember. Was. We'll put Nigel at the top, Wim here.'

On the verandah, sitting in the deck-chairs round the tin table, a candle flickering in the still air, the moon rising above the frangipani trees, a bottle of Geneva between them. Emmie suddenly stretched her arms above her head and clasped her hands like a winning boxer. 'Oh! This is so good. To be secure again, even like this, with patrols in the street and snipers sometimes . . . even this is so good. I suppose we should thank God. My Calvinistic upbringing, I imagine.'

'It has nothing to do with God. You should thank yourself. Your own faith, in yourself. That's why you are here. We are here. Our faith in ourselves. Three years in the camp taught me very clearly that there is no God. Religion, of any kind, is only for people who lack faith in themselves. People couldn't believe enough in themselves to create their own destinies so they invented gods for comfort. Buddha, Shiva, Mohammed, so on. I can't believe in God or in his discriminations, they are cruel, unfair and illogical.' Clair laughed suddenly and waved a moth away from the circle of light. 'What a way to talk! My father would turn in his grave.'

Emmie reached across and took the bottle. 'You said it was a celebration? Well, let us celebrate our new Faith. Ourselves! We are the gods. It has taken a cataclysm to teach me serenity. I suppose my father, who was a great deal more serious about God than yours, would say that the cataclysm came from God. As a punishment. Or a gift.'

Clair dismissed the thought with an impatient wave of her hand. 'Nonsense. The collapse of the British in Singapore brought you your cataclysm, my dear . . . and our own insularity and belief that the Japanese were nothing but a lot of bandy-legged idiots wearing glasses. That was the gravest mistake. I don't think that God had much to do with anything.'

Wim came on to the verandah, slid his arm round his mother's neck. 'Did you see my kite? I left it here. A truck is coming, I saw the lights.'

'Now we start in English,' said Clair, getting up. 'The kite's here. Where you left it.'

'Oh my God!' sighed Emmie.

'God won't help you. Just remember your grammar. Wim, go and open the door . . . he'll break his neck on the steps.'

'You don't mind if I propose a little toast, Clair, do you? To the new old house, to the new old company, and to you.' Pullen

43

had raised his glass. 'Your health, your happiness, and your future.'

'I never know,' said Clair suddenly, 'if one drinks to one's own health? Not, surely? So in fact we let you drink to us, and afterwards we will drink to you and the refrigerator and Emmie's job, and everything. A night for celebrations for us all.'

'The interview was all right, I gather? Nettles said he was very happy and that you had been to England, that so?'

'Eastbourne, you know it? But I'm very out of practice.'

'Well, Nettles was delighted. He found a couple of the other girls were fair . . . he'll use them as dispatchers for that news-paper. The General insists it is sent to all the Brigades. He's getting very steamed up about the bloody little thing. Terrible flap in the Mess this evening.'

Emmie looked blank. Pullen caught the look instantly.

'Flap. Umm . . . fuss, would you say, Clair? Yes, a fuss then. One of the chaps I had to meet in this morning, remember I told you? Getting frightfully high . . . drunk . . . rather funny in a sad sort of way. Nice chap as a matter of fact, but he's only been here twelve hours and the whole place has got him down already. Worried about having to go down to Pangpang. Can't say I blame him. They were all filling him up with champagne when I left. I suppose it is a bit of a shock to end up in the middle of another war just when you think you've done your whack. We all thought so. Still do. Never mind. But the fuss is rather good. Suddenly the powers that be have taken us seriously; realize we really can't cope alone here. Mountbatten is shuttling about the islands promising all kinds of support and morale boosters. Arrives here shortly with some bloody Labour MP to have a look at things. That's the Fuss. The Old Man is out of his skull with worry . . . having to entertain. Of course, as the way things stand here, he is the Governor, until your fellows arrive and take over.'

'And when will that be?'

'Well, not until we've got everyone out of the camps and sent off home, otherwise there really would be a full-scale war, and Heaven alone knows how long that'll take. Anyway everyone is very jumpy this evening up in "A" Mess. I was damned glad to get away.'

44

Emmie drew circles on the table with the handle of a fork. 'The officer who came with you to the Club this morning, you remember? Was he the one who is getting drunk?'

Pullen looked vague and then remembered. 'Of course. Yes. So I did. Yes, Rooke his name is, nice enough chap. Why?'

'Who is Noah Howard or Coward, do you know?'

'Noah Howard?'

Pullen looked puzzled for a moment, and then smiled.

'Do you perhaps mean Noël Coward? An actor fellow, playwright too; rather good.'

Emmie drew wider circles with controlled irritation. 'I don't know. Whoever he is he says a little English is not quite enough. And just before the interview.'

'I don't suppose he meant to be rude, you know. Perhaps you're taking it a little seriously.'

'It was a serious thing.'

'Oh! Come now! I imagine he was trying to be amusing, you know. He's a pleasant enough chap, I think. A gentleman, I have a feeling, even though he is an actor . . . you get all sorts in a conscript army. When do you start work for us?'

'On Monday week. The British don't like Eurasians, do they?'

'Beg pardon?' Pullen looked up swiftly; this time Clair saw the blush.

'Eurasians. Half-bloods. I think you call them chichis, don't you?'

'Never used such a filthy expression in my life.'

'Ah, not you. No. Not you, but an English woman in the camp. She escaped from Singapore just before the Fall and got caught here. Mrs Bethell-Wood. An English lady, from Surrey.'

'Contradiction in terms,' said Pullen mildly.

'Well, that's what she said. I don't know.'

'I can't believe she ever used that revolting expression.'

'Never to our faces, oh no! But that was her name for us. She was brave, I suppose, quite old. She never really complained, very . . . British, I suppose.'

'Brought up on a farm, you see,' she had said one morning in the camp while they were moving in a long serpentine trail slowly towards the only water tap which was working that day. 'So this sort of thing doesn't shock me. Cope pretty well. My father was a very progressive man; insisted that we children did our bit. Carrying, fetching, even making our beds occasionally. "You'll appreciate your servants better," he would say, "know how to handle them." He was right, as it happened. My name is Bethell-Wood. We haven't spoken before, have we? Are you Dutch?'

Emmie had nodded. 'Dutch–Javanese.'

'Ah! I see.' Mrs Bethell-Wood had grey-blond hair and white eyelashes. 'I wondered. Thought perhaps Spanish? Italian? That pretty olive skin. The Dutch are *so* white, aren't they? And all that blond hair.'

'They don't all have blond hair.'

'No, of course. I understand it is quite accepted in the NEI . . .'

'What is accepted?'

'You *do* speak excellent English. Mixed marriages.'

'Quite accepted. It bound the Colony together.'

'We found the reverse was true in India and Malaya. Rather unwise, we thought.'

'Why unwise?'

Mrs Bethell-Wood's hair had straggled out of its hastily pinned up bun, a long dry strand dropped round her neck. Impatiently she dragged it up and tucked it back with expert fingers. 'It's different here. But there *is* a prejudice. Anyway where I come from. The children, you know. They never belong on either side, you see. Very hard on them, so difficult to place them. They usually managed to find a job in the shops or the railways, that sort of thing . . . and that made the social acceptance even harder. And then resentment grows. Do you follow? Frightfully thoughtless of the parents. "Marry in haste, repent at leisure".'

The straggling line shuffled slowly under the blazing sun; some women had tin cans with wire handles, old buckets, petrol tins, saucepans. Mrs Bethell-Wood changed her canvas bucket from one arm to the other. 'Of course it's quite different here, one sees that clearly just by looking about. But it isn't the same in India or in Malaya. We were Government. So we saw a good deal of, shall I say, Social Problems. One really mustn't break the code, must one? Leads to such a lot of unhappiness and misunderstanding. Stick to one's own kind, much the best.'

46

'I never found that here. We were *all* our own kind.'

'No? Well, of course, as I said, it's different here.'

'It must be difficult for you in the camp, not to be with your own people, the English.'

Mrs Bethell-Wood laughed shortly, scratched her neck nervously. 'Mosquitoes. Frightfully bad in our house. No . . . no, no. I've always been a good mixer. I quite like foreigners. Well I mean, one *has* to, doesn't one? It takes all sorts to make a world. This camp really is a melting pot, isn't it? A very good lesson in mixing. I learned that during what my husband used to call laughingly my "busy times". The Bible Classes, Sunday Schools, Red Cross . . . I was very involved in all those things. One tried to help them, poor dears . . . they really can't quite manage on their own, can they? Haven't come down from the trees yet, my husband used to say: of course, many of them hadn't even gone up into them. But it's all patience . . . patience and no prejudice. The two "p's". Useful to remember. And patience is what we need here this morning. One water tap for the whole camp. So ill-organized. On purpose, I suppose. Teaching the whites a lesson. However,' she laughed re- signedly, 'that's one great advantage you have over us. You can take the heat so much better than we can. Never mind, put a good face on it. I really should have brought a handkerchief with me to put over my head.'

Emmie very nearly beat the head in with her bucket. She suddenly laughed at the memory and wiped out all the circles which she had made on the table top.

'It's such an awful name,' Pullen said. 'I almost can't believe it. But I do know the sort of woman. Convinced that they were doing right, and absolutely doing wrong. They were the worst things to happen to India; caused far more trouble than greased bullets, the mem-sahibs. It makes me furious . . .'

Emmie smiled across at his suddenly angry face. The little moustache, the wide angry eyes, the line of sweat across his forehead, his Adam's apple bobbing in his shining brown throat. His indignation.

'Please don't be angry. It didn't matter. It doesn't.'

'It did matter, and does. Bloody woman. You know, we were perfectly all right until they arrived, really managed frightfully well.'

And so did Adam before Eve tempted him, thought Emmie, with her wicked apple the guilty lump of which rides up and down in your kind, brown throat. Complicity. Clair started to clear the table, stacking plates and cutlery onto the tin tray. 'It's all over now,' she said, 'and anyway she died finally, last year. No one liked her, but I don't think she ever knew. She meant well.'

Pullen snorted angrily and handed her his plate. 'People who mean well cause the most awful mischief. I think it must be one of the saddest epitaphs a man could have engraved upon his gravestone. "He meant well".'

'Like missionaries, or Hitler or Gandhi, and the Americans with their bomb. I suppose they all meant well: for their countries anyway.' Emmie had taken up the bowl of pineapple chunks and was prodding the last three chunks slipping about in their syrup. 'You could even say that Dora Foto meant well. For herself.'

For a moment there was, for the first time in the evening, a neat, total silence. As small, as clear, as precise and well cut as a diamond. From the dark verandah Wim suddenly snapped it with a plunk, plink, plink, plunk and a smothered word of irritation. Clair continued on her way to the kitchen, Pullen looked at his watch; Emmie called out into the darkness.

'Wim, three pieces of the fruit left. Would you like to have them?'

Pullen got to his feet. 'Must be on my way. Relieve the Duty Officer in half an hour. I did enjoy myself.' He patted his pockets for his pipe and tobacco. 'I only hope to Heaven there isn't another case of rape while I'm on. It really is very distressing. Three in the last two weeks . . . it's getting quite a matter of course. Indian troops, no women, curfews and the perimeter. I do so hate having to ask the medical questions, you know. I'm not a doctor; not my style at all. Oh dear. It all is a rumble bumble, I'm afraid.'

The moon had risen, a shadowy garden; still. He looked up at the starry sky. 'You take care, both of you. Lock the doors and the shutters. The patrols are out, but don't risk a thing, and thank you both once again.' He turned suddenly to Emmie and took her hand. 'And thank you for joining us. I hope you'll be happy, I think you will. And we are really most grateful. I

48

don't know what you'll have to do just at first . . . interpreting, of course, as you know, but I expect they'll find you something more definite as soon as we all get sorted out. And don't hold that Bethell woman against us, will you? Just put her out of your mind.'

Emmie pressed his hand. 'I have already. Honestly.'

'That's excellent,' he said.

They stood for a moment and watched him bump through the potholes of Brabantlaan. Wim had started to bolt the shutters.

Her room, for which Clair had modestly apologized, was simple, sparse, and cool. Luxury after her own room in Chung Ling's little wooden hut in the Chinese sector, with its wooden boards, walls papered with old newspapers and magazines, a bamboo bed and the tin trunk which contained her few worldly possessions. Here the tiled floor was cool to her bare feet, the large brass four-poster draped in mosquito net like a separate, secret room. A chair, a table and, best of all, a wash-bowl in the corner with a large tin jug of water. She put out the dim light, opened the bolted shutters. Moonlight flooded in across her as she leaned over the balcony rail. It was high now. A steady white plate in the star-studded sky. To her left, the distant city, indicated only by the dull red glow of the still burning rubber dumps. Ahead, beyond the ragged silhouettes of frangipani, palm and bamboo, the hillside slipped down to the blackness of the plain where the arrogant moon reflected itself in a thousand broken fragments on the paddy fields; and rising high beyond them the mountains, a long row of knuckled fists thrusting against the stars. To her right, shining silent and deserted, the high tiled gables of the other villas in the street. There was no wind, no sound. The only sign of the war was the dull, wavering glow of the fire over the city. Everything else appeared to be at peace.

It had been a long time coming. She could mark the end of it by that humid February Sunday in 1942 when they heard on the radio that the British had surrendered Singapore. The unthinkable had happened, even though there had been warnings enough brought by the first shattered British women who, with hastily packed suitcases and frightened children, had managed to reach the Island, en route for Ceylon or Australia, by the last

49

of the big ships able to leave the doomed peninsula. In exhausted voices they spoke of the amazing speed of the Japanese advance, of the air raids, the vicious looting, the collapse of morale and the disarray and incompetence which reigned in Singapore. But nothing, it seemed, had shocked them as much as the cunning and might of the enemy.

A younger Mrs Bethell-Wood said, with three crying children and all her worldly goods in a couple of pillow-cases, 'There are millions of them. They came on bicycles! They simply swarmed down the peninsula like ants . . . no one *prepared* us for that. No one *knew* they were so strong. No one *told* us.' And no one told us, Emmie thought, that they would arrive so soon, landing so swiftly in the dark, taking us by surprise, not least the Saturday Night dancers at the Planters Club who, like the British in Singapore, had refused to believe that normal life could not continue and that They would be dealt with long before they could set foot in Java or Borneo or the Island itself. That the Island could be occupied was unthinkable until the unthinkable happened two weeks later.

At first they had been very polite and insisted that life in the city should continue as before. They appeared very fond of the children, surprised and delighted by blond hair and blue eyes, handing them sweets and fruits, correct behaviour towards the women, no raging, raping invaders, apparently; disciplined soldiers behaving less like the conquering Enemy than an efficient, if firm, Police Force. And then the first rumours that the slum area towards the dock was being evacuated, that wire was being strung around it, that a Reception Area was being made. A reception area for what, for whom? And then the orders to assemble in Rembrandt Plein one morning, one piece of hand baggage per person. The Male Europeans to the North area, women and children, 'male children up to fifteen', to the South area. It took all day to sort them out, the men into trucks, the women into lines, the men to camps far across the Island, the women walking through the silent city to their prepared camp at Molendijk, haggard, hot, exhausted and numbed with terror and grief. Even the children silent, subliminally aware of a deep despair.

But how absurd to remember it all now. In the peace, in the stillness, in the white light of the risen moon. She pushed away from the balcony gently, her hands cupping her elbows, arms tight across her chest. A little breeze riffled through the flame-tree branches filigreed against the paler sky and the dull glow from the rubber fire quickly lightened, flared gently, edging the lowering, loitering smoke with pink. The breeze dropped suddenly. The tree was still again, the fire waned. Crickets in the dry grass below. Not quite all peace. The fire reminded. Quiet but not yet peace. She closed the shutters slowly, bolted them, and felt her way in the sudden dark, to the folds of her bed.

Not so long ago there had been a bankruptcy of hope. Wasn't that the phrase which the El Greco angel had used this morning? His neat cap of tight auburn curls, the long grave face, the fastidious fingers which smoothed the pages of the book from which he dictated to her so precisely.

'What a bankruptcy of hope! I ask a few questions. Bachir is a *scullion* in a café; Ashour is *laboriously* earning a few pennies by breaking stones on the roads.' He had paused and looked up at her with indifferent eyes, closed the book.

'Went too fast for you?'

'No.'

'Splendid. It's Gide. *The Immoralist*. Do you know it?'

'No.'

'All I have at hand. You managed the Arabic names?'

'I think so.' She spelled carefully, 'B-A-S-H-I-R.'

'No. It's a "C".'

'I'm sorry.'

'No, no, rather unfair. Let me see.'

He had taken the notebook and read swiftly through the page, handing it back with a pleasant smile. 'Excellent. Apart from the two names, and there's a "c" in scullion, not a "k". You've done this a lot?'

'Not for many years. In England.'

'Oh. Where?'

'At Eastbourne; a convent, and then London with Pitman's.'

'Goodness me. Very travelled.'

'I wanted to be a journalist. My father was.'

'Where?'

'Here. He owned *Het Daag* — the biggest newspaper in the Island.'

'How frightfully interesting.' He folded his arms and leant across the desk. 'I suppose you know all about newspapers then?'

'Not all about. A little only.'

'You know we have one?'

'No. I didn't. I'm sorry.'

He rummaged about among some papers and pulled out a small double-sheet. '*The Daily Cobra.* We just started it. I think you'd do very nicely for it, don't you?'

'I'd try. I know quite a bit. Type-setting . . . you know.'

'I think it's a frightfully good idea! What a stroke of luck, Miss van Hoorst.' He handed her the blurry little newspaper and told her to take it and look it over. 'I'm sure you could be very useful. Shall we say you could start work, say . . . umm . . . say, on Monday next? You know where the Headquarters are, don't you? The old Anglo-Dutch oil buildings. Would eight o'clock be all right? Ask for me. Nettles, as in Stinging.' He laughed a clear, disinterested laugh. Seeing her face, he added, 'It's a sort of weed. Never mind. Such a stroke of luck to find you, I really can't believe it.'

'I think it is my stroke too.'

'Let's say half and half then. We really are in a hell of a jam here. No one can speak Dutch among us and then this silly boycotting business. We must get things sorted out. I mean after all,' he ran a long hand wearily over his tight auburn curls and glanced swiftly at his watch, 'the sooner we are all home and safe the better, don't you think?'

It was a rhetorical question and he had already risen offering her his hand. 'I absolutely don't blame your people, you know. I imagine I'd feel much the same. However, no one exactly *asked* the Japs to surrender the way they did, but who else was there with all of you still locked up in your camps and no brave Allies storming the beaches until two weeks later. I am sure they mean well . . . the Dutch. National pride, anger, bitterness, disappointment, all those things . . . but really, it is a bit idiotic, doesn't do much good, does it?' He had seen her to the door and called 'Next' and Pearl Ching had hurried past her.

She stared up into the dim folds of the sagging net which hung like a still vapour in the faint moon filtering through the shutters. No, it didn't help. Meaning well was something which the English seemed to think was a fault rather than a virtue. Pullen had said it was the saddest epitaph a man could have on his gravestone. A world of Bethell-Woods. Perhaps it was . . . a world of Bethell-Woods and Dora Fotos . . . two women with only one single link in common apart from their sex. Meaning well. Unaware of the destruction. It had been Mrs Bethell-Wood who, whispering snippets of news which she had gleaned from the secret radio (which Clair had hidden in a tin of paint) too liberally and without caution, had found herself betrayed and in consequence betrayed Clair who had refused to speak, so that Wim would bear the hideous scar on his arm for the rest of his life. It was Dora Foto who had hidden her four Australians, Mel, Dickie, Ron and Joe, in the foolish hope of getting them away by fishing boat one dark night and who, when her own unexpected internment faced her, had had to surrender them.

'They'll be all right. They are Servicemen. Soldiers. They'll send them to a camp. The League of Nations says so.' They beheaded them on the football pitch in the stadium at Rozendaal. No epitaphs for Bethell-Wood or Mel, Dickie, Ron or Joe. And Dora Foto was not, as somebody had once said, the dying kind. She'd bedevil Death if he should come towards her; she'd cheat, cajole and charm him, in her accustomed manner, to delay, postpone and finally evade him. Dora was the ultimate survivor. But when all was said and done she too had meant well. It is something, Emmie thought wryly, that I must avoid during my work with the Army. She stretched up and curled her hands around the coolness of the brass rail above her. I wish I could sleep, I wish I could. My head spins with too much talk, too much thinking, too much joy. I cannot sleep happiness away, there hasn't been so much of it that I can afford to simply accept it. I must cherish it and make it last. She left her bed and unbolted the shutters again.

The ragged garden was washed in light. A bat swung across the valley and was lost against the knuckle-fisted mountains hard and black against an immensity of stars. She could see the hands of her cheap tin watch; it was well after two. Another day had started. She scooped up her hair into a rough bundle

53

and held it on the top of her head, turning her naked body into the cool, still air, bathing in the night.

'No. I cook in it,' she said aloud, and laughed.

Three villas away up the deserted street Major Nettles lightly shrugged himself out of his kimono.

CHAPTER THREE

Hands behind his head, wide-legged on the rumpled bed, he watched her cross the room drying her hair vigorously with his khaki towel. Full breasts bouncing with the effort. A neat waist, plump thighs dimpling as she braced herself. He felt a swift surge of pleasure.

'You know, Dora, you've got the prettiest bum I've ever seen.'

She shook her hair, fluffed it out, threw the damp towel on to his belly. It's a paunch: looks like a little hat, she thought. She combed her fringe roughly with her fingers.

'Flanders mare,' she said.

'Nonsense. It's beautiful.'

'I'm Belgian. That's why. That's what they call me. I know.'

'Jealousy.'

'Maybe. Everyone is jealous of something here. I've left enough water for you.'

'I'm jealous too. Of you.'

'Ach . . . needn't be.' She blew a light kiss and padded over to a chair rummaging in her clothes. 'I know when I'm well off, Leo, a loyal woman; you'll see.'

He watched her pull a stocking over an arched foot, smooth it up her shin, round her calf. 'That makes me very excited, you know.'

'What does? Putting these on?'

'Yes. Terrific. Shiny, slinky, smooth . . .'

'You've had quite enough.'

'I could go again.'

'Disgusting. You're a naughty boy.' She snapped a garter round her plump thigh and started on the other stocking humming under her breath, ignoring the implied suggestion; dismissing him. He heaved himself off the bed, took the towel and waved it at her.

'Look! Not bad for fifty-seven, eh?'

She looked at him critically under her fringe. 'Naughty boy. Go and put cold water on it.'

'You'd get a stand out of a monk. You're a tease.' He tramped

55

into the bathroom, poured water into the basin, started to wash. You see; Peggy wouldn't have said that. Naughty boy. She'd call me Old boy ... Old boy. Not naughty. A world of difference. Difference all right, Christ! Where was she now? Banging about in her ruddy little flat in Moscow Mansions, Cromwell Road, that's where. Stuffing her bloody old mother with bread and milk and bossing the backside off poor old Daphne. Then committee meetings, badminton, Red Cross, ARP, making sure the Land Girls weren't getting screwed. Fat hopes. But she'd interfere anywhere she wasn't wanted. Bigot. Prude. Duff marriage, that was. Duff. Right from the start. First night in Darjeeling I knew we were sunk. 'Do it outside. I don't want it inside me.' What a bloody awful beginning for a lifetime of until-death-do-us-part. Died *that* night.

'You're my wife, Peggy.' He could hear the sobs now.

'If you want that sort of thing you should have got a girl from Whiteway and Laidlaws ... a tart.'

He had almost laughed in her face, but she'd never have seen the joke. Buying your conjugal rights from a Calcutta department store. And that's how it had been from April the third, nineteen bloody twenty-one. Otherwise, of course, a perfect wife. To the Regiment. Good at tennis, played bridge like a pro, chose the staff, ran the bungalows impeccably, good with the other wives, tough, firm, no nonsense there, arranged the choirs, the picnics, the Bible Class, sewing bees, the jumble sales, God! Those jumble sales ... A pillar of the Church, like her father, bossing the junior officers; only she called it Mothering. Christ almighty! Mothering! The last thing she'd ever know about. The only thing she knew *all* about was Class. 'Not quite our class, I'm afraid, but pleasant.' or 'Of course she married out of her class; as I did. Mistake, I always think. Leads to endless distress.' And that said in front of her sodding Sewing Bee. Loud as that, and me present: as if I were cellophane.

'You deceived me, from the first day we met at the DC's party.'

'Peg, I didn't, I swear.'

'I never *knew* your father was a Quartermaster Sergeant: you never said.'

'Didn't think it was important.'

'It was. Others knew. There were hints, raised eyebrows . . . I ignored them.'

'Good thing too.'

'Not as it turned out.'

'We manage.'

'I was too trusting. Where I came from gentlemen didn't lie.'

'I didn't lie!'

'Evaded. Avoided, whatever word you like.'

'And where the hell did you come from, I'd like to know? Bangor and a bloody Welsh parson with a bit of private money.'

'My dowry. And don't swear at me. At least he could read . . .'

'And so did my bloody father, he read too.'

'Figures.'

He nearly struck her, but she smiled blandly knowing he wouldn't dare.

However, she'd pushed him, he had to give her that; for her own sake, not his. Saw to his promotions, entertained enough, organized everyone around her.

He dropped the soap and had to chase it skittering across the tiles.

Organized herself too, knew when to lose a rubber at bridge, and to whom. And for what good reason. 'I know you'll mention it to Archie, Prudence. He can't possibly overlook Leo, I know, but a little word from you, you know, makes such a difference.' That barking laugh, the score cards crumpled quietly, the cheque written and pushed calmly towards the wretched Prudence who gently helped push him in her turn, towards his Majority. Oh, she was crafty at that sort of thing, cunning. Very Welsh. Shameless, she knew what she was after. They were all terrified of her, of course. She was beyond reproach naturally, knew who hit the secret bottle, who went wandering after the tennis matches, the picnics; and with whom. Bribed a whole fleet of loyal servants. Her Fifth Column, he called it, which sent her into white rage and twice to church on Sunday.

When he finally got his Division in '42 she suddenly decided that she had quite fulfilled any vows she might have made at the wedding and announced that she was off 'home' where she was really needed. 'You don't need me now: you've got a war to fight, old boy. That'll keep you busy and I'm not sitting about in this loathsome country rolling bandages and nursing the wounded. I'm going "home" now; about time. Daphne is at her wits' end with Edward dead, Mother's nearly eighty and almost blind, and I hate India and the Indians . . . always did, always will. Mean, spiteful, deceitful and sly. Don't try and stop me, Leo—as if you even would—my mind is quite made up. Booked a passage, compassionate grounds, pulled rank. Bombay on the tenth.'

He hadn't made a fuss. Didn't care much anyway. He didn't need her now, she was right . . . he'd done his best, he felt. Let her clear off. Good riddance to bad rubbish. Nanni Singh would look after him; best bloody bearer in the Army.

'Do as you like, Peg. It's your life.'

'Now it is. It's been yours ever since we married; all for you. Now it's my turn for a change. Taken long enough, old boy. I'm off.'

'Very well, Peg.'

'Don't call me Peg. My name's *Peggy*.'

'As far as I'm concerned it's Peg. Bloody wooden peg. Driven into the ground with a sledge-hammer, a sodding tent peg you are!'

She had smiled suddenly, looked almost gentle, hands folded calmly in flannelled lap, feet crossed neatly at the ankles, sharp nose held high, head to one side, a kind of bird, eyes bright, cold; killing the smile.

'That's it. Quite right. Driven into the ground. You know what tent pegs do, old boy, don't you? No need to tell you, I'm sure. Take up the slack. Hold things together. Didn't know you ever understood. Too late now. Bombay on the tenth.'

He dried himself briskly. Slack. Not he. One thing she was wrong about. Nothing slack about me, never has been. I've made it, all along the line from Quetta to Major bloody General. He picked up his ivory comb and ran it through thin reddish hair. I've done bloody well for Sergeant Cutts. A mention, and MC, now Governor of this ruddy Island, that's not to be sneezed at, for God's sake! Slack! Christ! I can still get it up twice in an afternoon . . . she'd have a fit if she knew that. But that's something she never found out once.

In the bedroom Miss Foto had finished dressing when he came back, fixing a neat velvet bandeau round her head, smoothing her fringe carefully under it.

She smiled a vague smile. 'What a time you have been.'

He pulled on his underpants. 'Big boy. Lots of me to wash.'

She flicked him a look: tall enough; paunch, sagging underdrawers, thinning red hair, slack breasts over a sparse mottled mat. Searching for his vest.

'I hate afternoon sex.' She turned towards the long mirror in the wardrobe, twisted about checking the seams of her stockings. 'I feel awful. Not tidy.'

His voice was muffled in the cellular vest. 'Only time, my dear. When else? Sunday's a day of rest, even here.'

'I feel like a whore. All the light.'

'Bugs and bombs at night, you know. Go down to the lounge. Nanni'll be bringing in the tea, a good cup of tea will make you feel better.'

She picked up her leather pochette. Why did the English always think that a cup of tea was the panacea for everything? Tea. She'd rather have a Bols. A beer even. She poked about, found a lipstick, pursed her lips into a false kiss, widened them into a dead grin, spread them thickly with two even strokes top and bottom. Scarlet.

'I don't like him. This Indian.'

'Good gracious me! Nanni? Marvellous fellow. Twenty-six loyal years.'

'He spies, I know he does.'

'Stuff! He just keeps an eye open. Anything you want. Very discreet.'

'He has a boy.'

He went red and unrolled his socks from a lumpy ball. 'Oh come now, Dora doll . . .'

'I've seen him, you know. A youth. Always in the kitchen.'

'Well, that's his affair. He's a grandfather three times over. Can't get a girl here, so . . .' He shrugged uneasily. 'Has to have a bit of fun, no harm.'

'Unless he talks too much. They'll spread it round the bazaar like a plague.'

'Nonsense. He *never* speaks; not that sort of fellow. I know.' He pulled on his shirt, buttoned the cuffs.

'I hope you're right. It's disgusting, I think.' She screwed the lipstick into its case.

'There's a song; you heard it, Dora?

> "There's a boy across the river
> With a bottom like a peach.
> But alas I have no boat." '

She didn't look at him. Slid the lipstick into her pochette and snapped it shut. Firmly. 'You British . . .'

'Indian actually. Old marching song.'

She went to the door, the pleats in her skirt swinging.

'You've got a bottom like a peach, Dora doll.'

She was on the landing and didn't hear him. Or chose not to. He smiled, rubbed his nose, looked for his trousers.

On the verandah tea had been laid already. Two cups, two plates, a lime sliced under a little net cage. Sunlight flickering through leaves. She wandered into the cool of the lounge, as he called it, dim with shuttered light. On his desk by the far window a neat pile of papers. Memos, Notes, Daily Orders, Information. She lifted the brass frog which held them down against a sudden breeze. Two replacement officers, Saturday, LST 3904.08.00 hrs. Convoy from Rozendaal, Major Caplan commanding depart Sunday 06.30 hrs. Nothing she didn't know already. Mountbatten: scrawled beside another name with a question mark. She looked up suddenly and saw Nanni Singh watching her motionless at the kitchen door. He held a tray, behind him a slim youth with a plate of sandwiches. When she had replaced the papers and the brass frog he moved, and crossed on silent feet to the verandah. The boy passing her, grinned in complicity. She felt suddenly irritated and taking up the papers again she crossed to the staircase and called up loudly. For Nanni Singh.

'Leo? When does this Mountbatten get in?'

He called something down, but the door was shut; she watched Singh carefully as he came back with the empty tray. He didn't look at her, but went over to the desk, straightened the brass frog neatly, and gesturing for the boy to go first, entered the kitchen and silently closed the door.

Game, set and match. She thought. To me. But I know him: he'll wait patiently before he strikes. I know the kind. Worked with them often enough, God knows. She replaced the papers under the frog and went out onto the verandah.

'You be mother.' He was spruce, shining, crisply starched into his fresh green uniform. A smell of talcum powder. He didn't look so bad dressed, blue eyes sparkling; the thinning red hair, now dry, seemed less meagre. And he was tall. That was always useful for an ageing man. He patted her silk knee, grinning inanely, as he sat before her. 'I *like* afternoon sex. Sets me up wonderfully. Like the tea afterwards as well. Very jolly. Bucks me up no end. You know, Dora doll, you really are a bloody good lay. Know how to please a chap, what? I feel in splendid form.'

She poured the tea steadily through a silver strainer, added a ring of lime, one lump of sugar, handed him the cup. 'You know, Leo, you speak very familiar to me.'

He laughed cheerfully, crossing his legs carefully so as not to crease the slacks. 'Speak the truth, my dear: haven't been able to say that for years and years, no idea what a pleasure it is for me, supposed to be a compliment to you.'

She stirred her tea, one finger neatly crooked. 'I accept it then. As a compliment. But I don't find the words attractive. Do you know what I mean? Never mind, you are a good boy, I think. Yes, a good boy.'

'Oh Dora doll, my little tease. I don't know what I'd do without you.'

And you'd better not, my dear, she thought, because I'm not leaving for a time. I stay on. No matter what. But you'd better have a smile from me, to assure you of my good intentions. She did, over the teacup, and added a wink, which threw him into transports of boyish glee, and joined him in whatever game he thought he was playing: by himself. You, my dear Major General Cutts, are this girl's life for the time being. My bread and butter, my roof, my security. With your help I'll get away from this bloody place and move on. Ten years is a long, long time, and I have outstayed the welcome. But when all is said and done, she reasoned, you've had a good run for your money.

Her mother, who had been known as the Belle of Courtrai, at least as far as the Hotel Terminus was concerned, had always insisted that you should get the most out of your investments,

61

whatever they were. She herself had been a bad investment which La Belle had turned into gilt-edged stock. Born of an unknown father, she had determinedly resisted every effort made to prevent her entry into the world and had opened her eyes defiantly almost before her lungs had forced out her first triumphant cry. Resignedly La Belle held her, cradled against a full breast, bewildered, somewhat irritated, but aware of a deep-rooted sense of contentment. And La Petite Folie, as she became known, proved to be a good, peaceful, pleasing child who grew into a shrewd, tough, amusing, good-natured girl, delighting her many 'uncles', singing indelicate songs charmingly in the bar, and finally, when the time came for which she had been well coached, taking over La Belle's varied batons from her wearying hands and placing them neatly, and deliciously, just exactly where they belonged. She also developed a particular gift for making dresses, and more importantly, for drawing them herself, in coloured crayons and simple, effective lines, so that her clientele, now extended to her own sex, arrayed in her original designs, culled from the fashion papers of Paris and Brussels, found their own profits much enhanced in the provincial towns of the area. La Belle was mystified by this fortuitous talent in her child, and wondered, constantly, where she could have inherited it, for she herself could do no more than make out a menu or a bill, in both of which she excelled. But to draw! To be able to suggest lace, satin, bows, buttons and taffeta ruches, that was a miracle.

'There was a photographer once,' she used to say. 'I remember him. Very, very refined. Only in Courtrai for a night or two . . . dark, with a fine moustache, a handsome rogue, Jewish of course, he took photographs of us all. We dressed in our very best and made a pretty group in the yard with carpets and chairs and a big bowl of peonies. But he forgot to send them. We waited and waited and waited and nothing happened. So of course he was Jewish. It was not long after that when you started. Oh my God the panic! Hot baths, exercises, bicycling for miles, emetics, they nearly killed me. But not you; you hung on, you little devil. Maybe it was him, that photographer, same eyes. He had an eye for composition as well as for all the rest. I'd like to think it was, I never got the photograph, but I got you. I'm not dissatisfied, my little Foto.'

And from then on, because she had reached a respectable age and position in her work, she was called Miss Foto. (The Miss being borrowed from Mistinguette as an added honour.) And as such, under that name, she had prospered exceedingly. In 1921, just as Miss Foto reached the age of consent, without which she had done remarkably well for a number of years, La Belle suffered a grave stroke upon leaving her bed one afternoon and aware that, as she put it, the sand was running out of her Time, she told her daughter exactly where her fortune had been hidden all these years (and for which her daughter had tirelessly searched ever since she was old enough to climb a ladder or lift a floor board), demanded an elegant funeral with 'feathers to all the horses', insisted that Courtrai was far too small a town for a girl of such rapidly developing talents and that, as soon as the To-Do had all been done, she was to take her fortune to 'Uncle' Albrecht in Brussels who had always promised that he would be more than delighted to assist a sorrowing girl through the tribulations and despairs of her mourning period. Having delivered herself of this list of instructions, La Belle folded her one good arm across her still-plump breast, and closed her eyes.

'Ah Mamma! Don't speak so. You'll soon be well. This is nothing.'

'This is everything. I sense it. I know.'

'No, no! It can't be true, it isn't so.'

'If I didn't know it was so,' said La Belle pointedly, 'do you think I'd have told you where I hid my money?'

'You'll be well again. You see. And then we'll go on a holiday. Deauville or Le Touquet.'

'I'll not get well; and the only holiday I'll get is in Heaven, God willing.'

Miss Foto's tears were nearly real. After all she had known her mother for a considerable time, and intimately. She also admired her. 'Don't speak so, Mamma. Don't leave me. What do I care for your fortune?'

'A very great deal!' snapped La Belle and died comfortably, in her sleep, as she had intended, later that evening.

The funeral was a modest affair. No plumed horses, and a plain, pine coffin. As Miss Foto knew only too well, dead was dead and that was that.

63

She was delighted with her fortune; La Belle had been very successful at her job, popular, prudent, expert, and, above all, diligent. She had also been thrifty. So armed with a not inconsiderable sum, a portfolio of sketches and designs, a becoming black cloche hat, monkey-fur coat and a pair of snake-skin shoes which she had long coveted and could now afford, Miss Foto set off for Brussels and the hirsute, if attentive, 'Uncle' Albrecht with La Belle's often quoted admonition ringing in her ears. 'Always go to the top, up and up: but remember! Never look down, for fear you become giddy and fall.'

Miss Foto obeyed this stricture to the letter, and on her rise, which was that of a rocket, she never once felt the least flicker of vertigo.

'Uncle' Albrecht owned a modest, but important, chain of provincial journals and very soon her elegant, imaginative little designs and ideas were appearing regularly and Miss Foto became so well-established, so hard-working and so determined, that a bemused 'Uncle' found himself purchasing a small dress-shop in a select quarter of the city, and Miss Foto was launched as a dressmaker and hat designer under the name of 'Dora Foto: Modes'. The Dora deriving from 'Uncle' Albrecht's name for her, a diminution of his word Adorable.

At about the same time that King Albert fell to his death from a rock in the Ardennes, clearly proving La Belle's advice to be correct, 'Uncle' Albrecht, worried by the state of affairs generally, the assassination of the King of Yugoslavia, Stavisky's suicide and an undercurrent of general European distress, jumped out of a sixth floor window in the Palace Hotel, leaving his affairs in disarray and Miss Foto minus her shop, for he had imprudently bought it in his own name and not hers. All this falling made her very unsettled, and shortly after Hitler conclusively came to power, she decided it might be a wise move to take what she had and put as much space as possible between herself and the shadows which were lengthening across Europe. To this end she packed up, took a train to Amsterdam, and from there she sailed, with three cabin trunks and a good deal of very useful experience one way and another, to Java. Enchanted by the islands, by the comparative ease with which she found herself accepted, with the great opportunities for a girl

64

who was so cosmopolitan in a rather backward European social society, she made her way to the Island (after a good look around from Bali to Borneo) and settled down to a comfortable existence in yet another little dress shop with a busy salon on the side, in a select neighbourhood, just off Nassau Boulevard, where she catered for the wives of the local diplomats, military, and naval personnel. And, after ten in the evenings, very discreetly, for their husbands. She had the prettiest hats and girls in town. And she had prospered very comfortably until the Japanese made their rather sudden, unexpected entry during the Saturday Night Dance at the Planters Club. But even then, by dint of sheer cunning, determination, and sense, she had managed to make her way; and although hats and ball gowns and sharkskin suits for the Sunday Cocktail Parties had had to go, the salon had, in greatest secrecy, managed to survive. For the Invaders themselves.

With more than a thousand women caged up in the Camp, deprived for a long time of male companionship and comfort, so essential to a woman's morale and well-being, it seemed a wanton waste of her organizing powers, her experience, and her small, but almost isolated, ground floor quarters which bordered, conveniently, the very edge of the perimeter wire. Everything was done with the utmost taste. Never a light allowed. Colonel Nakamura, the Commandant, was a perfect gentleman who spoke excellent French having studied at the Sorbonne, who realized the deep-seated need of his women 'guests' and also those of a number of his more intellectual younger officers. He also recognized his own. The ladies, when they arrived, arrived discreetly by the front door in the dark street of the camp, the gentlemen, quietly by the neat opening in the wire at the back. It was a perfect, well-organized, nearly elegant arrangement. And the ladies were always only too happy to show their gratitude for such an arrangement by leaving a little gift in Miss Foto's keeping. A lipstick, a powder compact, a ring perhaps, sometimes a little jewel, stockings or even, now and then and as the years drifted on, a treasured length of cloth, a dress, or a pure gold fountain pen; just little bits and pieces really. For they had not been able to bring very much with them to the camp in only one suitcase. But by the time the British eventually arrived and brought everything back

65

to near-normal, she was happy to see that her thoughtfulness, compassion and business acumen had helped her to accumulate enough assorted goods to open a small shop. Quite rightly, the ladies were only too delighted, once freed, to buy back their belongings. For very modest sums. There had been a few minor embarrassments, naturally, but she had managed to deal with those. No one, she felt sure, would want to dwell on the past; the present and the future were what mattered now.

She placed her empty cup on the tray, and reached out a hand to her 'security'.

'Another cup?'

He shook his head, 'No, my dear. Much as I'd like to spend the whole afternoon just sitting here looking at you but,' he looked at his watch, 'duty calls. There should be some news about that blasted convoy we sent out this morning from Rozendaal. Nettles said he'd probably have some information about now; he and the others are coming in after five.' He grinned slyly, 'Know not to disturb me, unless it's a big disaster, before that — otherwise engaged. My weekly rest, eh? With my Dora doll. You haven't had a sandwich.' He took one and stuffed it into his mouth. Miss Foto brushed her pleats, collected her little pochette, and got up. The movement took him by surprise. 'Where are you off to, my love?' His words were indistinct, coming as they did through a mixture of crumbs and Marmite. 'Don't go. Anything we have to talk about we could talk about in front of you, you know. Only military stuff, not secret.'

'No. I'll go home. Leave the gentlemen together.'

'As you like. Boring, I suppose.'

'Not so. But I wash my hair, and tell the cook about supper. You will come?'

'Of course. About nine-ish . . .'

'A little duck she got in the market. Curried, shall we?'

'Perfect.'

She bent and kissed his bald spot, he patted her bottom affectionately.

'Prettiest in the world. I'm a lucky boy.'

'You be good now. Nine o'clock.'

He sat watching her cross the verandah, down the steps, and across the brown grass of what had been a garden, to the hedge

of bamboo and the little gate which led to her modest
bungalow. Nice to have her right next door, and Tim on the
other side. Everyone on hand, but discreetly apart. She had
arranged all that perfectly: as well as being a perfect mistress
she was also a bloody good billeting-officer. Settled them all
in, knew every house in the area. Don't know what we'd have
done without her. He rang the silver bell for Nanni Singh and
stuffed another sandwich into his mouth, cupping his hand to
catch the crumbs.

'Nettles Sahib and Roberts Sahib are coming in. You have
beer?'

Nanni Singh collected his tray and nodded silently.

'And some of that American stuff in tins. Tomato, got that?'

'All ready, General Sahib.' He looked about the verandah as
if he'd lost something. 'The mem-sahib has gone?'

'She's gone.'

Nanni grunted, 'Only beer glasses then.'

'Only beer glasses. Plenty of beer.'

'As I said.' He moved silently across the verandah towards his
kitchen.

Tim Roberts had tight black hair, neatly parted in the centre,
and a small black moustache which looked like a smudge
beneath his nose and, thought the general, made him look like
Hitler, or a grocer, anyway common: however, he was a good
ADC and he'd miss him; and he could talk to him, didn't feel
uncomfortable with him as he did with Nettles who sometimes
made him feel a bit uneasy, although God knew Nettles was
damned efficient too . . . it was just the feeling that he was
smiling at some private thought all the time. Never quite came
clean with things, superior, reserved, a bit of a bloody snob . . .
too well-educated and knew it. A bit too dapper. Dora sensed
it, he could tell that. She always slipped away if Nettles was
coming in. Woman's intuition. If Nanni Singh fussed her, what
would Nettles do? Give her a seizure. Ah well . . . He poured
himself another beer and sat down behind his desk.

'And they reached them at Kampong 10?'

Roberts folded his map and stuffed it into its case. 'That's it,
Sir. Just in time . . . poor old Bob Holly copped it in the head,

67

six others with grenade splinters, nothing much, and two of the trucks on fire. But the extremists had buggered off.'

'With sixty women and children,' said Brigadier 'Bunny' Blackett. 'God knows where to. Hostages hopefully: otherwise it'll be the same thing as the Dakota business. Hack 'em to bits.'

'But the survivors are all safely in, eh?' Cutts sipped his beer.

'All in reception, two hundred and thirty out of the three hundred. It really can't go on like this much longer, Sir. We simply have to have air-support . . . can't deal with things otherwise, they just melt into the forests . . . got all the transport they need, all the ammo, damned well organized, and quite fanatical. Fanatical, screaming and yelling: what we need is the RAF to search out and destroy.'

'I know what we need, Bunny,' Cutts snapped. 'I've told Singapore, as you know. We'll just have to wait for Mount-batten, set it all before him. Facts, figures, casualties and so on. I know, as well as you do, that we're fighting a war with our hands tied; it's the same in Java, all over the islands . . . bloody bad luck for everyone concerned, but we'll just have to struggle on as best we can. I can't get another brigade up to Pangpang or a bloody Squadron from the RAF in ten minutes! They don't know what the situation here really is at SEAC.'

Blackett shifted slightly in his chair. 'Well, Sir, the sooner they do the fewer lives we'll lose. Of course we'll all do the best we can, but the men are getting pretty demoralized; a hundred casualties since we landed . . . not including Dutch civilians or Allied prisoners . . .'

'Look here, Bunny.' Cutts leaned forward, clasped his hands together firmly, narrowed his eyes, and straightened his back. Usually an imposing posture, he felt. 'I've requested a squadron, requested more field guns . . . made it quite clear we can't handle it alone. What's the result? Mountbatten's coming out to have a shufti. See for himself, can't do more than that, can I? The Supremo himself on a fact-finding mission? If he can't fix things we can't. Of course three brigades on an island two hundred bloody miles long isn't enough; but who expected a bloody civil war, eh? Who did?'

His patent anger left a singing silence in the shadowed room.

68

Nettles took out his cigarette case, received permission to smoke, and blew a series of little rings into the still air. The Brigadier poured himself another drink.

General Cutts relaxed, finished his beer, and carefully placed his glass on the desk. 'All get a bit rattled: no one's fault. We do the best we can. Bloody bad luck.'

Tim Roberts got up from his chair and wandered across to the verandah: it was starting to get dark, a flock of parrots wheeled over the garden and scattered quarrelling into the trees. The General watched him for a few seconds; making circles on the desk with the base of his beer glass.

'You're off when, Tim? Next month?'

'Fifteen days and ten hours time,' Roberts turned back, grinning.

'Just my bloody luck. Supremo arrives shortly, and some blasted Labour VIP. What do I do for an ADC? Indent for one? Ask 'em to bring one with them from SEAC?'

Roberts took up his cane and swished it through the air like a golfing iron. 'Been rather getting young Hall ready, Sir. He's a good chap, bright. I've been keeping him in the picture for a couple of months; I think he'd make it all right. Keen, presentable . . . you recommended him for mention.'

The General waved his hand across the cluttered desk. 'I may have recommended him for the MD but not for a bloody ADC . . . too namby-pamby—and stop wagging that bloody cane about, you're not at Gleneagles yet. I'm buggered if I want to start breaking in a new ADC. Got enough to do.'

Nettles leant forward in his chair and stubbed out his cigarette very precisely. 'It so happens,' he said deliberately, still stubbing the cigarette, 'it so happens that one ready-made ADC arrived in yesterday from Calcutta. He's up in "A" Mess. There's a thing!'

'Don't follow.'

'New arrival. Rooke. ADC to General Wade. The lie slid easily from his tongue. He watched Cutts carefully. Saw the flick of doubt. 'Very presentable, Wilmington, excellent Suffolk family, very keen.'

'Never heard of Wade. Wade, did you say?'

'North Grampians, I think.'

'No one I know. ADC was he?'

'Yes. Then he was asked for by Montgomery for 2nd Army Staff.'

'As ADC?'

'No, no. Trained as photographic interpreter. Very bright.'

Cutts rubbed his forehead slowly. 'Seems a bit of a muddle. Monty just *removed* him from this Wake, Wade, whatsisname?'

'Just that. Apparently. Wade was livid.'

'So I should bloody well think. Bloody high-handed! That's Monty if you like. Eh, Bunny? All gone to his head. Well . . . keep him around for a bit. Might be useful. Tim, we'll have a little party for you, how about that; farewell fling. Been a long time, eh? And a little party would do us all good. Get some girls along — somehow — a bit of beer, some dancing, we could all do with a bit of entertainment. What do you say, Nettles? Good idea?'

Nettles was smiling gently. 'Splendid idea, Sir; when and where?'

The General shuffled his papers together, stacked them tidily, placed the brass frog on top. 'You do all that. Leave it to you. Things are pretty quiet down here now. Shouldn't have much trouble now we're all deployed. 'Course if anything does blow up we'll have to can it . . . but get cracking, eh? Tim: stop whacking about with that bloody stick. Can't think . . .'

'Sorry, Sir. Sudden rush of excitement. A party. It's very kind of you, Sir.'

Cutts rose majestically from his desk, pulling down his jacket, pulling in his paunch. 'I am kind.' He smiled.

'Yes, Sir.' Roberts looked at him with wry affection.

'Been together what, two years, two and a half?'

'Just two, Sir.'

'Long time. I'll miss you.'

'Sir.'

Nettles let the tender little silence last a moment before he broke it, rising to his feet and reaching for his cap. He was smiling himself. It could have been mistaken for sympathy.

'Permission to leave, Sir?' The smile had faded respectfully.

'I don't think there's anything else. No. I'll hop down and see Caplan. Tim, come down to the reception area with me in ten minutes, must see Caplan and get all the details. Did they bring Holly's body back? I suppose so?'

'Yes. They got him back, Sir.'

'I'll come down with you, if I may, Sir?' said Blackett.

'And just one other thing, nip in next door, will you? Tell Miss Foto where I'm off to. Say I might be a bit late. Having supper with her at her place.' He looked oddly shy for a moment, fiddled with some papers. 'It's a bit lonely eating here by yourself every night.'

'Yes, Sir; will do.'

'She's currying a duck.' He grinned and winked, covering his momentary lapse into embarrassment. 'Currying it, Tim, not what you think!'

Roberts laughed obligingly, tipped his cap with his cane. 'I'll be off then, Sir.' He left whistling.

Nettles collected his maps and briefcase, stood politely in the centre of the room. Cutts came from behind his desk, rubbing his buttocks thoughtfully.

'Good chap Tim. Marvellous sense of humour. Quick as a flash.' He laughed; almost a high-pitched snort in the still room. 'What's that song he was always singing? Cockney thing, damned funny, can't quite remember it?'

Nettles' face was blank.

'Oh you know, come on! Whistles it all the time, did a sort of knees-up dance thing on VJ night, remember? Had everyone in stitches.'

'Oh yes.' Nettles examined the pattern of the rush mat at his feet. ' "Knocked Them in the Old Kent Road", I think.'

'That's it. First-rate. "Watcha' all the neighbours cried, who you goin' to meet Bill, have you bought the street Bill . . . tum tum tumpty tumpty tum and we knocked 'em in the Old Kent road . . ." Remember it now?' He was happy, smiling broadly, blue eyes suffused with remembered pleasure. For an instant Nettles nearly liked him.

'Of course, Sir. Silly of me. Quite forgot. Very catchy.'

Cutts' pleasant smile went swiftly. The eyes narrowed. 'Bet bloody Hall, or whatever his name is, or that fancy feller of Monty's you're talking about, won't know that. Too racy for them. It'll be the Eton boating song if I know the type. Tim may be a bit, well, rough, not top-drawer if you like, but he's not a snob. Can't take a snob, Nettles, had enough of them in my life. All that Mater and Pater business, all that damned Class and

Polo and so on. Can't do with that, thank you. "Went to school near Slough, Sir" — none of that shit, thanks.' 'Bunny' Blackett drained his glass.

Nettles carefully smoothed the flat of his cap with his sleeve. 'Don't think you'll find Captain Rooke like that, Sir. A gentleman, but not a snob.'

Cutts grunted, hands on hips. 'Never saw much difference myself. And I know men.'

'He's been around, Sir, done all manner of things, farmed a bit, did quite a stint with a printing firm in Birmingham . . . type-setting, photogravure . . .'

Cutts fiddled with his lanyard. 'What the hell for?'

'Very interested in newspapers.'

'Oh. Was he? Is he? Funny kind of mixture.'

'I thought, if you felt he could take over from Roberts, we might try him at *The Daily Cobra*. He's had enough experience, I gather.'

'Let's have a look at the blighter first. I'll make up my mind then. God knows, we need someone to jerk things up on that rag. Full of crosswords, sports fixtures, and bloody awful cartoons about NAAFI. Like "Tiger Tim's".'

'As you said, Sir, we need a bit of entertainment, you're quite right.'

'I *know* that! Now you get down to this party affair for Tim, right? Give him a good send-off, let's see it go with a swing, make it an evening to remember.'

Nettles inclined his head. 'I'm sure, Sir, everyone will do his best to make it that.'

Sunday night in 'A' Mess was usually the most relaxed, and certainly the most boring, night of the week. Unless there was a 'flap' on and some noble Fighter for Freedom chucked a couple of mortars over the perimeter wire, or hacked up one of the Mess cooks, as had happened a week or so ago when the silly fellow wandered down to the railway to pick some flowers for the Mess Table and was returned as ten perfectly butchered sections, in a sack. With the flowers. A nice touch. Otherwise boredom reigned supreme in the stuffy air. And since there was not the least possibility of a sudden visit by the General, for everyone very well knew that his knees were comfortably under the table down in Foto's digs, people relaxed out of the tensions of the week in slumped heaps, reading, drinking, playing cards or just sitting and listening, with glazed eyes, to the local radio station pleading for news of internees still in the camps from those who had, fortunately, managed to secure their release, an unattractive flow of Dutch interrupted, now and then, by the music of Tommy Dorsey or Artie Shaw. It had, thought Nettles as he moved quickly through the scattered groups of inertia, all the warmth and appeal of a cafeteria in a bus station.

Avoiding the dingy light, the stale smell of slopped beer, the wreathing vapour of cigarette smoke, he headed through the room for the verandah where, at the far end, under a rickety bamboo trellis covered with creeper, he saw Gaunt and Rooke together at a small table. Hooking a cane chair in one hand, he went along to them. They looked up. Gaunt smiled his neat cat's-smile, Rooke flinched: and reached for his tin of cigarettes. Nettles smiled coolly.

'Mind awfully if I join you? I mean, do say . . .'

Gaunt lifted his silver tankard, vaguely making circular movement, 'No. No. Do. Got a drink?'

Nettles settled himself comfortably, placed his briefcase on the plank floor, ran long fingers through neat curls. 'Got one coming, thanks.' He smiled at Rooke, put the tips of his fingers together forming a triangle under his chin. 'Had a good day? Settled in a bit?'

Rooke nodded pleasantly, lit a cigarette, spun the spent match into the darkness. 'Fine thanks. Found my way about. David here has put me in the picture.'

'Did my best,' said Gaunt. 'Div. history. Imphal . . . the Tennis Court, so on. He ought to know what he's joined, I suppose. Your meeting with the Old Man OK?'

'Fine. Usual wail. Hands tied behind our backs. Gone down to see Caplan for the de-briefing business; you know.'

'Hear Holly copped it?'

'Yes. Head. Bloody bad luck so near his Repat. After all this time.'

Gaunt nodded, looking gravely into his tankard. 'If your number's up, it's up.'

'And we've stood down the convoy for Tuesday, by the way. Old Man won't risk another for a bit, wants things to go off the boil.' He flicked a sharp look towards Rooke.

'So you're off the hook for a time, Rooke. No charabanc to Pangpang just yet. We'll have to find you something to do, won't we?' He turned and took his drink which had arrived from a silent bearer. 'Splendid. Just what I need.'

'Poor old Holly,' said Gaunt. 'Another old face gone.'

'Talking of old faces, Roberts goes in a couple of weeks.'

'Won't break my bloody heart,' said Gaunt. 'Tiresome chap, I always found, banging on about things. Bit too sparky for my taste, but efficient, I'll give him that, damned efficient. The Old Man'll miss him. God! Roberts practically wiped his arse for him. Don't know what he'll do. He was a good organizer, must say. Good in the field, death at the dinner table. Which reminds me, Mess P., what have you planned for Sunday grub? Ghastly stink in the hall.'

'Tinned salmon fritters or something. Peaches and tapioca pudding for afters.'

'Sweet Heaven.'

'Best lend-lease American. Cling peaches, I'll have you know. In syrup. Nursery treat. Can't eat curries every day.'

'I could. Disinfects the guts.'

'By the way, we're to have a party.'

'A party? What for? Where?'

'Roberts' farewell binge. The Old Man wants a party. Here, I imagine.'

'Well, that'll tax your imagination.'

Nettles sighed, 'It will. It will. What *am* I to do?'

'Think of something better than tinned peaches and frog-spawn, that's what you do.' Gaunt rose and drained his tankard. 'Going up to change. For the Nursery Treat. Christ!'

They watched him thread his way through the crowded room beyond, place his tankard, as usual, carefully on the bar, speak to someone briefly, laugh, then turn and disappear into the maze of jungle-green.

Nettles stretched his long legs under the table and smiled at Rooke. They looked at each other in silence.

'Cat got your tongue?'

74

'No. I was always told never to interrupt my elders—and betters.'

'That's a nice polite boy. Quite right.'

'No convoy then?'

'No. That's fun, isn't it? Immediately I heard that I started out on your salvation.'

'My what?'

'Salvation. I promised; remember?'

Rooke flushed, and reached for his beer. Nettles stirred his Bloody Mary.

'Oh, for God's sake don't go red in the face! It doesn't show, you know. You weren't disfigured. I made a promise and I stick to it. Here you sit; posting postponed, so what do we start you off with . . . to move you in the right direction?'

'God knows.'

'I do. The party for Roberts. You must know *something* about decoration, painting, scenery all that stuff. Theatre background?'

'Well . . . just a bit. In Rep ages ago.'

'Well, about the party. I'll do food and drink. Let's think of a motif. Have to have a motif for a party, you know. Why not golf? Golf for the golf-mad Roberts, eh? What comes to your mind first?'

Rooke shifted uncomfortably. 'I don't know. Golf clubs, I suppose?'

'My God you're so *quick*. Golf clubs, of course. A triumphant arch of golf-clubs for the guest of honour's entry. Like those delicious Life Guards at Knightsbridge weddings. What fun! Cover everything in yards of green material and have pyramids of little white balls, flags and pennants; that sort of thing. Marvellous idea.'

'Well, I'll try.'

'You'd better. I think it is safe to say that your future depends on it. Oh. By the way, do you happen to know a rather brassy little jingle, very ta ra ra stuff . . . cockney, I believe, something to do with knocking them down in the Old Kent Road?'

Rooke looked startled. 'Oh that. Yes. I think so, vaguely.'

'Well, un-vague it. Learn it by heart.'

'But what on earth for?'

'The Old Man. His favourite ditty, wouldn't you know. If

75

you get stuck get the words from Roberts. He knows it by heart.
All of it. Understand me?'

'I think so. You're not joking, are you? It's a leg pull?'

'I'm quite deadly serious. I think it's called Psychological
Warfare.'

'What am I to do, sing it in a spotlight?'

'No. No. Just little random snatches here and there, now and
again. Just a suggestion, occasionally. And you might brush up
your knowledge of type-setting while you're at it.'

'Type-setting? What the hell's that?'

'No idea. I only heard the word yesterday for the first time,
from one of my local "concubines". Very bright girl. Father ran
the Island newspaper, she knows all about it.'

'Well why don't you get her?'

'Because you are the one who'll tart up that dreary little
comic, *The Daily Cobra*.'

Rooke slammed the table with his fist. 'Oh for Christ's sake!
I don't know anything about newspapers.'

Nettles fished about for his cigarette case, chose one, tapped
it gently on his thumb-nail. 'As from this afternoon you do.
That's what you did in Civvie Street, or whatever the prole-
tariat call it.'

'But I didn't!'

'You did, in Birmingham. Sorry. I had to use every weapon
that came to hand. I said that you were an ADC, well-
versed in journalism, and frightfully keen. I also added that you
were not a snob.'

'Snob?'

'The Old Man is very sensitive. Been snubbed before, I
gather. By Class.'

'But it's not true—I mean about journalism. Oh, a poem or
two, wrote a play, but I don't know a bloody thing about
type-whatever-it-is.'

'Ask the concubine. She'll tell you all you need. You can have
her for a secretary. Why not? Splendid idea. She can help with
the party, interpreter, knows the city, all that stuff, it all falls
into place. She's coming to my office tomorrow. She's hired.
There!' He lit his cigarette with a happy flourish and placed
the spent match neatly back in the box.

For a few seconds Rooke looked at the table in silence, then

76

slowly bowed his head and cupped his hands about it, shaking it slowly from side to side. Nettles watched him amusedly, sipping his drink. After a moment the movements stopped and Rooke looked up, took a deep breath, shook his head as if he'd come up from a high dive.

'Look, what the hell is all this about? What are you up to?'

'I'm up to getting you replaced as the ADC, that's what I'm up to.'

'But going about it like this, you're bonkers, you know.'

'It's always possible. But I know my General. Know how to play it. You see.'

'But it's all based on false pretences. I hate bloody lies.'

'Not all lies. You were an ADC, you said? Oh! I have rather promoted your Brigadier, to General. An arrant lie. You can correct that later. Slip of the tongue. He didn't know him anyway, naturally.'

'That's just what I mean, untruths, all this Birmingham stuff. Why?'

Nettles leant across the table, his hands clasped together. 'Now look here, Rooke, if you had gone down to Pangpang you'd have learned pretty damned quickly that the cardinal rule for a Company Commander, or any kind of commander for that matter, is to consolidate your positions.' He leant back in his chair. 'And that's all I'm doing. Consolidating yours. It's all in the Field Manual: one is also advised to make use of all "natural features" which may offer themselves, which, after a fashion, I suppose I have already done—' he smiled briefly as Rooke took the implication and swiftly looked away, 'to further secure the positions gained. After that we come to camouflage. A *sort* of lie I suppose, don't you? Would you call camouflage deceit, lying, or merely a means of survival? You will realize, I know, that we are still in a war, and sometimes you have to fight dirty, as they say, like our friends across the perimeter hacking us all to bits in the name of Freedom. If the word lie really distresses you, Rooke, and your angelic conscience, why not soothe yourself with the word improvise?'

For a moment they sat in silence. The rumble of voices from the ante-room drifted into the still night air . . . through it the crackle of the radio and a soft woman's voice . . .

"I'll have to learn to walk alone again,
And heal my foolish heart"

Rooke got up suddenly. Nettles remained motionless in the shadows. Cigarette glowing.

"It was an idiot's delight, bound not to last,
Old Merlin and his magic wand are in the past"

'I'm not leaving,' Rooke said, 'going to get a beer. You want one of those tomato things?'

Nettles looked at his watch. 'Lovely. Say it's for me. Prepare us for the fritters.' He watched the tall figure as it went away. Stubbed his cigarette thoughtfully into the tin ash tray. A firefly drifted into the darkness beyond the wooden rail.

'... But in your September will you remember... me?"

The moon was rising and, whatever else, he was there to see it. Unlike Holly. Unlike a great many others. Really, he thought, war is a tedious business. It wounds in so many unexpected ways, it's not just a bullet in the head or a big bang and blinding eternity. There are other little forms of death. The tiny deaths which add up, after a time, to the whole. He couldn't be sure that a neat bullet, well aimed, in the head wouldn't solve a lot of problems. But perhaps Holly didn't have any? Didn't seem the kind who would. Breezy, jolly, a nice ordinary man who had once sold shoes in Hemel Hempstead.

Rooke set the glasses down carefully, spilling a little of his beer; foam spilled down the glass and puddled. He cursed lightly. 'No more Worcester Sauce. Sorry.'

'No matter. That doesn't give one the lift.' Nettles raised his glass in a small salute.

'Now look here.' Rooke lowered himself into his chair. 'I'll go along with all this, well, nonsense. I suppose I must seem a little ungracious? It just all seems mad to me. All a bit of a dream. I've only been on this island for, what? Thirty hours? Hardly got my breath. You've got it all buttoned up, haven't you?' He looked coldly across the table.

Nettles shook his head slowly. 'Not all. Some of it. Rest is up to you.'

'I know. But you've planned everything.'

'The best laid plans of mice and Intelligence Officers, Rooke . . .'

'Can often go astray. I know. I'll do what I can. And really, thank you. The point is, well, look, cards on table, all right?'

'Absolutely all right.'

'Well, you've been talking about consolidating positions. Absolutely right too. Camouflage, that sort of thing. I follow. I know what you meant about using "natural features" *available*. I got that.'

Nettles smiled gently. 'I know you did.'

'Well, that's all right too. I know. I'm aware. I'm not a complete idiot.'

'That's quite evident. I really wouldn't waste my time, or yours, or the General's. He may be all sorts of a bore and so on, but he's a good man according to his lights, and according even to mine. I'm not wishing an idiot upon a fool.'

Rooke opened his cigarette tin and took another, pushing it across the table towards Nettles.

'No. I know that. Thank you. But the point is, well, may I be absolutely frank?'

'You may.'

'We have discussed consolidating *my* position. What about yours?'

There was a burst of laughter in the room behind them, cheers and a thin voice shouted, 'Bloody bastards! Thieves and card sharpers! I knew you had the ace all the time!' A glass fell and shattered, the laughter rose and ebbed into a distant mumble of players dispersing, boots scraping on tiles.

'My position?'

'Yes. Yours. Last night was . . .'

Nettles raised his hand in gentle admonishment. 'I don't remember last night. All I remember is an immensity of yesterdays.'

'I'm sorry.'

'You needn't be. At least I lived them. My position is perfectly secure, thank you. It needs no consolidation. It is quite singular; you have no debt to pay.'

'Thank you.' Rooke, unable to return the steady gaze before him, fiddled with the lid of his cigarette tin. 'I'm sorry.'

'At risk of being flippant, and just so that you absolutely get the point, dear chap, I never take a bite of the same apple twice. That's rather more like me, isn't it?'

Rooke met the gaze and smiled suddenly. The smile became a soft laugh. 'Much more like. Thank you for coming back.'

'I have never,' said Nettles gently, 'been away.' He reached to the floor and found his briefcase and cap, took his glass and half-finished the drink. 'You were an actor, weren't you? So you'll know what Mr and Mrs Average look like, ummm? They come to see you, the actor, to be "taken out of themselves" as they call it. Nice, dull, plain, dreary, ordinary people. Humdrum: ten billion of them to every penny in your pocket. They run routine lives according to the rules they wouldn't know how to break even if they wished to. They conform. Herds, tribal, deathly. Plankton, Rooke, plankton; the universe is phosphorescent with their biological mediocrity. Remove them in their millions, and millions more sweep in to fill the area which they filled, seething, linking, joining, breeding, conforming, drifting, dying.' He placed his half-empty glass carefully on the table. 'Gobbled up by whales: whale soup, you see? The great mass leaves no mark on the face of time. It is anonymous in its very ordinariness. But sometimes, something quite extraordinary emerges from that tedious grey mass, blazing like a fiery sword. A Beethoven, a Wagner, a Cézanne, a Leonardo, a Turner or a Proust. Someone like that, you know? I do not speak of politicians or soldiers, you will note. They are destructive forces. I speak only of creators. You follow? And then the plankton is swirled about, is interrupted in its aimlessness, in its inertia, and it is illuminated, moved, embellished, enriched, bejewelled. For a little time. Oh dear! I'm using so many words, but do you really follow me?'

'I follow,' said Rooke quietly.

'And so, one tries to pull away from the mass to reach out to the light which blinds one with its force, its life, the promise of excitement. One removes oneself, for a little, from the indifference and mundanity. Attempts to leave the grey and beige, to walk in the sun. That's rather what happened to me yesterday morning when I walked into the bar at the Planters Club and saw, suddenly there before me, Donatello's David, in very short shorts.' He laughed at his own clumsy analogy and Rooke's shadow of disbelief. 'God! I do rattle on. That's the end of it.

80

No more. I must go and change. For the Nursery Treat. Can one face salmon fritters, I ask myself?' He rose abruptly, knocking the table hard, spilling the beer. For a long moment he stood quite still looking down on Rooke who had not moved, and whose face was partly silvered by the moon. Eyes wide, clear.

'I'm sorry. Spilled your drink. I got rather carried away, but as of course you know,' he smiled bleakly, 'that does happen to me. I get swept away. Perhaps I should have been a don? No brains. An anthropologist? No intellect. Perhaps a missionary? Alas, no zeal. If I survive this Island it's back to Russell Square and my troglodyte existence; nicely out of harm's way.' He tucked his cap under his arm. 'Stand forth, young Rooke. Illuminate and bejewel the common herd behind us, transform our humdrum lives. That's why you are here. I do hope I've made that quite clear? It may be putting a burden on your fine young shoulders, but it does not impose a debt as well. Remember that.'

He was still smiling when he turned away to his organic debris in the ante-room. His whale soup. Suddenly, at the double doors, he turned and looked back at the motionless Rooke. 'Incidentally,' he said, 'those shorts. Into your little tin-trunk or what-have-you, for the duration of this campaign. They simply won't do. And with that remark,' he added, placing long fingers on his left-hand breast pocket, 'I have just broken my own heart.'

His room was impersonal, spartan. Shutters closed against the moon, a chair, a wooden table, bathroom off, net-draped bed, a white catafalque in the very centre of the floor.

From the bathroom the sound of water being poured, the flip-flop of his bearer's sandalled feet on the tiles. He sat heavily in the cane chair, started to unlace his boots. A hard day, a wearying day; a moving day in some ways. He'd feel a great deal better after a bath, or a shower or whatever it was to be, depending on the amount of water collected.

'Bath tonight, Willie, or shower?'

'Enough for bath. Chota bath, Sahib. You sit all together, eh?'

Willie came flip-flapping into the room, the bottle of sandal-wood essence in his dark hand. 'You want, Sahib?'

'Very much. Lots.' Nettles pulled off his gaiters and slung them across the room wearily, eased off his boots, curled his toes in crumpled socks.

Willie fished about in a pocket and drew out a small brown envelope. 'This for you, Sahib. From boy.' He laid it on the table and flapped off to the bathroom.

Nettles took it up. 'Which boy?'

'Not knowing, Sahib,' Willie called. 'Not seen here. Young fella. Not good, I'm thinking. Maybe Tamil.'

'Where? When?'

'In street. Arriving from quarters. This hour.' He came back pressing the cork into the sandalwood bottle.

Nettles opened the envelope carefully. It was roughly addressed in perfect school-boy copperplate, pencil. His name, his rank. Inside a neatly folded square of paper. No date.

Wickedness is among you, close to your honoured General. Wickedness which has brought death to four brave young men, and defilement to women, sons and daughters. Remove this wickedness from your midst before your honour as British Soldiers is corrupted. We appeal to you as the Intelligence Officer of this noble Division to destroy this wickedness and bring the person to justice and punishment. You will know who we mean. You will not require a photo . . .

The S's coiled like snakes. It was unsigned.

CHAPTER FOUR

The eggs slid greasily together across the cold plate: siamese-twin eggs joined at the sides, flat beige corrugated yolks wreathed in a scorched frill of carbonized whites.

Pullen set them dejectedly aside and made an attempt at the shrivelled bacon: rind like a brown rubber band.

'He never gets it right. Never. Surely frying a couple of eggs is not *quite* beyond him. Morning after morning.'

'Orange juice and a bit of toast,' said Gaunt from the end of the table. 'Safer.'

'Damned hungry, for God's sake. Need my victuals. Got a full day ahead.'

'When I was a child,' said Gaunt, slowly spreading margarine on burnt toast, 'I got very put off fried eggs. My brother and I had an *ayah* who used to fry a bit of bread, cut a hole in the centre, bung in an egg and then fry it all on both sides. Called it "Pharaoh's Eye". Missionary trained, of course. Put us off for life.'

'Good God! What a fearful thing!'

'When you cut into the eyeball part, you know, the yolk, it spilled all over the bread. Bloody awful. Mutilation stuff, you know?'

'Awful.' Pullen looked across the empty table. 'First down again, I see.'

'I've been up since five, riding about the Estates. Best time of day. No one about . . . the Patrols, no one else.'

'Don't like your fellow man do you, David?'

'Not keen.'

'I didn't get to bed till damn near two. Old Man sent for me about eleven. On a Sunday. I ask you! In bed as it happened.'

'What for?'

'Dead beat: that's what for.'

'The Old Man?'

'Oh, got some idiotic idea of moving house.'

'Where to, for God's sake?'

'That thing up on the hill beyond Rozendaal. Chinese place.'

Gaunt looked astonished. 'You mean the Flack Tower, that

83

block? But it's right on the perimeter, sticks out into No Man's Land on three sides. He'll be mortared to buggery up there.'

'Just what I told him. Won't have it. Says we'll push the perimeter out a bit and double the guard. *Your* department. Duty Officer stuck up the order at one-thirty, it's over there on the board. Briefing at nine-thirty sharp.'

'We have quite enough to do protecting what we have here, without setting up a guard on a tropical Balmoral.'

Pullen screwed the lid on to the mustard jar. 'And I reckon that's who's behind it all. The Foto. He says the present house isn't quite suitable for his position when Mountbatten and the group arrive. Going to put them all up in his place and move up to Rozendaal. She probably told him it was more imposing.'

Gaunt laughed shortly. 'Imposing it is. He'll look like a bloody squatting duck up there. Highest point in the area. Marvellous target. Couldn't be better.'

'Well . . . it's empty, imposing, and he wants it. Or she does. This VIP visit is making him flap about like a tethered hen. Broaden the Rozendaal perimeter, he said, about a mile all round, nothing to it, area quiet now, easy. Just as if we were all sitting on our backsides in Aldershot doing a TEWT.'*

'Bloody women,' said Gaunt stacking his cup and saucer on his plate. 'God defend me from them. Always in the way.'

'Don't decry women, David! Where should we all be without them?' In a light haze of sandalwood Nettles settled himself crisply at the table and rang the little bell for his breakfast. He smiled brightly round the empty chairs. 'Not *here*, for one thing. That's certain. Every mother's sons we are. And, incidentally, where are the rest of the troupe? We first as usual?'

Pullen got up slowly and took his cup across to the side table. 'Always the same on a Monday after the glamour of Sunday night in the Mess. By the by, don't order fried eggs. I think we have the Inquisition in the kitchen.'

Gaunt sat upright, elbows on the table, hands supporting his chin. 'You heard we are about to extend the perimeter at Rozendaal?'

'No. Who said?'

'It's on the board. Pullen says the Old Man is moving house.'

Nettles raised polite eyebrows. 'Since when? No one told me.'

* TEWT: Tactical exercise without troops.

84

Pullen came back with his coffee. 'I tell you now. Flap late last night. All to meet him at nine-thirty sharp. Briefing.' He sat down and stirred his cup slowly. 'God. This coffee looks like bath water, which is something I haven't seen for a long time. I suppose it has a novelty factor therefore. But you must have a word, Geoffrey. Wag a stick or something. Really.'

'A magic wand? I do my best, I really do.' Nettles shrugged hopelessly. 'But why this sudden move?'

'Apparently that wretched woman gave him the idea. At least that's the feeling I got . . . her idea. Governor of the Island should have a Palace.'

A sullen bearer wandered in and Nettles ordered boiled eggs and orange juice.

'Boiled eggs!' said Pullen with quiet wonder. 'You're taking a frightful risk.'

'All he has to do is turn his little egg-timer upside down and watch. Simple.'

'Far too complicated for the Indian mind to comprehend. Seen them driving a taxi?' Gaunt wiped his lips carefully with a napkin. 'Or a bus? I mean, think of it, can you *imagine* the Indian Navy?'

Pullen took out his tobacco pouch and started filling his pipe. 'They made a pretty good showing at Kohima, Imphal. You must admit that.'

'With us behind them. Gurkhas and Pathans were the best. But I can't take the Hindu. Muslims yes . . . better . . . but Hindus. Only fit for licking stamps and counting their little money beads.' Gaunt brushed crumbs carefully from his lap. 'Jews of the East. Well named.'

Nettles locked his fingers together and examined his nails. 'Thought that's what *they* called the Chinese?'

'It's what I call Johnny Hindu,' said Gaunt with a flicked smile. He got up from his chair and adjusted a gleaming Sam Browne. 'Got to change. It's just seven a.m.'

'I can't really agree with you about the Hindu; don't know enough, I suppose,' said Nettles. 'But I do agree with you about women. I see now. Damn the Foto if it *is* her idea . . . A bit of a problem there, I think. Just a teeny one. Yes.'

'I should say so.' Gaunt smiled briefly, reached for his cap and riding crop. 'No need for them at all to my mind. Breed children. Stick 'em all in purdah, the only really sensible idea the ruddy Indians ever had. This should be a man's world entirely.' He crossed the shadowed room to the notice-board by the doors.

Utopia, thought Nettles wistfully, following the tall, military figure with admiring eyes. A splendid animal. The polished boots, well-cut breeches, crisply starched shirt, broad shoulders, strong neck, neatly cropped fair head. The traditional hero of every woman's romantic novel. A golden sheik to sweep you off your feet. But quite totally stone. Sexless. Sterile. Carved perfectly: from marble. Through the centuries men had produced beautiful *and* sensuous things from a block of white carrara, but not in Gaunt's case. Who the hell, he wondered, had carved him? The block of elegant, sexless, marble adjusted its cap, tucked its crop under one arm and left the room in a clatter of boots and spurs. Nettles shrugged and struck a marble egg.

'Thought you were taking a risk.' Pullen laughed and puffed smoke over his shoulder. 'Strange chap, David. Horse mad. Out since dawn riding about.'

'I wonder if he's a virgin still?' Nettles reached for the damp salt.

'What an extraordinary thing to say. Why?'

'Oh I don't know. So cold, distant, obviously anti the sex . . .'

'No, no, I don't think he's inexperienced. Fact is, I have heard he's a bit sadistic, I mean, you know, rather takes it out on them; gossip really.'

'Whips and things?'

'Good God, I don't know! What a conversation. But there *was* one girl in Delhi made a fuss. Got rather bashed about. Nothing came of it; tart, you see.'

Nettles hit his second egg and watched the slime slither down the shell.

'No go?' Pullen asked mildly.

'No go. One marble, the other mucus. Disgusting. What *does* he do with them? I really must have a word with him, but he'll only start to weep again. Oh God! And I've a meeting at eight with Rooke.'

'Rooke? The new chap?'

'Yes. Old Man wanted to look him over. Possible replacement for Roberts.'

86

'Ah! Not a bad idea. Good type, I thought. Any experience of ADC work?'

'Was one, to General Wade.'

'Well that's good: we've got a busy morning. This ruddy move.'

Nettles dipped a bit of toast into the congealing egg. 'I suppose David is what one calls a real professional soldier. The kind who made the Charge of the Light Brigade heroic rather than idiotic. Life bounded by the Regiment, glory and valour . . . horses, knights, King and Country. Goodness me.'

Pullen looked at his watch: 'I say, ought to be going. Seven-fifteen.'

'I must eat something. Those salmon fritters last night nearly killed me.' He stuck another rectangle of toast into the egg. 'We used to call these "soldiers" in the Nursery . . . soldiers! God.'

'Yes, as you were saying, I suppose David is very Regular: his great-great-whatever-he-was grandfather came out with Clive or something. One of them started the Bannou Horse up on the Frontier. Father of the Regiment, you can safely call him, with truth. My family knew them well, but I met David for the first time at Shillong when I joined the Division. Heard of them, of course, the two brothers, legendary young fellows, tremendous reputation with horses: jumping, polo, that sort of thing. Silver cups everywhere. And very pukka. Never set foot in the UK, I seem to recall. Tutors and so on, brought up by the Regiment from top to toe. Their life. Splendid soldiers: but not over bright really.'

'There's a brother?'

'Was. Robin.'

Pullen's pipe had gone out, he tapped it gently into the palm of his hand. 'Couple of years older than David. Same type. Identical really. Very Aryan, inseparable. Parents copped it in the Quetta business in '35, tragic.'

Nettles pushed his egg aside and folded his napkin. 'You said "was". About the brother?'

'Ah yes. Well. Rather an ugly business. Out on his horse up in the hills: went missing. Terrific search for, oh, can't remember, couple of weeks, say, not a trace. Tribesmen had got him. Kidnapped. Not infrequent incident up there . . . damned hard to trace, they just melt into the hills. Usually held for a ransom

87

of guns, cartridges, that sort of thing.' He tipped the ash neatly on to a dirty plate. 'But not Robin. Found him eventually, bound up like firewood, half-dead, in some gully miles away. Pretty dreadful state. No water, so on. They thought he was out of his mind for a bit, the sun, you know. Almost was. Apparently they had used him to serve some of the ladies. A sort of stallion.'

Nettles looked up sharply in astonishment. 'Stallion?'

'Yes. Frightful thing. The fair skin, blond hair, especially the blue eyes.'

'I simply don't believe you. Can't be, simply can't be.'

'Was. It's a fact. It had happened before. Fair-haired children *have* been seen running around up in the hills, you know, blue eyes sometimes, or with red hair, another much sought after effect.'

'What happened to him? I mean . . . Christ . . . !'

'Died, I'm afraid. Pretty soon after. Nothing much to do. There had been some pretty unspeakable things done. At the inquest it all came out: there had been, well, frightful thing to say; bestiality.'

'Dear God!' Nettles' voice was low with shock.

'And that was also the end of David. Never got over it, of course.' Pullen put his pipe away and wrapped up his tobacco-pouch. 'Well, you couldn't, could you? He's contained his hate, his disgust, but it's there all right. You can see it in his treatment of the men, sometimes a bit too harsh I think. And he fought like a dervish if you recall, every Jap was a tribesman. Retribution, I suppose.'

Nettles adjusted his belt. 'It's a perfectly splendid sort of character definition, isn't it? Couldn't be better.'

'I know. It is, isn't it? That is frightfully confidential, of course. Under all that he's a good man. Hard for us to understand, but then, we had very, very different backgrounds you and I, eh?' He smiled gently. 'Compassion, Geoffrey, just that, but don't ever let it show, will you? I say! We must be off . . .'

'It is all so splendidly improbable.'

'That's where you are quite wrong, old chap. Alas. It's true. Here comes the second shift. Let's clear.'

With a clacketting of boots and mumbled 'good-mornings'

they collected their caps and side-arms and left the rapidly filling Mess to find their transport.

In the brilliant sunlight Nettles shook his head. 'My dear,' he said aloud to himself, watching Pullen walk across to his jeep, 'you have led a very sheltered life.'

A small, dingy corridor. On one side rows of frosted glass windows, on the other a line of wooden partitioned cubicles with wire-grilled fronts. Each contained a desk, a chair, shelves and a filing cabinet. In one a couple of silent Chinese girls were bundling up copies of *The Daily Cobra* and a third, Pearl Ching, was laboriously typing, with two fingers, addresses from a fat book beside her. The other cubicles were empty. Nettles pushed open a door and they followed him in.

'Your office. Well, for the time being, that is, right next door to the newspaper; rather small, but I think you can manage. We'll get you a telephone as soon as possible. All right?'

Rooke nodded silently. Emmie leant against the door jamb, arms folded across her chest, eyes smiling lightly, bemused.

'You'll need pencils and paper and so on. My clerk will deal with that: he's running about now as a matter of fact. Now: I've given you the brief outline for this damned event, you've got the "chitty" for the Dump at the Docks and they expect you. Take what you need, make sure you find as many golfing symbols as you can; the motif is The Green, got it? Use my jeep until we get you transport of your own, I'll manage on my own. See you back in the Mess at noon sharp, all right? I must dash now, it's just on nine isn't it?' He didn't wait for a reply and brushed past Emmie with a vague smile. 'So lucky that you have both already met, isn't it? Saved all the introductions. Twelve noon, sharp.' He hurried briskly down the corridor.

They stood helplessly together in the silence. In the cubicle next door the Chinese girls looked up, smiled pleasantly, and went on folding and rolling: Pearl who was typing was bent double with concentration, her tongue flicking in and out like an adder's.

Rooke pulled the single chair into the room. 'Here you are, have this.'

Emmie leant away from the door, shook her head slightly,

and sat on the edge of the desk. 'No, this is good. I'm all right here.'

Rooke sat down deliberately, threw his cap on the desk, and sprawled back. 'I'm exhausted! Too early in the morning for so many shocks.'

'Shocks?'

'A new office, all his instructions.' He suddenly smiled across at her. 'And you.'

'I was a shock?'

'Well, rather. I mean. Well, I didn't think it would be you.'

'I didn't think it would be you either.'

'I'm sorry.'

'About?'

'Oh, I was pretty silly the other day, the banjo business. That.'

Emmie laughed, crossed her legs, and leaned back on the desk. 'Oh that. It didn't matter. I was very nervous for my English and so on. The interview. I can't play it, you know? I just found it that morning. I thought it was a lucky omen.'

'Was it?' He was still smiling.

Emmie looked at him gravely, pushed her hair from her face a little, shrugged, and drew her finger through the dust of the desk top. 'I don't know. I am too serious perhaps for omens like that. You see, I just made it up. It's not a real superstition, is it? I wanted it to be.'

'Well, if you wanted it to be perhaps it was. Anyway here we are. Very odd. But how the hell do we start?'

'We go to the Dumps.' She sat up and tucked her shirt into the grey cotton skirt she had borrowed from Clair that morning. 'I'm ready, I have my bicycle, I know the way.'

'I'd really like to have a bit of a think about things first. I mean, to just go into the Dumps, and look for stuff . . . it's hopeless. We must make a list, and the whole place, the Mess, has to be decorated, I mean painted, that sort of thing. I wish there was a café or something. A cup of coffee; we could just talk, you know . . . old Nettles bangs on so much I don't remember half of what he told me.'

Emmie slid off the desk and brushed her hand flat across a brightly coloured photograph pinned roughly to the wooden partition. 'Look. A mountain and cherry blossom. It's so dusty, but pretty, no?'

90

'So?'

'It's Fujiyama.' She turned towards him, almost a silhouette against the white glare from the windows beyond. 'Japanese. This was their Headquarters before you came. We used to wait in these little rooms for interrogation. But locked in of course.' She turned back and ripped the paper from the wall, screwed it into a ball and threw it into the corridor. 'It's so funny to be back again.'

Rooke sat up slowly, hands on his knees. 'You were here?'

'Yes. Many of us were.'

'What for?'

'Oh, things. Wrong papers, no papers, stealing, non-cooperation, mixed blood; you know . . . the usual things you do wrong for an occupation force. For the Victorious Occupation Force, I must say. That's what we had to repeat always. So many things to remember. It would make you very dizzy.' She laughed easily, hands on hips, long legs apart, relaxed, happy, dark hair tumbling about her shoulders, untidy from the wind and the journey on her bicycle.

'Why were you here? Do you mind my asking? I mean, don't say . . .'

'Oh, I don't mind. No.' She was laughing, the words liquid. 'All. Just all those things. I was very naughty.'

'For stealing what?'

'Motor cars.'

'Good God!'

'Silly, you think? We thought it very sensible. To hide them until liberation came, so that we could help the liberators fight. And petrol, we stole too . . . all hidden in the forests. What a good idea! Silly, *of course*. We were very young.'

'You still are.'

'No, no. I'm very old now. An old woman, you see?' Her smile had faded, the liquid in the gentle voice had hardened very slightly. 'You grow up, you know, it is a very good thing. If you survive. I did. I'm here. So I know I did. And I feel old.'

'I'm sorry. I didn't mean to ask things.'

'I don't mind, it doesn't matter. I've been asking myself things for a very long time. I am used to questions, you see?' The smile was back, the eyes bright.

'May I ask you what happened?'

91

'Nothing very bad. They sent me to the Kempei-Tai head-quarters, in the convent of the Sacred Heart on Amsterdames Weg, and put me in a cupboard under the stairs. In the dark. That's all.'

'A cupboard?'

'It was a little cupboard. Not high, you know, under the stairs? So I had to sit all the time. One year. So now of course I like very much to stand like this, to stretch up, like this.' She threw her arms wide above her head as if she could reach the cracked plaster above her, and then she let them fall slowly to her sides and leaned conspiratorially across the desk. 'And above all I like very, very much my bicycle . . . that gives me so much space; and I am very happy to see you here, Mr Englishman, you are my biggest space of all.'

Rooke got up suddenly. 'This room is too small. Really. Let's go. Outside, anywhere, I wish to God there was a little bar or something.'

Going down the wide stone staircase to the enormous entrance hall, four floors below, Emmie put her hand on his arm diffidently. It was the first time that she had touched him, they had both been too surprised at their meeting with Nettles even to shake hands and had merely stared at each other. Now, since they were to be partners, chosen by the El Greco angel unknowingly, she felt that fate was working its usual pattern of circle upon circle and that this was to be encouraged, and, at the same time, she quite suddenly and determinedly liked her partner. She had made up her mind to that. He would be good, he would be kind, and he would need her help.

'I have a good idea, Mr Englishman-Rooke.'

'Ben would do.'

'I have a friend, very nice, near to your "A" Mess, and she makes American coffee for us in her house, a good idea, I think?'

'Fine. She wouldn't mind?'

'She would be happy. She is a good friend of Major Pullen, you know him? Her name is Mrs Doorne. She is the translator for him and she also, and this is a very good idea of mine, she also knows all about the Dumps! She has been there herself, so we have coffee and we ask her about golf-things. You think this is sensible of me?'

'Very sensible, Miss van Hoorst, very sensible indeed.'

'Ah. If you are Ben I am then Emmie. That's also sensible?'

'And we take the jeep.'

'But my beautiful bicycle!'

'We put it in the jeep too. We'll all go to Mrs Doorne's together.'

The Dumps occupied a very large area of the dock complex, stretching, it seemed, for miles. Godown after godown crammed with everything from the contents of looted villas and shops in the City, to bales and crates of merchandise of every possible description ranging from refrigerators and typewriters to cases of cosmetics, silk stockings, clothing, sports gear, tinned foods and bottles of drink. The last imports from America and Europe to arrive before the surrender. All untouched. Ranged in neat alleys, in towering blocks, on endless shelves. Rooke thought, as Clair Doorne had thought before him, that he could easily lose his head in half an hour; the instinct for taking anything free and unguarded was not buried very deep below the fragile veneer of civilized behaviour. However, armed with his requisition form, and trailed by a nervous cackle of Japanese prisoners, and Emmie wandering amazed among the luxuries which she had almost forgotten, but not quite, he tried to find the godown which might, by some lucky chance, contain the things which he needed for Roberts' party. Golf clubs and general golfing paraphernalia. Nettles' bloody motif idea.

At the far end of an alley lined with cartons bearing warnings THIS SIDE UP or PERISHABLE and USE NO HOOKS he saw, huddled at a small table, a couple of figures in jungle-green who, he supposed, might just represent authority. So far the only persons they had seen, apart from the M.P.s at the gate, were the nodding, smiling Japanese officer and his flock of hissing geese waiting anxiously to do his bidding, to whom Emmie had briefly, and with some sign language mixed in, spoken.

'He says there is an officer here. English. Do we want whisky?'

The figures at the table looked up as they drew level: a sergeant with a red face, a worried frown, who saluted, and, to Rooke's intense displeasure, the pale face and blind eyes, and the thin mouth of Weathersby sucking a pencil. Standing beside him, hand on hip, head bent over a list of fluttering papers, was a plain girl in a brilliant silk dress covered in splashy flowers. Glass beads and earrings, a red paper flower over one ear. She also, Rooke saw with dislike, had a small, but pronounced, moustache.

Weathersby removed his pencil and wiped his lips. 'Ah. Rooke isn't it? Wondered what had happened to you.'

'Thinking the same thing myself.'

'No convoy, can't send us out. Typical, isn't it? All that panic and now no one cares. Shoved me here to get me out of the way. Silly sods.'

'What doing?'

'What doing?' Weathersby twisted his mouth into what he supposed passed for a wry smile but which looked, to the naked eye, as if he had bitten into a lemon. 'Doing an inventory. Can you imagine? Me. Got to sort all this bloody stuff out and check it against the original shipping lists and Japanese requisition orders. I'll be here for years.'

'But you're good at figures, aren't you?'

'Can *you* read Japanese?'

'No.'

'Well it's all in bloody Japanese or Dutch. I can't work it out. This girl is helping me. She speaks both, she says ... don't you, Ruby?'

Ruby swayed slightly from side to side, hand still on hip, wide carmine lips smiling. She nodded pleasantly. 'Just only a little. Is difficult to read, but I speak some. I ask Captain there from Japan, she reads. Is simple.' Turning, she said something rapidly to Emmie in Dutch, who nodded and pointed to Rooke, appearing not to be anything more than polite. Ruby smiled cheerfully and fiddled with her glass beads.

'Well, I'm here to find some golf clubs and things,' said Rooke. 'I don't suppose you have any idea ...'

Weathersby's glasses glittered coldly. 'I don't know where *anything* is. I don't even know where *I* am. They dumped me here this morning, that fellow who collected us on Saturday, just dumped me here; no consideration at all, ask the sergeant, he's been here a month, he tells me.' He turned back to the papers, hunching his narrow shoulders. 'What's this then?' he

94

snapped at Ruby tapping with his pencil. She leant over him and screwed up her eyes. Lips moving silently.

'Is Libby's Milk. 600 cases.'

The sergeant who had drifted away from the table moved back towards them. 'Can I help, Sir? Might be able to. Sergeant Morgan. If it's sports stuff, Sir, I found a lot of football shorts and jerseys in No. 17, just up the road. Kitted out the two teams, don't know about golf things though. Like to have a dekko?'

They followed him at a distance into the dusty yards and over the railway lines.

'God. Bloody Weathersby. He was on the ship with me. Who's the girl?'

'His interpreter. Like me for you. Yoko Oshima. Half-Japanese. Bad woman.'

'You know her?'

Emmie smiled brightly. 'We all know each other in this City. It's not a big place. Oshima was very clever, she was the close friend of Colonel Nakuma, who was very powerful. She was not in the camp, of course. Colonel Nakuma was in charge of the, what do you call it, the water, the electricity, the lavatories, those things.'

'City Engineer, or something. I know. So you mean she was a collaborator?'

'Oh yes. Very collaborator. But she didn't think so of course; her father was Japanese, he had a restaurant on Nassau. The Japanese paid him to watch us, to spy. Dead now. Dead the first morning of Liberation. The Indonesians shot him, but she hid. She will survive, Yoko, you see.'

'Not with Weathersby, she won't,' said Rooke cheerfully. 'Unless she plays chess.'

'She plays all kinds of games. I don't know.'

Sergeant Morgan's hunch was right. Crates and crates of tennis balls in tubes, footballs, track-suits, bathing-trunks, baseballs, dumb-bells, chest expanders, running shoes, golf clubs of every conceivable size and shape, golf bags, shoes, tees in boxes, pennants, balls and gloves. The crates, in this godown, had been ripped open and their contents scattered haphazardly across the dusty concrete floors. They trod through a wild tangle of coloured football shirts.

95

'Looters, you see. The roof's gone in parts, shelling I reckon, just help yourself, Sir, I should. Never be able to sort this muddle out, he won't.'

'It's the loot of Sporting America,' said Rooke in awe, rolling a tennis ball under his foot.

'The Japanese are very methodical. Everything they took. The pawnbrokers shops in all the city, the gold and silver, everything from the big shops and from the rich merchants' houses. Everything they put here to send back to Japan; some of it went, but then they stopped.' Emmie held a pair of white running shorts against herself, considered them, shook her head and dropped them back among the spilled clothing and scattered tennis balls.

'One day the people will want to come back, to take their things; but how will they prove?'

They stood for a moment silent among the litter. The Sergeant picked up a putting iron. 'This the sort of thing you had in mind, Sir?'

Rooke nodded. 'Yep. That's it. But not today. I'll come back. Just wanted to see if they were available. Thanks for your help.'

They went out into the sunlight of the yard. The Japanese officer hissed at his geese who all bowed low in their sagging loin-cloths and skip-caps, and then, on a high shrill command from him, hurried back into the godown and began sorting things. 'Like ants,' Emmie murmured dryly. 'Soldier ants.'

'What I don't understand,' said Rooke thoughtfully as they walked back to the jeep, 'is how the Ruby person is still free. I mean if she collaborated why hasn't she been arrested or something, running about like this, working for the British. It's a bit rum, isn't it?'

'What is rum?'

'I mean funny. Strange. Rum is a word we use for that.'

'I thought something to drink . . . ?'

'As well . . .'

'Confusing.'

'So is a free collaborator, or collaboratrice.'

'I think,' said Emmie and skipped over a pile of shattered tiles, 'I think it is too early perhaps? All is such a muddle. Maybe in time, people are not all free yet, and the ones who are, are too busy trying to start up again. But the time will come.

There are many, you know. Quite many. It was a difficult time.'

By the jeep a tall, glittering M.P. Corporal. Red armband flashing, his brasses and white belt brilliant, boots honed to patent leather. He threw a perfect salute.

'Do you know you've got a collaborator up there? Lady in a floral print and beads?'

The Corporal grinned. 'Ruby you mean, Sir? Oh yes, Ruby. She's well known in the area, Sir.' He shot a quick look at Emmie who was standing some way off tucking her shirt into her narrow belt. 'Call her the Meat-Grinder, if you'll excuse the expression, Sir. More use trotting about than being locked up, and we don't have any positive proof anyway. Funny thing, Sir,' — he had a wary eye on Emmie all the time. 'Funny thing, Sir, no one will actually testify anything. They'll all gobble about, nattering things, but no one will really point the finger. But we've got a nice little list coming along, nothing too big, no Goering or Hess you know, Sir.' He laughed easily, rocked gently on polished heels. 'But we have a list. Mostly small fish now that we have sorted out the Japs, we just bide our time. Wait for orders so to speak. But Ruby there: my word, Sir. Worth her weight in Sunday dinners, Sir, does a roaring trade."

Driving down the boulevard in the morning traffic, the bicycle rattling about on the back seat, they passed a small crowd of Europeans; mostly women, climbing the steps to a church, scarves or handkerchiefs over their heads. One or two carried bunches of flowers. A line of army trucks parked along the pavement. Emmie twisted in her seat.

'For the Dakota people. You know. Twenty of them. So near, so far. What a wicked, wicked thing to do for freedom.'

'All kinds of wickedness are done in the name of freedom, you know. I've seen it in France, in Holland, in Germany.' They turned into Rembrandt Plein. 'I'll drop you off at Mrs Doorne's, OK?'

'That would be kind. You will have a beer?'

'If pressed.'

'I press. You liked her this morning, Clair? She is pretty, no.'

'Pretty, yes: and nice. I do like her . . . the son?'

'Wim? He's pretty too, you think? Brave as well.'

'The arm?'

97

'Ah. That.' Emmie looked through the bustling carts and rickshaws.

'You prefer not . . .'

She shook her head. 'No. It's all right. But it is for Clair not me. She had a little radio set in a tin of paint. Very brave. In the camp. We would listen to All India Radio, sometimes. But it was discovered, not the tin, never did they find it because of Clair, but the fact. They took Clair away to the Convent and questioned her for many hours. She said nothing. They are very wise, the Kempei-Tai, they knew what to do. They took her to the garden and she saw Wim walking along the ridge of the big glass conservatory . . . you know . . . his hands out, balancing like at the circus. At the end they nailed his kitten. It was crying. The Colonel took his revolver and pointed it to the sky and asked Clair where was the Radio. If she refused he would fire, and Wim would fall: from the surprise. She watched him; Wim. When the revolver went off he fell, and they left her to find him in the glass. Afterwards she sewed him up with a carpet needle and some thin string. All his arm, you have seen? The guards brought her flowers.' She thrust her hands tightly into her skirt between her knees and shook her head. 'So silly,' she said in a rough voice. 'So silly. They didn't cry, then. But I do now. So silly.'

The desolate villas of Nassau Boulevard were shadowed in their jungle gardens under the noonday sun: a small pack of rangy yellow dogs with pale eyes tore through a ragged hedge and ran yelping down the crumbling pavement, their howls fading as the jeep reached the corner of Brabantlaan and swung into the weedy drive of Clair's house. She was on the steps and waved: smiling, fair hair across her face, a broom made from bamboo twigs in her hand. 'Something cool?' she called and went into the house.

Rooke touched Emmie's rigid arm lightly. 'You all right?'

'I'm well. Silly just.'

She looked at him for a long moment. Fisted her eyes quickly, pulled back her hair, smiled at him. 'Feminine weakness. We are unreliable creatures, don't you find?'

'Remarkable,' Rooke said easily and slid out of his seat.

The Palace, or Flack Tower as it was commonly known, an enormous, ugly, concrete block set about with stained-glass windows and heavy wrought-iron, had been constructed in the middle thirties for a Chinese merchant who had, with the sagacity for which his race is well known, prudently removed himself and his fortune to Ceylon the very instant that he heard that the Japanese had crossed the Causeway and were headed straight for Singapore.

It stood on a high piece of ground thrusting out into No Man's Land from the western perimeter like a finger, in a wilderness of once elegant gardens littered with plaster reproductions of Diana, Venus and Apollo. From time to time random shells had exploded uselessly against its concrete awfulness, chipping bits from the walls, shattering the storks and water-lilies in the stained glass.

On the maps in the Ops. Room the area on which it stood looked like an ugly appendix bursting out of the otherwise tidy line of the Rozendaal Front. It might easily become infected, since anyone occupying the imposing site could dominate the whole North-West area, and so it seemed therefore a very reasonable, not to say timely, thing to do to bring it comfortably within the area which the Division now controlled: it was to this end that the nine-thirty briefing to discuss 'Operation Palace' had been called at the General's villa. 'Tidy things up, square everything off neatly,' he said, fully aware that he was securing himself, his palace, as well as giving 2nd Brigade some useful, and necessary, exercise. There shouldn't, he reasoned, having digested his Intelligence Reports, be much, if any, opposition since the land about the 'finger' or 'appendix' was mostly long abandoned paddy and cane.

As the briefing broke up in little groups of enthusiastic chatter, he asked a number of his experts including Gaunt, Pullen, Nettles and Brigadier Blackett, the Brigade Commander, along with the ever-attentive Roberts, to stay behind as the others filed out into the morning, and outlined his detailed plans for command posts, wire, mine-fields, lines of communication and the ultimate restoration of the Palace itself. He asked for their thoughts and ideas as soon as possible, keeping any details pertaining to the house itself out of Daily Orders: didn't want the Other Ranks to start getting bolshie ideas at this stage of the war. It was difficult enough, he reminded them, to convince Indian Troops that they were doing the right thing by firing on fellow Asians who were struggling against Colonial rule for their freedom, while bloody Gandhi, Congress, and All India Radio were exhorting them to do precisely the same thing towards the British in India. There wasn't really very much to choose between Indonesia and India, just a question of four little letters. (He had used this same remark with great effect at a Staff Meeting in Delhi not long ago. It had gone down very well, he thought.) However, the blank faces before him very slightly unnerved him, so he picked up his little silver bell and rang it like a tocsin. Almost immediately, as if he had been crouching at the ready behind the door, Nanni Singh came swiftly into the room on silent feet, bearing a large tray of beer and glasses, followed by the slim, bright-eyed, boy carrying two plates of rice-cookies which he placed, as shown by a silent move of Nanni Singh's head, on the Benares brass gate-legged table.

Nettles, tucking away his maps and notebook in the little black briefcase, was instantly aware of the slim legs, narrow hips, glossy black hair, the one gold earring and a small tattoo of a single eye etched into a smooth, hairless forearm which deftly arranged the plates to its satisfaction. What I used to call 'dishy' in the days of my nubile youth, he thought appreciatively, and still do in the sear days of my middle age. Ah me! He closed his case just as Nanni Singh with his empty tray swiftly ushered temptation back into the kitchen and the swing door click-clocked gently behind them; but not before he had been rewarded with a swift appraising look through demurely lowered lashes. He almost laughed aloud, instead he snapped his locks shut and reached for his cap.

'Not good, I'm thinking,' as Willie would say. As Willie *had* said. Last night with the letter.

He froze.

'A beer for you?' Gaunt with glass and bottle.

'Ah no, no, thanks all the same. Not now. Must rush, it's almost noon.'

'Going to sort out your kitchen wallah?' Gaunt steadily pouring his beer.

'Hope so. Yes. Sort him out.'

'Good show. Those salmon things . . . Christ!'

Nettles rose to his feet. 'I'll get along, Sir, if you'll excuse me?'

'Yes, said all I have to say, off you go.' The General waved a dismissing glass towards him, and, as he passed, caught his elbow. 'By the by, that feller you were on about, new chap . . .?'

'Rooke?'

'Whatever . . . haven't clapped eyes on him. Ought to, don't you think? Tim's off shortly, damned inconvenient timing, I must say: still.'

'He's actually up at the docks, Sir. Got him started on the party.'

'Ah ha! The party! Nearly forgot! Good show, Nettles. Yes, Tim, your farewell "do". A real pisseroo. Your Repat and the success of "Palace". I drink to them both!'

In a polite murmur of 'Hear, hear' they dutifully raised glasses as Nettles, with a brief nod, left the room.

Willie with the letter!

He was sitting cross-legged on the little balcony darning when Nettles arrived. He got to his feet rapidly, wagging the sock on his fist. 'I'm thinking boot not good. Maybe nail. Many holies, Sahib.'

'Willie, my Gurkha treasure.'

Willie nodded and smiled happily, a wide gold-toothed smile. 'Sahib?'

'This letter? Remember?' He held it in his hand. 'Last night. Chota bath-time?'

Willie screwed his face into an anguish of concentration. 'Remember,' he said dully.

'Who from?'

'Ah. Chitty from boy. Fella. Not knowing. Not good, I'm thinking.'

'Why not good, you think?'

Willie looked down at his socked fist and shrugged silently.

'Why not good, Willie? Why bad fella?'

The silent shrug again, and then he looked directly up at Nettles. With his free hand he pointed to his own ear. 'Like mem-sahib here. And here . . .' he pointed to his right eye, 'is here.' Gently he placed his finger on Nettles' own forearm. 'So not good, I'm thinking?'

The rain, which had started in the afternoon, had stopped, and the day was beginning to fade. From where she stood on her balcony Emmie could see the pale light reflecting in the puddles below, the startling green of the datura leaves, the drips still splashing from the eaves of the house into the lush vine which sprawled unkemptly across the roof of the verandah. The rainy season, she reflected, was almost over. She folded the grey skirt neatly, ran her hands through her hair, and went downstairs to join Clair who was sitting at the kitchen table sewing on a button.

'Your grey skirt. Thank you. No marks.'

Clair looked up and bit off a thread, thrust the needle into a scrap of cloth, smoothed out the small shirt on her lap.

'Won't you need it a bit longer? You may, you know.'

'No. Today was First Impression day. Tomorrow I work. I wear this.'

'Looks like a blanket.'

'It was a blanket.'

'Won't it be terribly hot?'

'No. Really.' She reached out and picked up Clair's sewing box. A battered tin. 'Callard and Bowser's. Butterscotch', navy blue and gold lettering, much worn. 'You still keep this?'

'Very useful. All my sewing bits.'

'Mrs Bethell-Wood. I don't know how you can.'

'Her present to me. I treasure it.'

'Her apology. Not enough.'

'Her greatest treasure. She'd had it since she was very young. It was the only thing she had ever managed to keep. A reminder of the past. And her apology too, if you like.'

'For such a dreadful thing it is not enough.'

'It was all she had, Emmie. She didn't mean it about the radio set.'

'Silly, gossiping, cruel old woman.'

'She knew that. She said so.'

'And Wim? She knew that too? It is enough for Wim?'

'Wim is alive, so are we. She is dead. She knew. She knew I forgave.'

'Nursing her. You could have got typhoid too; Wim . . .'

Clair folded the shirt and closed the tin. 'Well, I didn't. She died in peace.'

'Still believing in her damned God.'

'Yes.' Clair carried the shirt and the tin into the hall. 'I think she did. I suppose I was her proof. Turn the other cheek. Never mind. Come and have a drink. And don't be so unforgiving, it's been such a good day. Have you seen Wim and his telephone set?'

On the verandah he was hunched over the tin table, his corn hair over his eyes, scraping the paper label off a round cigarette tin with a blunt knife. He held it up as they came through the wide doors. 'See? It's for the receiver, but I need another one and some string and then it'll be a telephone.'

Emmie lowered herself into a deckchair. 'Who said?'

Wim blew the paper scraps across the floor. 'The man you brought this morning. He said you need two cigarette tins, you knock a hole in the bottom of each, stretch a bit of string through them, pull it very tight and then you can talk to each other in different rooms. Something like that. He's going to show me when he brings the other tin; he's got one empty somewhere.'

'Rooke, do you mean? My boss.'

'Is he? I don't know, but that's his name. He came for coffee with you and gave me this. He said my English was excellent. You know? *Excellent.* I liked him.'

Clair helped herself to a whisky and pushed the bottle across the table towards Emmie. 'Help yourself. I never know about whisky, how much to give; too much, not enough.' She poured water into her glass. 'Tired?'

Emmie shook her head slowly from side to side. Leaned up and took the whisky bottle. 'No. Bewildered rather. Not tired. So many things in one day after so many days of nothing and no one. So much space, laughter, and kindness. Little kindnesses, like Wim's cigarette tin, you know? Thoughtfulness. I liked it all.'

Clair smiled wanly in the gathering dusk. 'Kindness takes a great deal of getting used to. I have found that. It should come in a liquid form at first, you know? Like when you have had no food for a long time, one should drink things, soup, milk, not eat a whole loaf. You can become ill so easily. Some people can really die from kindness, I imagine.'

Emmie held her half-filled glass in both hands and squinted

through the amber drink. 'You look very funny, Wim: like in a Magic Mirror, all horizontal.'

'Do I?'

'Yes, you do. We met Yoko Oshima today. In the Dumps. Can you believe it?'

'I can believe anything these days. Was she stealing?'

Emmie laughed shortly. 'Not yet. Working. Translating like us. A collaborator.'

Clair frowned. 'Don't say that word. It's so silly.'

'Rooke said she really was one. Because of the Nakuma business. I told him.' She shrugged. 'Why not? He was amazed that no one cared. Yet. But of course she knows the languages a little, and she knows the Dumps backwards, I imagine. I wonder if she is still in the flat they had? All the things they took; so much. Who will ever find them now? I wonder how she ever got the job there today, maybe the El Greco angel again.'

'I think it was Dora Foto. Nigel told me. She recommended her because she spoke Japanese, he told me.'

'But didn't you say anything?'

'No. Why should I? It's not my affair, they'll find out when the time comes, for the moment we must try to start living again. There is so little time for small jealousies, so much to do, so many people still to get home. You know? We have fought the war, now we have to fight the peace; it'll be as hard.'

'I hope not. Oh God, I hope not. And Dora?'

'And Dora? Miss Foto?'

'Ummmm.'

'Well. I don't know. Who will tell: you? Me? What for . . . anyway she is very close to the throne, she'll be all right, you see.'

'She'll be all right. Almost on the throne.'

From the valley below the frogs were croaking, the air was heavy and damp, the light had almost gone. Clair rose and snapped on the light hanging over the table in a warped grass shade; it gleamed sullenly on the bottle and glasses and a puddle on the steps. From behind the house the sound of a truck crunching to a stop, Rooke's voice calling. Wim ran swiftly into the house to meet him, the truck revved up and swung into the street. Clair pushed her hair from her hot forehead. 'I wonder what he wants?' She went into the house and Emmie heard

104

Wim's cry of pleasure: he came hurrying onto the verandah, a cigarette tin held high.

'He remembered! The other part of the telephone. Your boss.'

'Oh dear,' said Emmie. 'Now it must be all English again.' She put her drink on the table and eased herself out of the chair heavily.

'Don't move, please,' said Rooke. 'I only came for a moment, to bring him that. I'm walking up to the Mess. Please don't move.'

'I'm exhausted really. Are you still working all this time?' She sat back slowly. Rooke had his cap under his arm, light glimmered on his belt brasses.

'I was. Lists of things, you know. Paper streamers, golf clubs. I've been to a small funeral.'

Emmie raised surprised eyebrows. 'A funeral? Oh God, sit down, the chairs are safe, I think. Whose small funeral?'

'The chap who got killed on the convoy. Holly. Just Gaunt and me and the Padre.'

'Poor man. Did you know him?'

'No. But Gaunt was in the Mess while I was working, and suggested I should go . . . respect; you know. No one else came. He's very particular about good manners, the Division. I don't think anyone cared much, too used to it all. A small funeral in the hospital gardens, quite a few of them in there, white crosses for Christians.'

'And the Indian men?' Emmie looked worried. 'They burn them, I think?'

Rooke stuck his cap under his chair. 'I really don't know. Haven't asked.'

Clair came through the doors with beer and a glass. 'Or there's whisky, if you'd prefer? Nigel brought a bottle of the real one.'

'Beer is splendid. I mustn't stay . . .'

'What do I do with this now?' Wim held up the tin.

'Bang a hole in the bottom and put the string through with a big knot.'

'What's knot?'

Rooke took the string and tied it hard. 'That's a knot, so the tin won't fall off.'

'A knot. I know. I go to make the hole.' He ran lightly into the house.

'Rooke has been to a small funeral,' said Emmie. 'Such a sad phrase.'

'Whose?' Clair pulled a chair to the table.

'A chap called Holly. His other name, I gather, was Eustace. I never ever met anyone really called Eustace. From the convoy. Eustace Holly had a small funeral in the garden of The Juliana Hospital with just David Gaunt and me and the Padre, oh yes, and four English nurses who came in yesterday from Penang.'

'English nurses? I didn't know that,' said Clair. 'Poor things.'

Rooke laughed lightly. 'They didn't know either. A Sister Pritchard is in charge, very English and crisp and bossy, quite nice but no nonsense. Nettles said he'd rather bleed to death than let her touch him. I think David quite liked her because she rides or something, anyway he said he doesn't consider nurses as women. He says they are neuters.'

'He doesn't know nurses,' Clair laughed cheerfully. 'How many people for the party, did you work it out?'

'Ah yes. About a hundred at least; the Old Man has lifted the ban on women in the Mess and everyone can bring a guest. If they know anyone. So about a hundred, say.'

'Because I spoke to Yan Ho today and he and his sons could do all the food: they have no restaurant now as you know, with the curfew, so they would come to the Mess and cook everything, if that's allowed?'

'Gosh, you are kind to remember. I'll find out. Nettles would be delighted, he's at his wits' end already, so far it's either a giant curry or bully beef hash.'

'Well, find out if it's permitted and I'll tell Yan Ho. It wouldn't cost much.'

Emmie smoothed her blanket skirt carefully. 'What is neuter? I don't know this word.'

Rooke looked across at Clair. 'Sexless, would you say?'

Clair nodded, smiling across her glass. 'Yes, something like that. Cat's have an operation, don't they? Not masculine, not feminine. Awful.'

'And this man thinks this is good?'

Rooke shifted uncomfortably. 'Well, no, not good. Con-

106

venient. But I like him. He has been very kind. Funny chap. Do you know him, Mrs Doorne?'

'David Gaunt? Oh yes. Yes, I like him too. Very reserved, you know something? You look quite like him . . . not as old, but like him: physically I mean, not I think mentally.' She laughed suddenly. 'I get muddled in my English. So many "likes", but you know?'

'I know. Actually he said I reminded him of someone he knew. I'm riding with him tomorrow morning. My God! Half-past five! I ask you . . .' He turned to Emmie. 'You wouldn't like to come too?'

She shook her head so violently that her hair swung like a curtain across her face. 'Oh no! The bicycle is enough. And I must be at the Dumps early, remember, and meet that woman Ruby. She has the Japanese words so she can speak to the prisoners. I hate to. I still have fear you know?'

Rooke drained his glass. 'Of Ruby? Why?'

'No, no, not of silly Ruby. Of the Japanese men. When they go "hisssss" it makes me full of fear again. I remember the noise: the smiling, the bowing. Not Ruby, she's bad but I have no fear.'

'What is her real name again?' said Rooke. 'You told me?'

'Yoko Oshima. From Nassau Boulevard.'

'Ah yes.'

It was now quite dark, the weak glimmer from the hanging lamp cast deep black shadows on their faces, glinted on the glasses and the bottle, attracted a large black insect which blundered into the gently swinging shade, stunned itself and fell heavily onto the table, legs feebly waving. Rooke swiftly brushed it off and trod on it. It crackled under his boot.

'Her father had a restaurant once. Not very fashionable. The Golden Carp.' Clair reached out for Rooke's empty glass, her eyebrows raised in question; he shook his head and smiled.

'No thanks. Must be off, change for dinner, and get the list ready for you tomorrow.' He reached over and touched Emmie's shirt. 'That's pretty. It suits you.'

'It's just a piece of batik. Local cotton. Everyone wears it.'

'Why do you call her Ruby, Yoko Oshima?' asked Clair.

'I don't know. The Military Police call her that, I think. And another not very complimentary name.'

'Ruby is a jewel, isn't it?'

'Red. A precious stone.'

'Very good description,' said Clair. 'She likes jewels.'

Rooke got to his feet, searched in the shadow for his cap and put it under his arm. 'Thanks for the beer. I just came to bring Wim his other tin, and to see if you were all right after such a long day?' He looked down at Emmie, his head on one side. He is very tall, she thought, very beautiful with the light just on his nose, his forehead, the fine blond hair. I can't get up because I am suddenly too shy, but I can't say that. Instead she said, 'I'm very well. Lazy just. But I am very well, thank you. It's very dark now, will you find your way?'

'It's only four houses up, I'll count the gates. Until tomorrow then?'

'Until tomorrow at the Dumps.'

When he and Clair had gone into the house she rose from the chair and stood for a moment and looked at the squashed beetle which she gently moved across to the steps with her sandalled foot and kicked into the dark. Then turned swiftly and followed them into the hall: Rooke was explaining something to Wim who carried the two tins and a loop of string.

'We'll do it tomorrow . . .'

'Not now?'

'No. Really. Anyway you need more string, lots more. It has to be very long, so that you can be in one room and I in another, quite far apart. See?'

Wim clonked the tins together to hide disappointment. 'I see. Tomorrow?'

'Sure.' He ran his hand lightly through the child's hair. 'You get the string.'

I must touch him, she thought, I must tell him that I can't speak, can't say the words. I think them but cannot say them. I want him to stay. He could stand here for ever and I would just be content to look at him, to hear him, I would like him to put his hand on my head as he is doing with Wim, I'd like to feel his hand in my hair, against my cheek, on my heart. He'd feel it beating and say, 'Emmie, your heart is beating very fast,' and I would say, 'It's just a heart, a local heart, everyone has a heart which beats like this,' but it wouldn't be true. It is my heart, and it beats like this for him. Suddenly, happily, wildly, a lark rising.

I must touch him to tell him this. She clasped her hands tightly together, pressed them against her thigh. 'I have a long, long piece of string, Wim, in my room, you can have that.' She crossed easily to the polished staircase and started up, back straight, hand on rail; lark flown.

'Tomorrow then?' Rooke called up. She stopped at the landing and looked down into the hall. Three blond heads raised towards her in the soft glow of the electric light, smiling. 'Tomorrow,' she nodded. 'With bad Ruby.' As she turned to go on up Rooke suddenly broke away from the tableau and crossed to the foot of the stairs. 'Oh, I know. I knew I'd forget. Nettles asked me. Miss Foto, Dora Foto, Belgian I think, he wanted to know if you knew her?'

Emmie stopped and stayed quite still in the shadows. Then she turned and moved down towards the hall. 'Dora Foto? Yes, I know her. We all know each other here, we were all in the same camp together, why?'

Rooke shrugged. 'Don't quite know. He asked me to ask you because your father ran the big newspaper: must have known everyone in the city.'

Emmie came down three more steps carefully. 'Everyone knew Miss Foto. She had a dress shop. Everyone knows Miss Foto, even your General.'

Rooke swung his cap vaguely in a loop about his chest. 'So I believe. Anyway. Nettles just asked me, that's all.'

'Tell him I do,' said Emmie. 'It was a very chic dress shop.'

When he had gone Clair came back into the house, closed the front door firmly, ran home the bolts and, turning suddenly, saw Emmie crouched half-way up the stairs, arms hugging her knees, head leaning against the banisters.

'What is it?'

'Nettles,' said Emmie. 'The El Greco one. He's in Intelligence, isn't he?'

'Yes. The top one. Most senior.'

They looked at each other for a long moment in silence. Emmie broke it, and got slowly to her feet.

'I'll get that bit of string,' she said.

CHAPTER FIVE

The lengths of satin slithered across the table spilling into a rainbow of acid green, lemon yellow, crimson and bright blue. Confectioners' colours, thought Miss Foto disdainfully as she threw a length of magenta over one shoulder and gathered it at her waist. I'd look like an Ice Cream Sundae.

'How kind, Yoko. How thoughtful of you to think of me.'

'Metres and metres of it in the Dumps. I knew you liked plain colours, nothing flashy. I remembered,' Ruby said, happily rummaging about in a cardboard box producing a bunch of ostrich feathers. 'And these too. All colours. I like feathers so.' She threw them on the table. 'All for you if you like: I can get much more, anything I want. He doesn't care.'

'Your boss?'

'Doesn't know about anything. He's very cross nearly all the time.'

Miss Foto started to fold the lengths of satin neatly with expert hands. 'Well, you were very kind to think of me.'

'You got me the job after all. Thank you.'

'A good, diligent girl. You always were. A just reward: you and Pearl Ching were the best "cutters" I had; quick to learn.'

'You showed us, Miss Foto.'

'I taught you everything, eh? Remember how shy you were? In the Salon? A pretty face is not as important as a pretty . . .' she placed the folded cloth neatly back into the box, '*speciality*.' She gathered up the waving plumes and stuck them on top and closed the lid. 'There. My gift. And yours was very much a speciality. How successful you were, Yoko. Why do they call you Ruby now?'

'I don't know. He does, Mr Wizzerbee, I can't say it. Ronnie, I call him, he likes Ruby. The police called me that. Military Police. Red Light Ruby—pretty, yes?'

'Does he like you?' Miss Foto took the box and placed it carefully on the heavily carved sideboard, and took down a glass bowl of chocolate bars which she offered her guest. 'Have one, or two. I don't eat them, my hips, and this.' She patted her buttocks.

Ruby unwrapped her chocolate. 'Yes, he likes me. I've only done it once or twice with him. He comes to my flat.' She took a big bite and chewed for a moment. 'Nuts and creamy stuff. It's good.'

'American,' said Miss Foto lighting a Camel cigarette, 'like these. They have so much, it makes you almost ill to see.'

'I think the English are very like the Germans,' said Ruby chewing contentedly. 'Do you remember, years ago, Fritzie, he was so big and strong and I was very frightened that he would hurt me and he wanted *me* to hurt *him*! Remember! Oh, it was so funny. I almost couldn't for laughing.'

'I remember him. Very generous.'

'Well, Ronnie is like that. He doesn't touch me, only here and here . . .' She made a slight indication of her breasts and feet with the half-eaten Hershey bar. 'And then I have to spank him for being a naughty boy. On his bottom. And then he is very pleased and wriggles and it's all over. Pouf! Like that. Finish.'

'Easy money,' said Miss Foto dryly, blowing smoke.

'Oh he doesn't pay me!' Ruby laughed, her wide teeth outlined in chocolate. 'He just says he'll keep his mouth shut, about me, if I am kind to him.'

Miss Foto narrowed her eyes and stroked her fringe thoughtfully. 'Does he know about you then? How?'

Ruby shrugged and finished her bar swiftly. 'I think the police know. Because I am Japanese, half anyway, they think I am very professional. A real pro, one of them says, "Ruby is a real pro". It's very flattering, they appreciate me and they give me presents too, anything I like from the Dumps, all that.' She waved at the box on the sideboard. 'And other things, but they aren't like Ronnie . . . much quicker.' She looked happily about the room. 'I like your little house. So pretty, so many lovely things, so elegant.'

Miss Foto, still frowning slightly, adjusted a red silk scarf over the standard lamp. 'The General likes to be comfortable. He likes this room too. I have a soft light for him, and he likes my joss sticks burning, very refined you see. A real gentleman. And these, my ivory elephants all carved from one single piece, holding each other's tails.' She offered the yellow bridge of animals. 'Big, down to very little. So pretty don't you think?'

'Pretty as could be. Where from?'

Miss Foto replaced the elephants on her carved Chinese coffee table. 'From the same place as you get your things. The Dumps. I had to start all over again. My place was burned to the ground, on the Liberation Day.'

'All the fighting,' said Ruby, starting on her second bar, 'so much fighting. I saw many tanks this morning, tanks all over the Plein, and trucks and things, more fighting.'

'At Rozendaal, it's a big operation.'

'And in all this rain.'

'The English like the rain. They even keep things for a rainy day.'

Ruby crunched the second wrapping tightly in her hand and looked about for somewhere to put it neatly. 'Ah yes! Like Mel . . . remember?'

Miss Foto, rearranging a bowl of wax grapes which she had not been able to resist in spite of the 'only basic essentials' on her list, paused for a second. 'Mel? Who is Mel?' The grapes clonked against the side of the bowl and she reached out for the crunched wrapping. 'Give me that, and the other, I'll take them. Must be tidy, I consider. Mel who?'

'That Australian boy. I think he had red hair. He gave you fifty Singapore dollars. Money. All he had. You told me, you were crying. That last night, remember? Save it for a rainy day, he said.'

Miss Foto had gone into her little kitchen, put the wrapping papers in a tin under the sink, straightened up and placed her hands to her face. For a few seconds she stood quite still, and then shook her head quickly, combed her fringe into place with her fingers and returned to the sitting-room. 'Mel? Australian. He had some friends, I remember, of course. A nice boy, I liked him.'

Ruby looked up at her shrewdly. The last of the chocolate melting in her fingers so that she was forced to spread her fingers wide. 'He liked you too. You were very good to them, so brave you were to hide them, you could have been punished for doing that. Colonel Nakuma said so, he often told me, but because you confessed he said you showed true humility and respect for Nippon.' She ate the last piece of her sweet, and wiped her fingers neatly on the hem of her skirt. 'Mel, Dickie,

112

and two others, very young boys. I remember.' She got up from her chair and ran the tip of her little finger delicately across her lips. 'Is there a mirror? Ah yes . . .' She peered at her reflection, pursing her lips, pressing the red cotton flower firmly into her hair, rearranging the glass beads at her throat. 'I told him, Nakuma-san, you were very respectful of Nippon, and he was very pleased, I told him you were a very clever lady and that you liked to make his men happy and not to miss their wives and sweethearts. He was very interested.'

'You were very kind, Yoko, really kind. But you know,' Miss Foto carefully rearranged her wax fruit again, 'it is not always wise to remember too much.'

'Oh! Miss Foto! How could I forget you, so many things you did, so good . . .'

'That was then, Yoko.'

'All those poor women locked up away from husbands and so on.'

'They will not like to be reminded of the "so on" you understand?' Miss Foto was quite still, a bunch of blue grapes in her hand. Ruby looked at her with something akin to intelligence, and then looked away and fluffed up her lace cuffs.

'Oh that. Yes. But who will remember? No one will know. It was private. The silly English don't care, they don't know, no one knows that.'

'The Dutch do,' said Miss Foto unmoving, the grapes steady in her hand.

'They aren't here.'

'They'll come back.'

'You think so? Ronnie says not ever. All gone, he says. Freedom for all colonial slaves, he tells me.'

Miss Foto replaced the grapes to her satisfaction. 'The Dutch will come back to make things tidy, Yoko, they won't forget, and they will be very, very angry.'

'With you?'

'With us all, you and me, the others.'

'And what will they do?' Ruby's face was suddenly slack with alarm.

'To me nothing,' said Miss Foto crossing to the door to show her guest out, 'because I shall be in Singapore by then, maybe even America, who knows?'

113

Ruby was rooted to the floor. 'And me? Yoko? Your Yoko girl?'

Miss Foto leaned gently against the side of the door. 'Where did your father come from, originally, Yoko?'

'Japan, from Kyoto.'

'Exactly. Then my advice,' said Miss Foto opening the door gently, 'is to get back there just as fast as you can.'

'How?' cried Ruby, twisting her beads.

'Marry a Jap,' said Miss Foto brightly. 'There are so many to choose from here.' She went out onto the little verandah and took up Ruby's dripping umbrella. 'No: what you must do now is to stop remembering so well. The past is the past, what was, *was*. All finished. But thank you for the material, I can really look elegant for the big Party . . . are you coming?'

'Coming?' Ruby was still too troubled by the past to look towards the future with any degree of confidence or pleasure.

'The party in the English Mess, ask your man, he'll know.'

'I'll ask,' said Ruby.

'Now you go home and think of something lovely to wear, eh? And stop remembering everything so clearly; it is a dangerous thing to do.' She watched Ruby pick her way carefully through the puddles and, huddled into the rain, run untidily up the street.

He had thighs like tree-trunks, a waist which she could nearly span with two hands only, a chest like a bull and the tight red hair which so attracted her, skin as smooth and white as a lily petal. She leaned up from him and traced his throat with her finger.

'You were crazy to come here. It's getting more dangerous. Patrols, they even come to search now with no warning. Mel, don't again, please.'

'I manage. Take care, don't fret. Tall I may be but light on my feet.'

She ran her finger slowly down his chest, across his belly, down the smooth white thigh. 'There is something else. Serious. I think they will arrest all of us Europeans soon.'

He sat up suddenly. 'Who says?'

'One of my girls, she lives with Nakuma, the City Engineer or something. They have cleared all the people from the Molen-dijk slum, they are making a cage round it, Yoko says for European women, Nakuma told her; the men will be sent far across the Island.'

'Sure?'

'She says so. Soon. And then I wouldn't be able to get you food and things. You could not stay there in the forest without that. Alone. All of you.'

He scratched his chest. 'What to do then?'

'Well, when it happens you must put on your uniforms again and you must go to the Commandant and you will surrender . . .'

He swung off the bed abruptly and stooped to pick up his clothes from the floor. 'Not bloody likely, not us.'

'But you are soldiers, they will respect that.'

'Like fuck.'

'I do not like this word.'

'You like the act, my plump little sheila.'

'Stop it. Do you listen to me, Mel?'

'Sure I listen to you. Full of doom. They'd kick the shit out of us; want to know just who's been helping to hide us since February, right? Think I want that? We'll go it alone if it happens . . . make for the coast like I always said. A little boat, then down through the islands at night . . . if we get to Timor we'd be practically home, 300 miles to Darwin.'

She suddenly burst into tears, covered her face with her hands, shoulders trembling. He moved to her, put his arms around her naked body, kissed her head, she felt the rough cotton of his shirt, the hard hands on her back.

'Come on, baby. It's not so bad, we'll make it. We'll bloody try, you see.'

'No. No. You couldn't. I know better than you finally. What boat, where?'

'Can you get me some local money? Only got Singapore bills, the Indo's won't take that, guilders or Jap cash, could you?'

She wiped her face with a corner of the sheet. 'I'll try. Yes of course, I'll get it to you; don't come here again, please.'

He was buttoning his baggy cotton pants which she had bought him. 'One more time, eh? I take a different route each time, no danger, honey. In the meantime you try and find out if it's for sure, this slum business, eh?' He was dressed, pulling on his rubber sandals: she slid off the bed and dragged her dressing-gown over her shoulders. It was lace, and snagged on one of her rings, he helped her pull free, and tied the belt round her waist, kissing her hard on the mouth as he did so. 'Now don't you fret, honey, I'm off, until next time. Three raps on the window, count six, then two more. OK?'

'No, please . . .'

He took her chin in his hand and tilted her head towards him gently. 'What's all the water for? Look as if you'd had a shower?' He kissed her lightly once again. 'Can't have you in the forest very well, can I? Not a lady like you, all the bugs and things, not to mention my randy mates.' He laughed and pinched her nose, and went to the door.

'Your wallet, all your papers,' she held it in her hand towards him.

'Ah yeah. Get rid of it, will you, honey? Shouldn't have it on me by rights. Not in action. Only we weren't: hadn't gone in when we all scarpered. Burn it, bury it, okey dokey?'

She opened it, his paybook, a small snapshot of a smiling woman, tucked under the scratched mica, his blood group. 'But there's money.'

He stopped at the door. 'Singapore money. Can't buy a boat with that, couldn't buy a banana.'

'But keep it . . .'

'No, you keep it, honey. Save it for a rainy day.'

The room seemed darker when she came in from the hall. She snapped on the tall standard lamp and was comforted by the soft red glow through the silk shade. She opened Ruby's box of folded satins, spilled them onto the dark oak sideboard. I did what I thought was right. How could they have got a boat, where from? And one of them already had a poisoned foot, they couldn't have got far with him. She pulled out a length of yellow, slid it between finger and thumb, lining satin, not even good stuff, crease in a moment. And the colour. So vulgar. Like the girl. No sense of anything. White would be better. I am good in white. Sharkskin. A neat sharkskin two-piece, very simple.

116

Anyway it was all in the past. I did what I thought was the only sensible thing, the wise thing, for him. For Mel. No one can blame me. What did I know of army things? A prisoner of war is a prisoner of war. The Geneva Convention says so. This stuff is rubbish. Who but a half-caste Japanese tart would wear a bunch of ostrich feathers? She rammed them all back into the box. Poor child, a body of such beauty and the face of a baboon. I put her all in black, black boots, black apron, little black mask, and now she dresses like a circus pony. No brains, no sense. And senseless in remembering; remembering like that can be very disturbing, she thought, catching sight of herself in the amber tinted mirror before her: she traced a finger over the faint lines which already showed, even in the soft glow of the red light; at the corners of her eyes and mouth, smiled with her lips, wiped her tongue across her teeth removing a small flick of lipstick. Disturbing and dangerous. To comfort herself, suddenly feeling an urgent need of it, she shook a finger at herself in mock reproof.

'Never look down, remember, never look down,' she said aloud.

By mid-afternoon 2nd Brigade had secured the whole of the area surrounding the Palace and had even extended the perimeter line designated, since there had been, as expected, only very light opposition. An odd pocket of unorganized extremists here and there, a burst or two of automatic fire, a few poorly aimed mortars. Operation Palace had been a wild success, the Brigade had enjoyed the painless activity and the General's stock had risen effortlessly.

'We could have done the whole thing with a bunch of Boy Scouts armed with catapults,' said Gaunt. 'Easiest bloody Operation the Division has ever planned. I had hoped to offer you a bit more fun and games. Few more bangs and so on.'

'Had all the bangs I wanted in France, thanks.' Rooke followed him through the rain, soaked to the skin, steaming in the humid air, towards the gaunt block of the concrete monstrosity which had been the main objective. Wanton bamboo and banana thrust lushly through the scabby pebble paths, vines and creepers twisted and coiled about the rusting wrought

117

iron balconies, fragments of bright coloured glass littered the sodden ground winking in the fine rain like cheap jewellery; and in the hip-high grasses, one hand raised in plaster reproof, a tumbled Apollo Belvedere lay with missing fingers.

'Just look at it all,' said Gaunt. 'The whole grisly pile. What I could do with a couple of kegs of dynamite and a neat little plunger. Blow the bloody lot to smithereens. Christ! The things we have to fight for in a battle: tennis courts, bridges, crossroads, hill-tops and things like this, all in the name of democracy. Jokey.'

From the front of the house wide marble terraces shelved down the steep hillside linked by broad flights of steps, the final level, far below, hung out over the misty valley; a jutting semi-circle of pink marble surrounding a vast, empty heart-shaped pool flanked by twin pagodas with green tiled roofs, encompassed by a low tiled-wall. A Chinese merchant's vision of splendour gleaned from a thousand Hollywood films. They stared down unbelievingly.

'Shangri-la,' said Rooke under his breath. 'But what happens if you fall over the wall, do you suppose?'

'Land on your arse with a broken neck a hundred feet below,' said Gaunt.

'Probably where he tipped his concubines when he got bored with them.'

'Great idea. Sensible. One poke, then a good shove.' He shielded his eyes with his hands against the rain.

'What the bloody hell are they all up to? Running about down there . . .'

A scatter of soldiers scurried about the marble, peering at the void, running in and out of the little pagodas, throwing stones over the low wall, laughing, pushing, rifles wagging in the air like pick handles.

'Your Pathans by the look of them. Having a jolly time.'

'Bloody idiots. No restraint, you see. All so damned manly and proud and then they behave like a bunch of school boys. That's where they let you down in the end, no restraint, no sense of reason, bunch of school kids.' He turned on his heel. 'Come on. Don't stand about. I want the buggers back here.'

A burst of happy laughter as they turned the corner of the house, scattered applause and cheering from a circle of cheerful

118

soldiers who might well have been watching a cockfight. Which, in essence, they were. In the centre one of them, much taller than the others it seemed to Rooke, had thrown his arms in a passionate embrace about a buxom plaster goddess who, with head tilted back, patrician nose high, sightless eyes turned towards the lowering monsoon sky, rocked gently on her pedestal against the violently thrusting hips of her ravisher who crushed hard against her resilient form. Legs wildly splayed, arms tight about the waist, face pressed deep into the plaster neck, he drove and ground to the happy encouragement of his companions.

Gaunt's high roars of fury ripped through the fine rain. The laughter froze. A moment of stupefied shock, heads turned in swift surprise, bodies scattered hurriedly across the gravel towards the trucks and jeep leaving only the centre of attraction still hung about the neck of his goddess. For a moment he remained motionless, eyes closed, and then with slow deliberation he pulled away, turned his head and stared, heavy-lidded, at Gaunt, face drained, lips parted, arms akimbo, legs apart. He wiped a hand across his face, stooped for his fallen rifle in the trodden grass, checked the foresight, muzzle and safety catch, slung it carefully over his shoulder, looked back at Gaunt, held the look, and with a swift about-turn walked with a slow, easy gait towards his companions.

Gaunt thrashed a fleshy plant at his feet with his cane. 'Bloody animal.'

They walked over to the jeep.

'I think it was just a bit of fun, surely.'

'Fun? Bloody obscene. You saw what he was doing?'

'Yes, but . . .'

'No "but", humping a bloody statue. What kind of "fun" is that?'

'But really, David, relief or something; after the Operation.'

Gaunt raised his cane and tapped Rooke gently on the arm. 'It's just underneath that thin veneer of civilization. Not far down. Screwing a white woman, you realize that? Revenge.'

'Oh for God's sake! It was a joke.'

'No joke. I know. Frontier man. Bolshie sod. You saw that look? Watch out for him.'

They clambered into the jeep.

'Sorry,' said Rooke. 'Not my business, I suppose.'

'No, it's not,' said Gaunt evenly. 'You haven't been out here long enough for it to be your business yet. You'll see one of these days.'

They swung out between the high iron gates and headed back to the city.

I have never, thought Pullen, smiling down into the eager upturned face of Sister Pritchard, actually cared for women with hairy faces. Or rabbit teeth. This poor creature has her fair share. It's not really hair, I suppose, just a sort of down, and on the cheeks. Quite unattractive.

'Penny for them?' said Sister Pritchard.

'For what, Sister?'

'Smiling away. Happy thoughts.'

'Thinking how very well you dance.'

'Oh you! I do so love it, and you reverse marvellously.'

'I'm really not awfully good, frightfully out of practice.'

'Stuff! I haven't felt giddy once. What is it, the tune?'

'The waltz from *Rosenkavalier*, I rather think.'

'So pretty. I adore it. So swoopy don't you think?'

'Very pleasing, Strauss.'

'Romantic. He did the "Blue Danube" too, didn't he?'

'That was Johann, I venture to guess. This is Richard.'

Her eyes were wide with feigned interest. 'Oh! Are there two of them?'

'Yes, two. At least...'

'Ah well, it's all the same thing, isn't it? Waltzes from Vienna. Rather naughty and unpatriotic, I suppose.' She offered him what she had long ago been told was her tinkling laugh for she had momentarily lost his attention. She sought to regain it by giving his arm a sharp pinch.

'It's a wizard party. I'm loving it. Such a treat. A real treat. And it's all so beautifully done, all the golf clubs and green table cloths . . . the lanterns.'

He had seen Clair drift past him in a plain black dress, her hair in a tight glowing bun at the back of her neck; she had smiled at him as her partner turned her into the crowd. He had felt his heart rise with pleasure, a quite simple physical manifestation as if it had been attached to a cord like the weights in a clock, from somewhere in the region of his knees it had suddenly soared into his chest at the sight of her. And stayed there.

'You've seen someone you know?' Sister Pritchard wagged her head mischievously.

'My translator, interpreter. Pretty woman.'

'I was saying, the golf clubs and things, so original, but why?'

'Ah. Ah, that's in honour of the Guest of Honour, you might say . . . he's going home on Repat, he was a golfing pro in civvy life, I believe.'

'The ADC, Roberts, I think? A charming fellow.' She swivelled her short neck and looked about, they stumbled together, she laughed and apologized, and they swung back into the waltz. 'I must say,' she laughed conspiratorially, 'he looks just the teeniest bit woozey-boo.'

'Dare say he is. It's his night. I think he wants to be poured onto the boat when he goes, to deaden the pain he says.'

'Doesn't he want to go home?'

'I suppose so really. But we've all been together a long time, you know. He'll miss us back in civvy life, it'll be a big change.'

Sister Pritchard hugged him to her tightly. 'I simply *dread* going home. I simply loved my war, terrific fun . . . coming here was an absolute god-send to me. When they told me in Calcutta that we were coming here I absolutely cheered out loud! Bucked me up no end. Excitement, bustle, all that sort of thing. I simply dread it all ending. Aren't I wicked?'

He spun her swiftly and determinedly into four or five quick spins as the waltz came to its end, and helped her, slightly reeling, but laughing gamely, towards the bar and the hyena laughter of Tim Roberts and his companions who were busy filling his beer glass with champagne. Across the bar, a kind of canopy, an enormous banner in foot-high letters spelled out the legend, 'Tim! Knock 'Em In The Old Kent Road.'

'What fun it all is!' cried Sister Pritchard. 'Is that for him?'

'It is. And by the look of things,' said Pullen cheerfully, 'he will.'

Emmie wore a sheath of steel-coloured satin which fitted like a skin, and two long pewter cuffs on either wrist which she had

borrowed from a girl in the city. She moved with a fluid grace
and Rooke knew that she was the most beautiful creature he had
ever seen. And the most beautiful one present.

'You've done it all so well. Really. It looks marvellous.' She
touched his hand. He felt ill.

'So do you. You look marvellous, beautiful; there aren't the
words.'

'It's terribly tight.'

'I can see.'

'Very hard for me to sit down, you know.'

'I'm sure.'

'I could split everything.'

'I wish you would.'

'That's not polite. Where is your General?'

'Any minute now. He waits for things to warm up a little.'

'They are now. Look at Mr Roberts! What are they doing to
him?'

'Force feeding him with champagne, I imagine.'

'He'll be sick.'

'That's the idea. Then he can start again.'

'Such a pity. Poor boy.'

Nanni Singh, threading his way through the crowd with a
tray of glasses, gently touched Rooke's arm and inclined his
head towards the hallway, before moving discreetly towards the
verandah and the gardens, as Rooke went swiftly across the
room to where Nettles was engaged in a slightly strained conversation with a rather short, and very fat, Chinese lady who
was examining his outstretched hand with great interest through
thick round glasses.

'The General's arrived.'

'When? Here now?'

'At the door, I think.'

'Well, go and meet him . . .'

'I never have. You come. It's your plan, remember.'

Nettles excused himself from the Chinese lady and they
pushed through the dancers. 'Having my hand read,' he said,
'she says I have a long life line and had a serious operation
when I was sixteen.'

'Did you? Have an operation.'

'Not as far as I recall. A frightful turn-down from a ravishing boy at a swimming bath, wouldn't play, broke my heart. Didn't think it had left a scar.'

The General had just reached the hallway when they got there, tall, groomed, red hair neat, a pale blue stock at his throat, medal ribbons glowing, his face beaming, slightly flushed. Behind him a group of white figures laughing and chattering, handing their caps to the Bearers, assisting Miss Foto out of her floating chiffon coat.

'Ah, Nettles! There you are . . . the Fleet's in, what? Brought along the Navy for a bit of fun, show 'em how the pongos can whoop it up. All going well? Splendid noise.' He rubbed his hands together and looked at Rooke. 'You the new chap? Feller who fixed it all up tonight?'

'Captain Rooke, Sir,' said Nettles modestly. 'Done it quite splendidly. Come and have a drink, Sir, everyone is in fine form.' He led the way, the Navy following, Miss Foto drifting discreetly at the rear. She offered Rooke her hand.

'My name is Miss Foto. We have not met, I think?'

'No. Good evening, Rooke.'

'But now we do, finally. If we are late I am sorry. The Navy gentlemen, you see. They are from the big ship of yesterday, HMS *Seaford*, I think you say it? The General is most pleased they have come. For morale, you know. So we have a little cocktail and then we come to the Farewell Party, I hope it is not too many for you with no warning. You will take me in? I am a silly woman, so shy with so many people, everyone must be very exciting because this is our first party for so many years. Can I take your arm? It is most confident to hold it finally.'

They made an excellent entrance. She moved, thought Rooke, rather like a small monarch, slowly, calmly, with elegance and great dignity, one arm on his, the other raised slightly above her waistline, giving a silent benediction. Her smile, he noticed, was wide, serene, extremely confident, her back as straight as a ramrod in the simple white suit she had chosen to wear, a white silk ribbon bound round her forehead, a single strand of pearls at her throat. She was not unnoticed through the floating coils of paper streamers as they reached the dancing area.

From the corner of his eye he could see Nanni Singh, assisted by a slim white-clad youth, scurrying about with chairs

123

above their heads. On the verandah the General and his party, hands in pockets, laughing, blowing cigar smoke. Miss Foto placed her arm on his shoulder firmly.

'We will dance, I think? Then I will be less shy.'

'Not a drink first?'

Smiling demurely under her bandeau and neat fringe she shook her head. 'To dance would be beautiful.'

'It's just that the General and . . .'

She slipped into his arms neatly and took his right hand. 'The General is very happy. Nanni Singh is here, you know that already? And he has arranged everything on the verandah for his General. He is very devoted, so we dance together and you teach me, because after so many years I have quite forgotten, but if you are patient with me I will remember it again.'

They moved effortlessly into the throng, she was as light as a feather, held him pleasingly close.

'I think this is called a Slow Foxtrot, is it not?'

'I think so.'

'Invented for partners to talk to each other. Very comforting: you are very tall, you know?' She smiled sweetly up at him, her eyes on his, her lips just parted. She looked about thirty. He knew she was more.

'You must be used to that surely?'

She frowned, the smile still glowing. 'Why do you say that?'

'The General. He is tall also. Taller than I.'

The smile faded, the eyes darkened; suddenly she threw back her head, placed one gentle hand over his lips, and laughed happily. 'Ah! The General! Touché.'

'And I worry about him, the extra guests.'

'Why do you worry? I told you Singh is there, all is well, and you are not *yet* the ADC, I think? Correct?' The smile was there behind dark eyes.

'I'm sorry, no, I'm not. The ADC is getting very happy.'

'It would be very complimentary if the next ADC was also getting very happy; he should be, I think he has arranged a very beautiful party, so elegant, so happy, already I can feel that, you see?'

'You are very kind.'

'Not kind. So much. But wise. I can tell with my nose, also I can see. How pretty it all is. So many ladies, so many handsome

124

men, lights and music, people laughing again. It has been a long time here since laughter, you know that? So you must be very happy, you see.'

'Then I am. But I am not the next ADC.'

'No. Not yet.' Miss Foto turned her head suddenly. 'Ah look! My dear friend Yoko, so pretty all in red, and with the feathers, you see her? Red for a Ruby, that is what you call her, I believe, but so many feathers she makes me want to sneeze, and she is not dancing, poor child, always by the gramophone.'

'I think that her friend is working the gramophone, that's why.'

'The little man?'

'The little man.'

Miss Foto looked up into his face, licked her lips with the tip of her tongue, winked gently. 'So. The Ostrich and the Sparrow! Is funny, you think?' She pressed a little closer. Rooke's hand accommodated the move, slid gently down the waist, fingers riding gently on the firm haunch below them.

'It's funny,' he agreed, grinning slowly. 'And you are very naughty.'

Miss Foto's eyes were now clear of guile or darkness. She was enjoying herself very much indeed, a flat hard belly against hers, and a strong muscular thigh between her own, and she knew what to do. This would be an easy win, she thought, and half-closing her eyes, pressing a little closer, she used her clinching and, usually, irresistible phrase. 'I'm very naughty indeed,' she whispered, and was pleasantly relieved to find that they were both laughing delightedly.

Steady, he thought, not too much of the physical, that could easily upset your apple cart, 'softly, softly, catchee monkey', the plump bundle of joys you are holding here isn't Little Miss Muffet: she's The Red Queen. One false move and 'off with his head'.

She was still smiling up at him. 'You are happy? You were thinking?'

He nodded thoughtfully. 'Very happy. *Not* thinking.'

They were in the centre of the floor. 'It's so pretty this song, so romantic, you know it perhaps, I think is a new one for me? What is it called?'

' "More Than You Know," ' he said, and for reasons which

she didn't fully comprehend, but none the less found agreeable, she felt his arm tighten gently round her waist, and looking up at him saw that he was smiling to himself.

Clair patted the cushion beside her. 'Sit down. You've been on your feet all evening.'

Emmie eased herself carefully down beside her. 'It's so tight, you see. I am so afraid I burst out of everything. Idiotic!'

'It's beautiful. You've worked so hard here. Everything is lovely, is joy, are you pleased? Surely you are pleased?'

'Pleased for him. For Rooke. Yes, I'm happy, work makes you happy doesn't it? And you . . .?' She left the question floating gently in the smoky air, opened her chain-link purse and peered at her face in a little mirror, rubbing each eyebrow carefully with her finger, smoothing tiny beads of perspiration which shone like dew. 'And you? Are you happy too?'

Clair clasped her hands very tightly together as if to contain the pleasure which filled her. 'I am very happy. Very.'

'The sailors. You know we didn't expect them from the ship. I would have told you otherwise. He just brought them.'

'But does that matter?'

Emmie slid the mirror into her purse and closed it gently: a little cloud of powder drifted away. 'For the party, no: but I thought that perhaps for you . . .'

'For me? But why? I am a Navy wife, you must remember.'

'For that. I do remember.' Emmie placed the purse carefully on the bamboo table before them and smoothed the tight skirt. 'Reminding you perhaps; at a time like this.'

Clair nodded gently, leaned back in the little settee, her hands unclasped slowly, releasing the pleasure for an instant, catching it back almost instantly; she laughed softly. She has the kindest eyes I have ever seen in any face in my life, thought Emmie.

'Because of Pieter? Oh Emmie my dear. I do not need reminding. Every hour, every day, every night. He is so fine in his whites, do you remember that? The neat little bow, black, buttons shining, white so crisp. He is so good at making his bow: I never could, you know, like most wives are supposed to do . . .'

"Clair, it's this and this and this and then under and over and
126

like so." l was hopeless. He does it beautifully. Sailors are very good with knots of course . . . you see?' She placed her hand over Emmie's and pressed it. 'I am reminded all the time, my dear, every instant of the day I share with him, but with happiness, you see?' And then changing to English quickly she said, 'It is *always* there, and it is always here! Look! Happiness comes again, lovely glasses of wine.'

She reached out her arm and assisted Pullen to set down the tray he was carrying with enormous care, moving Emmie's purse, taking her glass, raising it to them both. 'I was longing and longing for this, Nigel, how did you know. So kind.'

'My God! It's a scrum, I think we'll be running out shortly, but all rather fun, don't you think? Frightful noise but everyone very happy. Poor Roberts has just gone out to the verandah to pay his respects to the Old Man but there's a good chance he'll never make it. I left, I'm afraid: tight as a fiddler's bitch, if you will excuse the expression.' He raised his glass in salute to them and sat in an unsteady cane chair with relief.

'What is a fiddler's bitch?' said Emmie.

He looked at her blankly, the sweat ran down the side of his neck. 'Oh Lor', I forgot. Well. Bitch is a lady dog, a fiddler is a man who plays the violin. Look here, rather complicated to explain, rather rude actually. He's just extremely drunk that's all; explain tomorrow, shall I?'

The music had stopped, the sound of raised voices and laughter broke upon them like an avalanche. Emmie raised her voice and leaned across to Pullen worriedly. 'Not Rooke? He's not drunk, you mean?'

'No, no, no, Timmy Roberts, ADC; no, Rooke is very chipper.' He turned in his unsteady chair and looked across the dance floor. 'I think he's being taken to meet the Old Man. Miss Foto has him by the hand, you see, very pleasant, if the boy knows how to play his cards I reckon we may have a new ADC by tomorrow.' He turned back grinning. 'Just a hunch.' Suddenly he fished about in his pocket and produced a crumpled paper napkin. 'Clair my dear. Before I forget and they melt on me, these are for Wim. Before everyone scoffs the lot, golf balls, I fancy, sugar and peppermint, hard as rocks, awful things, but I reckon his young teeth will deal with them;

all part of the decor, I gather.' He pushed the small package across the table to Clair.

'You really are very kind. He'll love them; anything sweet and awful.'

'Thought he might.' He was smiling cheerfully. 'Oh Lor',' he said, 'Miss van Hoorst, no criticism you know? I'm so sorry, the decor, I mean everything, you and Rooke have worked wonders, it's all splendid . . .' He floundered anxiously.

Emmie saved him swiftly. 'It's Emmie you know, my name, and I didn't do the cooking, just the other things, that's all.'

The music restarted, there was a scattered burst of applause and one or two loud whoops of pleasure.

'Oh God,' said Pullen. 'It's a conga or something: you all make a sort of snake thing and dance through the place. Too athletic for me, I just hope they don't go barging onto the verandah, that would really make a rumble bumble of things, what? Just as poor old Rooke is making his curtsey.'

'He is a very gentle man, you know,' said Miss Foto avoiding a laughing couple who were running to join the dancers. 'He is kind, just, and very brave, tonight he is very happy, you know, because of the success he had the other day for the perimeter and also, of course, because of this HMS ship which has come, it is a big honour, he is a good man, you will see.' She let go of Rooke's hand and pushed through the bead curtain which separated the verandah from the dancing. A soft wind jiggled the hanging paper lanterns in the garden, candles flickered on the scattered tables, Nanni Singh sped about on silent feet, cigar smoke eddied and drifted out into the velvet darkness of the gardens, there was laughter and a smacking of thighs, and somewhere in the dark just beyond the edge of light, two figures appeared to be battering the life out of a third. Miss Foto stood stock still, one hand holding a string of bamboo beads from the curtain, the other at her plump breast.

'What happens?' she cried anxiously, and then seeing the, by now, slightly ruffled red hair of the General comfortably seated on her left, she went to him: hands clasped for effect. 'Is it fighting?'

'It's Tim Roberts bringing up his heart,' said the General with a bark of laughter. 'Sit down my dear, he's nearly done.'

128

The figures on the edge of light staggered into darkness, the whooping and gasping grew fainter, the Navy sprang to its feet and shuffled chairs about for the Hostess, who sat down gratefully, fanning herself with a pale plump hand.

'This kind boy has danced me off my feet, finally,' she said. 'I would love a little glass of something cold: perhaps, Captain Rooke, you could find me a very small glass of cold, cold champagne.' She winked prettily and crossed her elegant ankles. Immediately Nanni Singh was at her side, salver poised, flute brimming, face bland, eyes just at a point above her head. She took the glass ignoring his disdain, raised it to the assembled company and sipped delicately.

'Danced her off her feet, have you?' said the General rising slowly from his chair and pulling down his crumpled jacket. 'Well, she could lose a bit of weight, not enough exercise, eh?'

'Oh you! How naughty in front of all these gentlemen.' She pouted demurely, as she had taught all her girls to do in the past. It never failed. Didn't fail her now, she was glad to see, the slightly sweating idiots before her raised hands of dismay and joined her laughter of disbelief.

'I could lose a bit of weight meself,' said the General to Rooke who was still standing politely at the curtain. 'Like to show me where to go?' He pushed past into the dance-room: a long serpent of squealing people wound past them, kicking legs to right and left.

'Where would you care to go, Sir?'

The General looked at him for a moment in steady silence. Blue eyes glinting in the red face, hands on hips, lips pursed. 'Dee da da da da da daa, Dee da da . . .'

'I want to pump ship. You know where, so show me.'

Nettles, leaning against the rail at the far end of the verandah being talked to by a Naval Lieutenant about fishing in the Kennet, watched the two men leave with a small smile of satisfaction, which changed to amusement as Nanni Singh moved after them at a discreet distance. Not called Nanni for nothing, he thought, and watched, with infinite pleasure, the progress of the slim, white-clad boy, as he undulated past him with an empty tray to the little bar Nanni Singh had concealed elegantly behind a camphor-wood screen in the corner. The relative weight of perch and pike in the Kennet River required

129

nothing more from him than an occasional, 'Is that so?' or 'How remarkable', leaving him plenty of time to reflect on how appropriately named a 'bum freezer' was, emphasizing, as it did, the delightful contours of slender buttocks taut in too-tight trousers as the boy slid easily behind the screen.

'Major Nettles!' The firm cool voice of Miss Foto. 'Could you ask him if he has any more of those little rice things for me? I am so starving.' She had caught his inattention in one kind of fishing and his interest in quite another: gravely he smiled at her holding the dark eyes, aware of the plump little hand sweetly extended towards him for sustenance. He excused himself from the hooks and rods of the Lieutenant and went down to the bar.

Behind the screen a neatly arranged set of tables carrying a wide assortment of glasses in serried ranks, plates of biscuits, nuts, rice cookies, bottles ranged, champagne chilling in tin buckets of melting ice like ninepins, the slender boy carefully pouring wine-cup from a large jug: 'Tuan?' eyebrows lightly raised, lips curled in a neat cat-smile, earring winking in the lantern light.

Nettles took up a filled plate. 'These. For the General's memsahib, so — OK?'

The boy nodded, went on pouring; just above his glossy head a meticulous list pinned to the screen. Bold Missionary School copperplate. 'Mowet Shandon. Twenty-six bottles', 'Booths Gin (London Dry) Six', 'Australia Sherri. Sweet. Four'. The catalogue was detailed down to one half pound of peanuts, the calligraphy exquisite. He bit absently into a rice-cookie: all the S's coiled like snakes. He rewarded the boy with a bright smile and carried the dish to Miss Foto.

Upstairs, discreetly standing at the far end of the long corridor, arms neatly behind his back, Rooke stood looking down the stairs into the shadowy hall where Nanni Singh stood in exactly the same position looking up at him. This is the Guardian Angel I suppose, thought Rooke. Too arrogant, too secret, too damned cool. 'I wait for the General Sahib,' he called down quietly. Nanni Singh inclined his head slightly, 'Roberts Sahib is not able. He cannot do his duty this night.' Rude sod, hit the bugger. 'You go and attend to *your* duty on the verandah, the General comes now.'

A heavy door slam, and feet along the boarded corridor.

Nanni Singh shrugged distrustfully and turned away as the General reached the top of the stairs doing up the last of his buttons, arranging the neat blue stock at his throat.

'That's better. Nettles tells me you did all this? Arranged it, so on. Good show.'

'With a lot of help, Sir.'

'Good organization, that's the thing. Done it before, I suppose?'

'Not much time for parties where I was, Sir.'

A baleful look.

'Not much time for bloody parties where we were either. Like Nettles?'

'Very much, Sir.'

The blue eyes glittered back at him. 'Known him long?'

'Only since I got here. His idea really, the party.'

'Stuff and balls! My idea! My idea for Timmy, get him pissed as a fart and send him off happy, I said. My idea.'

'Jolly good one, Sir, I think he seems very happy indeed.'

The General jammed his fists on his hips. 'He'll miss us. Miss the Division. Been together a long time, recommended him for the M.C., you know that? May not be much cop at the fancy stuff but he goes like a bat out of hell in action.'

'Which is what matters, Sir.'

'Exactly. Nettles tells me you were an ADC yourself . . . with whatsisname . . .'

'Wade.'

'Any good at it?'

'I lasted, Sir. Until Field Marshal Montgomery sent for me.'

'Montgomery? 2nd Army, right? Where were you?'

'All over. Normandy, Belgium, Holland, Germany, you know.'

'At HQ, what? Cushy job.'

Rooke looked at him for a long moment in silence. Letting it hold. Then he said very quietly, playing it perfectly, 'Not very, Sir. I was with the R.A.F. Forward Air Recce Wing.'

The General took the look, thrust his thumbs into his belt. 'It wasn't cushy here either. Far from. Suppose Nettles told you that too, good chap: bit odd, airy-fairy type, good head though, a gentleman of course, so . . .'

'That's a help of course.'

'You think so? Why?'

'Well, frankly, Sir, I think a soldier rather prefers a gentleman in charge of him, rather than someone up from the Ranks. There's a deeper awareness of responsibility, respect for the men, duty, Sir, sense of honour, family training, blood, so on.'

The music had stopped, there were loud shouts of 'Encore! Encore!' a burst of laughter and clapping.

'You sound just like my wife, for God's sake! Honour, duty, blood, stuff and nonsense! Damned snobbery.'

'Not really, Sir, I think. Tradition perhaps — but dying.'

The music started up again to loud cheers, someone ran through the hall with a handful of balloons.

'I've met some pretty shitty gentlemen in my time, Rooke, let me tell you . . .'

'I'm sure, Sir, I have too.'

'The shittiest of the shitty. I was a Ranker myself, so I know; what do you say to that?'

'I've met some pretty smashing Rankers in my time, Sir.'

A glint of humour flicked in the narrow blue eyes. 'Cheeky sod. You married?' The question was flat, the glint had faded.

'No, Sir. Not yet.'

'I see.' He turned away and looked down the staircase steadily. 'Anyone in mind, so to speak?'

'Matter of fact, Sir, yes.'

The General swung his look away from the stairs. 'Ah. Spoken for, what?'

'In a way. She doesn't know yet, actually.'

'A secret so to speak?'

'Deadly.'

'You told me.'

Rooke smiled into the fleshy face, the blue curious eyes. 'You asked me, Sir.'

'I did too. Someone in mind anyway, what, pop it to her one of these days?'

'One day, yes, Sir.'

The General started down the staircase, Rooke carefully two steps behind; half-way down they stopped as a tumultuous, wriggling mass of dancers swooped and swayed through the archway into the hall, legs and arms thrashing, hips and heads jerking, led by a sweating Brigadier holding a yellow sausage

132

balloon: the writhing caterpillar looped round the hall, past the stairs, back under the archway, someone at the tail of the line fell over, scrambled to his feet and ran to rejoin them.

'Good God! That was Bunny Blackett leading, silly buggers! They've all gone mad.' He gave a curious grunting laugh. 'Been at it all night, this tune. Dee da da da da da daa, Dee da da da da da daa. What the hell is it, Nigger stuff I suppose?'

'The conga, Sir. "I Came I Saw I Conga'd".'

'Yes, Niggers. Who *said* something like that?'

'Caesar, Sir.'

'Public School stuff; want to have a shot at it then?'

'Not tonight, Sir. Not dancing. Duty.'

'Don't mean bloody dancing. ADC?'

In a wild burst of cheering and laughter someone started throwing streamers into the air, one of them spun into the hall, hit the banisters beside them and coiled over the polished wood like a pink worm.

'Very much indeed. Thank you, Sir.'

'Have a shot. Soon as Tim is packed up and gone off. I want loyalty, understand, no shilly shally, still got a war on our hands here, obedience and keep your mouth shut unless I ask you to open it, got that? Just remember you'll be replacing a bloody good bloke. Trusted, Ranker and all. He knew all about your honour, duty and blood business even if he did go to a Grammar School, so just remember that. All you are is a bloody gentleman conscript. Clear?'

'Perfectly, Sir. Thank you.'

They started down the stairs again; as they passed the pink streamer Rooke took it and spun it discreetly into the air behind him.

'Your girl. Blighty is she? Running the estates in Wiltshire or somewhere?'

'No, Sir. Here, as a matter of fact.'

The General had reached the foot of the stairs, he turned slowly, one hand on the carved banister. 'British girl?'

Rooke shook his head slowly. 'No, Sir. Not British.'

'I hope you know what you're up to. Lot of girls about here, Rooke, flotsam and jetsam types, know what I mean? Only got one idea in their heads, you watch it.'

'Sir?'

'A passport.'

'Not in this case, Sir. I haven't spoken to her.'

The General looked at his watch. 'Well, just look out. An hour to curfew. Better think of getting this party wound up; look here, Tim won't be up to things this evening, his party after all, pour him onto his boat I said and I reckon that's what'll happen, that or carried. Nip out and check the Navy transport, don't want a fuck up at this stage of the game. I'll find my own way back and you come and give me the nod.' He turned and eased his way through the dancing. Rooke stood quite still. Above him a fan clickety-clacked, the pink streamer drifted slowly in the hot air, spiralling in the draught. He reached up and tore a piece off, wrapped it round his knuckles like a boxer's bandage. Punched gently into space. Done it. Done it. The General's voice spun him round suddenly. He hid his fist.

'Rooke!'

He was standing in the archway.

'Sir?'

'What's your name?'

'Benjamin, Sir.'

'My God. Hope that's your only drawback.' He grinned suddenly. 'Don't stand there like a spare prick at a wedding. Transport!'

'Promotion gone to my head, Sir.'

'My boot'll go to your backside. Skedaddle.' He left. Rooke wandered across to the wide front door onto the front verandah. The night air was soft, the black sky stabbed with pin thrusts of stars.

> 'You must remember this,
> A kiss is still a kiss,
> A sigh is still a sigh . . .'

If there was someone to tell.

'Skedaddle,' said Nanny Jarvis. 'And don't use that word in front of your father. It's not polite.'

'You used it.'

'It's all right between ourselves. What is it then?'

'It's a secret thing.'

'Well, don't come bothering me if it's secret.'
'But I want to tell you.'
'What is it then? I'm listening.'
'Daisy Rogers is going to have a baby.'
'Who said?'
'Fred Diplock.'
'Stuff and nonsense. Whatever next! She's not married.'
'That's why it's a secret.'
'And how, pray, does Mr Diplock know that then?'
'He gave it to her.'

> 'And when two lovers woo,
> They still say "I love you",
> On that you can rely . . .'

'Captain Rooke, isn't it? We're just getting a breath of air, so hot inside.'

They were sitting on a long white bench in the shadows, a woman in a billowing striped dress, a man beside her, balding, rimless glasses, wiping his forehead. Rooke went towards them.

'Sister Pritchard, remember?' She waved her wrists in the air to cool them. 'We met at the funeral a few days ago, a Major Beech or Ash or someone, name like a tree, remember?' She smiled happily swinging her feet.

'Major Holly.'

'That's it. Holly. Of course, and this is Mr Novak, Buzz Novak, he's American.'

'How do you do.'

'Pleased to meet you. Great party.'

'My feet,' said Sister Pritchard brightly, 'are simply aggers and mizzers. We've danced all night. Wizoo party, really. Mr Novak brought all the records, wasn't that kind?'

'Yeh. Your Lootenant, what is it, Ronnie Weathersby, said he was a bit stuck for the music, only had classical stuff, you know? I'm a friend of Ruby Oshima, you know Ruby? And I had this pile of stuff I brought from the States, said I'd be delighted, Benny Goodman, Artie Shaw, that kinda stuff.'

'It was very good of you,' said Rooke.

'Aw heck, nothing. Can't dance to Beethoven now can you, like I said to Sister here.'

'Wouldn't that be funny,' she laughed gaily. 'Now where's

that nice Major Grant who was with you that day? So good-looking.'

'Major Gaunt's Duty Officer tonight.'

'Oh poor fellow. Hard cheese!'

'He volunteered, hates parties and people, I'm afraid.'

'Well I just love them, I love company, absolutely harri-aggers if I'm stuck on my own. I always say that people are the spice of life. The utter spice. But it was a bit hot in there; Mr Novak knows all about hot and cold, don't you, Mr Novak? He's rather good at freezing things, aren't you?'

Mr Novak rose slowly to his feet thrusting his handkerchief into his breast pocket. He wagged his head kindly at her. 'I'd frankly say "cooling" rather than "freezing".' He grinned cheerfully across at Rooke. 'I'm with Freezy-Kool Incorporated, Chicago, Illinois. Air-conditioning, refrigeration and so on, offices, stores, private homes, you name it, we cool it. Just restarting here again now the war is practically over, *our* war anyway, that's to say.'

'Mr Novak is a civilian,' said Sister Pritchard unnecessarily. 'He's come from Rangoon.'

'And Singapore, Manila, Hong Kong. We have a lot of contacts in the East.'

Rooke said suddenly, 'Look, I'm terribly sorry, got to go and see about some transport, curfew's in an hour.'

Sister Pritchard jumped to her feet, settled a gauzy Indian silk stole about bottle shoulders and picked up her clutch-bag. 'My goodness, yes, the curfew. I must go and get my chicks together, they're having such a happy time. By the by, haven't met the General tonight. I do think I ought to just say Thank You and pay my respects as it were, don't you?'

'He's on the verandah at the back,' said Rooke. 'I'm sure he'd be very happy if you did. I really must go. Excuse me, would you?'

'Come along, Mr Novak, we'll just pop along and say Thanks together, I'm rather a shy one on my own, come and give me support, it would be harri-ruders if we didn't.'

Pullen watched her leading the tall American through the room; he turned his head away swiftly into Clair's shoulder. 'Oh Lor', the Pritchard woman's heading off to the verandah with some civilian chap. Hide me.'

136

Clair laughed softly and looked over his shoulder, moving gently with the music, holding him close, her hand pressed against his back. 'They've gone. She's rather funny, really, quite kind.'

'She's got hair on her face.'

'So have I. On my cheeks, you can see.'

Pullen looked at her, drew back his head, squinted, grinning, leant forward and kissed her cheek lightly. 'I love yours. I love every single one on your head, my dear Clair.'

She lightly ran her hand across his upper lip. 'And you have hair on *your* face. A moustache.'

'Does it tickle?'

'No. It's so fine. This must be the last waltz, I imagine, nearly curfew.'

'Oh General Cutts! Do forgive me, Sister Pritchard from the Juliana Hospital.'

He rose awkwardly to his feet, bewildered, polite, took the narrow hand like a handful of twigs.

'Just had to pop in and say Thank You for a wizard evening, so kind.' She turned, pulling Novak by the sleeve. 'And this is Mr Novak, from Chicago, he's longing just to say thank you; he provided all the lovely records, so it really is a *joint* Allied effort, you could say.'

'Most welcome, very kind of you, good of you I'm sure.'

'No problem,' said Mr Novak smiling around the Navy. 'Happy to be of help, all do our bit. Good evening, M'am.' His eyes had rested on the smiling woman who accepted his greeting with a polite nod. He put out his hand, which she took lightly. 'Novak, Buzz Novak, of Freezy-Kool.'

'This is Miss Foto,' said the General hurriedly, 'and, er, Sister?'

'Pritchard, Queen Alexandra's. So nice to meet you, it was just to say a teeny thank you for such a heavenly evening.'

'What is Freezy-Kool? Something to eat?' asked Miss Foto brightly, as if she really wanted to know.

'Air conditioners, M'am. Cover the whole East right now, starting up again.'

'Ah! A businessman. A traveller?'

'Yes indeed,' said Sister Pritchard happily, 'everywhere, Rangoon, Hong Kong, and Manila I believe you said, Mr Novak? He's all over the shop, but he's here for a while, now that things are more settled. Dear little flat, sweetly pretty. He gives lovely parties too, don't you?'

'Well, rather *intime*, you might say, it's a small apartment, but anytime you cared it would be just great to entertain you, my pleasure.'

Miss Foto regarded the bland, unfinished American face, the rimless glasses, the slightly stooping figure, crumpled drip-dry suit, enormous feet. She smiled her warmest smile. 'You are very kind, it would be so nice. From Chicago, you said?'

Mr Novak was slightly overwhelmed by her interest. 'The windy city! Great town, it's all going.'

'And so must we,' said Sister Pritchard firmly. 'Find my little chickadees, my nurses, lost in Heaven I have no doubt. Such a lovely evening, we do so thank you. Come along Mr Novak, be a dear and come and search for the naughty girls.'

When they had left the General sat down heavily, reached for his brandy and swallowed it down in one long gulp. 'Carpetbagger,' he mumbled wiping his mouth with the back of his hand. 'All the same, the Yanks: bash in everywhere the moment the real trouble finishes and set up shop. Soon as the guns have stopped, they're in. Bloody Yid, I shouldn't wonder: set up a stall in a piss-house.'

'Leo, really!' Miss Foto removed his empty glass neatly. 'I think Americans are very pleasant, very hospitable and generous, they are quite famous for it.'

'Oh they're famous for it. Generous! My golly! Got enough to spare, what? God! They hand out the Purple Heart for Herpes.' He looked up and saw Rooke at the bead curtain. 'Time to sup up, gentlemen; I think transport's ready.'

'All ready when you are, Sir,' said Rooke.

A clink of glasses, clatter of ashtrays, scraping of chairs on board floor, the Navy started to its feet, a shaking of hands, Miss Foto's pleasured murmurs, a buttoning of jackets. Through the white ballet Rooke saw Nettles far across the verandah, leaning easily against the railing, arms across his chest, tall, trim: wings folded, the journey done. Miss Foto's gentle voice broke their look.

138

'Captain Rooke, please to be so kind, my little white purse, on one of the tables, so silly of me, could you find it, possibly?' She smoothed her little fringe carefully, turned to receive a final compliment.

In a collision of small tables, half-empty glasses, dirty plates, empty cigarette tins, Nettles, with one long leg, pushed a table towards the searching Rooke. Among the debris a small white silk purse. He took it up, their eyes met, Nettles smiling gently. 'Here we go. Fetch and carry, eh? Position consolidated?'

Rooke balanced the purse lightly in his hand. 'I think so. Thank you.'

Nettles shook his head slowly. 'No thanks, I beg of you. Debtless, remember? Take her her little bag; you can't *imagine* how useful you are going to be.' The slim boy came fluttering past collecting dirty glasses and dishes clattering them into a tin bucket. 'The party's over now,' said Nettles, and eased himself away from the railing, whistling under his breath.

In the dance room the last people were leaving, streamers crushed across the floor, Weathersby stacking records sourly; someone burst a final balloon and there was a gust of laughter, a chair fell. Rooke found Emmie sitting alone in the corner of the settee, pushed a tumble of tangled coloured papers onto the floor and sat beside her.

'I deserted you all night. I'm sorry.'

'No, no, I danced three times, you know. I'm very out of practice, I preferred just to stay here and watch. A big success, I think? So much happiness.'

'Emmie. I want to come back with you. To your place.'

She looked at him silently.

'Will you let me come? Please?'

'I stay tonight with Clair. It's so near, four houses away, remember?

'At your place.'

'I always have a room at Clair's.'

'Let me be with you, Emmie. Please. Let me.'

'It's far. Almost in the City.'

'I have a jeep, if we leave now.'

'It is only a little place.'

'With you. Just you. Alone. Please?'

'Just me?'

'Just you.'

She reached out and touched his face, her hand rested on his cheek. 'Will you say it once more?'

'What?'

'Just you.'

He took her hand and pressed his lips hard into the palm. 'Just you.'

'We will not have any toothbrushes.'

When he looked up she saw his eyes were bright with tears. She rose quickly, pulling a satin scarf across her shoulder, slinging the chain-link bag over her arm.

'I will go to find Clair,' she said.

Gaunt stretched and yawned loudly as his Relief wandered into the Ops. Room rather blearily.

'Good chap. Bang on time. Good party?'

'Too much to drink. I'm swacked.'

'Sleep it off here. Quiet night. Coffee somewhere if you want it.'

'In a minute. Quiet, was it? Nothing on?'

'Nothing. No rape; routine stuff, a few signals, and this, this though.'

'What is it? Urgent?'

'No. Not urgent. 10 Brigade, Butan Pahang, came in about, oh, nine-ish. Apparently the extremists are bunging us down three hundred, I think it's three hundred, male European internees, by rail if you please! There's a thing! Want assurance of safe conduct, white flags etcetera, etcetera. No need to flap, it can wait till the morning. Not our pigeon, just let the repatriation chaps know first thing, right?' He slung the message onto the desk, shuffled his battered copies of *The Field* into a drawer. 'Typhoid or something, I gather, it's all there. I'm dossing down next door. If you want any coffee give Ahmed a shout.' He got up, stretched luxuriously, started to unbuckle his belt.

CHAPTER SIX

At the west end of Nassau Boulevard, where the broad thoroughfare bottle-necked into an ordinary street running among scattered tin and bamboo huts, clumps of cane, and the ruins of burned-out villas slowly strangling under billows of bright green vines, Nettles turned sharply right amidst a scatter of scrawny chickens up the rutted road to the Flack Tower, now known throughout the Division as the Residency, with Willie sitting in the bucket seat beside him, his Sten gun across his knees. Although things had eased considerably in the City since the glittering arrival of Mountbatten and his entourage of encouragement, the reassuring presence of the Navy in the harbour and, above all, the sudden and prayed-for arrival of a squadron of the RAF, together with the gradual build up of Dutch troops who arrived almost daily now from Singapore and Batavia, it was still essential to stay alert: especially on the very edge, as it were, of the extended perimeter. But, thought Nettles with relief, things have changed a good deal in the last few weeks, and apart from the extreme indignation expressed by a number of Dutch Civilians at the presence of Miss Foto at the reception in the Residency given for Mountbatten recently, about which the General was *apparently* unaware, relations between the Dutch and the British had simmered gently into a pottage of mutual effort and trust at last. Shutters had started to come down, shops reopen, bars and little restaurants began to proliferate, curfew was extended until 01.00 hours, the Convoys, under the umbrella support of the RAF, restarted and the tide, Nettles thought, had really turned: a swell of normality was ebbing back gently through the city.

One could almost say that it had started, astonishingly, with the evening of the party for Tim Roberts: suddenly there had been music and people dancing, people joining, people actually laughing again . . . absurd to think that a few paper streamers and balloons in a suburban villa could bring about such a metamorphosis, but then it only took a small twig to start a fire . . . and this time the fire was warming, comforting, casting light into dark corners, scattering the bats of depression and suspicion. Things were becoming resolved. One thing, however, had not been resolved, and could no longer be left unexamined. The note which Willie had brought him that evening, long ago now it seemed, and with which he was presently on his way to Nanni Singh in his kitchen at the Residency.

He presented his papers at the gates, received a neat salute from the corporal of the guard, spun easily along the raked gravel path, past tidied lawns, rough pruned hedges, and up-right Apollos, Dianas, and what might have been a hand-on-hip Narcissus, staccato with whitewash in the brilliant sunshine, as indeed was the whole objectionable cubism of the Residency itself. Ugly as it was, a coat of paint had wrought a modest miracle.

The kitchen was dim and cool, shaded by split-cane blinds splintering tiny bars of light across the table, the hunched figure of Nanni Singh sitting with his books and ledgers, brass cooking bowls, a piled dish of green limes, and the round face of a cheap tin clock which ticked loudly in the silence.

Nanni Singh looked up abruptly, closed a book, stood swiftly, a short jerk of his neck indicated a greeting. Nettles smiled, pulled out a cane chair, sat deliberately.

'Thought I'd find you tucked up on your little charpoy, no afternoon kip?'

'To better himself a man must study, Sahib.'

'Do sit down, Nanni Singh. What do you study? Recipe books, one hopes?'

'The Good Book. I am reading Matthew. I copy from the Book into my book, so that I may have things to ponder, Sahib.'

' "Matthew, Mark, Luke and John, bless the bed that I lie on." Is that right?'

'That I do not know.'

'Probably not. I'm a duffer at the Bible. Who taught you?'

'Mr Arthur Bishop, the Mission School at Kippapore, since I was very little.'

'And to write so well?'

A furrow on the bland forehead, the eyes flat.

'Mrs Amy Bishop. Very particular. Many times I must copy out.'

'She would have been very happy with this, wouldn't she?

So beautifully neat.' Nettles slid the opened note towards Singh across the table. The eyes flicked down, up into Nettles' eyes. Impassive. A nerve pulsing in the throat. 'And this too. The little list from your bar at the Party, remember? Exquisite. The little S's coil like serpents. No errors in the script, but no "W" in Moet, and Sherry has a "Y" not an "I", normally.'

The tin clock hammered in the silence. Nanni Singh's eyes rested steadily on his books.

'Why did you send it to me, Singh?'

Nanni Singh shook his head, raised eyes dull with agony, brushed his lips with a thin brown hand. Was silent.

'You send this by your boy to me. You want me to know; to take action. Tell me?'

'My boy is a good boy. He is not wicked. He was here only to comfort me, to help me attend my General. He has other work, not here. The woman sends him away.'

'I am sure he is a good boy. But is this true, this you say?'

'Is true.'

'How do you know?'

'Everyone knows. In the markets, everywhere. They know.'

'You dislike Miss Foto?'

Nanni Singh brushed the note with the tips of his fingers lightly. 'All this I steadfastly believe.'

'Miss Foto?'

'She is ungodly. I have seen the ungodly in great power, and flourishing like the green bay tree.'

'She is *not* in great power. She comforts your General as your boy comforts you.'

Nanni Singh's eyes flashed with sullen rage, all agony gone. He clenched his fists hard on the table, his nails pink against the brown skin. 'She sits in the seat of the scornful. She does not comfort General Sahib. She lies to him. I know these people; their throat is an open sepulchre, they flatter with their tongues.'

Nettles leaned gently across the table, his hand touched a clenched fist gently. 'She makes him happy, Nanni Singh; and you have no proof at all of all this you have written to me. No *proof.*'

'The General's mem-sahib was good. She made him happy. Since she has gone to her duty in Great Britain he is not happy.

143

She was dead unto sin, and living in righteousness, she was a light shining from Heaven. She who took me from the city, she who put me to Mr Bishop, she who taught me of God and his wonders, she who made me in the King's Forces to make me of his Empire, she who brought me to her house to be servant to her Lord and Master, and who I love with all my soul.' His eyes were rimmed with thin tears. Head held high. Shoulders square. A declaration of devotion, of honour, of loyalty. He looked beyond Nettles into a past which had gone for ever. Crushed with loss.

Nettles carefully took out his cigarette case, took a cigarette. When he looked again at Nanni Singh the tears had gone. The eyes gleamed strongly. 'It's a question of proof, Nanni Singh. Supposing this *is* true, supposing, can you imagine the shame which will come to General Sahib? He does not know this . . . so far as I am aware only you know this, from gossip in the market. From people who may be jealous of this woman, that is all you have.'

'I have seen. I watch. She looks at all the papers most private on the General Sahib's desk, she is rude with him and harsh, "she has caught him by his garment, saying, lie with me, and he left his garment in her hand" . . . but alas! he did not flee. She is too wicked, too clever. He is alone, without Peggy mem-sahib . . . he has need of comfort, but not from this woman.'

Nettles blew a stream of smoke patiently into the still air. 'You still do not understand. There is no proof of this. Bring me proof and I will try to protect our General, I respect him as you do. But bring me proof, or else we must forget this wicked accusation which you make.'

'The boy will tell you.'

Immediately he had said this, Nettles knew that he regretted it bitterly. He watched Nanni Singh suddenly fold gently before his eyes, shoulders sagged, the head bowed, he put his long thin fingers to his face and stared haggardly across the table. Got him, thought Nettles without pleasure.

'Where is the boy?'

'He is in his work. At Luk Chang's.'

'The barber's shop in the market? Sells scents and oils . . .'

'This I do not know. The scents. But is a barber, and the boy is there.'

Nettles rose easily from his chair. Nanni Singh looked up at him dully, both hands folded neatly on his Bible. Nettles re-folded the note, slid it into his breast pocket. Nanni Singh bowed his head.

'The ears of everyone that heareth it shall tingle,' he mur-mured. 'We will chastise her with scorpions.'

Nettles stubbed out his cigarette on the edge of the cracked sink, dropped the butt into a tin can of tea-leaves and egg-shells. 'There is just one thing on which you might care to ponder during your studies, Nanni Singh . . . a small thing but impor-tant. I shall go to see the boy now, don't worry, I shall be gentle . . . but you may just like to remember this, if you have forgotten it: "He who diggeth a pit shall fall into it". *Ecclesiastes*, I believe?' He turned and left the shaded kitchen, the ticking clock, the hunched figure. In the yard the sun hit him like a plank. 'Dear God!' he thought. 'I'm running a full tap into a spoon.'

Luk Chang's was on the north side of the market shaded by a skinny casuarina tree. A humble building, three storeys, scaling plaster, shuttered windows except for the two main shop win-dows which were shrouded by thick, dusty lace; above them an absurdity of a barber's pole, red, blue and white, twisted like barley sugar. Inside, the heavy odour of scents and potions, cedar, jasmine, coriander, cheap hair oil. Six barber's chairs, three to each side, gleaming mahogany, brass, white marble basins, rows of finely cut mirrors reflecting the two white draped figures being shaved. A fan spun wearily in the ceiling above, surrounded by floating figures in billowing draperies, a stork, a flight of blue birds, garlands of pink roses in yellow ribbons. 'When a man is being shaved his head is tilted to the sky . . . he must be refreshed by his imagination, so I provide substance for it on the ceiling. Sensible, no?' Luk Chang had said, and now hurried anxiously from behind his cash-desk in the corner, arms wide in surprised welcome, short legs hampered by a white apron.

'Major Nettles! In the afternoon! All the world rests now, but not you, you have much work to do. A shave perhaps?'

'An oil, I think.'

Chang smiled blandly, folding hands over his apron. Nettles looked round the room; all Chinese, elderly, preoccupied in lather and razors.

'A *special* oil,' said Nettles.

Chang bowed his head gracefully on a short neck, extended one arm deferentially. 'Then you would be wise to come and select that with me. These,' he waved the arm dismissively at a row of glass-stoppered bottles on the heavy mahogany counter behind him, 'these are not very special ones. It is difficult to obtain the ingredients today, but in the parlour . . .' He closed the door firmly, a small ugly room, red-wallpaper, a Chinese mask, a Varga-girl calendar for March 1942, a bowl of goldfish on a green chenille-covered table.

'Ting-Ting is not here, Major. Not until six o'clock. I am desolate!' Hands spread in false apology. 'A naughty fellow, now he spends much time elsewhere. What can you do? They give him Lucky Strike, Chesterfields, they promise to take him to America, to Hollywood! What can I do?' His eyes suddenly narrowed. 'It *is* "oil" you want? I am not incorrect?'

'Oil. He works here, I am told.'

'What name he has?' The eyes slits, fingers gently rubbing his sleeves.

'I don't know his name. But I will know him when I see him.'

'One of mine? My boys?' A slight jerk of his head upwards.

'So I believe.'

Chang shrugged gently. Smiled. 'Not all are here yet and three are new, not experienced. You want Short Time, Long Time?' He had opened a small cupboard in the wall beside the calendar, keys rattled on little hooks. He took one down, polished it carefully on his apron.

'Short time,' said Nettles.

'Twenty-seven,' said Chang, changing the key swiftly, and taking up a small pocket watch he altered the hands back to the hour. 'Four o'clock. I time from now. OK? You know where if you do not know who. I am curious.' He opened the door at the far end of the musty parlour and Nettles went through, up the steep dark stairs. He heard the door close softly below. At the top, a wide room, worn linoleum on the floor, wobbling fans, bamboo chairs scattered along the walls, one or two tables, mirrors, at the far end a heavy red silk curtain, no windows, a stale smell of powder, scent, and sweat, in the ceiling a chipped golden cherub swung disconsolately, bearing aloft two naked electric light bulbs glimmering dull orange. A rustle of cloth, someone sniggered, a glass marble rattled across the linoleum floor.

Nettles looked slowly round the sweltering room. Tableau. Five taxi-boys looked back in alert silence. He removed his cap and tucked it under his arm. The boy was sitting in a corner with another of about the same age, they had been playing chequers on a low cane divan; holding hands, like Rubens cherubim; two others sat bolt upright, wide lipsticked mouths, a glint of silver at neck and wrist; leaning elegantly against a sallow yellow wall a fifth, older than the others, in a drooping cream kimono which had fallen open revealing hard muscular legs, had been cutting his finger nails: the scissors sparkled in the amber glow. Only the fallen marble, rattling smoothly across the shining floor, moved. Nettles crossed to the chequer table. The boy watched him without interest, or sign of recognition, head turned, earring winking, tattooed forearm resting lightly on the table edge, a fine sheen of sweat glistening on his naked chest. Nettles gently lifted his key before the heavy-lashed eyes, the little tag jiggled, swinging back and forth. Twenty-seven. The boy nodded lightly, replaced a glass marble on the chequer board, rose, the tableau unfroze. There was a mild scatter of applause from the room, someone giggled and murmured quietly, the boy, with a slight shrug, smoothed his glossy hair and crossed Nettles moving like a cat towards the heavy silk curtain. As they passed, the elder youth in the cream kimono pulled it tightly about his long body and bent his head to his nails. Beyond the curtain a corridor of cubicles, on each door a number in Chinese and Roman numerals. The boy stopped at 27, leaned easily against the wooden wall, hips thrust forward, arms crossed behind his slender back. Nettles slid in the key.

A narrow wooden cot with a worn mattress; in a corner a metal stand with jug and basin, four hooks along the wall from one of which hung a clean cotton towel. Nothing else. Nettles locked the door, left the key in the lock, sat carefully on the wooden cot, his cap on his knees. The boy, standing by the wash-bowl, ran his hands lightly over his chest; he was naked save for a pair of tight white sailor trousers cut off roughly at the shins, one hand slipped down over his belly and started to pull at the buttons of the fly-flap. Nettles raised a swift hand. 'No. No. Not that. Do you understand me?' The boy's hand flew away as if struck.

'Not understanding,' he said.

'Not that.'

'This twenty-seven room. Short time room.' Wide eyes in perplexity.

'I want to talk with you. Just talk. Do you understand me?'

The boy nodded doubtfully, eyes clouded suddenly with suspicion.

Nettles patted the cot lightly. 'You come and sit with me, yes?'

The boy looked swiftly at the cot, the door, moved slowly back into the corner. 'Police?' The question was almost a whisper.

Nettles instantly shook his head. 'Not police, no, come here. There is no danger.' He undid his breast pocket and took out the note, held it towards the boy. 'You brought this to me from Nanni Singh, you remember? Nanni Singh tells me you are a good boy, that you will tell me of this letter. OK?' He watched the boy relax slowly, but instead of coming towards the cot he squatted, gracefully, on his haunches, bare feet together, back against the wall, head tilted, watching warily.

'I am not remembering the letter. I cannot read. Nanni Singh said to bring it, I do not know anything in there.'

'Perhaps,' said Nettles easily, 'if I read it to you you will remember.' When he had finished, and refolded the note in silence, the boy was looking down at his feet, curling one big toe over the other, then he looked up, pushed back a loop of hair, scratched the little tattooed-eye as if it was a sting.

'Now you remember? This is true in the letter? You tell all this to Nanni Singh, he says. Is true, is not true, you tell me now?'

The boy's eyes narrowed shrewdly. 'I do not see you here before, Tuan?'

'No. No, you do not see me before. But you are new I think here?'

The boy picked nervously at the tattoo. 'I am new. Since ten days. The woman say I must go. She is harsh with Nanni, he

148

cries, I go. I come here.' He twisted his shoulders hard against the rough wall. 'I must live.'

'The woman in this letter?'

'Yes, that woman. Foto. Very harsh with Nanni.'

'But what of the four young men in this?' He wagged the folded note. 'And all the sons and daughters. What is this?'

'Foreign soldiers. Four. It is a long time past, Tuan. But four. The Japanese come and make us all go in trucks to the race-course, it is for a good example, so that we will see the cowardly soldiers punished; we must struggle for our new country, the white man is a coward, he hides from Imperial Nippon, soldiers of the Emperor, he hides so he has no honour, thus he must die.'

'And?'

The boy clasped his hand round his right wrist, raised it high above his head, and brought the extended arm down in four savage swings. 'Chock! Chock! Chock! Chock!'

'You saw this?'

'Many see this. It is example. It is not good. But one is very brave. Tall, the last one, very white, red hair.' The boy stretched his arms above his head and slid down the wall until he was sitting, wide-legged, on the wooden floor. 'He was singing all this time.'

Nettles found that his mouth was dry. He clasped his hands together and cracked his knuckles; the boy raised his eyebrows and laughed suddenly. 'Crack! Crack!' he said pleasantly.

'How does this involve Miss Foto?'

The boy shook his head and scratched his arm again. 'I am not understanding.'

'Miss Foto. What had she to do with the four soldiers?'

'She hid them from the Nippons. I do not know more. Yoko tells me this, and all the rest, but I forget.'

'Yoko?'

'Is my friend. Yoko Oshima, she was kind to me. She is Nippon but only half. I have job in the restaurant, my belly is never empty all the years. You would like her, she is friend to everyone: even to the woman.'

'Where is Yoko Oshima now?'

The boy eased himself from the floor, he was becoming bored, he stood before Nettles, legs apart, hands on hips, rotating his

149

neck and pelvis, flexing the slender muscles of his upper arms. 'At Nanni Singh's house, you remember the party time?' He stopped swinging and stood still, smiling openly. 'You remember me, Tuan? I had uniform, Nanni bought for me. You remember me then?'

'I remember you then.'

'Yoko was making the music, with the machine of the English officer. He is good friend to Yoko, everyone is good friend to Yoko; Nippons, English, all, she is very lovely girl.' He moved slowly towards Nettles on the cot. 'And I am very lovely boy, isn't it?' He started to unbutton his fly. Nettles rose swiftly, took up his cap, went to the door. The boy caught his arm. 'If you do not have Short Time, Chang is angry with me. Is four dollars only.'

Nettles took out some notes, folded them carefully, tucked them gently into the half open fly. 'That is for the Short Time,' he said.

'God alone knows,' said Weathersby. 'Probably counting her small change in my office. You come to lock her up?'

'Not that I know of. Should I?'

Weathersby sucked the point of his indelible pencil. 'Somebody will one day.' He smiled with violet spattered lips. 'The office is across there. I shouldn't believe much she tells you, she's a slut, you know? A slut. Lived with the Japs, up to all sorts of shenanigans. Her particular bloke confiscated all the gold from the Pawn Shops, know that? Everything. Had all the rings, coins, teeth, even spectacles and things crushed into blocks the size of a brick. Shipped them all back to Tokyo, she says, but I reckon she's still got a couple of them somewhere in that flat they had. Payment in kind. Probably a few more, I shouldn't wonder.'

'What makes you think so?'

'Seen her bed? No, probably not. Brass bed, solid brass, knobs on. But it's *not*.' The speckled lips parted in a mirthless grin, he winked slowly, to emphasize his knowledge. 'It's covered in bloody gold-leaf, real. You can peel it off. I did.'

Nettles climbed out of the jeep. 'You wait a little while, Willie. Not long.' And turning back to Weathersby he said politely, 'Know your way about there rather well, I gather then? Brass beds and what not, eh?'

Weathersby coloured suddenly, stuck his pencil into the back of his note-pad. 'Well, have to have a bit of comfort. She's all right for that. Does my translating, they tell me. Speaks Japanese. Bloody hopeless really, but a business sort of relationship, you might say.'

'I might,' agreed Nettles starting across the railway lines to the office. 'I shan't keep her long.'

'One day,' called Weathersby, 'someone will come along and keep her a hell of a long time. Maybe twenty years or so, maybe more. She's on a list, for sure. Just biding their time, need the proof.'

Ruby looked up swiftly as he pushed open the door and a burst of sunlight ripped across the dusty office. A pale round face, not pretty, a black eye, a cut on her upper lip scabbing. She pushed a thick book away from her, shielded her eyes.

'Yes, Sir?' she had a low pleasing voice.

'Sorry. I disturb you. Major Nettles, Divisional HQ. You are Miss Oshima, I think?' She nodded, her hands at a shell necklace twisting worriedly.

'Yes. It is me. Can I help you, can I do something?'

'You were reading.'

'A dictionary. I must do translating. Many words I do not know.'

'And hurt your eye.'

'I fall over in the dark, excuse me. Silly girl. Is all right now.'

'You should put a raw steak on it, so they say.'

She grimaced gently. 'Ah no. Horrible, I think. I have pomade, very good.'

'In the market there is Luk Chang. He has many pomades.'

The silence whispered about them like singing dust. Outside a ship's siren blew three short blasts, a truck rattled across cobbles, a truck revved up somewhere, a door slammed with a metal clang.

She had stopped twisting the shells, hands still, eyes steady. 'You are Police?'

'No. Your friend at Luk Chang's told me that you could help me.'

'About what, Sir, please?'

151

'Four soldiers beheaded at the race course.'

Her hand flew to her mouth, she bowed her head at the brutality of his attack. 'Oh no! No! No . . .'

'But you do know?'

'No. I did not see. I did not see.'

'But you knew, Miss Oshima . . . your friend says you told him.'

'He saw. Yes. I did not see. Not see. He was very young then, maybe fifteen years.'

'Who were they? British soldiers? Dutch?'

'No. Not them. I do not remember. I must not remember.'

'What did you tell him? You must remember because you told him.'

Her head was still bowed and he knew that she was weeping, she had covered her face with her hands carefully cupping the bruised eye.

'And so you must tell me, please.'

She shook her head violently, tears glistened down her bare forearm. 'All questions,' she sobbed. 'All so many questions. I cannot. I will not. No. It is all ended, so far away, all is ended now, please.'

Nettles settled himself in a folding wooden chair, crossed his legs, cleared his throat. Women made him uncomfortable at the best of times. Emotional women made him ill.

'I think that you are wrong, alas. Nothing has quite ended yet. Perhaps something is just beginning, who can say? For someone you know well, Miss Foto. You do know her, I believe?'

She sat upright, hands before her like a begging dog, plump face a ruin. 'There is trouble for her?'

'Did she hide these men, Miss Oshima?'

'Yes. So they could go home to Australia: maybe find a little fishing boat; she was so good, so brave for them.'

'But hid them?'

'It was much danger for her.'

Nettles unfolded the note and handed it across the desk. She took it listlessly, a post-office clerk accepting a telegram, read it very slowly, shook her head in silent disbelief, handed it wordlessly back.

'And what do you make of that?

152

'It does not say her name here,' she said simply.

'I assume that "photo" is intended to indicate Miss Foto. A "Ph" instead of an "F".'

Her eyes were voids of incomprehension.

'Well. You do see?' He put it back in his pocket. 'And there is much talk about in the City also. What do we do, you and I?'

Her hands wrenched at a handkerchief. 'It is lies. All is lies.' She wiped her face carelessly, tucked the handkerchief into her little puff sleeve. 'So I must remember now.'

Weathersby was standing checking a great pile of stores by the quayside in the dazzling light, a square of blue cotton stuck under his cap falling round the back of his thin neck to protect it from the sun, his pipe-cleaner legs sticking out from baggy shorts.

'Powdered eggs, for the RAPWI lot: they're bringing them out in hundreds now, too many mouths to feed. They need Jesus and his bloody loaves, not me: made me a Quartermaster, for Pete's sake, you imagine that? Me. No consideration, used to be in your mob, Intelligence, before I got landed here.'

Nettles slid lightly into his jeep. 'I am absolutely shattered to hear that.' He adjusted his cap carefully on auburn curls. 'But I am absolutely sure you are a splendid QM. Good eye for details, eh?'

'I've got that all right. Still . . .' The violet lips almost smiled. 'Ruby tell you what you wanted to know?

'Ruby? Oh. Yes. Miss Oshima. Yes, yes, most helpful. Now *she*'s got a spiffing eye. For details. Memory of a true historian.'

Weathersby wiped his neck with his cotton square. 'Bully for you, Major. Can't remember a ruddy thing when I ask her, you must have the right touch.'

Nettles switched on the ignition. 'A light one, Mr Weathersby, very light. Doesn't leave a mark.' He smiled at the startled face with its spotted lips, started the engine, and swung round towards the main gates with such speed that Willie almost dropped his Sten gun and had to hold on to his hat.

Rattling of teacups, clink of spoons in saucers. Ordinary sounds. But what do they remind you of, thought Rooke? Oh, I know. I know. I remember. I know so well. All the clichés:

153

security, warmth, comfort, love, cosiness — that funny word that only the English could invent — like home, or nice, or naughty. A fire-guard with a shirt to air, crackle of a shifting log, hot toast, crumpets in a covered dish, ginger snaps. Over the high mantelshelf, the stuffed squirrel in his case, Beachy Head lighthouse in cheap china, *Pip, Squeak and Wilfred*; *Doctor Dolittle*. Nanny Jarvis nudging open the door with one raised knee, tray held high in strong arms.

'We've got a visitor today. Miss Grimwade has been persuaded, persuaded very hard I may say, to stay and take a comforting cup.'

Miss Grimwade of the red nose and ear-phones, books bulging in her satchel, pulling off a rabbity coat and a woolly glove. 'Well, I really shouldn't, you know, but such a horrid day, rain and that. And we have done well today, haven't we? Mastered twelve times twelve and now we remember, don't we?' The thin smile and wagged finger. 'That it is *always* "I before e except after c". So I just let myself be persuaded: can't wiggle away from Miss Jarvis when she's made up her mind.'

'Dish in the hearth, Ben, keep the crumpets warm, and draw up a chair for our guest, there's a good chap,' said Nanny Jarvis.

'Is tea, Sahib,' said Nanni Singh.

Rooke turned slowly in the wide windows, raised one hand in salute. 'Good afternoon, Nanni Singh. What have we today, I wonder?'

'Marmite. General Sahib likes very well.'

'He's upstairs at the moment, down directly. The engineers come about the taps up there?'

Nanni Singh set the tray carefully on a low carved teak table, set out the cups and the plate of wafer sandwiches.

'Engineers came, Sahib. All is correct, they tell me.' He checked his tray silently. 'Also Nettles Sahib came.'

'Major Nettles? For the General? But he knew we were at the hospital?'

Nanni lifted a small jug. 'Is tinned milk, but I put much water in. I think he is forgetting this.'

'Leave a message?'

'No. No message. He leave.' He closed the door gently behind him and the big room was silent. Rooke started to whistle. Nettles knew damn well we were out. Oh well . . . draw up a chair for our guest, there's a good chap. He pulled a heavy carved chair across the parquet floor, sat down facing the tea tray, spread his legs, looked about him: at the high walls, the carved furniture. Apart from the walls it is all my own work, I never cease to be horrified by the utter perfection of its monstrousness. Look at it! Crushed mauve velvet set in wide panels surrounded by heavy lacquered frames inset everywhere with chunks of semi-precious stones cut as birds, beetles, flowers and bamboo. Inlaid, among this rioting jungle of lapis, coral, amethyst and jade, an ivory leopard, life size, snarls on a jagged rock of malachite, cornelian eyes blazing, studded all about with lumps of amber like a rich fruit cake. And here we have heavily carved chairs, cushions in scarlet silk, Nanking jars, celadon bowls, brass lanterns, onyx pots, Persian carpets, all of it I looted without a by-your-leave from the Dumps.

'If anyone wants his stuff back,' said the General, 'he can have it when I'm finished with it.' Oh! It's a joy! It is truly frightful and he loves it, a dazzling cross between the Delhi Durbar and the second act of 'Aladdin'. No one can say I didn't try and I succeeded beyond my wildest dreams. Hey diddle-de-dee, an ADC's life for me . . .

At the slam of the door he sprang to his feet, adjusted his webbing belt.

'Mindless! Bloody mindless, that's what,' said the General.

'Mindless, Sir?'

'That whistling. What do you do it for?'

'Wasn't really aware, Sir. Sorry. Happy, I suppose.'

'Well, get unhappy for a change. Gets on my wick, but if you must whistle, try and change the tune. Mindless noise.'

'Hey diddle-de-dee, an actor's life for me. From "Pinocchio" —a film.'

'Silly bloody tune. And that other thing, Tim's song.'

'Old Kent Road.'

'Drives me up the wall.

'Got rather stuck with that, sorry.'

'Well, get unstuck. You've got the job now, what? Sandwich?' He picked up the silver teapot helplessly, waving it unsteadily over the tray. 'This is where we really need a woman's touch, not my line.'

'I was thinking of nursery teas. That's really what started the whistling.'

'Humph. Nursery teas, good God. Nanny stuff, I suppose.'

'I had one, yes. No mother so one has to have a nanny.'

'Spare me the story, Ben. What's *this* awful stuff?'

'Tinned milk with water. We do need a woman's touch. So that's why I had a nanny, you see.'

'Christ almighty. Nannies? Substitute mothers. Don't hold with them.'

'What else then?'

'All Class stuff really. Snobbery. Good tutor and a kick up the backside.'

He settled carefully, cup in one hand, Marmite sandwich in the other, into a low armchair, stretched long legs before him. 'Sit down, not on duty here.'

'I was just thinking, Sir, one does need a woman in one's life.'

The General lifted his smallest finger in a delicate crook, sipped his tea in a parody of daintiness. 'Oh, one does, doesn't one. One really does.' He snorted cheerfully. 'All this "one" business, why don't you just say "I", that's what you mean, isn't it?'

'It'll do,' said Rooke.

The General drank his tea normally and looked comfortably round his monstrous room. 'Feel like a Nabob sitting here.' Satisfaction shimmered from his happy smile. 'You did a splendid job, most impressive: that Labour chap, whatsisname, Wagstaff? Arthur Wagstaff, was it? Something like that, came from Burnley or somewhere; at the Reception, he said it was very impressive. Quite took his breath away, he said. Tried to make some kind of a joke about Imperialism and exploited natives. Labour stuff. I didn't bat an eyelid of course.' He reached for another sandwich. 'Mrs Cutts would have appreciated all this. Marvellous taste she had, knew absolutely what was what about this sort of thing. Every Service House we lived in from Lahore to Barrackpore she made a home, marvellous touch, much admired everywhere.' He grinned over his sandwich. 'Playing into your hands, aren't I, what? *One* does need

156

the feminine touch, doesn't *one*?' His little blue eyes sparkled
with relaxed amusement.

'One does indeed. Pity she's not here to see it, Sir.'

'Well, you know what it is. Woman of honour, my wife. "No
point in me rolling a lot of bandages with the girls while you are
off in Burma or wherever it is, can't do any good that way."
Home to England she went, pulled rank, got a passage, off to the
Blitz and all that. England in a state of siege you might say . . .
she wanted to do her bit. Must say she had her priorities right
there. Take off my cap to her, she found me Nanni Singh,
y'know, priceless chap. He all right now by the by? Seen him
today, haven't you? With the tea?'

'He's all right, Sir. But glum still. Hard to tell really.'

'Glum, is he? Yes. Well, I suppose so, he'll get over it. That
boy, is it?'

'I feel so, Sir. Yes.'

'Well, there you are. The feminine touch. Miss Foto didn't
care for him, had an instinct, she said. Up to no good, she felt
. . . caught him poking about on my desk, you know. I said he
couldn't bloody read, but she said you never knew, so off he
went. She gets something into her head, it sticks.' He rattled his
cup on to the tray. 'Pour me another cup, will you? What
happened at the Reception that afternoon? You know, Ben?'

Rooke poured steadily, added the watery milk, handed it
back. 'Reception? No, Sir. Not what I recall . . .'

'Something upset her, I don't know what. Won't say . . . she
was pretty damn angry, I can tell you, wondered if you noticed
anything? *I* saw nothing, stuck with the Supremo, but she was
definitely upset about something. Well, you know women,
brooded for a bit then it all seemed to pass over sort of thing. But
it's odd. Funny, she's only been up here a couple of times since,
she was so interested in everything once, her idea really.' He sat
stirring his tea thoughtfully, lips pursed in recollection.

Rooke poured himself another cup, avoiding the milk. 'It is
quite a haul here, Sir, half an hour up, half an hour back to the
Cricket Club . . .'

'But I always send the Packard!'

'Perhaps, Sir, she doesn't care for the journey after dark.'

'Always has a driver for protection, even sent Nanni Singh
along with her.'

'Unwise to ask him to go at present, don't you feel?'

'Damn right. Course not. A bit jealous, I suppose, natural really. He always did everything for me, y'see. Then she rather took over, my fault. I liked it. But you see it was a bit easier down at the other house. Just across the garden, didn't bother about curfew, that sort of thing . . . know what I mean?' He flushed suddenly and wiped his lips, aware that perhaps he was saying too much. 'Anyway, not much fun for her up here really, too quiet, I fear. More life going on down in the City now that things are easing. Planters Club is full every evening, they tell me, dancing, got a band there even. Not much at the dancing myself. Case of three left feet, if you follow me. Anyway difficult for me to just barge in there, makes everyone uncomfortable, can't relax, "Old Man's got his eye on me" stuff. I know the feeling. Still.' He put his cup down suddenly. 'Dancing. Well, we saw a few chaps today who won't be dancing again, didn't we, eh? Bloody senseless business. Havildar Lalbuka with no bloody legs from the hips down, and the other chap, Irish, one leg gone at the knee, the other at the shin or something. It's a bloody war here still. Chaps being maimed, chaps who made it all the way from Burma with me without even a head-cold! Every time I go round that hospital I never know what to say to them. What do you say to a chap who's lost his legs driving his jeep over a sodding mine four months after the war is officially over, eh? What do you say to a chap blinded by a mortar fired by some ruddy terrorist yelling "Freedom from colonial oppression"? How do you explain that to a *blind* Indian Corporal, I'd like to know: couldn't even explain it to that pompous prick from Burnley or Huddersfield or wherever he came from, the MP. He just said it was not our affair, just hand things over to the Dutch to deal with. Not *our* affair!'

He got up angrily from his chair and walked heavily across the room to the wide bay windows, standing there for a while in silence, fists clenched on his hips, chewing his moustache, swaying slightly, controlling his anger. 'And all that!' He waved an arm in wide embrace over the plains below, the far smudged ridge of blind volcanoes on the skyline, the pink tiled roofs of scattered villas spilling down the ridge, the City a gridiron smouldering in the afternoon sun, stretching away to the sea, the south spiked with spires, cranes, factory chimneys, and in

158

the centre, the gutted dome of the Opera House like the carcass of a partridge. 'All that *is* our affair . . . all of it, and they're still across there with their damned mortars, field guns and fanatics with pangas, biding their time for the next bash. It'll come: but we'll teach the buggers a lesson, this time we'll get them.' He cleared his throat roughly, shook his head, ran fingers through sparse red hair. 'A lot of potty little gangsters, all of them. Mindless! Mindless nit-wits. My God! The things they do in the name of Lenin. He's got a hell of a lot to answer for, had a Rolls Royce!' He opened the keyboard of the glittering Buhl grand piano which crouched beside him in gilt and scarlet splendour, jammed his fingers furiously a couple of times at the keys. 'A lot of mindless bloody gangsters hacking away at my chaps. Come and play something, come on. Do your party piece.'

Rooke got up slowly, flexing his fingers. 'Music to soothe the savage breast, Sir?'

'Don't know what the hell it does. Just play something.'

'Usual? *Warsaw Concerto?*'

'That'll do.'

'Only by ear.'

'I know it's only by ear. Don't have to be told.'

'Just the theme.'

'The part I like.'

Rooke played imperfectly, foot hard down on the base pedal, the General stood staring down across the plain, hands in trouser pockets, head bowed.

'You're damn right, of course,' he said over his shoulder, 'about the feminine touch business, nannies, so on, I'll give you that. No good pretending.' He looked round at Rooke, his blue eyes on the keyboard. 'That Yankee. Novak. The carpetbagger, know who I mean?'

Rooke looked up from unconfident fingers, the General turned swiftly back to the windows.

'Apparently sees quite a lot of him these days . . . Chats her up, I suppose: but at a time like this, need a bit of comforting myself, y'know, as you say, the feminine touch. I miss her popping in and out.'

The piano was hideously out of tune, jangling like a barrel organ. Nanni Singh tip-toed into the room, eyes averted, took

159

up his tea tray, melted reverently away in silence, convinced that he was hearing a hymn.

Weathersby clumped into the office, slung his pad and invoices onto his desk, took a bottle of Tiger beer from a cupboard above his chair, opened it and filled a tin enamel mug until it brimmed.

'What did he want then? Nettles? Want to know your war history?' He took a long pull, pushed his cap to the back of his head.

Ruby stacked her books neatly in a pile. 'Nothing. If there was a recent list of internees from Butan Pahang. Was I all right? Nothing.'

'And you said yes? Good girl, all tiggity boo and shipshape.'

'What is that? I don't know.' She lifted a wide-brimmed hat from the desk and pulled it slowly on to her head, one hand searching for a cotton rose.

'Never mind. Too long to explain. Give you a lift, shall I?'

'No, thank you.' She pulled the rose and the brim down low over her eye. 'I take rickshaw to market. You have bad marks on your mouth.'

'You can talk!' He spat into a handkerchief, rubbed his lips hard. 'A stubborn girl, you are. I'll pick you up about eight-thirtyish then, OK? At the flat?'

Ruby shook her head, the cotton rose flopping loosely. 'I don't come to the party tonight. Not like this.'

'Oh, Buzz won't notice. No one will. Wear a veil or something. Come on, it's Thanksgiving, there's a turkey, he says.'

'No, I stay at flat. Tell Mr Novak I am sorry, I say sorry to be rude.'

'Washing your hair?'

'If you like.' She collected a straw bag and a paper fan. 'Maybe I go to my good friend Pearl Ching, she is needing help with her dress she makes for tonight. Maybe I go there from market.'

'A girls' gossip, eh? Sob on her shoulder.' He opened a drawer in his desk, threw a neat bunch of short leather straps on to the scarred wooden top, swivelled himself into his chair. 'Brand new. Double buckles,' he said.

160

Ruby looked at them from below her flopping brim with dull eyes. 'What are?'

He took another pull at his beer, set it down. 'Got them this morning. Want to try them on that solid gold bed of yours. Easier for you, see? No knots to break your fingernails. See how I think of you, Ruby?'

'Not this night, Ronnie, not this night, please.'

'Why not this night? Have a try. After the party; I'll be around about half past ten, that do?'

She stood quite still, the straw bag at her side, tapping the fan against a firm thigh. 'I go to my friend Pearl.'

'After then. She's going to the party, isn't she? About ten-thirty, OK?'

The fan stopped tapping and was still. 'OK. OK,' she said. 'If you want. Not before that time. At half-past ten I will be ready.'

He winked up at her, twisting one of the leather straps in his hands. 'There's a good girl.' He suddenly slapped his open palm hard a couple of times. 'Then you can pay me back, can't you? Oh, what a cruel girl you are. Dead cruel.'

She stared at him silently from shadowed eyes. 'I'm not cruel, Ronnie.'

He wagged a strap towards her, face screwed into his lemon grin. 'I know all about you, Ruby girl. Remember? Heard lots of stories about you, a naughty, naughty girl you are, and I've been a naughty boy, haven't I? So you pay me back for it, eh?'

Suddenly, as if she had collected a jumble of disconnected thoughts and reached a happy decision, she smiled a brilliant smile, which was all that he could see from under the shadowy brim. 'Yes. I pay you back. Is so, that is so. Now I go, OK?'

He watched her cross the room, her body undulating gently in shiny pink satin, hat brim flapping, buttocks swinging, bag swinging. At the door she turned and raised the paper fan in a soft adieu. Grinning, he slapped his hands three times, hard with the strap. 'Later then,' he said. But she had already closed the door.

The little maid hurried after her worriedly through the pretty

161

shaded room with its lingering scent of joss sticks, the curving bridge of ivory elephants, scarf shrouded lamps.

'Mistress is resting. I must not disturb now.'

Ruby threw her straw bag into a chair and walked out onto the verandah. 'You say that I am here, that I will wait.' She sat in a rattan chair and opened the paper fan as if she had all the time in the world.

The verandah was cool, shaded by bamboo blinds beyond which the long-abandoned garden dazzled in the late sun; a pair of oriels flashed like yellow darts across emerald banana leaves. The little maid had not moved, still stood uncertainly in the doorway, hands clasped in anxiety.

'I wait,' said Ruby. 'Tell Mistress.'

The maid wagged her head, hissed worriedly through her teeth, flip-flapped away across the dim room behind. Silence and solitude fell about Ruby like a soft sweet vapour. A green lizard scuttled onto the wooden planks, stopped, head alert, eyes gold, swung about and scurried up the scaly stem of a twisting vine. From the beamed roof hung a stuffed macaw in a brass hoop, a shawl of fine dust over its crimson shoulders, twisting idly in the almost airless gloom. Ruby watched it for a time, the lifeless body, dulled glass eyes, dusty feathers, crippled feet wired to its improbable perch, then she closed her eyes and let two large tears slide aimlessly down her bruised cheeks.

'Yoko! What is it? You are inconsiderate coming at this time, I have to rest a little. I am no longer as young as I pretend, you know.' She was there in a flurry of lace and ribbons, shaking long wide sleeves down to plump elbows, her head a billow of bows and lilac net. 'Now what is it? What is the matter?'

Ruby had her head turned away, fanning herself wearily, staring under the blinds into the brilliant light.

'I am sorry, Miss Foto. But I must speak with you.'

Miss Foto plumped up a cushion in irritation and sat down by the bamboo table, folding her lace dressing-gown around her securely.

'Well then, what is it? Here I am; I am listening, but you must be quick, I have to dress shortly for the party. Thanksgiving Party, the American Feast, Mr Novak is celebrating; but this you know! You are invited too, I think, no?'

162

Ruby pulled off her flopping straw hat and dropped it to the floor beside her, shaking her hair so that it fell loose about her shoulders; then she turned and faced Miss Foto directly for the first time. 'Like this? You think I can go like this? To the Thanksgiving?'

Miss Foto raised a hand to her mouth, eyebrows crescents of surprise. 'My God! Yoko chick. What happened; what did you do?'

'I fell over.'

'A clenched fist?' Miss Foto regained composure. 'I have seen too many of those in my life time, who was it?'

'He cut my mouth.'

'I can see. Why? Who, this Wizzersby?'

Ruby nodded miserably, tears welling.

Miss Foto snorted. 'That little runt! Impossible. I thought you had to hit *him*, not he you.'

'He hits me because I will not tell.'

'Tell what?' said Miss Foto sitting rather still, her eyes narrowed. 'Tell what?'

'About Nakuma-san, about Tassa Nakuma who was so good to me. Ronnie wants to know all about him, about the gold from the pawnbrokers, you remember?'

'No,' said Miss Foto firmly, 'I do not.'

'Tassa gave me a bed, just for my pleasure you know, it was covered in gold leaf, very fine, like paint, you could say. The Chinese did it for him, it was a gift for my pleasure, a nothing, very pretty only. This Ronnie discovers.'

'How does he discover?'

Ruby wiped her face with a listless hand, searched in her puff sleeve for the handkerchief, found it, blew her nose. 'Well, sometimes I must tie him to the bed, sometimes he prefers the other way, he has put hooks in the ceiling.'

Miss Foto waved a hand dismissively. 'Yoko, please. So unpleasant.'

'One time on the bed he says, "This is not brass, it is gold!" ' She stuffed the handkerchief under her sleeve. 'He scratches and scratches, he can see. He knows from the Military Police about the pawnbrokers' gold from the Occupation, he knows about Nakuma-san, what he did, he thinks that Tassa has hidden some maybe in the flat, not sent it all to Japan. He wants to know

163

where. He says he will search until he finds it. He wants to know where, and for that he hits me, Miss Foto.'

Miss Foto folded her hands calmly. 'And did he?'

'Yes. Yes, he hit me. You can see.'

'No, no, Yoko, no . . .' said Miss Foto impatiently, for this was clearly a lovers' quarrel and nothing to concern her. 'No. Did Tassa Nakuma hide some gold in the flat perhaps? It is possible . . .'

Ruby fanned herself urgently. 'Tassa. A good man, so gentle, so kind to me, what have they done to him? Taken him away like a beast, why? He harmed no one, he was a sweet man; in Hamamatsu where he lived, his life was only for his little trees, his bonsai. He said that he would be good to me like the little trees, to care for me, cherish me, tend me solicitously, those were his words, and it was true, he was so tender with me, a gentle man.' She put her bruised face in her hands and sobbed wretchedly, which irritated Miss Foto who rose impatiently.

'Yoko! Now stop this! You are being ridiculous. You wish to be a dwarf tree of one hundred years old in a too small pot? You are mad; now please stop. It is disgusting all these tears. What can I do, pray? This is not my affair, you must report this Wizzersby to your friends in the Military Police, if he assaults you, you have the right to complain. They will listen, it is *their* business, not mine.'

Ruby twisted her fan. 'You know what they call me? Red Light Ruby. You think this is pretty? It is a kind name? At first I thought maybe yes, so pretty, but Ronnie says it is a whore's name. A whore, you see. So how can a whore complain about a British officer; who will listen? He says I am a half-caste whore, traditional! Traditional, he says!' In her distress spittle had collected on her wounded lip and she spattered it across one pink satin knee.

'I can tell you nothing,' said Miss Foto adjusting her many bows. 'This is a most disagreeable exhibition, and now you are spitting; it is not agreeable at all and I do not like it when you raise your voice to me in this manner. It is most ungrateful of you, I have been good to you, Yoko, remember. I recommended you to the British as a loyal, diligent, trustful girl, and also because you spoke some Japanese to help, as we all have done, with the translating in a difficult time. And now you rile at me and spit and behave disgracefully. The British didn't want you, they know your association with Tassa Nakuma, they know what he did, they did not take him away because he was a gentle little Japanese gardener, my chick! Bonsai! Little trees! Ha!' She wagged a pale finger before the ravaged face. 'I know too. I have seen his dossier.'

Ruby lay back in her chair and stared up at the macaw twisting slowly above her head. 'They know about Mel. The British.'

Miss Foto, whose impatience had been growing, and whose hands had been fluttering like a host of little butterflies about her frills and ribbons, froze.

'What is that?' she said in a remarkably sweet voice.

'The Australian. You remember? Rainy day.'

'No . . .'

'There is a letter about you. Major Nettles gave it to me today. About Mel. And the others, all is there, even the little salon in Molendijk.'

'Little salon! In the camp? Who is mad? Who sent this letter?'

'It does not say. There is no signature.'

'Then it is just gossip! Evil gossip, nothing more.'

'He is worried, because of the General.'

'Why?' Her voice now flat, cool.

'Because if they investigate and it is so, the General will be in disgrace, he says.'

'Investigate! Investigate gossip? If they start doing that the entire City will be in disgrace, as you call it. It would be in ruins!'

Ruby rolled her head from side to side against the chair back, eyes closed. 'I have told him this. All lies. I said so. I said everything I can remember, how good you were, how brave, the risks you took. He was very impressed, I could see.'

'Ah Yoko,' said Miss Foto softly. 'I think you have been perhaps remembering again, eh? And who told you *not* to remember?'

'I know. But it was for you, all for you. You were so sad, you told me, the last night he came with the dollars. "Keep it for a rainy day," he said. You gave me his wallet when my Tassa said the Kempei-Tai would come to your house. "So little

165

time!" you said so sadly. "So little time, take it away, burn it."
You were so frightened. Remember?'

Miss Foto, who had been standing as if carved from granite,
suddenly clapped her hands and went swiftly into the sitting-
room calling for the maid.

'Some wine, don't you think? A glass of cool wine for your
poor eyes and lips. We need, I think, what the British call a
"little pick-me-up".'

After three glasses, and the full story from Ruby, Miss Foto
had almost completely recovered her wits, if not composure. Her
hand was perfectly steady as she fitted a cigarette into a jade
holder, lit it, placed the match tidily in the ash tray before her.
'Poor Yoko. Such a day. So many questions, your head must
quite be spinning. It was right of you to come and tell me,
quite right. Now we must take some action together.'

Ruby raised hopeful eyes. 'Together?'

'You and I,' said Miss Foto taking up the bottle with care and
refilling the glasses. 'The letter must have come from that old
goat, Singh; he hates me. The boy probably told him all these
lies, he hates me too, because I had him sent away, and what is
his evidence worth? Fifteen at the time of the race-course
happening! Fifteen, so many others were there, all impression-
able children, but there is no proof, Yoko, you see? No proof of
my hiding Mel and the others. Only you and I know the truth.
I only trusted you because you were my good, safe, Yoko and
because you knew how much I suffered; of course there may be
rumours but who will take action to investigate such silly
things? Jealous people, and many too afraid to open their
mouths because they know that *I* know a few things also! I can
point a finger too! This they know.' She raised her glass and
took a sip. 'When I suggested to you that you might warn Tassa
Nakuma where they were, it was because I was desperate with
worry and grief, as you remember well. What could Mel do
with one man lame, and two idiot boys trying to get to the
coast . . . a boat to Timor! Madness, they would have perished,
and what could I do then locked in the camp, how could I help
them, you remember my agony . . . oh God! The decision to
make, help me, I implored. Mel would not surrender . . .

so . . .' She settled her glass on the table, tapped the ash thoughtfully off her cigarette. 'But only you and I know this. You and I.'

Ruby shook her head gently. 'Emmie van Hoorst knows.'

Miss Foto raised polite eyebrows which did not betray the slight tremor in her hand. 'The van Hoorst girl?'

'She took food once, when she was working with the people hiding the petrol, the cars, you remember. So she knows also.'

Miss Foto smiled and wagged the jade holder slowly at her guest. 'Yoko, you remember *everything*! What a girl you are. I think now that we should consider you.'

'Consider me? How?'

'I think, truthfully,' said Miss Foto staring into her glass, 'that it would be best if you were just to, well, slip away quietly for a time.'

'Away? Where? There is nowhere to go!'

'Just for a time. For both our sakes, yours as well as mine.'

'But where?' Panic had stolen into Ruby's voice suddenly.

'The Chinese sector is the best place. It is packed now with refugees from all over the island, they are from the north, the south, all over. You could be perfectly safe there. We must get you away from these people who question you all the time, it is so unfair for you. I will find a nice family to hide you for a while—I will pay well.'

'But my job: Ronnie, he will ask questions, you see.'

'One morning you just don't go to the Dumps. You will stay in the flat for a day or two, because of your eye, to rest. That will give me time to arrange things comfortably for you. When things have settled down, as they will, my dear, as they will, you could even go away to Sumatra, to Java, maybe even Malaya, you'd like that, eh?'

Ruby looked at Miss Foto in dull fear. 'Sumatra? Java? But why, how would I go? Oh no!'

'Oh yes! It is easy. Now listen. Buzz Novak—you know him well—Buzz has many, many connections, his friends are everywhere. He could slip you on to an American boat as easily as anything, there would be no questions, you would have nothing to fear, and he has American friends who would be very happy to help you. He would make sure of that.'

Ruby suddenly burst into sobs. 'But this is my home here, I have never been away, I would die.'

'Nonsense!' said Miss Foto briskly. 'You wouldn't die! So silly! Do you want to stay here when the Indonesians take over? What then? The Dutch will never come back, not to stay; that time is all ended. Now we have an Indonesian president in Java! Soekarno. Dear God! Yoko, we must all think of leaving one day. Even I will leave. So, it is wise to go when there is still time . . . Mr Novak has very kindly offered to help me when the time comes, you see? He has ideas for me where I could be useful. He is a very persuasive man, but this is still a secret, Yoko.' She wagged the holder at the sad face once again. 'This is one secret you must keep for me; I tell you only to encourage you. So. Tomorrow maybe you decide not to go to the Dumps . . . and you stay quietly at the flat. And then we will arrange it that you slip away one day. It happens all the time, you know very well, people just get, shall we say, forgotten for a time? And it is only for a time, until Novak has made his plans. This, I think, is a good idea all round. You agree with me, I am sure? No more questions.'

Ruby leaned forward and reached for her floppy hat on the floor, laid it on her knees, smoothed the cotton petals of the rose listlessly. 'No more questions,' she said softly. Then looking up, her eyes rimmed with tears, she said in a meek voice full of weary submission, 'You will tell me when?'

Miss Foto nodded briskly, stubbed out the cigarette and got to her feet. 'I will tell you when, my chick. I must go and change, they'll be here to pick me up directly.'

'You will tell this to Mr Novak?'

'I will tell him, maybe even this evening.'

'And tell him sorry that I cannot come tonight.'

'I will tell him.'

Miss Foto suddenly stooped and kissed Ruby's hot brow. 'You are my good Yoko; there: how good you were to come and tell me, so sensible, so full of thoughtfulness. You must tell Wizzersby that *I* know where the gold is hidden which he seeks!'

Ruby looked up into the smiling face with a start of fear.

Miss Foto placed a soft hand on her left breast.

'It is here,' she said kindly. 'Tell him it is here. Hidden in your heart.'

168

Although Weathersby arrived at the flat half an hour before the time he had agreed with Ruby, he was quite unconcerned, since he had his own key, and let himself in quietly. The tiny hall glimmered in the soft glow from the buddha-lamp in the corner. He took off his cap, threw it onto the fur-covered 'pouf' as usual, and went into the stuffy little sitting-room, switching on the light and the fan which started to revolve in the ceiling, wobbling unevenly, with its usual rhythmic squeak, stirring the stale air, fluttering the tall pampas plumes in the big china jar. Looking through the archway to the bedroom he could just see the faint glint of the brass bed beyond, and his heart gave a little jump of pleasure as he fiddled with the buckles of the haversack he had brought and which contained, apart from his pyjamas and razor, for he fully intended to stay the whole night, the four little straps which he placed with loving care on the table. Loosening his belt, and pulling off his bush jacket, he crossed to the draped archway and snapped on the light, bathing the bedroom in a deep red glow: the bed, he suddenly realized, had been dragged into the centre of the room and stood like a sacrificial altar with its shining knobs and tight orange rubber sheet tucked smoothly all over. On it, he saw with a gleam of pleasure, three black whips of varying sizes, the four coils of thick white cord spread neatly along its length, and looking up suddenly, as he stepped out of his trousers, hanging from one of the hooks which he had long ago screwed firmly into the ceiling, Ruby: swinging gently in the draught, as lifeless as a bolster.

CHAPTER SEVEN

Gaunt rested easily in his saddle in the freckled shade of a giant
banyan tree and waited for Sister Pritchard to catch him up:
which presently she did, trotting easily down the slope through
the canes and scrub, waving brightly when she saw him. With
her hair tied roughly back in a bit of string, a loose khaki shirt
and flapping khaki slacks, she looked sexless: which as far as
Gaunt was concerned she was. He waved his hand about to
disperse the persistent flies swarming about his mount's sweating
head and neck as she drew alongside and reined in under the
tree.

'A wizard run, that was, simply wizard. Blown all the
cobwebs away,' she said.

'You do very well. Most women are usually pretty awful
mounted. Bums out of the damn saddle, legs all which way.
You ride quite like a chap.'

She accepted the compliment, slapped her horse's neck,
fanned away the flies. 'Used to do it a lot. Terribly out of
practice, I'm afraid. But I do love it.'

'Where did you ride?'

She shrugged vaguely. 'Just about; nothing special. I was
never with a proper Hunt, that sort of thing. We had a house
outside High Wycombe. Chilterns, all a bit suburban really.
Ridden since I was a girl, my original passion. Just bashed off on
my own most of the time. Had a horse called "Atta Boy".' She
laughed lightly, did up a button of her shirt. 'Absurd name for a
horse. Came with it. What are all these bits of rag hanging
about the tree for?'

Gaunt squinted up into the glossy leaves. 'A holy banyan.
Moslems. All rather primitive this emerging New Country.
We're under a sacred tree.'

'Goodness me. You live and learn. Smelly little rags. Prayers,
I suppose.'

'Something like that. Rather thought you'd be at Church
yourself. Sunday, on your knees confessing or something.'

'Not me. Only go when forced. Always have. Don't believe
in God or any of that larky stuff. It's pretty hard cheese to be

born the only ugly duckling in a family of raving beauties. I went off God pretty early, I can tell you.' She laughed lightly, swatting at flies. 'Two brothers like gods, a sister like Isadora Duncan and me. Jolly unfair really. End of the litter, I suppose.'

'Bit hard on yourself, aren't you?'

She looked at him sharply. 'I'm not a complete fool, I know what I look like. Behave like a fathead too, that's timidity really, but I'm not actually as daft as I look.'

'I didn't think so.'

'Funny thing is, about God, I mean. He sort of levelled things out. Marvellously inconsistent. Alan and Rupert both died in some dried up river-bed in Spain fighting Franco, and Alice got peritonitis, leaving me, poor old Deirdre, to look after Mother and Father. Stuck. Hence the horsey-porsies, the local Red Cross, the Good Works.' She grinned at him suddenly. My God! he thought, she looks like something out of *Just William*. 'Do you wonder,' she added, 'why I joined up on September the 1st, 1939, and never looked back?'

They left the shade of the banyan and headed slowly in single file down the dusty track which led to the sad, scabby land surrounding the old race-course. Kites scimitared lazily through the still morning, dust rose in little puffs from the horses' hooves, the flies droned and zigzagged constantly. Ahead rose the rackety white wooden clock tower of the course, hands permanently stopped at a quarter to twelve; the stands, sagged and bleached by sun and rain, stood empty and forlorn in the dazzling light.

'Another thing about God which is fearfully interesting,' said Sister Pritchard riding up beside him as they reached the open scrubland, 'is the fact that every time a chap is on his way out, as we say in our job, he *never* calls for God. Mum, perhaps; his wife, even me. *I* sit there holding hands; they want a woman's touch, not God. Even bossy Sister Pritchard will do. And does. I've held more hands that way than any other. Funny, isn't it? My compensation, I presume.'

'You must be pretty used to it—the dying, I mean.'

'No. Never! It's not ordinary at all. One moment you are holding something which is full of pain, or grief, bitterness, hope, longing, awareness, belief, anything . . . and the next instant it's a shell. Empty. *The next instant.* That's the only time I

171

ever do a quick re-cap on God. But it soon goes.' They were walking slowly through a long-fallen wooden arch into the deserted stadium. 'It's a bit like this place really, isn't it? Once so full of life and hustle, people cheering in all those stands, horses sweating round, whips flying, colours flapping . . . look at it now: desolate. Empty. A corpse. You don't get used to it, Major Gaunt.'

'You said timid, just now. You?'

'Me? Oh yes, terribly timid, hadn't you guessed? I mean, I can carry a severed leg, drown a rat, hold down a screaming man, even embalm him if I had to, it's not too jolly, I'm bang on at all that; but stick me down at some party, or in a crowd and I just go to bits, inside. Drink too much, talk too much, irritate; can see it a mile off. I know I'm doing it, feel it happening, the defence mechanism getting to work. I know that the inside of me is all right really, it's just the outside that I have to come to terms with.' She suddenly grinned her monkey's grin again. 'I'm not exactly Frankenstein, Major Gaunt, nor Helen of Troy by a long chalk. "Deirdre Drear". Had it all my life. Something you get used to, as my Mother used to say. Like the Sailors and the Drowning.'

'Don't seem very timid to me, I must say.'

'That's the whole thing. I'm not frightened of you. You're not frightening to me. Do you mind awfully?'

'Not in the least. Glad to hear it.'

'The moment we met I felt a sort of kindred spirit thing: only you don't need people and I'm afraid I do, worse luck. Which is why I nurse. If they won't come to you — and I don't have much to offer, do I, let's face it? — you go to them. People need you like billyho when they're ill, even if you do look like a cross between Plain Jane and the Queen of the Willies.' She laughed cheerfully into the still morning. 'How I go on. You are so wonderfully strong and silent, aren't you? But I bet we are both bung full of private little deficiencies of our own: a mutual love of these beasts helps, doesn't it?' She leant forward and slapped her horse's neck briskly. 'Good old boy. What a wizard morning we've had, quite set me up.'

'I hate parties too,' said Gaunt. 'Bloody awful things, awful people, yacking.'

'Oh, I don't go to many really: there was an American, do

172

you know who I mean? Mr Novak. Came to us first because he had a touch of Delhi Belly, thought he'd got amoebic dysentery, you know how Yankees panic. We fixed him up in a trice and he asked the girls and me to a few parties. Short of white women to begin with, but it all got a bit, well, a bit vulgar. Not the right sort of people at all, all kinds, Chinks, Indians, Americans, some rather rum Dutch: I think there was opium somewhere, at any rate, a frightful stink, and people did behave in a very extraordinary way. Not our class at all. That girl who hanged herself the other day, you know her, Ruby Something, quite a jolly girl, but not one you'd actually ask home to meet mother, poor thing. That friend of the General's is there quite often, very much the life and soul of the party; she's a cold fish.'

'Miss Foto?' said Gaunt mildly.

'No idea. They all have special names at Novak parties. She never spoke to me.'

They had reached the long shadow of a shabby wooden hut at the far end of the deserted track, two white-shirted syce scrambled to their feet and took the horses. Gaunt swung easily out of his saddle, adjusted his cap, dusted his pale breeches and walked over to a straggle of soldiers who had emerged from the wooden hut and shuffled into a line measuring the distance between each other with raised arms and clenched fists and come to attention, heads high, rifles pressed flat to their sides. He murmured something to them, saluted with a casual tap of cane against cap peak; they relaxed. Sister Pritchard, standing in the sun, watched him walk slowly along the line of men, speaking to each one individually; he must have cracked a joke, she thought, because one or two of them laughed suddenly and some smiled. Only a naik, taller than the rest and at the far end of the line, remained stiffly to attention and made no move. Very much in charge, she thought, quite the little soldier. Gaunt spent longer with him than the others and although he appeared to reply to the questions promptly and quite civilly, Sister Pritchard was interested to note that his eyes remained fixed on a distant point somewhere just above the Major's head: it was only when Gaunt turned and started walking back to her that she saw the naik's eyes drift into focus and survey the departing figure from the top of his cap to his spurs. They raked the body slowly up and down a couple of times: filled with contempt.

In the jeep bouncing and lurching over the rutted tracks towards the main road, Sister Pritchard searched for, and found, a squashed packet of cigarettes in her breast pocket and lit one. 'Aggers and mizzers in that place. Beastly feeling, so sad, silent. Evil almost. Horrid atmosphere. Don't you think?'

'Be all right, full of people again. Thought I might try to start up a kind of little gymkhana thing. Got the mounts . . . we'll find the riders easily enough.'

'Wizard idea. Spot on.' She removed a shred of tobacco from her lip. 'Sort of exorcize the place. Gives me harri creepers; don't know why.'

'Probably,' said Gaunt, swinging out onto the main road, 'probably because it's where the Japs held their executions and so on. Got all the Chinese and whatnots herded together and then sorted out those who had helped the Dutch or any of the Allies before the Occupation, profiteers, black-market, that sort of thing. Or anyone who had openly denounced the Emperor. Made 'em all dig their graves and machine-gunned them in bunches behind the stands.'

'Charming, I'm sure. I knew there was death there. How did they sort them out?'

'Collaborators. In canvas masks so they couldn't be identified later, just walked along the lines, pointed at Tom, Dick or Harry and that was his lot.'

'So much hate. Good grief.' She thrust her hand into wiry hair, pulled off the bit of string, shook her head, raised her throat to catch the gentle draught in the moving jeep. 'By the by. That naik you were talking to just now, tall chap, rather fine-looking.'

Gaunt drove over a snake streaking across the road, turned back swiftly, grinned. 'Got him. Can't stand bloody snakes. Naik? Kalik, you mean, Patrol Commander?'

'I suppose so. Rather impertinent, I thought.'

'Oh, he's all right. A bit pissed off with me. Bolsie bugger, as a matter of fact, had a bit of trouble with him up at the Residency early on, with the lot of them as a matter of fact, mucking about in the gardens. Nothing serious, but I didn't care for it myself. Bit of obscenity with a garden statue.'

Sister Pritchard's laugh became a snort as the jeep crashed

into a shallow hole, and she swallowed cigarette smoke. 'A garden statue. Whatever next!'

'Randy lot, Pathans, in their nature. So I'm keeping young Kalik out of temptation for a while: in the quiet areas. Sex-mad the lot of them.'

'They say that's what happens in a war, don't they?'

'Do they? Don't know.'

'Oh yes. A natural instinct to re-create, reproduce the species or something. A natural urge.'

'All waffle. Just an excuse if you ask me, everybody coupling with everybody else. Not my style.'

Not mine either, thought Sister Pritchard, as they turned into the empty width of Nassau Boulevard towards the city; first time ever for me, had filthy breath, kept on his socks, and hurt. That was that. But she said brightly, looking at her large service watch, 'Good idea to cool 'em off so to speak. And now I'll just have time to cool myself off. A nice shower if I'm lucky, a cup of tea, and I'm on duty at nine. It's just gone eight, by the by. I feel quite refreshed though, thanks to you, kind sir. Wizard morning, only had a couple of hours shut-eye last night. Got a bunch of Dutch internees suddenly from the Butan Pahang camp, RAPWI sent them over, awful state: malnutrition, beriberi, sores as big as plates. We don't usually take civilians but these were all Military, Navy, Army you know, so grateful, it was pathetic, can't believe they're free. Letting them out in droves now that this Soekarno chappie says he's President of Indonesia. We live in a changing world, don't we?' She flicked a glance at Gaunt from the corner of her eye, threw her cigarette into the dusty road. 'There I go. Chatter-baggers. Just tell me to shut up.'

'Shut up,' said Gaunt.

She grinned, folded her arms, and leaned back contentedly.

Emmie lay on her back like a corpse. Arms folded across her chest, legs straight, a slight smile on her lips, a smile of infinite pleasure and contentment. She stared up into the milky folds of the mosquito net watching the sunlight throw wandering, wavering shadows across the drooping canopy, heard Rooke's low voice murmuring to his bearer in the little kitchen across

175

the hall, the clatter of a kettle, water bubbling. Stretched, raising her arms from her breasts high above her head, pointing her toes like a dancer towards the brass rail at the foot of the bed.

'Get up. You lazy slut,' said Rooke with his tray, drifting the scent of coffee lingeringly across the room as he went out onto the terrace.

'It's Sunday.'

'It's nearly nine. It's all ready. God knows why *I* have to do the coffee, it's your job.'

'You do it so well. That's why. You look so pretty in your little skirt.'

'You put yours on immediately, it's a beautiful morning out here.'

'It's a beautiful morning here too; in your bed.'

'You are a lazy bitch. Really.'

'If I came and had my coffee in the sun naked, would you be shocked?'

'No. Probably spill something. Shaking hands. Kim might lose his head on the other hand.'

'You said he was a very discreet servant.'

'So he is. Very. But there's no need to take him to the brink of sanity to test it. Get your bottom up, come on.'

She heaved herself off the bed, fumbled through the floating folds of net, found a white cotton shirt on the chair beside her and clambered into the sun-striped room, pulling the shirt over her head. The pebbles on the terrace were already hot under her bare feet; she slid her arms round Rooke's neck, bent and kissed his head, he turned and found her mouth. She laughed, wiping her lips with the back of her hand.

'You taste of coffee.'

'You are molesting me at my breakfast.'

'I love molesting you. Do you like me molesting you?'

'There's a time and place.'

She poured herself a cup, sat with her elbows on the table, blowing steam into the soft air. 'Always a time and place. Everywhere is a time and place. You are so beautiful.'

'So are you.'

'I am a very lucky woman.'

Beyond the wall of the terrace the rough-cut lawns, mowed three times a week by a team of sweating Japanese prisoners,

176

folded softly up the gentle slope to the harsh, angular bulk of the General's house shimmering in the brilliant light as if carved from giant blocks of chalk. The terrace where they sat was discreetly sheltered from direct view by tall palms whose spiky fronds speckled them with fretwork shade, and by a darkly gleaming giant hibiscus starred all over with deep vermilion blossoms. Far below, in the blue haze of the morning, the plains spread wide across to lavender mountains, light winking on shards of paddy like broken mirrors.

Emmie looked up at the house. 'Does he know that I am here?'

Rooke broke a biscuit. 'I haven't actually put your name in lights on the roof.'

'He would mind?'

'What the eye doesn't see the heart won't grieve over.'

'I see. Very English, I think. No?'

'Yes. Very. That's how we built an Empire.'

'Perfidious Albion.'

'Anyway, today's Rest Day: until the evening briefing, and he's got his lady there.'

Emmie set her cup down gently. 'Miss Foto? Is there now?'

'No. Cocktails at eleven-thirty. Then she's there.'

'It's a pity. Because I would like to stay here all the day. Not go to the beach.'

'All day?'

'All day. Look how beautiful it all is. So calm.' She reached across the table and took his hand. 'I could molest you all the day long. Why must we go to that dirty beach?'

'Because I promised Wim. He wants to, so does Clair, so do I. So you must.'

'I don't. Not me. Poor Emmie. But because I am your devoted concubine I obey.'

He pressed her hand to his lips, bit her knuckles gently, she curled long fingers round his cheek. 'You must shave.'

'I must shave.'

'It is very soft, very fine, but like a field after the corn is cut, you know?'

'I know. You look very happy.'

'Oh, I am. I am so happy that I am terrified. Perhaps it is wrong to be so happy and to let it show like this, maybe the

177

Evil Ones will see and say, "Ah ha! That Hoorst woman has too much fortune, we will take it away." You think?'

'Is that what it says in your cards?'

'The Tarot? Oh no. No, I do not look at them anymore, I am too afraid; they might say "yes" and I believe, you know.'

'Why should they? What can be wrong about it?'

She pulled her hair roughly over her face as if to hide the delight which glowed there, shook her head, mumbling.

'Don't do that!' said Rooke sharply. 'You look like a Yeti, for God's sake. Awful at breakfast.'

'What is that?'

'Too complicated.'

She sighed and pushed the hair away, brushing it back into place carefully with long fingers. 'Oh dear. You cannot explain things because I am too stupid for you, and then you say I have no sense of humour, I am too serious, too literal, I am also a slut, I am a bitch even. I have no good qualities at all.'

'Oh yes you have.'

She nodded happily, smiling through lowered lids. 'Oh yes I have.' She leaned towards him, tracing one finger along his lips. Suddenly withdrew the hand, hunched her shoulders, folded her arms tightly and looked up the green rise to the ugly house.

He sensed the change immediately with amusement. '*Now* what is it? Where have you gone?'

'I think of the people up there. Miss Foto, the sad General, he is sad, I think, no? And Yoko Oshima too.'

'Oh Emmie! For God's sake, my darling. Not now, not her or them, not this morning. Be sweet.'

'Well, she was a little bit bad, Yoko, but not so bad. Why? Why will she do such a terrible thing. Why would she be so unhappy.'

'I really don't know. But if you'd ever met her bloke you'd have one good reason.'

Emmie crumbled a biscuit and threw the crumbs towards a quarrel of sparrows along the terrace. 'That thin little man? Oh he is a harmless little fellow, he is so transparent he doesn't even cast a shadow, no woman would kill herself for him. I am thinking it was for something else.'

'The harmless little fellow without a shadow beat the living daylights out of her, if you want to know. Nettles as good as said: saw her that afternoon.'

'Why would he do that? She was so simple . . . stupid, quite.'

'Maybe that's why; stupid people *can* drive you mad.'

'Like me?'

'Well, I could give you a good thump now, if you don't stop.'

'But why should she do such a wicked thing, Rooke?'

'Oh Emmie! I don't know! A lovers' quarrel, who cares, it's not our business.'

'Even so. Maybe that's why he went by himself to Mr Novak's and left her all alone, and he was punished, you see, because the next morning when she did not come to the Dumps he was very worried, he was distracted, and then he went to find her. And so, Pearl told me this, Pearl Ching was her friend, she said all this and that he was crying, this officer, and the flat was like after an earthquake when they got there, everything smashed . . . all her dresses torn to pieces. Poor Yoko,' she swung her coffee spoon sadly over the cup. 'They were awful dresses, but . . .'

Rooke put out his hand and grabbed the swinging spoon firmly. She looked up at him with troubled eyes.

'Now look here, my girl. Enough. The hell with Ruby or Yoko or whatever she was called. You're mucking up the day already. We are going to the beach for a picnic, all right? With Wim and Clair and Nigel, and we'll have a lovely time.'

She nodded, the smile had come back. 'Yes. We'll have a lovely time. And you will wear the swimming costume I brought you?'

Rooke sighed softly. 'I will wear it. Have to, all I've got.'

'And you will stun everyone with your beauty!'

'And,' said Rooke levelly, 'I will stun you with a black eye like Ruby's if you don't start moving.'

Emmie gave a little cry and covered her face with a hand. 'Oh no! She had that? He punched her?'

'Emmie, that's enough, my love!' said Rooke. 'Come and get dressed.' He crossed behind her chair, leaned down and thrust his hands into the open neck of her shirt, cupping her small breasts as she reached up and pulled his head down towards her parted lips. 'Before I strangle you,' he said.

They had built a shelter from the sun out of driftwood bamboo poles and a thatch of bleached palm fronds; the beach was a wide crescent bounded on the left by a tangle of mangrove which concealed the Dock Area two kilometres away, and on the right by a lushly wooded point which marked the limit of the perimeter. As Emmie had said, it was not the cleanest of beaches, owing to the nearness of the docks; the tide line marked by a ragged line of flotsam and jetsam, broken wood, old tins, balls of tar and dead jellyfish; but the sea was clear and stretched before them to Borneo on the far horizon, broken only by the stark wrecks of two sunken ships, the bridge and masts of one, the tilted stern of the other, breaking the white satin sheen of the gentle swell which slid towards the curving beach and broke in a whispering flurry, curving up the steep slope like frayed white lace.

Emmie, in a shiny black, skin-tight swim-suit, sat cross-legged threading beads on a length of string. Clair lay beside her, indolently drifting fine sand through her fingers in handfuls, one arm across her eyes: where the sun burned through the gaps in the thatch it lay like golden coins scattered across their bodies, polka-dotting the baskets of food and drink, and Wim's neatly folded pile of clothes. Clair threw a scurry of fine sand and shells into the sunlight.

'You look as sleek as a seal in that suit,' she said. 'Where on earth did you find it? Loot?'

Emmie nodded. 'From the Dumps as usual. Boxes of them. American. I brought a big bundle away. They all have them now, all the officers. After all you don't pack a swimming-costume to fight a war, do you? Rooke looks very fine in his, don't you think?'

'Very fine. I don't think that I could persuade Nigel to wear one though, do you?'

Emmie laughed and threaded another bead onto her string. 'No. Not for Nigel. Something in wool, with a modesty skirt. He should be here soon, it's nearly noon by the sun.'

'He said noon.' Clair sat up on her elbows, thrust her bare feet into the sand. 'He always checks when there is a Convoy, likes to be quite sure.'

'There was no trouble last night? No ambushes or anything?' She slid on another bead.

'No. Quite easy, I think. He didn't say, but I think so. Two hundred came down, he said. Some are ill.'

'All civilians?'

'All. But no women or children. From the men's camp at Butan.'

'Do you want a drink?' said Emmie suddenly. 'We brought lime juice and a huge bottle of English gin. Booth's. I did the lime juice myself last night. I got six kilos in the market.'

'I'll wait for the men. You have one if you like.'

'No. I'll wait too.'

Clair sat up, brushed her hands, pulled down her wide cotton skirt, hugged her knees, laid her cheek on them, looked at Emmie. 'It's a pleasant phrase, isn't it? "Waiting for the men". There's a security in it. A feeling of promise.'

'But it doesn't really mean anything, does it?' Emmie's snake of beads lay in a turquoise coil across her naked thighs. She had not met Clair's look. 'It just means that it will be pleasanter to drink with them than without them, a social thing, isn't it?'

Clair nodded, head still on her knees. 'Social, yes. Yes, it's social. Terribly much so. Companionship you can say. Being together. Nothing more.' She laughed softly. 'Do you love him?'

Emmie held her bead snake high above her head, slowly counted each blue sphere under her breath. 'Twenty-eight, twenty-nine and—thirty. That's enough, I think. Rooke you mean?'

'Rooke, I mean.'

'Oh no.' She started coiling up the beads in the palm of her hand. 'No. It would be so obvious, don't you think? "Madame Butterfly".' She laughed, fisted them into a tight ball hard against her breast. 'I do not allow myself that.'

'Allow?' Clair was smiling gently but her eyes were clear of amusement.

'Yes, allow. Allow myself the humiliation.'

'Humiliation, Emmie? Why?'

'He will go away. Mr Pinkerton always goes away, remember?'

Clair sat up and looked out towards the sunken hulks; sea birds screamed and swung about the twisted rails and buckled davits. Far along to the right she could see two figures walking across the shore from the wooded point. One tall, one small, and the small one waving arms like a windmill. 'Mr Pinkerton *came* back, remember?' she said.

Emmie crawled through the coins of sunlight, pushed the beads into a straw basket, rummaged about in it. 'Oh, all that wisteria and wailing, and the dear little boy in the sailor suit. He was too late, Mr Pinkerton, far too late, in time for the final aria. No thank you, I don't want that.'

'You're being absurd,' said Clair lightly. 'Quite absurd. That was Victorian nonsense, things are different today, there is no wisteria and wailing now, or little boys in sailor suits. You *are* impossible.'

'No, I'm not impossible. Practical.' She had found what she sought, and crawled back to her place on the runkled towel. 'And if there ever was a dear little boy in a sailor-suit, you know what, don't you?'

'No. What?'

'Mine could be black.' She opened the book and ran her finger down the index lightly.

When Clair spoke, her eyes still following the two nearing figures along the water-line, her voice was low. 'That is madness, Emmie.'

'Not madness at all. My grandmother was as black as black, from Molucca, my good grandfather as blond as a field of corn, my sweet mother, you will remember, pale as an Italian which is exactly what Mrs Bethell-Wood thought that I was, as you may recall; and my father, my adored father, as ice-white as the Frisian Islands from which he came. But where in my body do I carry the Moluccan seed, my dearest Clair? Can you tell me that? Can you even tell me, for certain, that it is *not* so?' She opened the book at the page she required. 'So I do not "allow" myself. Listen to this, it is a book of Rooke's and I found this, it is very sentimental, but so am I, but it's very beautiful too. I will read in English, so please excuse me.'

Clair stared unmovingly along the beach, her eyes blurred. The figures coming along the shore suddenly stopped, she saw Rooke swoop Wim up into his arms and race swiftly with him into the sea where they crashed together in a towering spume of spray and sparkling drops, two heads bobbing, arms thrashing, laughter rising in the still air.

182

'. . . the thought of thee waits, hidden yet bright;
But it must never, never come in sight;
I must stop short of thee the whole day long.
But when sleep comes to close each difficult day,
When night gives pause to the long watch I keep.
And all my bonds I must needs loose apart,
Must doff my will as raiment laid away, —
With the first dreams that come with the first sleep
I run, I run, I am gathered to thy heart.'

She closed the book slowly, first marking the place with a shred of palm, and threw it lightly back into the basket.

'I know,' she said, 'that I don't read very well in English. But it is good, don't you think? It's right too, yes, Clair? "Must doff my will as raiment laid away'', that is surely right?'

The two figures were chasing through the shallows scattering showers of crystal drops about them, then, turning swiftly, Wim raced along the beach.

'They're coming back, Wim and Rooke. Yes, it's right, I suppose.'

'I know so.' Emmie lay back, arms behind her head. 'And when I feel that I am "allowing'', you know? I stop myself. I have worked out quite a good campaign for myself. I do things which I know will irritate him. Try, sometimes, to make him a little cross so that he will think, "Oh God! This idiot woman. So lacking in humour, so literal, so serious: she is so predictable that one day she will drive me mad." You see? A female campaign for self-survival. I do it very well now; he is quite unaware.' She sat up and hugged bare knees close to her chest. ' "As raiment laid away." I know it's best. For me. And for him.'

Clair reached out, found a towel, rose stiffly to her feet. 'It seems to me such a needless thing to do. And cruel. To you both.'

'It would be far crueller the other way.' Emmie leant over and closed the lid of the straw basket. 'He will never know.'

Clair stood out in the sun, her cotton skirt flapping round her legs in a sudden timid breeze which whiffled and rustled the palm fronds of the shelter. 'I cannot reply to that.'

'Of course not. Things are not like this for you and Nigel.'

'Not like what?' The towel snapped in her hand like a flag.

'You are in love with him, that's so?'

'I love him. I am not in love with him.'

'There is a difference?'

'Profound.'

'Not so much.'

'How could I be? You are absurd, you know.' The little breeze faded.

Emmie was busy with bottles and glasses suddenly. 'I only know that three years is a very long time,' she said.

Wim crashed to his knees in the fine sand before the shelter, ignoring Clair's proffered towel, holding a closed fist towards her.

'Treasure!' he said in English. 'Treasure. Rooke said so; look!' In his open palm one small coin, a jagged triangle of broken pot. 'He says it is real porcelain: you said so, Rooke is right? Porcelain? Maybe it comes from China even, you can see, look there is a bird on it quite clear. The coin: well, we don't know. It has a hole in the middle, you can have it if you like.'

'Did you swim far?' She rubbed his hair briskly with both her hands, he ducked away and wriggled into the shade.

'To the Japanese ships, almost, Rooke will say.'

She turned helplessly to Rooke smiling, shaking the towel lightly. He was standing, long legs apart, hands on narrow hips, blond hair sleek to his head, the salt already drying on his shoulders.

'Really to the Japanese ship? No, surely not.'

'No.' He shook his head. 'Not so far, not quite. But you did an amazing job on that arm, he swims like a fish.'

She folded the towel neatly into four. 'He always did. Like his father. He was very lucky really. No arteries severed, and we did exercises day and night, day and night. My God! That was an ordeal I can tell you, far worse than my poor surgery ever was. How he hated it. But we persevered, so he swims. I'm happy.'

Rooke flopped onto the sand, arms wide. 'He's exhausted me, that's certain.' He rolled onto his belly and called into the shelter, 'Emmie! Come to my side, this very instant, you sluttish woman, with refreshments.' He heard her laugh and the clink of glass on glass and watched her with deep pleasure, as she trod through the hot sand towards him bearing two glasses on a piece of driftwood as a tray.

'Why didn't you come to swim? It was so good.'

'I will, promise you, before lunch.' She raised her glass.

'I want to see that thing wet, you see.'

'Clair says that I look like a seal in it.'

'Clair is out of her mind. No seal has a bottom as pretty as yours.'

'He loves me only for my bottom, Clair! Not for my intellect.'

'You have more of the former and less of the latter,' said Rooke.

She threw a handful of sand onto his back and he grabbed her arm, pulling her down roughly to him; she cried out that her glass was spilling, and he silenced her with a laughing mouth.

Wim, watching curiously, gently kicked his mother's foot. 'They behave so stupidly, don't you think?' And then, turning, gave a high cry of pleasure at the sight of Pullen picking his way awkwardly through the trees at the far end of the beach. He raced to meet him, caught his hand and dragged him laughing to the shelter. 'He's got all his clothes on! Look.'

Pullen wiped his brow, took off his cap, embraced Clair lightly, and fanned himself. 'My God! What a journey! Got lost of course, I would.'

'I told you, my dear.' Clair was pouring him a drink swiftly. 'I told you, turn left at the little track after the eight kilometre post.'

'I never saw the ruddy post! Never mind, I got here. Cheers!'

'Come and sit in the shade, and take off those great boots, and your gaiters. You can do that, can't you?'

'Well, not for the moment. I'll have my drink first and then move the damned jeep. Parked it in full sun, wasn't sure this was the place, you know.' He grinned up at Rooke who had come to join him.

'Hullo, Rooke. What on earth are you wearing?'

'The very latest fashion. American. They stretch.'

'Reached bursting point, I'd say.'

'A present from Emmie.'

'Thought they *were* hers.'

'What's the matter with them?'

'They give a singular impression of total nudity.' He half-finished his glass, handed it to Clair and heaved himself out of the sand. 'Go and deal with the jeep. Rooke, be a good chap, come and have a look will you? Carburettor trouble, or plugs. I'm really not much good at the innards; put something on your feet though, it's up the track behind.'

They clambered through the mangrove trees, out onto the dusty track scattered with old tins, broken ammo boxes, rusting coils of barbed wire; a little way along, neatly parked under a cluster of tall palms, the jeep: in deep shade.

'It's not that. Jeep's all right. An excuse really. I need your help.'

Rooke leant against a palm, arms crossed. 'What's wrong? Trouble?'

'Of a sort.' Pullen eased himself sideways onto the front seat, hands between his knees. 'A convoy last night, you knew that? Butan Pahang . . . I always check them in, as you know. It's not really trouble, rather good actually. For Clair. Her husband's here.'

'Here?'

'Juliana Hospital. Bit bashed about, malnutrition you know, the usual. Said who he was, and the Pritchard woman sent for me. So along I went. Pieter Doorn. Alive.'

'Dear God!' said Rooke, joining him by the jeep.

'I've got to tell her, tell her now, you see, don't quite know how to do it, but I don't want to do it in front of the boy, Wim. Y'see? Terrific shock for both of them. Three and a half years after all. Or Lor', what a rumble bumble it all is. Oh hell! Here he comes . . .'

Wim scrambled bare-footed through the trees, picking his way carefully among the tins and wire. 'Can I help you? Nigel!'

'Get him away, can you? Emmie and you? Take him for a walk, anything, just for a bit. It's all done, Wim, thank you. Dirt in the carburettor; come on, let's go back to the beach, I rather think Rooke is going to take Emmie for a swim. That's right, isn't it?'

'That's right. Come on, Wim, a final swim before lunch.'

'To the ships?'

186

'To the ships.'

Emmie had just spread a thin grass mat on the sand. 'But not now, really, Clair and I are just getting the food.'

'Yes, now. I insist. A swim before food, just what you need; you promised you know, and Wim wants to and so do I.'

'Oh Rooke! You're so selfish.'

'Off you go,' said Clair. 'It can all wait. Nigel, you only took half—another glass?'

'It would be very acceptable, my dear.'

'And take off those awful boots.'

'Come on,' said Rooke. 'Don't hang about, girl. Let poor old Nigel have a bit of a rest after his drive; down to the point we go.'

'But it's so far!'

'To the point.'

'To the point!' cried Wim, and ran ahead.

She suddenly realized that something was not perfectly right with the morning. Rooke was over-bright, over-alert, his eyes steady, very cold. Instinctively she took his hand and let herself be led away. 'Clair! I am being bullied by these men, forgive me.' They almost ran down the sloping beach to the sea, Wim joyously ahead, splashing through the little waves nudging listlessly along the smooth damp dand.

'Goodness me. I need this, my dear.'

'It's not very cold. The ice has all melted.'

'Perfect. Nectar.'

'Those boots . . .'

'In a second. When I've got my wind back.'

'A bad night? The convoy?'

'No. No, as a matter of fact, absolutely no worries.'

Clair was kneeling beside him, hands folded neatly in her skirted lap. 'Why did you send them all off for a swim?'

'Send them off? They just went.'

'I'm not a complete fool, or else Rooke is a very bad actor.'

'Well, I'm not an actor at all.'

'Tell me.'

He took her hands in his. They were lifeless. 'Pieter is here. He's well.'

A great shudder ran through her body.

'I wanted to tell you alone.'

'I know.'

'He's well.'

'Where?'

'Juliana Hospital.'

'But you said "well".'

'Not maimed, not blind, my dear, malnutrition, that's all.'

'Not maimed?'

'No. All together. But terribly thin, of course.'

'Of course.'

'Lost a good deal of his hair, too, bit of a scarecrow.'

'When can I go to him?'

'When you like.'

She looked over her shoulder to the three distant figures. 'I must tell Wim.'

'Of course.'

She looked at him steadily, eyes wide, no tears. 'Thank you for telling me like this.'

'Rather clumsy, I'm afraid.'

'He spoke of me?'

'Of you, and Wim. I told him how well you were, how happy.'

'Three years and a half.'

'A long time.'

'A lifetime.'

'Oh come now, it'll seem like days only; you'll see.'

'Can he walk?'

'No. Not yet. Dreadfully, dreadfully thin, I warn you, very weak.'

'But he will walk?'

'Yes, yes, he will, pretty soon too, you'll see. Just feed him up, you know . . .'

'And not maimed?'

'No, no, not maimed, your husband is all in one piece, my darling.'

'Oh sweet Christ!' she cried in anguish. 'Don't call me that! Don't call me that!' And reached blindly for his arms.

Nettles sank back thankfully into a bank of cushions on the low divan, undoing the buttons of his creased bush-jacket and approving, with a gentle nod, the elegance and comfort around him. Cane chairs, a low carved table, a soft glow from the tall standard lamp, rush mats on the cool marble floor, a Chinese cabinet with bottles and glasses; on one wall a long scroll of a tiger and guinea fowl, on an ebony chest a portable gramophone, records, and a carved wooden bird on slender legs which appeared to be devouring an egg.

'I couldn't like it more. Divine,' he said.

Rooke was stretched out in a low cane chair across the room by the wide windows open onto the dying light of the day, the leaves of the hibiscus bush were jet against a crimson sunset. He felt utterly drained.

'There's a bedroom next door, a titchy kitchen, bathroom, and a hole in the wall where Kim dosses. I must say it's not bad; this is all the stuff the Old Man rejected for the Residency up the hill, as you'd imagine. Too simple by far. I just carted it here, it was the Guest Pavilion.'

'Bit near for comfort, aren't you?'

'Convenient really. Hundred yards. I'm on tap if he needs me, he doesn't intrude, damned reasonable really. He knows Emmie drops in, turns a blind eye.'

'Well,' said Nettles, reaching for his drink, 'it's all a very far cry from your first digs. With the crocodile. Nearly broke my foot.'

'A very far cry indeed. It all is . . .' He really didn't want to talk. Just be still.

'How depressed you were, poor boy. Talking of depression, what about the briefing this evening? I mean, what *about* that for depression? Reading the Will and everything's left to a cat's home. The Old Man sunk in gloom, Pullen a heap of weary indifference, and as I arrived, the Foto drove away in a gigantic Packard dressed in black, my dear! I ask you. Ibsen in the tropics.'

'Clair Doorn's husband came down on the convoy last night.'

'So I heard. I should have thought that was a moment for rejoicing.'

'Not for Pullen.'

Nettles tapped his glass with a long finger. 'I see. Had expectations, had he?'

'Possibly.'

'Frightful luck. Know the feeling all too well.'

'The Foto's in black because of the Oshima girl.'

'As well she might be; if she didn't exactly dig the grave, she gave her the shovel.'

'Oh Christ! Come on, that's going it a bit.'

'It's as murky as a cess-pit. And Mr Weathersby's lily-white hands aren't exactly delicate. He's got a punch like a mule, saw the results, as you know.' He got up and wandered slowly across to the gramophone, flipped through some records. 'A catholic taste: Mozart, Delius, Franck, Favourite Arias by Lili Pons, the Lambeth Walk, and Vera Lynn.' He slid them back on the pile. 'No. The Oshima girl took off on her own, no doubt about that, poor bitch. I am given to believe that it is becoming increasingly common in the city these days. Quite a lot of people really did think that the Japanese were here to stay. Can't blame them; it did seem rather permanent at the time, but now that the Dutch have started up shop again, so to speak, the questions are becoming more difficult to answer.' He picked up the wooden bird, smoothed the sleek curved back. 'And this? Rather good, isn't it?'

'I don't know, I like it. Emmie found it. Carved from a single piece, Balinese.'

'A sort of crow eating an egg?'

'She says it is a symbol of avarice.'

'Perfect. Not many people free from the taint of that here, are there?' He replaced the bird carefully. 'When you come to think of it.' He wandered slowly over to the windows, leant against the open frame. It was practically dark. A bat swooped away into the shadows, fireflies sparkled beyond the terrace wall, up on the hill the lights blazed from some of the Residency windows. Nettles laughed under his breath, a half-sigh. 'What do you suppose the Old Man's doing up there in your jewelled cave? Planning the next move to power? This *idiotic* idea to move into the south of the city.'

'That came as a bit of a surprise, I'll confess.' Rooke got up and went to the chest of drinks. 'I didn't expect that.' He opened a beer and poured it slowly.

'Neither did poor old Bunny Blackett, gave him a frightful shock. Gaunt even paled, and he never shows emotion on principle, and poor old Pullen almost climbed out of his wellingtons.'

'I was just beginning to feel like a civilian again.'

'Back to battle. I don't know. 'Course it does need cleaning up, jammed with nig-nogs, the main base they've got now. Ground Sources say they're pretty strong, tanks, field guns and all the rest, but they couldn't possibly launch an attack, not now, we're too well in; I think there is a bit more behind it. It was, after all, the main factory area. Industry was down there, still is, empty and waiting, and there's a bloody great electricity plant.' He finished his drink and walked back to the divan, settled into his cushions again. 'I think that there might well be a bit of "avarice" behind all this. We're going into the south for Big Business is my guess, the place can't function normally without its factory area, can it? We've got the docks, all right, but what use are they without the factories? And the bloody place is crawling with suddenly arrived business-executives from all over the place waiting to start up shop again. But where? Can't build new depots, new railway lines. It's all there, in the south. I think that the Old Man is having a bit of pressure put on him, if you ask me. We've secured the perimeter for the city, now we'll secure its economy from the Communists across the railway.'

'A Capitalists' War?'

Nettles snorted cheerfully. 'That's what it's been all the time, didn't you know?'

'I'm getting the idea now.'

Nettles yawned and stretched his arms high above his head. 'We really shouldn't be talking like this, you and I, not our job, is it? "Have a think about it, please gentlemen," he said. "Bring me your ideas in a day or two." The only people present who looked anything but glum were the RAF. Itching to strafe the place to bits I suppose. Rugger Bugger Lot. And the Dutch: naturally.'

'He's worried about our casualties: that I do know. Not just here, but up north, up at Butan Pahang, everywhere. Snipers, mines, grenades, ambushes, all the rest of it. We really are collecting quite a packet all round. I think he feels that we should bash in there, clean them out, and teach the sods a lesson all round.'

'Not our job to teach lessons, Rooke. We are here simply to keep the peace. Not to bash off and attack the peasants.'

'But shit! This is a ruddy war!'

'Tell that to the British Government. They don't want any part of it.'

'Well, I think that's what's behind this idea, casualties.'

Nettles started to button up his bush-jacket slowly. 'I must be on my way. But I just want to leave you with a tiny thought, just for your own amusement mind, a bit of a riddle to worry at while you're in your shower. It's this, Master Rooke. Whose idea was it really, do you think, to widen the perimeter and secure this splendid little bungalow and its imposing Residence above with a few extra kilometres to patrol without, I must admit, too much loss of wind and limb? And who is it who is fluttering about nightly at the Planters Club in the arms of half the American wheeler dealers from all over the States who have suddenly descended on our sunny shores in crumpled drip-dry suits, bristling with glossy green dollar bills, and absolutely roarin' and ready to start up Trade again? And who is it who knows, without question, that they have the adoration and the open ear of God Almighty, as far as this Island is concerned, at their disposal in a wide double bed? Do you follow me, or are my profundities flying over your golden head?'

Rooke stood perfectly still. His tired face glazed with surprise. Nettles buckling his webbing belt looked up and grinned. 'You look exactly like the Princesse de Lamballe confronted with her first lobster.'

'It couldn't be . . .'

'*She* went rigid for half an hour they say: do come back, Rooke.'

'I can't believe it.'

'I didn't give it as fact. Simply supposition. I have an evil mind, and you know I tend to despise the sex, but consider, Rooke . . .' He rose nimbly, smoothed down his jacket. 'Consider all those clever little things like Dubarry, Lola Montez, Magda Lupescu, irresistible, powerful, the mistresses of strong men or weak men, makes no difference really. There were so many of them through history, but they were the ultimate power; because of them armies were raised, kingdoms were toppled, their men made and ruined with equal felicity: they

192

were the power because they possessed it, Rooke. Nestling coyly between pink and pearly thighs.'

'Oh for God's sake, man.'

'It is so typically English of you to avoid the main issue. But if you'll just think it over you'll realize that I am astonishingly right. The name of the game is Sex. We all suffer from it in one way or another; whatever our genders.' He picked up the wooden bird again and smoothed the polished back. He balanced it on the palms of his two hands. 'Avarice, you said? Well. We all know that avarice is the spur of Industry, and when some *jolie* ladies make sex their profession, you will very often find that avarice is not far behind the bed-head; it becomes second nature, and no one knows this better than that extraordinary little survivor with the highly improbable name who is presently speeding back to town in her master's commandeered black Packard, industriously weaving away at her little web, and stitching up a shroud for him. And one other thing . . .' He replaced the bird and wiped his hands as if to remove a stain. 'What she equally knows is that just before poor Ruby Oshima jumped off her bedside commode to kick up her heels in the Elysian fields, she made me the custodian of all her unsavoury little secrets.' He tapped his fine forehead with a slender finger. 'I have enough in here to fill ten editions of *The News Of The World*. But no *absolute* proof. Which, as you must admit, places me in a very unenviable position. The thought of coming to terms with south-east Asia's answer to The Dubarry fills me with awe.' He took up his cap and his briefcase, in his accustomed manner and wandered to the door. 'I'll see myself out, as they say. I can see that you have had quite an exhausting day.'

Miss Foto hurriedly unpinned from her bodice a spray of black cotton roses, which she had dyed the day before in Indian ink, slung two ropes of fake pearls round her throat and felt immediately better. Mourning, she knew, did not suit her, she was happier in light colours; however, black was slimming and the pearls took the sombreness away, and in the soft glow of the sitting-room lamps, to which she made her way trailing a white chiffon scarf, she was aware that the stress lines, caused by an

193

emotional and exhausting day at the Residency, would be pleasantly smoothed away. Which they were; causing Buzz Novak, mixing her first, and his second Martini with professional care, to raise eyebrows above rimless glasses, glittering in the shaded lamp glow like sheet lightning.

'Hey there! My! My! Very sexy, very sophisticated. You look great in black. Joan Crawford.' He offered her her glass beaded with moisture. 'Real dry. As you like it.'

'I'm so sorry, Buzz, to be so late; it is so far, you know, from the Residency.'

'No problem, they let me in, know me by now, eh? I know where the drink is, they brought the ice, we were just fine. Tough day you had?'

She shrugged gently, spreading the white scarf casually across a silk knee. 'It was a difficult day. But I will be strong after this.' She sipped delicately at her chilled glass. 'But your Martinis make me very sentimental, you know? And today I feel most sentimental . . . Finally I really could weep, I am thinking.'

Novak shifted uneasily. 'Come now, honey! It's a while since Ruby . . .'

She shook her head thoughtfully. 'No, no, no, not Ruby. Ruby is over now. I am quite strong from that. No, it is not Ruby.' She set her glass down on the brass table beside her. 'I suppose that a woman always feels sentimental when she has had a, what is the word you use? Proposal?'

He looked at her in consternation. 'A proposal? A marriage proposal?'

She nodded sadly, eyes lowered, fingers pleating the scarf on her knee.

'You had a proposal of marriage? From Cutts?'

'Poor Leo, it was so moving.'

'He asked you to marry him? You just *have* to be kidding!'

'You are extremely impolite. Most rude.'

'Hell, I'm sorry. No, I didn't mean to be rude. I mean, how could he?'

'Why couldn't he?' Her voice was as chilled as her glass.

'Well, for chrissakes, it just seems crazy. What age is he?'

'What difference does age make between a man and a woman, I would like to know?'

194

Novak nervously fingered his bow tie. 'No offence, Kodak sweetie, no offence.'

'I think it is very offensive of you. It was a very moving compliment.'

'Of course it was, I'm sure. Sure. Yeah. What did you say?'

'He is already married, his wife is in England since 1942. And before that it was quite tragic, quite tragic.'

'Well. So what is the point, if he's already married?'

'He proposes a divorce.'

'And you'd be the General's Lady, I take it?'

'I suppose so, yes.'

'I really can't see you shooting grouse in a Burberry, Kodak.'

She looked at him with eyes of deep dislike. 'I do not understand this expression, and I detest this name Kodak. My name is Dora. Even to you.'

Novak swallowed his drink in one gulp and hurried across to the tray of drinks, narrowly avoiding a collision with the draped standard lamp.

'I'm sorry, dear, I'm sorry. It was just a silly joke. Kodak is my personal name for you, that's all, you know that. I like to "own" the people I am fond of, see, sort of personalize them.'

'I am not a packet of book matches. You will call me Dora.'

He nervously swilled ice cubes in his glass, spilled them into the bucket, squeezed a sliver of lime peel. 'Right, so it's Dora. And I apologize. It was a mighty shock, is all. The last thing I ever expected to hear.'

'It was a shock for me too,' she acceded softly, hands to pearls. 'I know I can make him happy, but how much I did not realize. How much. He says to me that he has never been so happy in his life before. I give it to him, he says; life. I am his sun and his moon. It is a big compliment to a woman, you realize. I am most touched.'

Novak carried his brimming glass back to his chair avoiding the scattered occasional tables, supporting bowls of wax fruits and candy bars. 'You must feel *truly* sentimental, Dora.'

'I do. I do.'

'But perhaps not sentimental enough to say "yes", I guess?'

'Guess what you like: do you show your hand at the bridge table?'

'Correct! That's my girl.' Novak relaxed slightly into over-stuffed cushions.

'I was very tender with him. He was happy, so happy, even I was happy; after all a proposal is a proposal, married or not.'

'So I would imagine,' said Novak, stirring the slip of lime peel in his glass with a nicotined finger. 'So I would imagine that there just wasn't the time to make that suggestion of mine? Went out of your happy head with all the wedding bells and so forth . . .'

'Nothing went out of my head. Nothing ever does.'

'You said about the south? The factory area?'

'I just hinted, very lightly . . .'

'And what did he say?'

She placed her glass neatly on the brass table. 'That he was not Wellington.'

'And what did that mean, do you think?'

'What do you think it means? That he is just a simple British General, he is not out to conquer the world.'

'We weren't talking about the world, honey. Just south of the railway.'

'I know. He knows. That is enough, no more.' She pulled the scarf into a rope across her knees.

'You want to take that nice boat trip to Yokohama?'

She looked at him flatly. 'You become ugly, finally.'

'A deal is a deal. Did you mention the other interested parties? Northmount Oil, Kline and Klinger, I mean apart from Freezy-Kool, and . . .'

'I didn't mention any names!' Her eyes snapped with fury. 'Do you think that I am mad? What would they mean to him? He is a soldier, not a business tycoon . . . all you Americans think of is trade. He called you carpet-baggers! Maybe he is right to say that! You buy and you sell, it is nothing to you that we still are at war here? No! It is not *your* business, all you want is for the factories to start, you do not conquer, you Americans, with flags and honour but with dollar bills and bribes.'

Novak raised his empty glass thoughtfully in both hands and pressed his full lips to the rim. 'Now it seems to me that you have been a bit upset today, I don't like you to talk to me this way, Dora honey, it is not couth of you. America cares very much for the world. We want to help heal it after this long, long war, to

196

rebuild it in a brotherhood-of-man spirit. We are richer because we trade, we are a trading nation. What's wrong with that? We have the knowhow, we have the ideas, the energy . . . we have the money. We want to help. For fuck's sake, Dora! We just saved Europe!'

Miss Foto sat very still. Then she picked up her glass and held it out to her guest. 'I think we stop this conversation. I am aware of what you say, and I have sown a seed: now we wait for the germination, is that right? You must be a little more patient. And give me, please Buzz, another delicious Martini. I am a feminine woman you know, not political. I have no head for those heights, be sweet to me, please? Such a sentimental creature, such a day.'

He rose and took her glass, the sweat shining on his balding head, the front of his shirt ruckled with damp. At the drink tray he paused in pouring and jerked his head towards a bulky paper package on the carved buffet. 'Oh, by the way, this package. It's records. I thought maybe you might care to have them, short supply, and I don't need them anymore.'

'How kind,' murmured Miss Foto, who had drifted back to the Residency for a moment.

'Ronnie dropped by just as I was leaving the apartment. I gave them to him and Ruby a while back, just dance stuff, you know. But he says they're too heavy to pack, so he brought them back.'

Miss Foto sat upright slowly. 'Pack?' The Residency erased.

'Yeah. No room in his luggage. He brought me a portable gramophone he had, and some books. Light stuff, but in English at least; you need a copy of *Forever Amber* or *No Orchids for Miss Blandish*?'

'He is leaving, Wizzersbee?'

'Posted, Pangpang or some damn place, don't recall the name. Tomorrow's convoy.'

'That is sudden, I think?'

He handed her the drink and went across to his chair. 'Well, the Dutch control the dock area now, so I guess that's goodbye to the Dumps, don't you? And he doesn't have a job, and anyway without Ruby . . .' He cleared his throat and avoided her eyes. 'I gather he's redundant. He's due for repatriation in eight weeks anyway so they're shipping him south until he goes

197

and he says he'll just travel light, take his bed-roll and chess set, shipping off his personal effects from the Docks. Hadn't room for this stuff.'

Miss Foto struck a match and lit a joss stick in a little holder on the table beside her. 'What are personal effects?'

'Oh shit, I don't know, stuff he's collected on his travels; clothing, stuff he won't need right now, you know.'

'There is a boat from here to England? Surely not?'

'No, no, to Singapore. You remember Mo Hyman and that great guy Al Kalovski from Commodore Coffee? Well, they're taking it, they want out from here, like I said, too British, too damn slow, and what's going to happen with this Soekarno guy, you know, and the plantations are all to shit. They're going to try Manila, open up there, or Singapore, but that's *still* British too. I think they'll do better in the Philippines myself. I said so. More opportunity.'

'Oh no!' said Miss Foto wistfully. 'Don't say to me that funny Mr Kalovski is leaving too? And his tricks, you remember his tricks at your parties? So funny with the burning dollar bill, and then he found it, all intact, in the top of my stocking! You remember! How we laughed. And with the cards he was so good too, and now he leaves? We will miss him. When do they sail, I must say goodbye, I think that would be proper, no?'

'Tuesday morning, as I recall.'

'And on what ship?' said Miss Foto, sadly twisting her pearls.

'The *Prince Bernhardt*, I think,' said Novak.

CHAPTER EIGHT

A salvo of shells ripped into the centre of the city at eleven a.m. precisely. One hit the Opera House, tumbling a Doric column like a rolling pin, another smashed into the second floor of the YMCA building, wistfully called Lyons Corner House, on the north side of Rembrandt Plein, others thudded into the market and one whistled like a fast express just over Nettles' head, as he swung his jeep into the forecourt of the Planters Club, and exploded in a scatter of broken tiles and brick dust in a neighbouring empty villa.

He brushed the grit and shards from his cap and went into the cool, black and white chequered hall, in which two un-happy Indians in lopsided turbans huddled, clutching each other, under a table.

'It's all right, you can come out now. Went next door.'

In the bar room with its long counter and tired chairs, no one had taken any notice, and there was such a crush in the gloomy room that he found it difficult to thread his way towards the bar. Halfway across he felt a hand on his shoulder and turning, looked into a plump, shining face with a fat black moustache under a button nose.

'Nettles? I'm Holt, Don Holt, Military Police: we're over there, I ordered you a beer, hope that's all right? Or anything else?'

'No, no a beer is splendid,' said Nettles brightly, dismissing any idea he might have had of a Bloody Mary. 'Good of you to find me: the place is like a Cup Final suddenly.'

'Well,' said Major Holt, indicating a sagging chair by the beer-ringed table, 'I wasn't sure that you'd remember my face. We did meet, briefly, some time ago at the Docks during Mountbatten's trip. Anyway, here we are. That's your beer, might be a bit warm, I fear.'

'Sorry I'm late. Bit of a tizzy in the market.'

'They hit that? Bloody sods.'

'They got the YMCA too. Rather a mess.'

'This is the third day in a row; the natives are getting restless, what? Been good as gold for ages, why this sudden Hate, I wonder?'

'God knows. Nuisance raids. Your health.'

They drank, replaced their glasses. Nettles threaded his fingers into a cat's-cradle.

'I got your bumph,' said Holt wiping his lips, 'about the letter and all the rest of it. Good of you to let me know. Of course we have heard rumours, gossip, chitter chatter, that sort of stuff, but nothing really concrete. I mean, quite honestly, old man, what do you want me to do, I mean, what next? There *is* a war on, you know.'

'All I want you to do is take it off my shoulders. It really isn't my area. I got this letter personally, that's why I acted on it, started rummaging about, you might say, and came up with a few clues. I agree nothing much, but I thought it was something for your chaps to deal with rather than me. Puts me in a frightful spot, I mean, you do see that? I do know there's a war on: actually.'

Holt rolled his glass thoughtfully in a puddle of beer. 'It's the Old Man who worries you, I presume?'

'First and foremost. I mean, if there is any truth at all in all these rather hysterical accusations just think what'll happen to him. He's quite unsuspecting of it all as far as I know, but he's in pretty deep. She's at the house quite often, he's commandeered a car for her, furniture, a house, she has the run of his bloody Palace place, he takes her advice, I swear to that; she has access to all the personal papers in his office. I mean, that's a bit steep, don't you think? And you remember the shindy there was when Mountbatten was here and she swanned about at the party like the Queen Mother. Caused terrific offence among the Dutch. They simply can't understand it. There must be some pretty good reason why.'

Holt drained his glass. 'You're suggesting that she's a War Criminal, I take it, from your papers here.' He patted a small leather case on the floor at his side.

'No. I'm not suggesting it, Major Holt, but it is a possibility. If she did give away four wretched Australians and they were beheaded because of that action, doesn't that put her in a slightly uncomfortable position?'

'Decidedly so. But where is the proof? The one person who you say told you all this, we used to call her Red Light Ruby, strung herself up. We knew all about her, a pretty harmless

200

tart, dim-witted; masses of them about, MI6 is stiff with them. She may have opened her legs obligingly to every Tom, Dick or Harry from Tokyo to Sydney but that doesn't make her guilty of anything more than excessive carnality, does it? Or a passionate devotion to duty. And now she's gone.' He spun his lighter ineffectually. 'Flint's gone too. You got a light by any chance?'

Nettles placed a lighter on the table and fumbled for his cigarette case.

'Of course,' said Holt, lighting a small cheroot, 'there's this boy you mention, the main witness, so to speak.'

Nettles carefully tapped a cigarette on his thumbnail. 'He's gone too.'

Holt looked surprised for the first time. 'Gone?'

'He worked at a barbers' near the market. Hasn't been seen for over a week.'

He had been checking through his Weekly Intelligence Report when Corporal Batt brought in the morning mug of tea and a pile of routine Signals.

'The General's servant is here, Sir. Wants to see you. Says it's personal.'

'Where? Here?'

'In the hall, Sir. Won't come up. Shall I say inconvenient, Sir?'

In the immensity of the hall below, Nanni Singh looked like an exclamation mark, stiff to attention, arms by his sides.

'I would be pleased to speak to you, Nettles Sahib.'

'Fine. What is it? What can I do?'

'There is perhaps somewhere...?' Nanni Singh looked anxiously about the wide hall.

'Private talk, that it?' Nettles pushed open a door marked 'NCOs Only'. Some shabby chairs, a ping-pong table, empty bookshelves, a camp bed in one corner, a dartboard, a cardboard lid stacked with dirty cups. 'Now what? Take your time.'

'The boy has gone away. My boy.'

'How do you know?'

'For three days he has not been to the Residency. Always he came to see me after the lunch-time. Always on the Sunday also, to help me with my labour.'

'But he was forbidden.'

'Nevertheless he came. She is not in the kitchens, the woman.

201

That I can prevent. But always he came, on his bicycle. He is good, honourable boy.'

'I am sure of that, Singh. Perhaps he is unwell.'

'Not unwell. Is gone. I ask at the place he works. He was well, but was sad, very sad for his friend who is dead. After that he does not come.'

'But where can he go to? Have you an idea of this?'

Nanni Singh shrugged slightly, stacked a dirty cup into another. 'To the south, I think perhaps. That is where; across the railway.'

'That is difficult to do.'

'Not for the boy. It is possible.' He turned and faced Nettles squarely, arms to his side again. 'You did this, Sahib. You ask him those questions; because of this his friend is killing herself and for this he weeps; this is a cruel thing which you do.'

'I venture to remind you, Nanni Singh, that the boot is on the other foot. *You* have done a foolish and irresponsible thing. If you had not written your tiresome letter none of this would have happened at all. None. I would also remind you of what I said the last time we met. He who diggeth a pit shall fall into it. It would seem to me that this is something which you have overlooked. I am sad that your friend has left but there is nothing that I can do.'

Nanni Singh smoothed his cap between long brown fingers. His eyes on a point far beyond his shining boots. 'Unless, Sahib, my boy is dead also? Like his friend is dead. If you know this, Sahib, through my wilfulness that I have caused this to happen, please you will tell me?' He looked up slowly into Nettles' face. 'It is a small matter, Sahib, but if you find it to be true, if they find him to be dead, you will say to me?'

'It will not happen. But I will say.'

As if satisfied, Nanni Singh crossed slowly to the door, put on his cap, snapped a salute. 'I shall go softly all my years in the bitterness of my soul,' he had said.

Holt signalled through the crowd to Pram at the bar. 'Probably pissed off, if you ask me. Gone to the south, lots of lovely free guns and ammunition with the rebels. Doesn't want to get involved; probably knows he said too much now the girl's dead, can't trust anyone in this city at present, he knows that, everyone is whispering about everyone else, not actually

202

declaring, you understand, that would be too damn easy, just whispers and suggestions. They're all at it. Makes our life hellish tricky deciding what is just spite and what is hard fact.'

The beers arrived spilling foam. Miserably Nettles started to pour his; Holt, catching his look swiftly, misunderstood and offered a confidential apology.

'Oh look here, old chap, no offence meant. I mean, I am sure you are right about your wretched letter, know the source of course, and no smoke without a fire and so on. No, no, we'll have a crack at this of course. It's just that people are getting pretty irritating at the moment, and remember, we're still coping with the bloody Nips. Of course some tips we get are absolutely spot on. One yesterday. Chap you might know, Weathersby?'

Nettles looked up in startled surprise, his glass halfway to his lips. 'Weathersby? Worked at the Dumps?'

'Exactly. At the Dumps. With Ruby whatsername. The dead girl. Yes, same fellow. Off to Pangpang on the convoy, left as a matter of fact; we got a tip, like you, a letter. To the point. "Have a look at his Personal Effects sailing out on the *Bernhardt*: shipping them home. Something of interest may be found." Well, I ask you!' Holt spread an expansive arm across the cluttered table. 'A British officer? Inspect his luggage? I mean, after all, what's the world coming to? Christ! Then I thought, well, he worked with this Ruby, lived with her more or less we gather, suicide and all that.' He took a long pull at his beer. 'Long and short of it is we had a look at his trunk. Rotten thing to do, absolutely rotten. Hauled it off: guess what?'

Nettles trod his cigarette under his foot. 'I am beyond imagining; the Island's supply of senna pods?'

'Gold,' said Holt with satisfaction. 'Three bloody great blocks of it, bigger than bricks. Crushed gold. Coins, ring settings, false teeth, eye glasses, cigarette cases, you never saw such a collection. All crushed together in these compressed blocks, neatly sown into sacking covers. We thought the trunk was bloody heavy: but Christ! All part of the stuff the Japs took from the pawnshops when they arrived. And Mr Weathersby had three lovely chunks all addressed to his Mum in North Finchley.'

'And where is Master Weathersby?'

'Well, he can't get far, can he? Got our tabs on him, he knows that. Had the bloody gall to say that it was loot. *His* loot! Spoils of war, booty. Quoted the ruddy *Oxford Dictionary* at us.'

'He'd do that all right.'

'But can't quote the War Book, y'see? Fact is, whose is it? The Dutch Government's? The Chinese pawnbrokers'? Individual owners' whom we'll probably never trace, or whose? It's a bit of a pickle. But you just see: these tip-offs *can* be useful, I mean like yours.'

'It was anonymous too, I suppose?'

'Oh strictly. Neatly typed in block capitals on a piece of graph-paper. No date, no signature, no errors, nothing. Even spelled his name right. And his number. Someone who knew him. What can you do?'

'Abnormal times,' said Nettles quietly.

'Absolutely. It's all very, very nasty, old chap. Now, look here: this business of yours, ours, I suppose. I'll keep an eye on things, get the boys out so to speak, but I don't really see what we can do at this minute. Both your witnesses, we might say, are out of the way.'

'I gather a hell of a lot of people witnessed the executions.'

'I bet they did. They held them at the race-course once a week, like a ruddy sort of circus act. God knows how many Chinks they dealt with, Malays, Eurasians, blackmarket fellers.'

'And four Australians,' said Nettles patiently.

Holt thumped his fist suddenly on the table and clanked the bottles. 'We can't be absolutely positive of that. Yet. No one knows how many Australians or British or anything else were here, a lot of chaps deserted, it was all a state of flux after bloody Singapore. They may have got away, lost in the jungle, died of fever, anything.'

'If the boy I speak of saw it, and described it very clearly, there must be a great many others who saw it and remember it as well.'

Holt sat back in his chair, his small moustache bristling with irritation, the cheroot dead in stubby fingers. 'What are we to do, put up posters? Question the whole bloody city? Shove an announcement in the ruddy *Daily Cobra*? What *do* you suggest then?'

'Open up the graves behind the race-course.'

204

'But there must be hundreds of bloody skeletons, they were mass graves, and after three years or so in this climate, what do you expect to find, for God's sake?'

'Four headless ones,' said Nettles reasonably.

She heard him whistling cheerfully far along the stone corridor. Loud and as piercing as a one-cent flute, high above the scrape and slither of studded army boots and the constant flip-flop of the Chinese clerks in their rubber sandals. It was a sound for which she waited instinctively every morning in life at HQ and which, once it came, steadied her restless heart. Especially on this morning with the shelling, which had rattled the windows and, with one near miss, brought down a large piece of the dusty plaster cornice, causing Pearl in the next cubicle to shriek with terror and cringe under her desk, uttering little idiot cries like a distressed hen.

She didn't look up as he swung into the room and slammed to a stop with a crack of boots and a smart salute when he reached her desk.

'Good morning. Captain Rooke reporting, all well and are you?'

Then she looked up from her typewriter slowly, pleasure and relief well-contained. 'Quite all right, thank you. Busy. Heard the bangs. Nothing very near, some plaster, the windows shook, Pearl in there had hysterics.'

'But you just went on with your duties. Which are what?'

She read from the top of her page. 'Exciting match. Div. HQ scores over 3rd Indian Field Ambulance.'

'No wonder you carried on: it's enthralling.'

'And now I'm trying to write the report from someone called CQMH Dalip Singh who has written it all in pencil, I imagine on his knees, in the dark. I dare not make a mistake, so I didn't hide under my desk, you see.'

'That's a brave girl. They hit the YMCA, did you know? Char-time, quite a few casualties, anybody gone down to get the facts?'

'Corporal Batt went off with his notebook an hour ago.'

'My God. Our efficiency staggers me.' He sat on the bent wood chair, put his cap on her desk. 'Do the shelling for tomorrow's paper. "Terror Shelling of City Centre". If anyone comes up with a snapshot of it before we go to press we'll use that, if it's clear, otherwise suggest to Bainbridge that we use No. 2A Betty Grable, and give her two columns, full length. What about the daily poem?'

Emmie was writing down her instructions. 'There's something sent in from someone in one of the Field Regiments, it's there, in the correspondence tray.'

He reached in and sorted through the letters. 'I yearn, I yearn, to see; the nodding daffodils, so free.' He replaced it gently. 'Try my *Oxford Book of Modern Verse*. Use a bit of Yeats or something, no hope, I suppose, of this evening?'

Emmie shook her head slowly. 'I'm sorry. Really no. I have Wim: I can't leave him alone.'

'How long is he staying?'

'Until Clair is back to normal routine. She tries to spend a lot of time with Pieter, it's difficult for her with the boy. Only a day or two. She came in this morning; looking really well, much more like Clair, you know? And she asked me to ask you that when you see Pullen today would you tell him that she would like to see him this evening about seven, if he can? It's not urgent, just if he can. Will you?'

'Of course. Thank God she's pulling out of it.'

'She'll be all right, you'll see. She is a strong woman. Stronger than me.'

'He's been very tactful, keeping away. Not easy, I imagine.'

Emmie stuck the point of her pencil deep into her note pad where it broke. 'None of it is easy. It was a very dreadful day. Pullen is most correct. It was the right thing to do.'

She looked up suddenly as Gaunt arrived at the wire-grille door, back-lit in a halo of sunlight, and rattled his cane down the mesh. Rooke opened the door.

'Welcome to our little Press Nest.'

'Not intruding, I trust?'

'Not in the least. Have the chair; you haven't got a tiny poem up your sleeve, have you?'

Gaunt looked at him coolly without comprehension.

'Or perhaps a sonnet, even a rhyming couplet would do.'

'Don't quite follow, old chap. Poetry's not my line.'

'We need a little bit of culture for tomorrow's edition.'

206

'Can't help you there. No culture. I'm a soldier. Know a few riddles, those do?'

Rooke sighed heavily and sat on the edge of the desk. 'Far too many riddles in this sheet as it is, thanks all the same. Too many riddles in the whole damn City, and not enough answers.'

Gaunt settled himself in the chair. 'Haven't got a poem I'm sad to say, but I have got a little bit of info you might be good enough to pop into your penny-dreadful, if you can?'

'What is it?'

'Well, an idea I have, think I told you about it long ago, a sort of gymkhana thing? Everyone is bashing about at badminton, tennis and all that hockey going on everywhere, but some chaps might quite like a ride. I have it in mind to start up the old race-course again, out at Rozendaal. A bar, some beer, you know, got the mounts, horses, well,' he ruefully smiled at Emmie across her machine, 'ponies really, but they go damn well. Thought if you put it all down in your penny-dreadful, in your own words of course—I'm no good at the writing business —and there was a terrific burst of excitement, I'd get onto the Old Man. He's all for normalizing-the-situation, isn't he?'

He stopped suddenly and looked out through the grille at Pearl next door who stared back at him in silent awe. He waved fingers at her, she uttered a little cry of delight and hid her face in her hands. 'Just like damned monkeys, aren't they? Sitting in a cage. Bring her some peanuts next time I come. Well?' He placed his hands on his knees and looked at them both with cool grey eyes.

'Well,' said Rooke thoughtfully, 'snag is that now the shelling seems to have started up again, not sure that a race-meeting will go down all that well with the Old Man just at present. He's a bit fidgety already. You know they got the YMCA this morning?'

'Been down there,' said Gaunt. 'Foul mess, right through the window, but the race-course is well out of range, I imagine, otherwise the Old Man would be in trouble. So would you, come to that, on your hill. Anyway it's all a risk here wherever you go, and whatever you do; we wouldn't do anything about it all until we clear the south of course. Just put out feelers, that's all, get a reaction. Think you could?'

'Sure. Stick something in for you tomorrow, I'll work something out.'

'And put it in the Indian Section, will you? Not just for the British chaps.'

'No. Do both.'

Gaunt rose, waved fingers at Pearl, rattled the grille with his cane. 'Bring you some bananas next time I come.'

Pearl pulled her hair over her face, and turned away with a muffled cry.

'Bloody odd lot,' said Gaunt. 'No sense of humour.' At the door he paused to adjust his lanyard and belt. 'The Old Man's upstairs, I take it? Saw his Packard in the car park. Whose is the pea-green Buick?'

'Mine,' said Rooke shortly.

Gaunt stared at him. 'Very nice. Drop-head '38, I think. You're doing well, going it a bit, isn't it, commandeering civvy cars? Roberts only had a jeep, ah well, we live and earn.'

'Saves wear and tear on Military Transport, releases them for other duties. Sensible to me.'

'So it should be. Lucky fellow. Next thing we'll have is Nettles swanning about in a crystal coach drawn by four white rats.' He gave them both a mock salute, and strode off down the corridor.

'He's very sarcastic, isn't he?' said Emmie. 'And rude, Pearl's had too many frights in one morning. A very rude man, Pearl!' she called in English through the wire.

'Very pretty man,' said Pearl brightly.

Rooke laughed softly. 'Women! Honestly, you are the most unpredictable creatures!'

'Pearl simply doesn't understand European manners. The Chinese are very polite, it would be beyond her comprehension that a man could be so rude to her.'

'Beyond her sense of humour, that's all.'

Emmie had started to read through the pencil-copy of the Exciting Match. 'She hasn't had very much experience in a British Officers' Mess.'

Rooke, stung with anger at Gaunt's remark about his pea-green Buick, was busy looping elastic bands round stretched fingers. 'More experience of the Tarts' Parlour in Molendijk, I presume.'

208

'I don't know what you mean.'

'Oh don't be so damned prissy!' A band snapped and stung him.

'And prissy is what?' she looked anxiously through the grille at Pearl who was dutifully addressing labels for *The Daily Cobra*.

Rooke selected another band and strung it round his hand. 'She was the Oshima girl's best friend, wasn't she?'

'Yes. I think so.'

'And didn't they both work for Miss Foto?'

'Before the camp. I didn't know them then.'

'Wasn't there a little salon in the camp, too?'

'I do not know. Anyway they were not in the camp. They are non-Europeans.'

'But there was one?'

Emmie slid the Hockey Match into the pending file. 'I don't know! I don't know! If there was, what does it matter? It is all in the past, we try to forget all that time now, if it happened, it happened, and no one was hurt.'

Rooke slipped the bands off his fingers and dropped them singly into the pen-tray. 'Some were.'

She pulled the lid over her typewriter, closed her dictation pad. 'I think I will go out.'

In the long corridor they walked side by side in silence to the vaulted landing and down the giant staircase to the hall below.

'I cannot work when you speak like this.'

Rooke's anger had gone as quickly as it had come. He took her arm gently. 'I'm sorry. Gaunt. It's my fault.'

'We mustn't speak like that before Pearl. Who was hurt?'

They had reached the wide floor, crossed to the high arched doors.

'Four Australians, I believe.'

She pushed through them and down the steps into the fore-court: the sun hit her like a furnace.

'Where are you going?'

She looked vaguely about her, shading her eyes. 'Just out. In the air.'

The pea-green Buick was parked in the shade under a spreading flame tree; she followed him across to it and sat beside him in the front, hands between her knees. For a little they stared across the car park in silence; trucks roared in, bicycles wobbled

209

past on the unraked gravel, someone ran anxiously up the steps with a roll of maps.

He put his hand on her knee lightly, pressed it. 'I'm truly sorry. I didn't mean to distress you: I love you far too much.'

'It distresses anyone to be forced back to that time. We try to forget it in the day, because it always comes back in the night; it was not a good time, terrible things were done, Rooke, terrible mistakes were made, it was not a normal time. I do not think you know what it was like here and at Molendijk.'

'I saw Bergen Belsen. I have a fair idea.'

She looked at him with a faint hint of amusement. 'Oh, Rooke. You said you went there for *two* days, to look, not for years, to die. Does that give you a fair idea of anything?'

'I apologize. I accept that. But I did see. There were terrible things, and people were punished for those things.'

'The Japanese have been taken away and punished for Molendijk.'

'But there are still others.'

'If you mean that vain and vulgar woman, what was so terrible?'

'Running a brothel in the camp . . .'

She cut him short with an impatient hand. 'There was no brothel. That is nonsense. I don't know; there was "an arrangement", people say, but I didn't hold a candle there.'

'You'd hardly call that a normal affair, would you?'

'Normal! What is normal in a war? Keeping two thousand women with small children herded into a camp, starving, frightened, alone for years, is that normal?'

Rooke took out a tin of cigarettes from the glove pocket. 'No, of course not.'

'People are not all saintly, you know, just as the Japanese were not all wicked, or ugly. Hunger and isolation do strange things: when you see your child swelling up with hunger what do you do? Half a cup of rice, maybe a bit of fish. If you can obtain a little more by using the only means you have, is this so terrible, Rooke? Do you preach to me sitting here in your pretty car smoking your cigarette?'

'It's not preaching. Asking.'

'And what right have you to ask? What does it concern you if some women have done this thing for a little more rice, some

210

medicine' — she ran her hand roughly through her hair — 'even *one* banana.'

Rooke hunched forward unhappily. 'Oh shit, Gaunt was unforgivable. I'm sorry.'

She interrupted briskly. 'Oh, there was the other side too, of course there was. This was not a city of shining angels, Rooke, it is a Port City, all kinds were here. We were not all perfect little ladies, you know. A woman has her needs and her instincts just like a man, perhaps you still do not realize this? But it is so, some of the officers were attractive; can you believe that? They were correct, polite, discreet. In a camp there is only one main idea. To survive. And if some could only survive by this method of nature, must they be blamed for not behaving like Nuns? I think that you ask too much. I think that it is you who are "prissy".'

'This vain and vulgar woman, as you call her, is supposed to be responsible for the deaths of four Allied soldiers.'

'I do not know of this. Nothing.'

'That was betrayal, that was criminal.'

'And so?'

'And so? Where does that place the General if it is proved to be true?'

Emmie ran her finger round the dust in the dial of the speedometer, wiped her finger on her skirt. 'And what does that matter? About your foolish General? That is his fault that he chooses such a person, do you think that *that* is normal? Why do you care? If he has made a stupid mistake he will pay, so is that important?'

'Yes.'

She lay back wearily in the scuffed white leather seat, closed her eyes in the fretwork shade. 'All armies are the same, it seems to me. You come and you go, you invade, you liberate, you plunder, you give orders, you take the whores for your beds, you make your own rules and we must bend and bow to you. If your General is sent away another will come until all of you go, and then the Dutch will come back, and there will be more revenge and more rules and more fighting until the Indonesians come. And so it goes on for ever and ever.'

In a scatter of gravel and a plume of dust a jeep raced across the car park and swung to an abrupt stop at the steps. Nettles got out, said something to Willie in the passenger seat, and mounted the steps with the dignity of a crane.

'It is he who makes you ask all these questions, I think. Nettles?' Emmie smiled softly. 'The El Greco angel. Do you really think that he cares what happens to that stupid General?'

'Yes. I really think he does. He's thinking of the disgrace.'

'He's thinking of you,' she folded her arms across her chest and looked up into the spreading branches.

'Sometimes you really do go off your head, you know.'

'It's true. He's in love with you.'

'Read all this in your tarot cards?'

'All this I read in his eyes. Like a sad old dog, you know?'

'You're off your pretty head.'

'No, I watch. I am a woman, it is not so difficult to see.'

'And what has the General's disgrace got to do with all that?'

'Nettles just wants you to be close to him, to run little errands for him, to report what you learn from me, from Clair, anyone, about this "scandal", so that he has an excuse to be with you, to see you, to, well, love you from a distance. He has arranged all for you, isn't it? The ADC, the newspaper . . .' She stretched her arms high above her head, turned to him smiling. 'And even me, you remember? You are obliged to him.'

'It is a debtless obligation.'

'There was a price?'

'A very minor one. Shock you?'

She folded her arms in her lap, shook her head slowly. 'Oh no. You are so beautiful how could I blame him? Or you. There is always a price to pay for survival, you see? Like the women in Molendijk. You can understand a little?'

'In a rather squalid way.'

'All war is squalid and what we do in war. To pay your debt is right, even if you say you have no debt: but it is not right to ask these questions all the time. You are turning over stones, Rooke, and you must say to Nettles that you will not do it any more, because under the stones are many ugly things and they do not concern you.'

Rooke jammed his cigarette into the ash-tray, wiped his fingers. 'They do, however, concern my General.'

'That is not your fault.'

'I am his ADC. I respect him. I do not want him disgraced.'

212

'If he chooses to share his bed with this woman, what can you do?'

'Warn him when we know the truth, or get rid of her.'

Emmie looked at him for a long moment in silence, then opened the door of the car and stepped out, closing it firmly behind her, leaning over it on folded arms. 'You will never know the truth, Rooke, no one will ever tell you, no one will ever say for sure. No one will admit; and what happened in the camp does not make her a criminal.'

'What happened to the Australians could.'

She started to walk away slowly towards the building; he followed her. As they passed the General's Packard she ran a finger along its gleaming length. 'He is a foolish man, very foolish.'

'Sad, unhappy, perhaps a foolish man, but not a foolish soldier.'

'There is a difference?'

'To my own surprise, yes.'

They went up the long flight of steps slowly, and into the cool of the enormous galleried hall filled now with hurrying people going to lunch. 'I'm so late,' she said. 'The Hockey Match, I must do it before two o'clock. You come with all these senseless questions.'

'Oh, leave the bloody thing until tomorrow; no rush.'

'No, I will do it. You will remember to speak to Pullen? About Clair?'

'Yes.'

They reached the foot of the main staircase and she stopped, one hand on the rail. 'About these Australians: if it is so, I don't know. When I went to the camp later, an English woman told me a story. Mrs Bethell-Wood, but she was quite old, and now she is dead. So you cannot ask her.' She smiled at him slightly and started up, passing Nettles on his way down who gave her a polite, 'Good morning' and joined Rooke on the black and white floor.

'Christ, what a morning! Shells falling like confetti, warm beer with the most porcine member of the Military Police, a fit of the vapours from the Old Man because I do not know the precise number of terrorists who may possess sub-machine guns, and Nanni Singh's boy wonder has hopped it across the railway line.

213

What about that for a tale of woe? What had Emmie got to say? Saw you huddled in your limousine.'

'She had nothing to say except stop asking questions.'

'Were you heavy-handed, Rooke, dear boy?'

'I didn't think so.'

'Anyway the heat is off as far as we are concerned. *I* am concerned, perhaps I must say. Handed it all over to the M.P.s. I really was starting to feel like something out of Dorothy L. Sayers. Too tiring. Not my role.'

They reached the car park, revving with engines and crunching wheels.

'I thought Nanni Singh was a bit glummer than usual. When did the boy go?'

'A week ago. The suicide upset his tender little heart. So he's probably joined the Other Side and sworn allegiance to Freedom and the Revolution. Nothing like a bit of over-emotion to ignite your ideals.' He slipped into his seat, switched on the ignition, leant out smiling. 'By the way. Extraordinary thing. Weathersby of the Dumps, you recall? Just heard he's been found shipping half the Island's gold to his Mum in North Finchley; another anonymous little letter, acted upon. It really does get murky, doesn't it? I wonder if The Dubarry could type as well?' With a cheerful wave he drove swiftly away just as the General arrived at the top of the steps with a varied collection of weary officers including 'Bunny' Blackett looking fretful.

'Three extra for lunch,' said the General in a loud voice. 'Go ahead and warn Nanni Singh, will you, and take these with you.' He threw down a roll of maps and his briefcase. 'Tell him we need a good stiff drink before, and get that all sorted out.

'What a bloody awful morning!' he said to no one in particular.

Clair closed the lid of the butterscotch tin: smoothed a hand across the scratched blue and gold lettering on the lid, placed it carefully back on the table. Time past. Time lost. Not time forgotten. Mrs Bethell-Wood's final, humble gesture of apology, filled now with needles, thimbles and buttons, stood there as a symbol to remind her for the rest of her life of what now seemed, in retrospect, a hideous three-year ride on a run-amok

214

carousel. The blurring faces, wheeling colours, clashing cymbals of pain, grief, uncertainty, and terror, the juddering ups and the staggering downs, the swirling vertigo, cries and shouts: all these had now come racketting, lurching and staggering to a slow stop, in a screech of metal upon metal, and whisper of weary steam. The ride had ended. On the beach.

Now, in the still of the evening, the deepening blackness silent but for distant frogs and the low chatter and complaint of night birds in the trees about the verandah, she moved to a chair as a sleepwalker, the ground uneasy beneath her feet, arms outstretched to seek support, her body light, disconnected as if her very joints were linked together with hooks and rings. The chair gave her some sense of stability, she lay back looking up into the dark roof, gripping the cane arms lest they too might crumble beneath the weight of her uncertainty.

'So you would count it as a success, a perfect trip?' He had danced so easily that all she had to do was follow, and this she found exceptionally pleasant.

'Perfect. The best three months ever. I never knew it could be so beautiful. This is, after all, a sort of Paradise, isn't it?'

He was extremely tall and very blond, and even in the sullen heat there was not the least sign of moisture on his brow, or in the hands which held her. A cool man. In all senses.

'It depends very much on how you see it.' The eyes were brilliantly blue, rather grave at this moment. Four years older than I?

'I see it very clearly.' As indeed I see you, the white uniform, gold braid and buttons. I am dazzled: of course. Twenty-three perhaps—even -five?

'I gather that you are from The Hague?' It is extraordinary that he can steer me through this crowd so effortlessly without once taking his eyes from mine.

'Yes. But we have a house near Zutphen in the east: do you know that?'

'Well. And Apeldoorn, I have family there. The Doornes, do you know them?'

'No. But I know the Apels well.' Polished trivia. I am *so* sophisticated.

215

'And you have to go back so soon?' His hold firmer. Do I imagine this?

'Alas! It all comes to an end.' Like the music now.

'Would you like them to play it again?' They swung to a gentle stop, applauded, he spoke briefly to the band leader who smiled and rapped his music-stand, they went into each other's arms once more.

'Think of Zutphen now! Ice, snow . . .' And still the eyes were grave.

'We could skate on the Ijssel you know. So thick. But I prefer this very much more.'

'Then don't go back. Stay.' His hand hard.

'Stay? Impossible. In one simple question, Lieutenant Doorne: how could I explain, what would I do here?'

'That is two questions.'

'Very well. First. How could I explain?'

'That you love the Navy.'

'All of it. The fleet?'

'Just me.'

'And what would I do here? Second question.'

'The third if I may correct you? You'd marry me.'

'Am I asked?'

'Yes.'

'It doesn't happen like this.'

'It has.'

'Are you sure? I thought it was just me.'

'No. Very often it is quite instant.'

'When was the instant?'

'Four nights ago on the terrace here, your aunt was describing the recent delights of Bali. In particular the Bat Cave Temple at Goa Lawa.'

'She said they were vampire bats, and I laughed. But I think she was right.'

'It was then.'

'I know. It was then for me too.'

'So we might postpone the skating at Zutphen?'

'But one day perhaps, later on, we could?'

'One day. Later on,' he had said gravely.

The absurdity, the banality of it. But that's how it was then,
216

simple, young, uncomplicated, sure. Oh God, how sure! A shadowless dance of delight together, he and I, which never stopped until the music broke away raggedly ten years later at the shatteringly sudden presence of the neat little man in the tight grey uniform at the top of the ballroom stairs.

'Please.' The hissing sibilant. 'The General commands that you dance until the hour of midnight. There will be no National Anthem.' And when the music falteringly started once again it was the music of the carousel and there never was a later-on-at-Zutphen.

White, barred with filtered light, the clinging scent of antiseptic, wincing squeak of soft rubber soles on polished stone. Sister Pritchard starched and trim beside me.

'He's in a little room on his own. We felt that was more tactful. The other men who came in don't yet know where their wives are, you see? It would be upsetting for them and, Lordy knows, they've had enough to upset them for the time being. You are a lucky woman, Mrs Doorne, but I expect you know that, no need to tell you.'

'No. No need to tell me.'

'Can't allow you more than ten minutes, he tires quickly, they all do . . .'

'I understand.'

'And no distressing news, nothing sad, ummm? All light and jolly.'

'Of course.'

'You don't look an emotional type. Keep the tears for after, will you?'

'I have none left to shed, Sister.'

'Good. Just keep it light. He's along here.'

At a chipped white door she stopped, a finger to her lips, one arm lightly on mine. 'Ten minutes only. I'll knock. I know how you feel, I really do. Head up. That's it. Splendid. Good girl. Good luck.'

The headlights of Pullen's jeep raked through the black trees scattering the night birds. She got swiftly to her feet, hurried through the hall to meet him, instinctively pulling her hair back, altering the pace of her walk as he opened the paint-blistered door. For a moment they stood quite still, the door

217

swinging slowly shut with a mild click-clock. He raised a hand in a half-salute.

'It's all right, isn't it? Rooke gave me your message. He said about sevenish, it's all right?'

'It's all right. Yes. It's fine. Thank you for coming.' She took his cap, led him out to the verandah.

'I wasn't going to butt in, but Rooke said you'd asked me to come.'

'I did. Yes I do. I wanted to see you. Want to. I'm so bad with my tenses.'

'Please don't be . . .'

'What?'

'Don't be tense, not with me.'

She laughed suddenly, put out her hand. 'No. No, I'm not. *Tenses*. Grammar, I mean.'

'Oh thank God for that. For laughing.' He took her hand. 'It would have been quite awful.' He kissed her hand gently. 'When you said I was to come I thought I'd bring this along. It came yesterday. It's for Wim, he about?'

'At Emmie's for a day or so, a change for us both.'

'Good idea. Give it to him when he comes home.'

'What is it? You always come with gifts, like Santa Claus.'

'It nearly is.'

'Christmas! My goodness, of course. We call it St. Nicholas's Day . . .'

'It's a book. *Treasure Island*. He said he'd like it. Islands, treasure, pirates, all that stuff. You know. My sister sent it out. Taken weeks.'

'Nigel, sit down, I beg you. We behave like strangers.' She sat down herself, running a finger over the bright wrapping of the gift. 'Holly and mistletoe. I'd almost forgotten . . .'

'That's Muriel, my elder sister; loves Christmas, the stockings, all that.'

'We have shoes. Wooden clogs in the fireplace.'

'Are you all right?'

'I'm all right. Yes. Now I'm all right. It was bad.'

'I know.'

'No, my dear, you can't know. I hope that you never do. I was thinking just now that it was just as if I had been on a carousel for years and years, spinning out of control. My head

218

is light, my feet don't behave well, I have no limbs. Look!' She laughed gently and raised a drooping wrist. 'I need an enormous whisky, and you shall pour it immediately, is that a sensible idea?'

'Splendid idea, I need a "strengthener" myself by this time of day.'

'I feel so absurdly weak. I almost haven't the courage to walk. So silly.'

'A matter of feeling filleted; you know what I mean?'

She took the offered glass, shaking her head.

'Filleted, you know, no bones. Do it to fish.'

She laughed, nodded. 'Fish I am.'

'You all alone here now? Without Wim. Door unbolted? Is it wise?'

'No, no, Minnie, my old servant, came back with her daughters. Now they aren't afraid to work for us. They were threatened. Very terrible things would happen to them if they assisted the Colonials; to be a servant to Europeans was humiliating. But it was all she knew how to do, and she didn't think it was bondage; she was so brave when we were in the camp. Smuggled things through the wire, an egg, fruit sometimes, cloth for bandages, good kind people taking such terrible risks for love. There is no love left now. It is madness.'

'Like the shelling. Slam them anywhere, dotty. I hoped like hell you weren't near anything, I worry for you so . . .'

'Quite safe. One takes the risk. I was at the Juliana.'

'Of course.'

Cocktail party conversation, thought Pullen; wooden clogs, *Treasure Island*, kindly servants. Putting off the main issue. I long to hold her: instead he found his tobacco pouch and pipe and started the ritual of filling and pressing.

'How is he?' he said.

'He's stronger, much stronger. They are so good there.'

'Take a little time, I reckon.'

'They made him plant tobacco, and coca for the cocaine . . . sometimes rice; all over the Island he went. He is so thin, Nigel, so thin, a wisp of straw. This tall, golden man you could almost blow away with a breath. And he will not smile, you know? He has no teeth much, he said a rifle butt in the mouth twice for answering back. Which he would. Now he is so ashamed of no teeth. Men are so vain!'

'Of course we are! Goodness yes.'

'And almost no hair now, that makes him very distressed of course. But you saw all this, you told me.'

'I saw all that. He'll mend, promise you, it'll take time, but he'll mend.'

'I wanted you to come so that I could apologize.'

Pullen looked up with steady eyes, folded his pouch neatly, laid it on the table, rummaged for a match. 'What for?'

'The beach. The things I said.'

'No need to apologize, my dear, none at all. You made me very proud.'

'Thank you. I know that you love me and that gives me the courage I must have for what I will say to you. That very day, it was strange, Emmie asked me if there was a big difference between "in love" and "loving". I didn't tell you this. But I said that there was. A profound difference.'

'And so there is. I know.'

'But I thought that I loved you and was in love with Pieter, which was wrong. This you also know.' She leaned forward, put her glass on the table between them, her elbows on her knees, cupped her face in her hands and looked beyond him into the night.

'All the years I have pretended to myself that he was alive somewhere, that he would not die, that he would come back one day and it would all be as before. I spoke of him in the present tense to give myself courage, to have his support, to reassure Wim, to get us through the camp, to exist just. But I *pretended* I believed.' She picked up the brightly wrapped book and pressed it between her hands. 'And when you came that day, so long ago it seems, with your first wondrous gift, the refrigerator, remember? I told you that one day you would also give me the courage to face what I instinctively knew all the time, that deep in the very most secret pocket of my soul I had searched and found a tiny seed of treachery.'

'Oh God, Clair. Treachery is a terrible word, you don't mean that at all.'

'I do. It is to betray trust, isn't it? Every single day in that hospital I betray him.'

'You simply cannot say that. You cannot know.'

'I am a woman and I can say that because I do know. I

know when the heart is empty. All women do; my heart is as empty and as echoing as a cave.'

Pullen sat back in his chair, crossed his legs, bit firmly on the stem of his pipe, held onto every shred of reason he possessed. 'You feel like this now, my dear, I understand very well, it is perfectly normal, you know? You have struggled for so long alone in an abnormal terrifying life, and suddenly, as you said, the roundabout thing has stopped. Of course you feel as you do, you will for a while. But it'll come back, just as his strength will return, so will all the rest of it. It is bound to take time to adjust, for you both.'

She laid the book carefully on the table, patted it softly. 'And for Wim. For him it must seem as it always did; and will. I shall make sure of that, have no fear. My treachery will only be known to you and me. For Pieter I am filled with pity, with compassion, with tenderness and admiration. I brim with all these things, I love him as a child, as a wounded animal, as the helpless creature they have made him, and these things and the knowledge of your love will be the fabric of my strength. I shall be so strong, you will see. But what I am not strong about, just at this moment, is the terrible knowledge of the profundity of the gulf between "in love" and "loving". I cannot put a bridge over it, I cannot cross it, and now my guilt makes me wonder if I ever did? Did I ever reach that side? Did I only ever love, passionately, blindly, willingly, unaware, a silly girl? With nothing else to give? It all seemed to be such happiness; and perfect happiness, we know, even in memory, is not so common. But I know now that it was not so. In the camp there was very much time for thought, I am not the only woman who will suffer this, be sure of that; it is the great hidden wound which women suffer in a war, the withering of the heart.'

Pullen swung himself out of his chair across to the verandah rail, leaning hard against one of the wooden pillars, looking up into the darkness.

'As long as you secure Wim. You must do that.'

'I'll do that. I promise you.'

'I can still be a sort of uncle, can't I?'

She closed her eyes for an instant, opened them, reached for her glass. 'Of course. You must, please.'

'Then we'll just let it all peter out, fade away. The odd post-card, that sort of thing. You must tell me his birthday.'

'Yes.'

He had let his pipe go out, tapped the bowl gently on the rail, scattered the dead ashes, and with the blade of his pocket knife scraped carefully at the residue. 'I'm jolly glad you asked me to come; said all that. Don't feel quite so unsteady, if you follow me. Stronger because I know that you are strong, and that you'll go on fighting the way you always have. Trouble with a war, well, one of the many troubles with them, is that they are such damned emotional things, do you know what I mean? I'm a Regular, been a soldier all my life, always knew it was something to do with emotion, banners, bugles, splendid uniforms, King and country, death and glory, all the rest of it, knew that. Knew I might cop it one day, or get a bullet in the backside, lose a leg, couple of fingers, that sort of thing.' He changed his position, slid the pocket knife away, leaned over the rail, his back still towards her. 'Ordinary wounds. You know. Didn't expect the others. The ones you speak of, the, what was it, hidden ones? Worse than the others in a way. I do see that. I suppose I really thought, as so many of us do, that there was only a sort of surface emotion to it all. No idea it could go so deep. Hurt so much.' He turned and faced her. 'Just wanted you to know. So that you know I share it. All. Bit unfair with so much to worry you already, just another burden, but it might just help with that fabric you spoke about, in the days to come.'

'It will. Thank you. It does.'

He slipped his pipe into a breast pocket, crossed slowly to the table and took up his tobacco pouch, reached for the wrapped book. 'Might as well take this along with me, bring it back a bit nearer the date, don't you think? A real uncle.'

She was no longer looking at him, and did not speak as he finished the last of his drink, turning her head only a fraction as she heard him cross the wooden boards to the hall. He stopped in the doorway.

'Sure you're all right here? I mean alone.'

She shook her head. 'Not alone, three strong women.'

'Ah, of course. Minnie. Odd name.'

'Her real one is very complicated.'

'I love you very much.'
'I know.'
'Nothing will ever change that.'
'Yes.'
'You can't make a crab walk straight, can you?'

She heard the front door close gently and the pattering of anxious feet as Minnie hurried through the hall to bolt it securely against the night.

South of the railway line, in the labyrinthine cellars below the Convent of the Sacred Heart, lately Kempei-Tai HQ, the boy sat attentively watching a tall, thin girl, with burning eyes, a sallow skin, and the dexterity of a conjuror, assembling and disassembling with astonishing rapidity a Japanese machine gun, Mk 92, on the table before her. Above her head on the whitewashed wall a grainy photograph of Karl Marx, and her own body throwing puppet-shadows from the naked lamp hanging in the centre of the room.

'You can see it is very simple to do. Now you will try individually.' She balanced the gun lightly in her hand, waving it vaguely before the intent faces of 23rd Cadet Corps of the People's Democratic Communist Action Group, of which the boy now found himself a member, uniformed, in baggy blouse and trousers, a small red star sewn on his collar, and a burning resentment against the people whom he considered, with some validity, had tricked him into causing the death of his loved Yoko.

'You will try,' continued the sallow girl. 'And when you are proficient, Comrade Suka will come among us and you will try firing with live bullets at the target which you see behind you. Turn.'

Dutifully the six members of the Cadet Corps turned in a quiet shuffle.

At the opposite end of the room, before a high planked, sandbagged wall, hung a rough figure of a man, made from sacking, stuffed with sawdust: a round head, sausage arms, legs, chest and pelvis delineated by a piece of rope. In the centre of the head a red cross, one at the heart, one at the exact centre, one at approximately each knee. She pointed the 'bull's-eyes' out

223

with a thin cane. 'Head, heart and belly will kill. These two,' indicating the knees, 'will maim, but you can finish him off easily. It is hard to miss with this machine, and you must remember that every European you drop is one less to come against us and the liberation of our Island for the People's Democracy. In Java they have the Fascist hyena, Soekarno, who will amalgamate us with his so-called empire. Soekarno is no better than the Dutch and the British, all are Fascist, all are ready to destroy the Cause. At first the British came as police, but now they encourage the Dutch Army to return; soon the Island will be overrun again with Colonial rulers, and that is why your leaders decide to extend the struggle; we must resist, we must kill every Dutch soldier, we must destroy their morale by secret infiltration, we must make them unsafe, so that they will walk in fear; we must burn their houses, destroy their women and children, and drive them into the sea like rats. You are the chosen group, for all of you have come from the north and you have lived among them, you know their ways. You are young and brave and you will go across that evil boundary of the railway again and again to burn and kill and then to melt away like the morning mists above the fields; you will sow bad seed in the crop so that it will wither and fail and the harvest will rot. Already we have destroyed all the plantations which brought the Imperialists power and money but brought us only starvation and shame. The coffee, the tea, the sago, all is torn away; the rubber bleeds, untended, from the cuts of our knives; the dykes and walls of the paddy fields have all been breached; the land will not sustain the Fascist jackals any longer, it is scorched by the hatred of the exploited worker with his own toil-worn hands. And now we will destroy and scorch in the cities . . . and you will be the heroes of the Action Group. When they have been vanquished we shall prepare ourselves against the Soekarno fascists. Cry, Ho! To the People's Democratic Communist Action Group! Death to the supporters of Fascism! Life to the Liberating Workers!' She threw a thin arm into the air, clenched her fist, and on her hoarse cry of 'Ho!' the entire Cadet Corps involuntarily cried out, thrusting arms high, standing stiffly to attention. Not that any of them had taken in much, if any, of what she had said. It sounded angry and exciting, and the sooner Comrade Suka arrived with his box of

224

bullets the fun could really begin. Even the dimmest witted of the group realized that they had been given full permission to kill without punishment, and that was a heady enough feeling.

After an hour of assembly and disassembly, a number of bruised knuckles, cut fingers, and pinched thumbs, the six earnest students managed a creditable performance, and the final slamming of the magazine into the slender weapon in their eager, if fumbling, hands sent an undeniable thrill to their untrained killers' hearts.

Comrade Suka, watching attentively the final and individual assemblies, was well pleased and praised them warmly. He also praised his lady Comrade who threw back her long hair and glared proudly up at Marx on the wall behind her. He dumped the wooden box of ammunition on the table, clapped his hands above his head, commanded the Cadet Corps to remove the long benches on which they had been sitting, to the back of the room and line up behind the table, as he reverently removed the empty magazine and replaced it with a full one. Not exactly full, as he explained, six bullets per person for the first attempt. He warned them about recoil and heating, jamming and safety catches; they listened with impatient eyes as the Lady Comrade plugged her ears with tufts of cotton wool against the bangs and reverberations which would burst upon them in the confined area of the vaulted cellar. The first youth shot wild, the gun bucked about in his hands like a live snake: he shattered a plank, winged the foot of the dummy which swung, and jiggled on its rope, and handed his smoking weapon to the boy.

The magazine replenished, he stood, legs apart, body braced, and aimed with deliberate care at the still-swinging target. He trained his sights intently on the red cross which marked the head, and when it became almost motionless, lowered the sights to below the centre-cross at the point where the two sausage legs joined the bulging trunk. Took aim.

Comrade Suka exclaimed thinly, 'No! No! You are too low. Aim for the heart, the heart!'

The boy looked over the top of his gun. 'I am, Comrade. I am. Excuse me. That is where this man's heart lies.' He aimed again and fired. The dummy swung into a frantic dance of flying limbs, as a cloud of sawdust and shavings exploded into the air.

225

CHAPTER NINE

Shortly after take-off the scattered villas of the suburbs slipped away and the coastal plain started: flat as a games board, chequered in paddy-fields, criss-crossed with irrigation canals, veined with lanes and dyke roads, starred by the vermilion roofs of huddled houses in the kampongs, and here and there the darker green squares of bamboo, banana or sago plantations. Running through it all, as straight and shining as a steel ruler, the main highway from the City up to the foothills and Pangpang.

A deserted landscape below them. No movement in the fields, on the roads, no smoke drifting from the kampongs, no oxen or buffalo in the paddy, no paper kites soaring gaily into the morning air: everything still, silent, serene in the early sunlight. An abandoned land across which the shadow of their Dakota passed swiftly like a ghost crucifix.

The General looked about him comfortably: he saw nothing of what lay below since he suffered from vertigo and preferred not to look beyond his own confined area of the 'plane, its passengers, and the cargo piled down the centre aisle, supplies for 14 Brigade. The one good thing about flying, he thought to himself, is that you don't have to talk to anyone. Can't. The rattle and drone of the engines see to that. A pleasant insulation from conversation, and he'd felt he'd had quite enough of that during the last few days of briefings and meetings. So now I can turn off, pull my thoughts together: which might astonish a few of my retinue sitting strapped-in down the length of the fuselage. Like a lot of bayonet-dummies. How many of them think I *have* a thought in my head beyond Standing Orders . . . original thought, that is? Most of them don't think I have an idea in my bloody cranium. Well: not quite fair. The ones who are closest have, perhaps. Nettles over there: sitting beyond the cluttered aisle, head in the air, long legs crossed easily, arms folded over his knees, staring blankly into space. Apparently. A loyal bloke. Arty farty, but bright. A bit over-anxious, superior but damned sound. Couldn't do without him. Gives me a feeling of security, somehow. Comforting. Been together a long time of course.

Seen some mucky moments together, and he's never flinched for all he looks like a piss-elegant pansy. Which he is. Not my affair. Never put a foot wrong from the Chindwin to Ipoh. Ah. Well. Ipoh. Ipoh was a bit bloody tactless, confess that. Euphoria of Liberation or some damn thing, I suppose. After all, if a fellow prefers Hansel to Gretel it isn't my business as long as it doesn't get in the way of his duties, and it didn't; no, Nettles is a good chap, glad I've got him, he got me Rooke. He stared thoughtfully at a large cardboard crate stamped with a red cross on the floor at his feet. Wonder how he got hold of him? I can guess. No great harm done, I should imagine. Master Rooke is all there, you might say. He can take care of himself and takes care of me bloody well: if you forced me I'd say he was better even than old Timmy. Makes me feel comfortable, easy. I think he actually likes me. And he makes me laugh. My God! But *that's* a thing. Not bloody great belly laughs, like Timmy when he was pissed and danced about with someone's knickers on his head, but easy things. He knows who he is and that's the point. No shilly shally. Direct. Honest. Suppose it's all the Public School shit, breeds confidence with good manners. But no real action yet. That's where we'll see what he's made of. Test his mettle on the South crossing. Separates the weak from the strong, a few bursts of gunfire up the backside. No point in having a good Court Jester who craps in his pants and fucks up the map references at the first big bang. So we'll wait and see, but I do like him, and I think he likes me.

The plane suddenly shuddered in an eddy of turbulence; he risked a covert glance over his shoulder, glanced down for the first time at the deserted land uneasily. Some way ahead the foothills rose in ridged terraces; to the west the long dark immensity of the jungle, a glint of water, a scatter of small white clouds floating below, spotting the plain with drifting shadows. He looked swiftly back at the Red Cross box feeling instantly giddy. Never look down, Dora said, damn right. Funny feeling, quite queasy. He looked up at Rooke's head framed neatly in the oval window just up the aisle. Good-looking bloke, we'll just have to see how you manage on Operation South next week. Get it over before Christmas, get the Dutch up to Pangpang and let poor old Lulworth pull his Brigade out and get shot of things. Been there long enough taking the shit. Let the Dutch do their

227

bit, their ruddy Island, their affair. That's what the MP from
Huddersfield or Burnley said. Their affair. Normalize things.
Dora was perfectly right, get things moving again. Mind you,
my idea, not hers. My idea. She just gave me the push to make
up my mind that the risks are worth it. *Her* idea about Timmy's
party; 'Let's have a party,' she said, remember it well – 'a little
music, dancing, let the girls come, party dresses and so on.' It
worked, have to admit that, it worked a treat; and taking
Rozendaal, she was right there. You could see it in the way
things went during the Conference. Mountbatten was damned
impressed, we looked as if we meant business and we did. And
did business what's more. Women know these things count.
Odd, even Pegs knew that sort of thing was important, the
Outside Details, she used to call them. She knew. When to
push, when to pull back. Closed the bloody bedroom door but
opened the one to Promotion. Pushing me. Us, really. And
when she got what she wanted she just pissed off home. All right
by me. Fine. Good riddance. Wonder how she'll take my
letter? That'll be a sight I'd like to see, her face at the breakfast
table or wherever she gets her letters. 'Mother! Leo wants a
divorce.' I can see her old mother's face dribbling, bread
and milk. Of course she'll wonder why. Reasonable. But
I kept Dora out of it all, just said I would supply 'the
grounds', and she'll know what that means all right. Dirty
filthy thing! *Shuddering* as if she'd trodden in a dog turd. I
can see her now. He grinned, and as if discovered, looked
up quickly.

Nettles had taken a book from his briefcase, brown paper
cover, SHELLEY printed in red ink. Some kind of poetry it
seemed. Would be. He looked vaguely across the piled sacks of
rice, mail, and bundled copies of *The Daily Cobra*, jumbled
among the ammo boxes and Red Cross cartons, crossed his feet.
All those years of distance and dislike. Mutual dislike, corroding
like acid on a pickle fork. No affection, no laughter, no sex.
Groping some damned Calcutta whore when things got too
difficult, a kind of medical release; never touched each other
even at the dinner table; only time I think I ever laughed was in
the Mess with the others, wasn't really allowed at home. Like
smoking. 'Smoke on the verandah; it'll smell in the curtains, if
you must smoke, do it outside.' Do it outside! Cripes! That first
228

corking remark of our marriage. Corked me all right. Corked me tight. Until Dora.

He had leaned up on one elbow in the bed, parted the ruffled fringe on her warm forehead, kissed the tip of her nose. She had twisted away slightly, wiped her face with the back of her hand.

'Leo. Behave. Don't. I'm so hot.'

'You were hot. Juicily hot.'

'You are a coarse man. That moustache tickles.'

'And you love it.'

'No. No, I don't. So rough. See? My breasts: I will have a rash finally.'

'Best pair of tits in the world.'

He bent his head and kissed them. She slapped his head gently.

'I hate this word you use. Now I will have to wear a high dress you see.'

'For your Mr Novak?'

Her eyes narrowed, she put a plump hand on her forehead. 'You speak very familiar to me you know? Why this *my* Mister Novak? You are jealous of him?'

'Jealous of everyone.'

'He is harmless. He is amusing for me. We dance, we play mah-jong, I like his parties, you do not. So . . .'

'I like you. To myself. He's a ruddy carpet-bagger, after all the loot he can grab, but he's not going to get you.'

'You talk very silly. He is here to trade. A strong country is a country which has a strong trade. He said so.'

'I can ruddy well hear him. What else does he say; while you're playing mah-jong?'

She folded her arms behind her head, aware that the gesture would tighten her breasts. 'He thinks that if the British open the south, industry can start again and make the Island very strong; everyone will come back to invest here.'

'Every ruddy American he means, out for grabs the lot of them, take over the damned place, run the Dutch out. Greed, that's all, greed. They'll boot us out of India and Malaya and take Asia. You see. Busy taking over the Philippines at this minute—and Japan.'

'You are boring me; you are the most greedy man I know.'

'For you I am.' He stroked her body tenderly. 'I love you very much, Dora.'

She pulled his head down to her breast to stop him talking, ran her fingers carelessly through his short hair.

'Then you must not be so ugly with me,' she said indifferently.

'I can't bear to share you, you know. I want you to myself.'

'But Leo! How is that possible? I am a free woman, I must have a little pleasure now, it was not so much joy in the camp, you know.'

He hugged her closely and when he spoke his voice was blurred by her breasts. 'I know, my dear, I know, but I don't want you to be that sort of free. I want you to be mine always.'

'Now that is selfish; also it is not possible.'

'If you would marry me . . .'

Her hand which had been idly smoothing round his hair and had slipped down to his cheek suddenly froze.

'Marry you?'

'Yes.'

In the intensity of the silence he could hear her heartbeats under his right cheek.

'You are making me a proposal, Leo?'

'Yes.'

'When you are already married?'

'I will get a divorce. She left three years ago, it's ended. Ended the day we married. My life began with you, Dora. I would look at you and say all this but I can't.'

'Why?'

'Shy. Sorry . . .'

She suddenly reached down with her free arm and dragged the sheet high up her body covering herself almost entirely. He sat up and turned away.

'Funny thing to say, Dora, but I mean it.'

She sat up slowly in the bed, holding the sheet tightly across her body with one arm, an almost prudish gesture of respectability. 'You can look at me now, not be shy, I am quite decent. If you like.'

He kept his back to her, hands clasped between his knees, head bowed. She saw a fine dust of freckles which she had not noticed before, caping his shoulders.

230

'There's a bit more. I love you. I want you. You are the light of my life and if you left me I don't honestly know what I'd do. I know I'm not young any more, not much of a catch, apart from the rank business, but I'd do everything in my power to make you happy for the rest of our lives. I don't want to force you, not a bully really, give you time, think things over, can't rush into it like a silly girl, I know. But if you would? Think about it, could you?'

Miss Foto was so unexpectedly moved that she was forced to remain silent. All she could do was nod her head a couple of times which rattled the headboard. Still turned away from her he suddenly looked up.

'What did you do?'

'I nodded my head.'

He turned swiftly and reached for his cotton dressing-gown in a crumpled heap on the floor, pulled it on, wrapped it tightly round him. 'Thank you. Take your time, not a bully really,' he said gruffly and went into the bathroom.

That was the gist of it, how it was. Like a cinema screen, I remember it clear as clear. Things like that stick. The 'plane was rising and falling like a shaky lift, probably over the hills, he thought, coming in soon. The carton at his feet slid along the metal deck. He stopped it with a foot. Said to give her a little time, she was very moved, I think. Funny thing; no one ever asked her before, she said. 'Course people don't like her. I know that. Nanni Singh, those bloody stuck-up Dutch, don't think Nettles likes her either. Can't think why. So kind that day, didn't laugh at me. I expected it rather, but she didn't. People are bloody snobs, it's all class, that's what, Colonial snobbery just because she worked in a dress shop or something. The plane suddenly banked steeply and he spread his legs to steady himself.

Across the aisle Nettles looked up from his book, peered out. Under the starboard wing Pangpang tilted away below him, tumbling down the mountainside, right-angled streets, a large square, spires, a temple glittering golden in the sun, far beyond the town the sinuous terraces of ruined tea plantations. The 'plane straightened out and started its descent. He hoped it was to be a nice, flat, landing ground. Sliding Shelley into his brief-case he realized that he was extremely glad that the flight was

231

over, at least until the return trip later on; a forced landing in
that area could only result in being chopped to pieces and
tumbled into a pit somewhere in the name of Freedom: a very
disagreeable way to go.

The sudden sight of the boy standing silently in the barred
light of the kitchen gave Nanni Singh such a fright that he cried
out and held a chair for support.

'Oh oh! It is you? It is justly you?'

The boy nodded, 'It is I.'

Recovering himself as quickly as he had lost himself, Nanni
Singh hurried to the door, slammed it shut and locked it. 'How
are you here? The Patrols in the gardens did not see you?'

'No one saw me. It is not so difficult.'

'You have come from the south, is it?'

'I walked. It is quite far but not so hard, there are many
places we can cross, the Indians are lazy and all Indonesians
look the same to them.' He came over to the table slowly. 'I am
unwelcome?'

Nanni Singh sped to him, embracing him with shaking arms.
'No, no. Not ever! I am so astonished. But fearful also because
there are two women now who work here, two young girls, if
they come . . .'

The boy patted the elder man's shoulder. 'If they come I will
speak with them and say I am your old friend from the City, I
am bringing fruit for the General.' He swung a small cloth bag
onto the table beside them. 'I am well prepared, this is what
they tell you in the south, you have to have "cover" to be safe,
this is my cover. Some fruit.'

'You are thinner,' said Nanni Singh.

'We train very hard. There is not so much to eat. Rice,
noodles. It is very interesting, I am happy there.'

'I have eggs?' said Nanni Singh suddenly starting to busy
himself among his pots and bowls.

'I am thirsty first of all. I am very good at the machine gun,
and I can also now throw grenades: did you know that from an
empty bottle and a bit of cloth you can make a fire bomb?' He
took the glass of lime juice and drank it down in one long gulp.
Nanni refilled it immediately, hovering anxiously at his side.

232

'With a bottle? And what else?'

'Petrol. Gasoline. It makes a fine explosion. This I find very exciting.'

'It sounds not very safe, this playing with guns and bombs.'

'We do not play.' The boy shook his glossy head. 'It is not for playing that we do these things.'

'You will have eggs? If you do not play what do you do?'

'We prepare to drive out the Imperialists and their lackeys.'

Nanni Singh cracked three eggs deftly into three saucers, spun the shells into a tin by the sink. 'Communist talking.'

'Cry, Ho! For the People's Democratic Communist Action Group,' said the boy with a wide grin. 'That is how they talk. It is very curious.'

'You do not know what it means, I am thinking?'

'I know about the machine gun.'

'And who are these Imperialists?'

'All in the north and those who support them.'

Nanni Singh slid the eggs into a tin frying pan. Above the splutter of ghee he said mildly, 'I am in the north, I am a supporter. Therefore I am your enemy too?'

The boy stretched back in his chair, his hands behind his head grinning. 'No, no, not you. You are my friend, isn't it so? I will only shoot the Dutch, because we must drive them away and make the Island free when you have all gone.'

'You talk nonsense, I think. Always war; you do not know war, it is not a game.'

'I do not play a game, I tell you.'

'You take such risks to come and tell me this? If the General was here and the house full, you would still have been so stupid?'

'The General is not here.'

Nanni Singh turned quickly from the stove. 'How are you sure?'

'The General and all the Staff have gone this day to Pangpang in the flying machine. This we know.'

'Who tells you this?'

'We know all that happens in the north, there are many of us to find these things out, boys and girls; we listen and we watch and we hear, even in the Headquarters we are there.'

The eggs bubbled and spat, Nanni Singh spooned out a bowl

233

of warm rice, tipped the eggs on top, pushed the dish across the table.

'Eat this; I will make tea. Who in Headquarters will say these things? You make a fool of me because I am old, I think. But not so old.'

'There are many Indians in the Headquarters, is right? They do not like so much the British, you are our brothers in the struggle, and soon they will throw all the British from India and we will be a United Nations of Asia together.'

'I am Indian,' said Nanni Singh, warming his teapot lovingly. 'I am Indian and I do not want the British to go away. I do not want to be brothers of the Chinese or the Indonesians or the Malays. That is what the Japanese planned to have, a United Asia, but it will not work, it cannot work.' He poured the hot water, put on the lid, took two glasses from the sink and came across to the table. 'We are all different, Buddhist, Muslim, Hindu and even Christian. I, even I your friend, I am Christian and I love my God, I will not denounce him.'

The boy looked at him steadily over the eggs and rice, his lips yellow at the corners. 'And you love also me and will not denounce me?'

Nanni Singh stirred his tea with a fork. He did not look up. 'I will not denounce you.'

'And you do not love your boy? Is that it?'

'You do a wicked thing; you make me your enemy. You come as a spy to this house, I am thinking.'

The boy finished his meal, wiped his mouth with his fist, put the bowl aside, leant across the table and placed his hand gently on the veined arm before him. 'I am not your enemy, Nanni, I do not come here to spy. I come only to see you, to be with you after so many days. It is wrong of me? I will ask nothing of you.'

'I will give you nothing.'

'I come only to see you, to show you that I am well.'

'My heart is filled with joy to see you but my ears are saddened by the song you sing. To run away because of that girl I understand, but to join with the heathen people brings me grief.'

'I must eat! I must live! Is it better to be in the barber shop to pleasure ugly white and yellow men? You say this is better than to fight for my land?'

'I do not say that! But they will teach you vile things and wickedness, to kill, to maim, to burn; you bring down my grey hairs with sorrow to the grave.'

At that moment there was the high chatter of women's voices coming towards the kitchen door; as swiftly as a deer the boy was on his feet and Nanni pushed him to the door of his bedroom. 'You go in there, soon they will leave.' He shut the door and took the bowl and glass from the table, unlocked the door.

The women entered shyly, buckets and rice-grass brooms clattering, laughing and nodding, a flash of gold teeth, demure eyes, flapping sandals. When he had paid them from his little petty-cash tin, they bowed and waved and laughed and hand in hand wandered into the sunlight. He shut the door, locked it again, poured his half-empty tea-glass into the sink as the boy opened the bedroom door cautiously.

'They have gone?'

'Yes, they have gone. They will not be back. Only morning time.'

The boy pulled his tight cheap cotton shirt over his head and threw it into the bedroom behind him. 'You are angry with me?'

Nanni Singh rinsed the glasses in a bucket of grey water. 'I am not angry, I am only sad.'

'And you do not look at me, therefore you are angry too.'

Nanni Singh looked up gently. 'I look at you.'

'And I am pretty, isn't it?'

'You are pretty.' He carried the two glasses carefully past the boy and set them neatly on the dresser, wiped his hands on his trousers.

'I am a little thinner,' agreed the boy. 'But I have muscles from my work, see!' He flexed his arms, sucked in his belly. 'And my legs, from running with guns and jumping, and the exercises, I will show you.'

'Unstable as water, thou shalt not excel.'

'I do not understand.' He suddenly slipped out of his trousers and stood in the doorway naked. 'You see now? So strong! I am a fine boy, isn't it so?'

'It is so,' said Nanni Singh softly. 'Now he was ruddy, and withal of a beautiful countenance, and goodly to look at.'

235

The boy leant slowly against the doorway, smiling through his lashed eyes. 'It is of me you speak?'

'It is of you I speak.'

The boy reached out his hand. 'Then you must tell me that you are not angry with me? I am your boy still.'

Cross-legged in the corner of his room, Nanni Singh sat quietly watching the sleeping boy in calm adoration. The splayed limbs, tumbled hair, lightly parted lips, gentle rise and fall of his chest, the smooth skin shining in the dim light of the shuttered room.

A wondrous creation of God the Father whom he would soon have to awaken since the afternoon had come, and he had slept long. The thought of awakening this resting youth saddened him deeply, but not as deeply as the thought of the slender body being crushed by a tank, ripped up by shrapnel, charred, burned or exploded into reeking chunks of flesh: He had seen those things happen to many brave young men during his long journey into battle; the sights which appalled him had, on quite a number of occasions, almost cost him his belief in Mr Bishop's God, and all his earnest teachings. They put the very Book itself into doubt, but his faith had come to his rescue in time, and he still was able to Believe. It was, he admitted wistfully, an awesome test. His faith had been beaten constantly by the flails of truth, fact and reason, and this boy was possibly the cruellest flail of them all, the beating which he was presently taking was the hardest he had ever had to bear, for of course the boy would die. Of that he felt certain. An heroic death chasing the Imperialists into the sea. He would die in a burst of gunfire, or the explosion of a grenade, with the word '*Merdeka!*' exultantly on his lips, and for what reason? He would never see the freedom for which he had fought, the young, golden idealists always died for the Cause whatever it was, only the old and evil survived Wars, stepping over the piled bodies of youth who had given their lives, shedding false tears, uttering patriotic cries like the parrots of the jungle. Only they ever entered the treasure houses of Power.

The boy stirred gently in his sleep, dragging one slender hand across his hard, flat belly. Nanni Singh sighed softly, bowed his head, tears pricking, clasped his hands tight to his chest. And I, he thought, am I as evil as these men who are old and sere? I who covet this youth, who love him and who cherish him. I take the beauty which he offers me so freely, but I do not destroy it, I do not harm it, I did not corrupt it, I will not betray it. I find no place of repentance though I seek it carefully in tears, for he has been happy with me and I have shown him joy, and I have been as a father to him. Oh! treacherous tongue, for a father is not a lover and in this I sin. But I do not betray him, only myself, and my penitence I shall make when God demands, and only I at this moment have the final chance to save him as now I will do.

He rose from his corner and leaning across the sleeping youth laid a gentle hand on his arm, just above the little tattooed eye. Instantly the boy awoke and sprang from the bed, arms and legs braced, eyes wide.

'Who is it?'

Nanni Singh opened his arms wide. 'It is no one. Be calm. I awaken you since you have slept long and the shadows grow, it is late. That is all.'

The boy slumped onto the bed, rubbing his eyes. 'And I must go?'

'And you must go. Where?'

'Back to my friends; to the south.'

'There is great danger in the south for you, you know that?'

'There is no danger there for me, we are united and strong, we are armed.'

'And against flying machines? You are strong against them?'

The boy smoothed his thighs, laughed, shook his head. 'We fear nothing; we will shoot them from the skies, but if they bomb us we will fight from the cellars and the holes . . . we will arise to fight.'

'I will make you some tea; and find you some food to take for your journey.'

'They will not come: they will not provoke us and we shall come among them quietly, and cause damage to them in their midst. This is what is planned.'

'It is planned that *they* will come. That I know.'

'The British?'

'Yes. They will come soon with fire and 'planes and they will destroy you; you must not go back.' Nanni Singh knelt suddenly

237

at the boy's side, placed a hand on his arm. 'Do not return. Stay here with me. Do not go back for it will be certain death and I shall never see you again.'

'When will they come?' The boy was almost contemptuous.

'You will see. Very soon. It is planned, this I know, for days now all is being arranged and discussed, it will be a big operation, they will cross the railway and destroy all resistance once and for all. This they say, this I hear.'

The boy lay back on the charpoy, hands behind his head, legs spread wide apart. He grinned, his head on one side.

'And who will come? All the British?'

'And the Dutch also. They will come with tanks and guns, you will have no chance.'

'They will find us ready. We will resist to the last. We will fight them in the forest, in the ruins. And we will conquer.'

'You speak the nonsense as you have been taught. Heed what I say: there is little time for you. A week, less maybe, five days before the Christian feast of Christ, this I know.' He touched the smooth knee before him hesitantly. 'Do not go back. Stay here.'

The boy's eyes lowered slowly to the hand, the grin faded to a slight smile, beneath the heavy lashes a gleam of triumph. He looked up directly at the thin, anxious brown face in front of him, the pleading eyes, the little flecks of grey in the smooth black hair.

'It is my duty.'

'You have no duty to these people, these people have a revolting and rebellious heart, already they corrupt you.'

'You have told me always to do my duty, now you say that I must not go to do it, but must stay and hide here behind an old man. It is my duty to fight shoulder to shoulder with my brothers and sisters in their struggle.'

'I am not an old man,' said Nanni Singh softly. 'And I do not ask you to hide behind me, but to take heed of my warning. I am wiser than you, I know what you risk. I do not want you dead or maimed because of foolish words which you truly do not comprehend. Your life is ahead, you are young, it can be full and rich and good. This I want for you with all my heart. If you go back they will surely destroy you.'

'I think,' said the boy raising one leg and prodding Nanni

238

Singh's shoulder with a gentle foot, 'that you want only my body, isn't it? You would not like this boy with only one leg, one arm, or with *this* cut off, hey?'

Nanni Singh rose slowly to his feet and looked down upon the sprawled figure regretfully.

'You offered me your body, as you do now, but it is truly your happiness and your soul that I would have.'

'You are a greedy man, that is it! You have told me that greed is wicked, so?'

'Is it wicked to love?'

'I do not know. I loved only one person, Yoko Oshima, and she is now dead by her own hand. I do not know of any other love.' The boy rose from the bed, reached for his clothes and started to pull them on slowly. Nanni Singh stood immobile, as stone, arms by his side.

'You will not stay?'

'I will not stay.'

'Thus you have no love for me?'

'No,' said the boy tucking in his shirt tails. 'You are kind, you are gentle, but also you are foolish and full of vengeance: you have cared for me and fed me, you have bought me fine clothes, you have given me much. You gave me the letter to take about the evil woman who is sometimes in this house, and because of that letter Yoko is dead.' He buckled the belt about his slim waist. 'It is for her that now I fight, for I too have learned vengeance, from you. I will fight the evil of the woman, of the English officer who came to ask me all the questions, of the other one who beat her. I fight in her name. That is my duty.'

Numbly Nanni Singh turned away and went into his kitchen reaching out for his teapot automatically, eyes blurred with sudden tears of despair, loss, and aching guilt. 'Oh God,' he murmured. 'Is it such a feast that I have chosen? A day for a man to afflict his soul.'

The boy came through, tying a strip of bright cloth about his neck. 'You speak to me, is that it?'

Nanni Singh did not move or raise his head, the teapot held between hard lean fingers.

'I have no thirst,' said the boy simply. He took up his bag of fruit from the table and swung it easily in his hand. 'You will not denounce me?'

Nanni Singh shook his head slowly. 'No,' he said softly.

'But you weep? Why do you weep?'

'For myself. I am your enemy now, my friend.'

'You are not. No, no, not my enemy. You are my good friend Nanni Singh. I know that you meant me no harm, you are a good and saintly man, I think.'

'I am a foolish man, and I wear the mark of Cain.'

'This I do not understand. But now I will go, the shadows are growing long, down by the swimming pool and through the bamboo grove I will pass. There was no guard there this day.'

'If you do not love me, then I ask another time, why did you come to this house, to take such a grave risk?'

'To show you that I was well after so long, that is all! It is not so difficult, and I will return one day. *After* the Christian feast: to show you that I am well and strong and that I have still my legs and my eyes also; that will be good, yes?'

Nanni Singh placed his teapot carefully upon the table. He looked up at the smiling boy. 'The Christian feast?'

'As you said. After. It is not so long, I think?'

He came very close to Nanni Singh, placed a light hand upon his stooped shoulder. 'A saintly man, a good man, you have given me much.'

'I have given you nothing.'

The boy leaned forward swiftly and lightly kissed the tight brown face. 'I will come back. You will see.' Taking up his bundle he crossed to the door, unlocked it, winked at the still figure standing in the shadows, and let himself quietly into the afternoon. The faint click of the closing door hit Nanni Singh like a blow, his body slumped against the table. 'Now,' he said aloud to the teapot before him, 'now the axe is laid into the roots of the trees.'

The General and his entourage boarded the return flight from Pangpang to the City, at about four-thirty, with intense relief after a heavy day of inspections, discussions, presentations, facts, figures and lunch with the ebullient Brigade Commander, 'Sonny' Lulworth, in his immaculate Mess in the commandeered villa of a leading tea-planter who was, it seemed, still, as he had put it neatly, 'shut away' somewhere. Although the

240

Brigade was in an unenviable position, high in the hills, surrounded on all sides by hostile extremists, in contact with the City only by the weekly convoys which the RAF shepherded along the ambushed highway, or the lumbering Dakotas flying in supplies and flying out tired and frightened internees, everyone appeared to be in very high spirits generally, which had risen even higher when the General had assured them that very shortly their days of seclusion, strain and tension would be over for they were to be replaced by a Dutch Brigade which was already on its way out to relieve them.

There had been no overt demonstrations against anyone on the streets of the shabby town, nor, on the other hand, had there been any cheers, bands, or clapping. Sullen groups glared as the General's car had passed with pennant flying and gold braid glittering, a few banners had been jogged up and down bearing the familiar slogans of '*Merdeka!* Death to Slavery!' and less comfortingly perhaps, 'Freedom from Colonial Fascists!', and an hour before the touch-down someone had thrown a couple of hand grenades into a truck full of Europeans heading for the airport and, they had presumed, their own freedom. Otherwise, things were as calm as usual in the sulphur-scented air of the restless town high among its volcanoes.

Lunch had been a pleasant affair in the cool villa at a long mahogany table sparkling with silver, crystal and bowls of slightly frivolous orchids. 'Sonny' Lulworth knew what was what. Everything he ever did was done with great polish and a passionate eye for detail. Although he gave the impression of a rather ageing boy-scout with cropped hair, blue eyes which had the intensity of a goat's, no chin much to speak of and a healthy rush of teeth to the head, a bravery and energy which exhausted his senior officers and terrified the wits out of his juniors, there was a good deal more to him than that. Not only could he supervise his own flower arrangements, design his own uniforms (today in crisply starched cream cotton, shorts and jacket, long white socks, gaiters and brilliant brown boots, a red and white polka-dot handkerchief tied round his throat, and an Australian bush-hat ablaze with rank and red-tabs), he could fight like a tiger, go for long periods without food or water, march effortlessly for miles, and lead his adoring troops to whatever death he deemed necessary for the success of any operation he was required to perform. In a limited time he had gained almost the same degree of awe and devotion among his Other Ranks as the legendary Orde Wingate, but realized, with due humility, that as yet he was as a trout to that salmon. However he had his ambitions absolutely intact. In short, a man who knew his way about, who was at least an individual and at most a crashing bore.

But brave with it. Or foolhardy: it very much depended on one's rank as to one's opinion. The lower orders worshipped him as a leader, but then, as Nettles thought, all sheep follow a goat; while the Seniors waited in tactful silence for him to thunder into the ravine.

However, he served a splendid lunch and a pleasant wine which was not, as he himself admitted, 'too emphatic', and although his conversation during the long courses was mainly composed of the pronouns 'I', or 'We', when referring to his glorious Brigade of sheep and doubters, this was felt to be allowable since he was the host after all and must surely be glad of new faces around his table as so much of his time, and his officers', was spent in an almost complete state of siege.

As far as General Cutts was concerned he was perfectly happy to let the fellow chatter along as he wished, and what was wished was that no form of 'business' should be discussed at the table. At table one could talk of as many topics as one liked ranging as widely or as narrowly as one's own intellect. Gardening was a good one, Fishing another, Hounds, the delights of a pony trek through Connemara or the absurdity of Fatehpur Sikri; he was also quite knowledgeable about Early English silver spoons.

Rooke, for his part, sitting opposite Nettles well below the salt as befitted any good ADC, spoke politely when spoken to and got on with his excellent lunch in a rather preoccupied manner. He had other things on his mind: earlier in the morning, having inspected a rather 'safe' strong point on the edge of some tea-gardens, they had returned to a Battalion HQ for the customary General's chat-up, and among the assembled spit-and-polished officers present, far across the room, Rooke had been astonished to see the pinched face of Lieutenant Weathersby peering across at him with yearning intensity. Seeing that the General had made himself comfortable with a

242

large tin mug of tea, and was fully involved with Nettles and the Battalion IO he moved across to the solitary figure who had been his travelling companion of many months ago on the trip down from Calcutta.

'Merry Christmas,' said Weathersby, offering a damp hand. 'Two weeks off. Merry Christmas.'

'You finally made it then. To Pangpang.'

'Finally.'

'And I made it too. Funny thing isn't it? Both here after all. Where we were coming to at the beginning, remember? Replacements.'

'I remember. Things all right?'

'All right.' Weathersby shrugged indifferently. 'I'm sweating it out. Not long now.'

'Thought you were, well, locked up or something?'

'Can't get far here, can I? It *is* being locked up. Anyway I'm in the clear, you know, no one can prove a damn thing. Personal effects are personal effects, don't give a bugger who says not. Just bad luck. Anyway, I'm off to Blighty pretty soon, thank God.' He scratched his head. 'It was a tip-off, you know that?'

'No,' said Rooke. 'I didn't know. Just heard there had been a bit of bother with your luggage or something. You seem to be luggage-prone, don't you?'

Weathersby looked at him steadily through round glasses. 'Don't follow.'

'First day we arrived you dropped your suitcase, bust it open, the chess set spilled, remember?'

'Oh that. Yes. The MO here plays a terrific game. Had one running five days.'

'That's nice. Keep your mind alert.'

'My mind is fine. Great, couldn't be better. I know who did the tipping-off.'

'I honestly don't think anyone did, you know. Just a random search, they do that from time to time.'

'To an officer's luggage? Pulled my bloody trunk out of the hold. Random? Why mine only? I know who it was, hated me because I was shacked up with one of her ex-girls. Ruby Oshima. Full of sweetness and light she was to me at those parties at Novak's, full of fun she was, said she knew all the Oshima specialities, and hoped she was doing a "correct" job

243

for me. Full of ruddy innuendo, as if I was some ghastly pervert or something. She hated my guts.'

'I don't know who the hell you're talking about.'

'The General's Lady, that's who. Ask your chum Nettles, he'll tell you.'

'You're being bloody offensive.'

'It's all offensive, as you call it. Nettles badgered poor Ruby to her death, you know that I suppose? Questions. Grilled her silly the day she died. Asked him?'

'I think you've gone dotty up here.'

Weathersby smiled his sour smile. 'They've all got something to hide, the whole lot of them, all so bloody la-di-dah, a real shitty lot, all of them, corrupt as hell.' He suddenly fished about in his trouser pocket and produced a small, wrapped, packet which he thrust into Rooke's unwilling hand. 'Have a look at this on the trip back to Sodom and Gomorrah, might amuse you. It'll give old Lot's wife over there a bigger thrill than a "shave" at the barber's in the market.' He looked uneasily over Rooke's shoulder at the General and his little group round the table at the far end of the room. 'They were going to send her away, you know? Ruby? She left me a note the day she killed herself, said they were making her clear out because she knew too much, told me where *that* was,' he said, indicating the packet in Rooke's hand with a jerk of his head. 'Asked me to give it back to Miss Foto, but not to tell anyone.'

'They said the flat was ransacked,' said Rooke mildly.

Weathersby looked at him steadily. 'It was. Stripped, everything ripped about, but we always left notes for each other in a . . . secret place. They didn't find it. In the lavatory cistern, if you must know. With that.'

'Why didn't you give it back then? Why give it to me?'

'I would have. Until the tip-off business. Then I opened it and I knew what to do. But I don't want any part of it, thanks: got enough worries of my own now. Glad you came up, knew you were coming anyway, so I just waited. You'll see why. Sort of checkmate. That,' he said turning away as the group in the background started to break up, 'is a term we use in chess.' And with a quince smile he had drifted out of the room.

Nettles leant across a shallow bowl of pale orchids, tapped his spoon lightly on a wine glass to attract Rooke's attention. 'Lost

244

your appetite for tinned mandarins in syrup?' he asked quietly.

Rooke snapped back to the sparkling table. 'No. Well, yes. I've had an elegant sufficiency, as my Nanny Jarvis would say.'

'Isn't it "delicate' sufficiency? I can never remember.'

'Enough anyway, thanks.'

'Weathersby seemed in form. Saw you get trapped, briefly.'

'Coincidence, really. Tell you later.'

'Not frightfully sure I want to know, thank you.'

Rooke pushed a slice of slippery fruit round his plate. 'No. I'm not frightfully sure that you will.'

Coffee was served on the wide verandah and terrace, scattered chairs, small white tables, thin Dresden cups handed perfectly by silent bearers in trim cream jackets.

'Don't you think it is all too splendid? All this? Must have been utterly divine before the idiots went to work with their pangas and hacked everything to bits. Absolutely senseless destruction, do look at it.'

'Sonny' Lulworth stood with the General by the rail looking over the shaggy lawns of the villa to the terraces falling away like steps below. Row upon row of massacred tea-bushes draped across the little hills like a throwing of dark green corduroy velvet. 'Destroyed everything they could lay hands to, coffee, rubber, hydroelectric works, and the tea. The Japanese started it, of course, ripped up the tea to plant coca for the cocaine, had some idea they could ship it all to China and drug them into submission!' The goat eyes remained wide, the teeth, like a handful of peeled almonds, glistened in the brilliant light. 'And now we have the Marxists screaming for "scorched earth", to get rid of the hated Colonials, and how, pray, do they intend to survive after they've thrown us out? Can't run it themselves; indolent people here, jolly, charming, lazy, fly kites as soon as pick a tea-leaf, full of inner violence. Of course, at base, it's simply avarice.' He sighed and sipped from his thin Dresden cup. 'Know what Kipling says, don't you? Utterly true of course.'

The General shifted uneasily, put his cup on a table, folded his arms. 'Not so good at Kipling.'

'A soldier like you; Sir?' The eyes still wide. The pause between the 'you' and the 'Sir' nearly measured.

'Not my cup of tea, if you'll pardon the pun.'

'Oh, pardoned indeed. Frightfully good! Kipling: no, my wife, Olive, simply detests him, far too jingoistic she will say. But I think he's rather good misself.'

'What did he say? I mean about all this sort of business . . .'

'Oh. That, well, yes. He said, and I do so think he was right, sure you'll agree, you've spent your life out here, haven't you? India, so on. Well, he said . . .' Quite suddenly he turned and sought a wider audience than the General and threw a beckoning arm towards a crushed-looking middle-aged Captain in an over-new uniform who had been standing alone at the end of the verandah, and who now came cautiously towards them.

'General Cutts, this is Captain . . . my dear fellow, your name! Too frightful! What can you think of me? Forgotten your name, Lewis, Lanning, do forgive me.'

'Levine,' said the crushed Captain. 'Daniel Levine. Public Relations.'

Lulworth set his cup on the table, and rubbed his hands. 'Public Relations. Quite forgot. Fleet Street before, wasn't it? Came up here last week to have a look round the Brigade, get down to facts, so to speak, that's it, isn't it? Captain Levine had a rather wretched night last night, didn't you?' Without waiting for the unhappy Captain to reply, he turned to the General with a wide wink. The Goat had altered focus for a split second. 'A little too much of the grape, I fear. That was it, wasn't it, Captain?'

Levine managed an uncomfortable grin with effort. 'Bit of a hangover this a.m., Sir.'

'Too much of the grape, as I said. It's the altitude, you know. Two thousand metres up here. Goes to one's head in a second.'

'As I found out.'

'Sonny' Lulworth patted the over-new uniform warmly. 'Yes, you did. First time I've ever seen a Jewish fellow the worse for wine. Curious thing, isn't it? One never sees a really drunk Jew, does one? Quite marvellous, but I suppose that's the religion, isn't it?'

'About Kipling,' said the General with a face like red sandstone.

'Ah! Kipling! Yes, I was saying to General Cutts that Kipling had an answer to all the wanton destruction which I am
246

sure you have been aware of during your little holiday with us here; the tearing up of the tea; rubber destroyed, all that idiocy. What I wanted to say was this: Kipling wrote the following, I'm quoting strictly from memory remember, might have got it a bit wrong, but in fact he says, "The 'eathen in 'is blindness bows down to wood an' stone; 'E don't obey no orders unless they is 'is own". Pretty fair, I venture? Can't do the Cockney bit, but you can get the idea; he goes on, and this is the best part, " 'E keeps 'is side-arms awful: 'e leaves 'em all about, An' *then* comes up the Regiment an' pokes the 'eathen out." Do you see? Marvellous, don't you think? But the final part is what I really feels fits all this . . .' He waved a lean arm angrily at the ravaged country side below them, ' "The 'eathen in 'is blindness must end where 'e began." '

A small silence broken only by muted murmurs on the terrace and the clink of a spoon against a fragile cup. Lulworth threw wide crisply-starched arms. ' "Must *end* where he *began*." Absolutely true, don't you think?' He turned to Captain Levine, 'You could jot that down in your notebook. It might be immensely useful. By Kipling. Rudyard.'

Taking the General's elbow with extreme care he led him down the steps onto the white marble terrace glaring in the sun. 'I've got one of my chaps to have a word with your ADC about a place back with you for Captain whatever-his-name is. Can't really cope with another moment of him. Do hope you won't mind, but the morale of the Brigade is at stake, you might say! God knows what he came here for . . . as far as I can see he's merely snooping about, probably for some Sunday Dreadful in London. Madly class-conscious, of course, they all are, aren't they? Jews, I mean? Can't understand the set-up here. Silver, good food, the discipline, this house . . . manners, behaviour. Simply no idea of what *behaviour* means. No idea how my fellows fought coming down from India and Assam . . . no idea of the deaths, the filth, the Japanese, the utter, utter carnage.' He stopped at the edge of the terrace glowering over the ruined terraces below. 'We'll never teach them, the "professional observers", they go home and write their memoirs but they never knew the fellows who got left behind. Stuffed into slit-trenches, swamps, scattered into bits, burned, dragging themselves to death with dysentery. Can't stick the breed personally.'

247

He suddenly looked at his watch and brightened up. 'Suppose it *is* a bit of a paradox, all this, but they deserve it after all they have been through. It's not war here, really, is it, General? Rather more of a spiteful hit-and-run affair, nothing heroic about any of this; a shifty, mean, cowardly business, and morale does sometimes get just a teeny-wee bit wobbly. One still gets killed, that's the rub. Not as soldiers, as policemen.'

He scuffed the terrace edge with a glinting amber boot. 'So one tries to spoil them a little after all they've done. Splendid job. A little civilization is due in the middle of this extremely un-heroic non-war. One sets a standard, gives them an image, something to emulate, put on a show, lift them up a degree or two; if I say *I* can do it and *do*, then they know they can also.' He looked at his watch again, buttoned up a pocket. 'Now then; we should be off, if you can cope with the rest of the day? West Dorsets, Patialas, then as you rightly suggested a quick look at RAPWI HQ who will so appreciate it, and if there is time at the end of the afternoon, over to my devoted Nuns at the Orphanage, coping amazingly. Reverend Mother is a perfect darling even though she does happen to be Italian: unfortunately.' He turned and led the way back to the verandah. 'Really can't say how splendid it is of you to have made this little visit, boosted everyone's morale tremendously, terribly good of you, General . . .'

The General looked into the goat-eyes beside him with his own small blue ones. 'Behaviour; you'd say? Am I right?' He brushed his moustache with a finger.

Lulworth dipped his head like a sipping bird. 'Correct, Sir: behaviour. That's it absolutely. So few people know what it means.'

On the verandah the staff from Brigade and Division waited in polite anxiety. The cast of a play lined up for the finale. 'Sonny' Lulworth clapped his hands briskly. 'Action stations, chaps! Phase two: West Dorsets first.' Suddenly he took up a crystal jar of brilliant orchids from the table and thrust them at the General. 'Look here! Too perfect, aren't they? Like a branch of tiny butterflies: look here, let's send them off with you, don't you think? Plenty more here where they came from, trees festooned with them. So delicate, so fragile, there must be some pretty young creature down at HQ who would be delighted to

248

have them, I venture, eh? Not wrong I'm sure? Where's your ADC?'

'Very generous of you,' said the General. 'Most thoughtful, very kind.'

Rooke spent the rest of the afternoon worryingly occupied by two unwanted burdens. Orchids wrapped in damp paper, and Weathersby's slim packet heavy in his breast-pocket. The afternoon passed swiftly, if exhaustingly, and the journey to the air-strip, when the time finally arrived, was welcomed with keen relief, although it turned out to be not entirely comforting. There were many more people on the streets than in the morning, rather more banners and placards waved, and far more noise, Rooke noticed with slight apprehension, which had nothing whatever to do with cheers or happy applause at the sight of a braided GOC riding stiffly to attention behind his pennant and two outriders from the Signal Corps. There was a rising and falling swell of sound rather like angry bees in a hive, and here and there thin brown arms flew up with fists firmly clenched.

Looking back a couple of times he saw that the crowd spilled into the road after they had passed, and swarmed behind them, banners wobbling and dancing, keeping, however, a discreet distance between itself and the Bren-Gun Carrier which brought up the rear of their small, but heavily armed, convoy of cars. Suddenly a stone spun out of nowhere and whanged harmlessly against the bonnet of the car in which Nettles and the unwanted Captain Levine rode together with the Brigade IO and another young officer. Rooke was horrified to realize that the action, although trivial under the circumstances, had brought him out in a fine cool sweat. He had just had time to brush his forehead casually as the convoy turned, through the barbed wire gates of the air-strip which then swung firmly closed against the murmuring crowd pressing forward with its banners. He had never been so thankful to see a 'plane in his life. The Dakota stood full square on the centre of the strip, engines idling, dust swirling behind the last of the internees climbing aboard, who would accompany them on the trip back to the City. Farewells were made swiftly but individually.

'Sonny' Lulworth walked across the grass with his General. 'Full load today, afraid you'll be a bit squashed on the trip, try to keep away from the ones who are air-sick. Frightfully disagreeable business, most of them have never flown before; by the way, Sir,' he laid a hand briefly on the General's arm, 'I must just say thank you again. We are a very proud Brigade as you will have seen, I hope, and your visit to us today has made us *all* even prouder.'

The General tipped his cap lightly with his little cane. 'It was an honour and a very great privilege: I have been very impressed and most touched.'

Suddenly Lulworth whipped off his bush-hat and made a deep and sweeping bow with the elegance and splendour of Sir Walter Raleigh before the realm. 'It is we who have been honoured, Sir,' he said with a wide grin.

The General laughed shortly. 'And that I take it is also behaviour, eh? Jolly good!'

With a final salute he about-turned and climbed aboard behind a harassed woman whose two children and large straw hamper had just been hauled up with an effort.

Brigadier Lulworth waved his hat in circles over his cropped head, red-neckerchief whipping in the slipstream, as the 'plane rumbled along the grassy track and then he was lost to sight as they rose steeply, gained height, banked and the town tilted away below, spreading out into squares and streets, the airstrip suddenly growing as small as a cigarette card while they climbed steadily so that all they could finally see were the scattered cars of the little convoy glittering in the late sun and the dark mass of people gathered at the gates looking, from this comforting height, like a milling swarm of frantic ants.

The General had pushed his way forward where a seat had been held for him. Rooke struggled through the worried women and bewildered children aft, finding a place among piles of straw baskets and rolled blankets where he wedged himself beside Nettles and a hollow-eyed girl in a Mickey-Mouse shirt. At this moment he rather wished the General was not so damned democratic, and had not insisted on sharing everyone's discomfort. The day had been pretty tiring, even fraught, and huddled up in the packed 'plane, with the yelling of small children and the roar of the engines and the staggering rise and fall as they lumbered over the hills made it impossible to relax; however, he rested his head wearily against the shuddering fuselage and left the orchids to tremble on his knees, thankful to be leaving.

Nettles poked him lightly, leant forward to be heard. 'That, dear fellow, was Pangpang. Now *aren't* you glad you were not a replacement?'

'Deeply.'

'Two days of "Sonny" Lulworth and you'd have been a corpse.'

'Curious fellow. Rather splendid.'

'A cultist. Wildly dangerous creatures. Destroy everyone but themselves.'

'Poor Weathersby.'

'Deserves not a grain of our pity. What did he want?'

'Didn't actually want anything. Gave me something.' He patted his pocket.

'Presents?'

'Not for me. Miss Foto.'

Nettles removed his cap, ran his hand through tight curls, pulled his nose thoughtfully with long fingers. '*How* that woman keeps cropping up. I can only imagine it must be cyanide.'

'Could be.'

'Haven't looked?'

'No. Supposed to, before I give it to her. Or you, as a matter of fact. He said that you'd get more of a thrill from seeing it than having a shave at the barber's, whatever that means . . .'

'I know,' said Nettles easily. 'Oh, I do indeed. Nasty little fellow. Quite splendidly foul.'

'Called you Lot's wife; rather funny.'

'Presuming that I shall be turned to salt when I see it, is that it?'

Rooke unbuttoned his pocket, slid out the wrapped packet. 'Shall we try? See if you do?'

'I really can't wait. I'll do my best to restrain myself, this is hardly the place for a grand Transformation Scene. Open it.'

The packet was tightly wrapped in a piece of brown paper, bound about with black adhesive-tape which Rooke started to unpeel. Across the crammed aisle, crushed between a quietly weeping woman in a faded print frock and a bulging sack of mail, Captain Levine was writing busily on his knee in a small

251

notebook, now and then looking up vacantly, sucking the end of his pencil. The 'plane suddenly lurched to port, lost height, climbed again, the sunlight probing through the small windows fingering the taut, pale faces of alarmed children for instants like groups by De La Tour. It bucketed up and down for moments, baskets slid about, a child cried out and was hushed, someone further along vomited with loud, harsh, sobs as Rooke slid a battered leather wallet from the wrappings.

A worn paybook, some Singapore dollar bills, a Kodak snapshot of a smiling woman in a bathing-suit, a Blood Group Number, the stub of a cinema ticket. Roxy Kinema. Melbourne.

'Oh Christ! Oh Christ!' said Rooke. 'Look what we have here.'

Nettles' slender fingers examined the shabby pieces. 'Whose? My word! Melvin Alfred Wills. Sergeant. 149274. Date of birth February 16th 1918. Hair: red. Height: six feet two inches. Distinguishing marks: none. So they say. But singing to the end, I am informed!' He ran his thumb lightly over the small photograph in the paybook. 'Very male. Stubborn face. Why did he have this with him, I wonder? Will of his own, Mr Wills . . . no pun intended. Anything else?'

Rooke silently handed him a folded strip of paper. 'It's in Dutch I think. You can see "Miss Foto" at the start and it's signed "Yoko". Weathersby's girl at the Dumps, Ruby.'

Nettles turned abruptly to the girl beside him in the Mickey-Mouse shirt. 'Do forgive me, but can you speak English? English?'

The girl nodded tiredly. 'Just a little, not well.'

'I wonder if you could be angelic and tell me what this says.' He handed her the slip of paper as Rooke grabbed his arm, 'Geoffrey! No, you can't.'

'I can,' said Nettles. 'And have.'

The girl was reading slowly, holding the paper close to half-closed eyes, her lips silently moving. She looked up. 'You would like I read this? It is in Dutch.'

'I know. It must be important; someone gave it to me, a message for a friend in the City. Could you tell me what it says?'

'It is for a Miss Foto, is right? It says: "You told me to burn this but I could not . . ." ' She stopped, bit her lip. 'I continue? It is very personal.'

252

'Do please.'

The girl read on slowly, her voice so low that it was almost drowned by the noise about them, they leant closer to her. ' "... But I could not because you loved him so very much so I kept it for you always forgive me your Yoko." ' When she had finished she handed the slip back. 'I am sorry if it is bad news. It is also very sad, I think?'

'Very sad,' agreed Nettles, folding it into the wallet. 'But thank you most awfully, terribly kind of you, I had to know before we get down.'

'You are from the City, not Pangpang?'

'No. The City.'

She locked her fingers tightly together. 'In the City do you know Delftlaan? It is very near the Cricket Club?'

'I'm afraid I don't.'

'It doesn't matter. Maybe it is not there now. My parents' house ...' Her voice trailed away and she turned and looked over her shoulder through a crack of the window.

'Your affair, my noble Rooke, knight in armour, off you go to your crusades. I have washed my hands of the whole sorry affair. I have far too much to handle at the moment. Given it all over to that porcine member of the Military Police, Major Holt. Suggest you do the same; you've got a hell of a week ahead, bangs, alarums and excursions all that sort of stuff, no time for sordid little private follies now. We have a battle, a real one, ahead. But I should tell him just how you came across the little packet of delights, he'll be frightfully interested.'

Rooke slid it into his pocket, took up the bunch of orchids, clasped them tightly between his knees. 'I feel quite sick,' he said. 'Quite bloody sick.'

Nettles looked at him anxiously. 'Don't give way to your feelings, I pray. The whole place is awash as it is. I trust your remark was metaphorical, we're nearly there.'

A perfectly ordinary landing, an orderly disembarkation. Which rather disappointed Captain Levine who had already pre-written his captions. 'Emotional Scenes at Air Strip', 'Tragic Reunions of Weeping Families', 'Panic-stricken Refugees Land'. But there was nothing remotely like that taking place as he pushed his way through the tired, orderly, patient crowd in a mixture of relief at his arrival and irritation at his

253

loss of saleable 'copy'. Nurses, nuns and brisk, uniformed girls hurried about carrying children, bags and bundles, shepherding everyone with bright reassuring smiles towards the Red Cross huts and RAPWI tents across the strip. The General had marched ahead on his own, and Rooke, who had been hindered by bags and baggage and the girl in the Mickey-Mouse shirt, whose suitcase had got lost somewhere, saw to his relief that he had already been met by a small group of officers from the staff, among whom he instantly recognized the kind, worried face of Nigel Pullen: quickening his pace, leaving Nettles to assist the Mickey-Mouse girl with her burden, colliding with people and their belongings, holding the orchids high for fear of their being damaged at this final stage in their journey, he reached the General just as Pullen had turned away with the others and was hurrying to the assembled cars.

He was standing suddenly quite alone, perfectly still.

Rooke reached his side. 'Sorry, Sir. Got held up.'

General Cutts turned slowly as if he had just awakened. He looked curiously at Rooke who held the orchids towards him.

'Shall I take care of these, Sir? Or will you?'

The General put out a hand and touched the shimmering flowers vaguely. 'Ben, get down to HQ will you? Jump to it. Just got a signal.'

'Yes, Sir?'

'Murdered Brigadier Lulworth. Point blank range, fifty minutes ago.'

CHAPTER TEN

Rooke sat listessly on the terrace, back against the stucco wall of the house, legs thrust before him, arms at his side, head back, staring up into the black filigree of the vine through which the great white moon probed lancing fingers, speckling his naked body with shifting fragments of light.

Behind him in the darkened room Emmie lay motionless, under the enormous pale drapery of netting which fell about their bed. She was not asleep, he knew, but as awake as he, listening, waiting, alert, aware of his need for solitude.

In a banyan tree hidden from view by the thickness of the vine above, the sound of restless birds, chuckling, murmuring: sudden shrill squawks, a scolding among themselves although it was still an hour until dawn. A leaf dropped to the tiles with the sound of a falling card. He looked at his light-speckled legs. White wounds on the dark flesh. Giant measles. Chicken-pox. Lupus.

'It's lupus,' said Nanny Jarvis. 'They all have it . . . now come away do . . .'

A tramp was sitting on the steps in the stable yard, a slender stack of ragged clothing, matted hair and beard, a sack, a stick, boots tumbled beside him, unwinding a stained grey bandage from his leg, wincing with over-acted pain before Rooke's startled eight-year-old gaze. The bandage fell away in loops like old potato peeling, exposing a china-white shin glistening with a scatter of sores as large as pennies and halfpence. White-rimmed, deep, puckered, pus oozing.

'Come away, Ben, do; let the poor man get on with his bathing the thing. Jessie'll have to scour out that bowl before she uses it again.'

'Is he poisonous?'

'Verminous I'd say; now come away, he's got water and boracic, a loaf and a quarter of cheddar. Can't do more.'

The tramp looked up suddenly, folding the bandage deliberately into a neat pad.

'Does it hurt you very much?' Rooke asked politely.

'Piss off,' said the tramp, dipping the pad into the bowl of water. Rooke turned swiftly and followed Nanny Jarvis across the yard.

'I asked him if it hurt him.'

'And . . .'

'He told me to piss off.'

'Ask a silly question and you'll get a silly answer.'

'Will he die?'

'Very likely.'

'From them?'

Her black and white pinafore bellied in the breeze, a laundry basket under one arm, chickens scattering distractedly before her path. Rooke looked back as the tramp looked up and stuck out his tongue.

'He's very rude.'

'And so were you: staring like that.'

'How did he get the lupus things?'

'Dirt,' said Nanny Jarvis stuffing a handful of clothes-pegs into her pocket. 'Dirt and plain laziness, that's about it.'

'And he'll die from them?'

'We all have to die sometime from something. He'll die like the rest of us: comes to us all in the end.'

In such a diversity of ways. The diversity of death.

But he didn't know that then. In those shimmering days of halcyon innocence the word dying had a vague meaning. It was something which happened tidily in your bed, painlessly, comfortable, with a loving family gathered about you and a flutter of blissful-faced angels to bear you aloft to something called Heaven when you had fallen into the deep sleep. The long sleep. Dying was altogether a very ordered affair. Aunts and Uncles did it, people one didn't know very well did it, it was remote and in any case it only happened to those who were very much older than you were. It didn't happen when you were young. Killing was, of course, quite a different thing. Only animals got killed. Rabbits in a gin trap, otters in the stream, dogs by motor cars, cats by foxes, and soldiers were killed fighting for their King. But those soldiers were made of lead and didn't make a sound if they lost a leg or an arm fell off; and if they should lose their heads, as sometimes happened in nursery wars, you just stuck them back on again with half a matchstick.

256

However, you couldn't do that with Brigadier Lulworth, they said: his head was splattered across the back of his car in an explosion of brains, teeth and close-cropped hair, the goat-blue eyes jelly-balls on the drenched upholstery. No lead soldier this, but one of mortal flesh. He had not died merely. He'd been killed; and only the headlessness made them parallel, except that on the nursery floor you could repair the damage while on an ambushed road to Pangpang all that could be done was to chuck a couple of hand-grenades into the yelling crowd, as someone had done, and in the confusion lurch desperately towards safety, covered by the angry chatter of the gun in the Bren Carrier bringing up the rear.

Although they had eventually got back with their bloody load, the two grenades and the savage murder had been as tinder to the fire and under cover of darkness the Freedom Fighters attacked with wild ferocity, hurling mortar- and fire-bombs, raking the night with tracer bullets. The charming Mess in the elegant villa which had been the setting for such a pleasant lunch only hours before, crumbled, splintered and burned furiously, while a little way along the road, caught in their jeep by a hail of exploding petrol-bombs, two figures blazing like torches ran zig-zagging through the tea plantations tearing at their clothing, screaming with high, shrill sounds which cut through the chattering machine guns until silenced by a racket of bullets, slamming them into the tall canes where they sprawled smouldering in supplicating agony. One of them was Ronnie Weathersby.

A diversity of deaths. And they were only the start: others had followed, to which he was witness, and to one of which he was the deliberate instrument of death himself. Bloodied at twenty-four by a badly aimed revolver, and the wide spreading stain in the fork of the tight, grubby trousers. Oh shit! Oh shit!

She was beside him instantly, her body smelling sweet and warm, two thin bracelets clinking as her arms enfolded his bowed head and pulled him to her breast. 'I am here.'

He nodded, reaching for her.

'It will soon be dawn, there is a red line in the sky, then it will be light and the dreams will go.'

'It is light now. With the moon. And they haven't gone.' His voice muffled by his own cramming fist.

257

'But the moon makes dark shadows where the dreams hide. The light is like reason, when the shadows go so too will the dreams. When I was in my little cupboard below the stairs I would wait for the day to come. There was a very little crack under the door and I could just see the first grey line of dawn arriving; as the day grew bolder and the sun rose high the light beneath the door was so clear, so strong, that I could touch it with a hand; but I could not hold it, so it slipped away again and soon would come the night. So I know.'

He laid his head against her shoulder looking out into the black and white garden.

'It'll go. It'll go in time. It's just when I close my eyes; in the dark. It's so damned silly, I've seen a great many deaths in these years, I'm not new to it really.'

The sprawled American soldiers on the Normandy beaches, drifting face down in the incoming tide, boots and gaiters, helmeted heads bobbing, grey-green humps like drifting seaweed swinging idly on the swell. The youth curled up in the hole in a hedgerow, mouth agape, eyes misted, maggots inching across his spilled belly like little grains of yellow rice; the kilted body in the buttercups, buttocks obscenely in the air, head crushed helmetless into the sorrel. A baptism in high June.

He touched her lips in the white light briefly with his fingertips. Her eyes were very bright, almost smiling.

'I don't think it's the death that worries me, Emmie. The guilt perhaps. I never killed before.'

She pressed his hand hard to her mouth, kissing the hollow of his palm. 'This is a war, you are a soldier, you have a gun, you have an enemy. It is you or it is him. You make the choice. There is no guilt in war: win or lose, survive or die. Do you feel guilty for surviving?'

'Sometimes.'

'I do not.'

'No. Perhaps, oh, shit! It was having to shoot him twice; it was shooting him twice, Emmie. Once is quite enough.'

Smelling of talc, and having just buttoned up his stiffly starched bush-jacket, Rooke had reached for the silk stock which Kim was expertly folding for him as the telephone rang. In his

258

pleasant sitting-room with the cane furniture and the Chinese scroll of guinea fowl the handset shrilled insistently, and in his hurry to silence it he collided with the low table and cracked his shin.

The General's voice appeared to come from an echo chamber forcing him to hold the receiver some way from his head. 'Ben? Thought you'd gone to sleep.'

'Changing, Sir.'

'I'm changing too. Plans. Want you up here this evening.'

'But Sir! You said I was clear until tonight's briefing.'

'I know I did. Sorry. Things have altered, need moral support at dinner, come up about seven-thirty, half an hour's time. Tikh-hai?'

'Difficulty, Sir. Emmie van Hoorst is on her way up.'

The silence ached.

'What's the difficulty? Don't follow. Say you're on duty.'

'Hasn't got a telephone, Sir. Probably left by now, she was coming to supper.'

'Look here: Miss Foto's coming to *me*, just called to say she's got a lift from that blasted Yank, the Boxwallah chappie: not my arrangement, she wants him to see the house and so on. I'll need support, can't stick the chap; get yourself up here in half an hour, bring your girl with you.'

'Miss Hoorst?'

'If you like. Presentable, isn't she?'

'Yes, Sir. Don't think she'll be in a long frock, she's coming on her bike.'

'Look: I don't care if she's coming on an elephant, it's not a Burra Khana, just a light supper; my evening's been buggered so there's no reason why yours shouldn't be either. Got it? Seven-thirty.'

'Very well, Sir.'

'And Ben, no mention about the other day. Lulworth, Pang-pang, so on, keep off that, and tomorrow's operation naturally; this is a Civilian Benefit, you can slope off after it's over until final briefing.'

Emmie arrived a few moments later, parked her bike and, carrying her music-case under her arm, came up the terrace steps brushing back wind-blown hair. 'The journey seems to get longer and longer, especially at dusk; for Christmas I would

259

like a nice car and a driver, please.' She kissed him gently, dropped the music-case into a chair and took the John Collins which he offered. 'You are sad?'

'Pissed off.'

'What is wrong?'

'We have to go to the House for supper. Both of us.'

She looked at him in mild shock. Took a quick sip of her drink. 'To the House? With me? Why?'

'Apparently Miss Foto's got a hitch from the Novak chap, buggered up the Old Man's plans and he wants moral support.'

'Oh my God! But I can't go like this: a skirt and blouse.'

'You look very nice; he doesn't mind. It's a light supper-affair . . . do your hair up, put it in that bun thing I like.'

'It takes ages to do, pins and things . . .'

'Don't take ages: he wants us there in a few minutes. Go on, hurry.'

'Oh Rooke, you bully me. I'm exhausted already. And Miss Foto: get me a flower for my hair then. I'll go looking like a real "putain": white for my shirt . . .'

'No flowers. You look beautiful without them.'

'You bully, you see.' She took up the music-case and went off to the bathroom emerging a few minutes later with her dark hair pulled severely back into a tight knot at her neck. She drained her glass, clattered the ice. 'Another for courage. I am terrified suddenly.'

'You look marvellous. Very elegant.'

'What will we talk about?'

'Anything except army matters; no mention of the Pangpang business, Lulworth, Weathersby or anything like that, or about tomorrow. Tell them about your exciting experiences in Eastbourne.'

'Who else will be there?'

'Just them and us. And the Old Man. He won't bite you, you know.'

He rose to greet them, hand outstretched, small blue eyes smiling, red hair glinting with brilliantine.

'How good of you to come, Miss Hoorst. At such short notice.'

'I'm sorry to be dressed like this.'

'You look very handsome. Sorry to have had to change your

260

plans, but a soldier's life is all changes and duty. Ben, see to a drink for yourself, and Miss Hoorst. What do you think of my room, pretty fine, don't you agree?'

Emmie looked slowly round the Coromandel Room, the mauve velvet walls, malachite, ivory leopard, bowls and carpets. 'It is like a treasure-cave! So many fine things.'

'All done by Master Rooke here, found all the things himself, took him days to get it just right. Did a magnificent job, I think.'

'Incredible.'

'Wait till you see the dining-room. That's really very fine, windows fourteen feet high, marvellous view of the City, you'll see at supper. Where did you get the table, Ben? Enormous great thing.'

'Must have come from a board-room, I imagine, Sir.' He handed Emmie a glass.

'What's she drinking?' said the General.

'John Collins, Sir.'

'Full of sugar. Awful stuff. There's champagne there, you know. Miss Foto likes a glass or two.'

'Started on gin, Sir, wiser to stick to it.'

'Quite, quite. Seen my piano, Miss Hoorst? Now what about that for a beauty. Do you play?'

'I did. Not for a long time.'

'Like to try? Anything'll do, a little music.'

'Dreadfully out of tune, Sir,' said Rooke.

The General turned to him with sudden suspicion. 'Out of tune? You never told me! Perhaps after supper. Cheers!' He raised his glass, drank, and settled himself into his chair. 'You help us out on *The Daily Cobra*, I understand, Miss Hoorst. Know about newspapers?'

'My father owned the main one here.'

'Ah, ha! Going to start up again soon?'

'He's dead and the building is destroyed, mostly.'

'I'm sorry. In the war?'

'In the Occupation. He refused to collaborate.'

'Just so.' A veil of discomfort slipped across the small blue eyes.

'They wanted him to continue, but he refused to print the things they asked him to.'

'Very brave chap. Shot him, I suppose?' He flushed suddenly with embarrassment. 'Do forgive me . . .'

'Please!' Emmie smiled pleasantly and set her glass down on the carved table between them. 'It is all over now. They didn't shoot him, no. They hung some big bags of type, you know? Printing type from the presses, round his neck and threw him in the river. I didn't see it.'

'My God! What a frightful thing. I'm so sorry, so sorry.'

'I'm sure, General, that you know very well what a war is? Shall I try your beautiful piano? But I think I will make a horrible noise after so long.'

Whatever Miss Foto expected to find in the Coromandel Room on her arrival it was quite certainly not the odd little Victorian tableau which revealed itself as Nanni Singh ushered them wordlessly into the room. Emmie van Hoorst at the piano, Rooke and the General standing on either side respectfully, apparently entranced by the Chopin waltz which jingle-jangled from the immense piano under Emmie's hesitant fingers. But her composure was as intact as always (only Buzz Novak appeared uneasy among the amber, ivory and malachite) and she advanced on the unaware group, for the piano was hideously loud and they were far across the room in the great bay windows, hands outstretched in delight, a smile of pleasure on her amiable, for this evening, face.

'A party! It is such a *wonderful* surprise! Oh, General! What a rogue not to tell me! And I am dressed but in rags!'

The piano stopped abruptly, the General took the offered hands in warm greeting. 'My dear Dora. How fine you look.'

She turned swiftly to include Buzz Novak. 'You remember Mr Novak? He gave us all the music for the party. This is Emmie van Hoorst, how are you, Miss van Hoorst? And this is Captain Rooke who is the right leg of the General.'

'Right arm, I imagine you mean,' said Buzz Novak easily, shaking it limply. 'Pleased to know you, a great pleasure. My! But this is quite a place? Or should I say Palace? It sure as hell is stunning . . .'

'Not too bad,' said the General. 'What'll you drink?'

'Bourbon: but if you don't have it, Scotch is fine. I just can't get over this room. Wow! Is all this stuff for real?'

262

'All is real,' said Miss Foto with delight. 'A Palace, you know.'

'Fit for a King,' agreed Mr Novak.

'A General,' corrected Miss Foto. 'And that's what I said at the very beginning, didn't I? We must make it fit for a General, and he was very brave, you know, he said, "Dora, I give you a free hand, a free hand. Do as you like." ' She took the champagne from an astonished Rooke with a cool smile and placed her arm on that of the General. 'To be so trusted! To be among lovely things once more, to be able to select and to discard, what fun I had!'

Rooke opened his mouth to protest at the blatancy of her lie but, receiving a sharp look from the General, closed it firmly.

Novak looked hard at the snarling leopard, the Nanking jars. 'You did all this? It's just stunning.'

Miss Foto smiled serenely. 'Blending of colours and so on is a *professional* job, Buzz, and the General knew that so well. Each little thing must answer to the other. Harmony, that is the general rule. Miss van Hoorst! How nice you look, your hair is most attractive. I remember that in the camp you sometimes had it cut *right* off, so mannish!'

'To avoid lice,' said Emmie amiably.

'Look at the view from here,' said the General quickly, avoiding Rooke's furious face and leading Novak to the windows. 'Right down to the City: and across there the mountains; pretty good, eh? Better from the dining-room next door. Show you later. Ben, Miss Hoorst's glass is empty.'

Emmie placed the palm of her hand over the glass. 'No, it is very well, thank you, no more at present. It's a long time since we met, Miss Foto, how pleasant it is to appear to be civilized again.'

'That is one thing I always tried to maintain for myself, even in that camp, to be civilized, it is so important, don't you think? Ah! Captain Rooke, how trim you look, so young and golden; don't you envy them their age, Miss van Hoorst?' She turned to Emmie with a bright smile. 'They are babies, all of them. Not even grown up yet. They don't worry about civilization and survival, do they? With so much youth and beauty and so much time ahead why should they? But the past was ugly and the future is beautiful . . . this, of course, he does not know: yet!'

'I'm learning *very* quickly,' said Rooke. 'The scales fall from my eyes every day.'

'What a funny thing to say. Scales . . .?'

'Like a snake. They fall away from one's eyes and things become clearer.'

'We are getting so serious, Captain Rooke! Goodness me, and it is really not the time. I am getting so exciting, you know, because almost it is Christmas! Our first Christmas in freedom for a very long time, so let us not speak of scales and snakes and ugly things, the future is so attractive!' She raised her glass and took a roguish sip, her little finger elegantly bent. 'A party! What a surprise, but so naughty of the General not to warn us, don't you think, Miss van Hoorst? In rags we both are; I am just out of mourning for poor Miss Oshima, you remember her? So tragic.'

'You must have been very sad,' said Emmie. 'She worked for you for so long.'

Miss Foto turned her head from Rooke slowly and smiled kindly at her. 'She was very good with ribbons. She could tie exquisite bows.'

'*And* knots?' Emmie's eyes were steady.

'Lovers' knots. So pretty.'

'Ben,' said the General across the room. 'Just check the table, will you? The ladies right and left . . . just family tonight, you might say.'

In the echoing dining-room with its immense table gleaming like a mahogany lake, Rooke scribbled place-cards and set them on frilly lace mats. Nanni Singh placed a bowl of hastily arranged flowers in the centre, wiped a knife slowly on his sleeve.

'You managing, Nanni? Short notice, I'm afraid.'

'I am managing. There are two fowl and American black bean soup in tins. That is all.'

'Put some sherry in the soup?'

'No sherry, Sahib. I put port.'

'Don't suppose they'll notice. How long?'

'I ring my bell, maybe ten minutes. The fowl were old.'

'You see what I mean by the windows? The height?' said the General easing himself slowly into his chair at the head of the table, Miss Foto on his right, Emmie on his left. 'Best view in the

264

Island, I'd say, see the whole place. Come up one Sunday, if you like, for tiffin, got a damn great swimming pool right down there somewhere; bring your water wings, what?'

'Be a pleasure,' said Novak as Rooke poured him wine. 'What a stunning room, so high, and the marble. Tiffin? May I ask you what that is?'

'Lunch,' said Rooke. 'Or brunch as you call it, I think.'

'Oh that! Great. Glad to, thank you, I take it that tiffin is an Indian word?'

'Correct,' said the General, concealing his surprise at the taste of his soup.

'I get confused, the British have so many different words for everything.'

Miss Foto crumbled a biscuit elegantly into her plate. 'You know, I find it so easy to talk to Americans: they have such a limited vocabulary. Where did you pick up your English, Miss van Hoorst, it is so good, that pretty little lilt. Singapore? Batavia?'

'Eastbourne,' said Emmie, laying her spoon discreetly in the purple soup and folding her hands in her lap. 'Do you know it? It is not very gay perhaps, but charming. There is a pier and a bandstand, donkey rides on the sands . . .'

'And the Palm Court, remember that?' asked Rooke, sitting beside Miss Foto determinedly ignoring his soup. 'Albert Sandler and the Palm Court Orchestra. Lots and lots of violin music, "Land of Smiles" and "Roses of Picardy".'

Emmie laughed with delight. 'I remember, oh yes! But we were never allowed into an hotel, you see, so I only heard about it, and on the wireless on Sundays after homework.'

'Why were you not allowed?' said Miss Foto sharply.

'Reverend Mother said that hotels were really brothels.'

Rooke jumped in swiftly. 'But not in Eastbourne! Far too respectable.'

'Captain Rooke,' said Miss Foto suddenly. 'Do you think you could be sweet and turn out this big chandelier? It is so harsh, look at poor Miss van Hoorst, it is not the least bit flattering to her. The side-lights would be kinder finally.'

Dinner progressed in shadow, which was probably just as well, for the enormous bowl of mutilated bird which Nanni Singh sullenly presented was not the most appetizing sight.

265

However the rice was good and the poppadums crisp, and the wine flowed under Rooke's thoughtful care so that, to all intents and purposes, the stifling supper party had every outward indication of pleasure, and by the time that the dessert had been served Novak had gained sufficient courage to embark on the rather long story of a canoeing trip he had taken just before the war in Nova Scotia. 'It's the damnedest place, you know, a wilderness; it was all Indian country not so long ago, and they left some pretty stunning ideograms up there on the rocks, it gave you such a feeling of history. Majesty, you know?'

'What are these things: ideograms?' said Miss Foto.

'Well, it's the same as petroglyphs: that's the name we know them by.'

'But what are they?'

'Oh. Ah, well, kind of scratchings on the stone. Pictures of birds, deer and sailing ships, things like that. I took a million photographs.' A distant rumble made him turn his head towards the high windows. 'Thunder?'

'Somewhere over the mountains, far away,' said the General. 'I've never been to Canada, maybe one day . . .' There was another rumble, this time closer, which rattled the windows in their metal frames.

'Storm coming up,' said the General. 'You usually see the lightning.'

The door behind him suddenly swung wide open and Nanni Singh sped across to his chair, arms raised in alarm. 'Burra Sahib!' he cried in a loud voice. 'Dekho!' and ran down the room to the windows. In an astonished clatter of spoons and forks the General and Rooke rose from their chairs and followed him as a third, and louder, rumble reverberated through the high marble room. Miss Foto rose swiftly in alarm, her hand to the pearls at her throat.

'Guns. That is guns, not thunder.' She moved halfway down the long table, Emmie and Novak sat quite still. 'What can you see? What is it?' She had reached the far end of the table as the General turned sharply.

'Fires,' he said. 'In the south of the City.'

In the black night, far below on the plain, beyond the motionless silhouettes of palm and frangipani the City burned. Three immense blocks of crimson light throbbed and flickered,

266

stuck about in the night like blazing lanterns, and as they watched a fourth suddenly ripped into the sky, a great rush of curling smoke and scattered debris which spun through the night like handfuls of brilliant jewels. The sound reached them seconds later hammering at the windows, bringing Emmie and Novak from their places, jingling the dead crystals in the chandelier.

'They are firing the City,' said the General in a low voice. 'Someone has tipped them off.'

The telephone rang, Rooke turned and ran to the hall fumbling in his pocket for a pencil, dislodging, as he did so, a slim scuffed wallet which fell open on the table top before him just as he reached for the receiver, the name Melvin Alfred Wills shining through the scratched mica. He swiftly folded it and stuck it back.

In the dining-room Novak nervously took Miss Foto by the arm. 'I'd better get you the hell out of here: maybe they're attacking, how can we tell?'

'They aren't attacking,' said the General mildly. 'Burning. We'll all go down together in convoy.' He turned kindly towards Miss Foto. 'Don't be frightened, it'll be contained, not near you, you know, across the railway. Did you have a coat?'

'A bag,' said Miss Foto vaguely. 'In the Coromandel Room, I think.' They moved out into the hall.

Emmie stood quite still, her arms folded, looking over Nanni Singh's drooped shoulders at the livid sky beyond and the tumbling, billowing smoke rising slowly in the still air until it flattened out and spread wide across the city, floating like a vast orange veil in the night. She turned as she heard Rooke call her name. 'Go back to the house. Wait for me.' She nodded and he left, buckling on his revolver, carrying the General's cap. At the window Nanni Singh leaned against the glass, his forearm across his eyes, head bowed. She knew that he was weeping and with a swift gesture took his arm and turned him to her.

'Mr Singh! Ah! Mr Singh, do not weep, please, you make me so sad, and there is no need, no need.'

Nanni Singh shook his head gently. 'Oh Sahiba, yes there is need, and for that I must weep.'

She had fallen asleep in one of the cane chairs which she had dragged to the open windows so that she could look out across the terrace to the burning city far below, an open book on her lap, a half-filled glass of cold tea on the floor beside her, her hair, freed from the tight pinning, tumbled across her shoulders. Rooke stooped gently and kissed her brow. She was instantly awake, her hands half-raised in a gesture of protection. The flicker of alarm faded to a soft smile. She took his hand and held it to her lips.

'What time is it? I've been asleep.'

'Three something. You've been all right?'

'Perfectly. I read. Watched. Is it very bad?'

'It's very big. Difficult to tell, the place is swarming with refugees. Chinese mostly, kids and bundles, women wailing, never seen such a muddle, trying to get them all across the railway before we go in; that's all we'll need, bloody civilians mixed up with the tanks.'

'And you do go in?'

'As planned. At first light. Got to now, anyway, obviously someone gave them the tip-off. Easy to do. The Old Man's hopping mad about Security, but you can't have complete security when you employ a swarm of civilians, anyone could have given the plan away. Bloody senseless.'

She got up. 'I'll make some tea perhaps? You are covered in dirty marks.'

'Oil smuts. Terrible stink down there. Burning rubber or something, and oil. I'd rather have a Scotch, big and strong.'

'Won't it keep you awake? You should try and sleep for an hour.'

'Too excited. You know? Don't think I could sleep. The Old Man is quite calm, gone up to bed: I'm to call him at five sharp. Nothing he can do for the moment, they're all milling about down at HQ. Everyone is prepared of course, the RAF standing by for first light. Excited as hell. Funny lot, the RAF.'

She brought him a whisky. 'And Mr Novak and Miss Foto?'

He laughed shortly. 'A bit of a panic for him, she was fine, very cool. But he's scared they've burned the place to ruins, kept saying it was a disaster, a terrible disaster, British security was all to hell and if that's the way we ran our wars it was mighty lucky we still had America to get us out of our 'snafu's'. I just could have hit him, but he was really scared shitless, you

268

could see that, full of piss and wind and damn all else. He really is a ruddy Boxwallah, that's all.'

'What's that?'

'Tradesman.'

'Of course. And the south is where all the factories and the plants are, also my Convent. I wonder if they've burned that, I hope so.'

'The Kempei-Tai HQ? I'll make a personal check for you.'

'Don't risk anything for me. Nothing, please.'

'I won't. You go back when I leave, get down to HQ as soon as possible, I'll get news to you as soon as I can. Somehow.'

'It'll be a long time?'

'Depends what they do. Stay and fight from the rubble or pull out: maybe they have. Can't tell yet. A day, two days: maybe longer.'

Maybe for ever, she thought. Maybe you won't come back. Perhaps this is how it ends, Pinkerton doesn't return after all. She sat quietly at his feet; he yawned and fumbled in his pocket, gave her the wallet which she opened incuriously.

'Meant to put it away, keep it for me, will you?'

'What is it?'

He told her briefly; she looked at him with surprise.

'Read the little note inside. In Dutch.'

'Yoko? Yoko Oshima? She kept this?'

'Apparently.'

'But why do you? It proves nothing.'

'Proves she knew the man. Miss Foto.' His eyes were heavy-lidded with fatigue.

'But that's all, only that maybe.'

'It's enough. We'll see.'

She closed the wallet and laid it on the table beside them. 'Oshima, Weathersby, now this. Wills. We are haunted by the dead.'

'Put it in my safe, will you, in the morning?'

She nodded and looked out into the livid night sky, dull crimson beyond the black trees; when she turned to him he was asleep, head against the back of the cane chair. She gently removed the whisky glass, reached across for her open book, the soft arc of lamp-light touched his ear, the stretched tendon in his neck, the smut-stained hand lying on his thigh, the white

269

pages of *Cranford* on her lap. She looked at her watch. Three thirty-five. They had one hour left together: she pushed her hair from her brow and addressed herself to Mrs Gaskell.

The railway line which divided the City also invested it with a subtle social difference known best to those who lived there. The south, for want of a better phrase, was the wrong side of the tracks. Wilhelmina Boulevard cutting through from north to south abruptly changed its name to Amsterdamse Weg the instant it crossed the railway, and its tree-lined length gave way to banks, office blocks, shipping companies, a department store called 'Arkadia', blocks of shabby flats, the Convent of the Sacred Heart some way down in ugly red-brick gothic, shops, or packed warehouses. The heart of this commercial district was a vast square formed by the intersection of Oranje Laan which ran directly east and west. In the centre stood a battered concrete lady symbolizing Commerce with a cornucopia, the Arkadia and the Bank of Nieuwe Celebes, both of which were still burning brightly as the first Japanese Tanks of 2nd Brigade reached the place; their first objective. They had moved without much hindrance, apart from snipers, mortars, fallen masonry and the jostling throngs of refugees, eyes red-rimmed from the acrid smoke, dragging yelling children, aged parents, and anything which moved on wheels. This ragged river of unhappy people poured up the wide street and across the railway into the capable hands of the Military Police and exhausted members of RAPWI. By eight a.m. the tanks had deployed about the area of the rubble-littered square and a temporary Brigade HQ had been set up in the offices of a shipping firm, Nettles securing the lower ground floor room as an Ops. Room where he hurried about, aided by Corporal Batt and a sweating group of Signallers. At the same time the 16th Indian Grenadiers, with tank support, pushed on down Amsterdamse Weg to the south in the hopes that without too much fuss and bother they would eventually link up with the first elements of the Dutch VI Brigade who were, according to the General's plan, sweeping down from the dock area in the north, thus to contain any extremists foolish enough to hang on in the wide pocket which they would make. That there still

270

were extremists in the area was proved by intermittent bursts of automatic fire from roof tops and windows, and also by still more explosions and barrelling columns of smoke which rolled up into the hot morning air beyond the red-brick tracery of the Convent spire, a kilometre and a half down the road.

The General was a Fighting General. He didn't believe in sitting comfortably in his Ops. Room at HQ, but uncomfortably, and happily, in that provided by his IO Major Nettles in the heart of the battle. With the clatter of tanks outside, the shouts and curses of Signallers stringing cable and wires everywhere, the hot crackle of the burning Arkadia, the smell of cordite and smouldering rubber, he felt far more at home and relaxed than he ever did in his opulent Coromandel Room at the Palace. He sat at a makeshift desk on a dining-room chair prodding at a large blow-up map of the area.

'Now let's see. That's the shop across the square still burning, right? We are about here, I'd say on this corner, and this place with the X beside it is the Convent building: why a question mark, Nettles?'

'Because we can't be absolutely sure it *is* their HQ. All we do know from Ground Sources is that they train most of their commando recruits there.'

'Who do?'

'The PDCAG.'

The General sighed. 'One has to presume that is the enemy, I gather? All these bloody initials. I got on better when I knew it was simply Jerry, or Wops, or Japs, even ruddy Wogs. You need a blasted directory to find out who is who now. Communist, I suppose?'

'Marxist–Leninist.'

'Oh God. Spare me. Once Kempei-Tai HQ, I take it?'

'So there must be plenty of facilities.'

'Let's try and take the place intact, shall we. All that bumph for you to clap your beady eyes on.'

'Unless they've pulled out and burned the lot. They have had advance warning, remember.'

'I don't need reminding. Let's look on the bright side, Nettles, only thing to do.'

'The bright side,' said Nettles rubbing his hands together, 'is just arriving.'

'In what form, may I ask?'

'The invaluable Rooke bearing tea, Sir.'

'Spot on!' said the General taking his tin mug. 'Simply splendid! Set up already?'

'Cookhouse practically in business next door,' said Rooke. 'Tea's a bit tepid, it came in a container, I'm afraid. Be fresh stuff in a moment or two, Sir.'

'Never mind: it's wet,' said the General and raised the mug to his lips at the exact moment that a tremendous explosion roared through the square outside. The blast tore the mug from his hand, hurled Nettles into a whirling hurricane of files and papers, spun Rooke wildly into a far corner, and brought down half the ceiling in a cascade of dust, rubble and plaster. Three more giant explosions followed almost instantly, filling the wrecked room with smoke, dust and flying shards of glass which ripped across the mahogany counter of the office, slicing across it like the teeth of a saw. And then there was a sudden and abrupt silence. Dust trickled: a brick toppled with a thump onto a metal cabinet. In the square someone started screaming.

Rooke stared up at the shattered ceiling, the gaping hole, steel girder, hanging lamp still swinging wildly on its cord, a piece of paper eddying through the dust. He struggled to sit up but was jammed under a table top: through the dust he saw that Nettles was on all fours clawing his way over tumbled debris to the General who was slumped against a marble pillar, head on his chest. With a tremendous effort he flung the table top aside, and, to his astonishment, found that he was on his feet lurching over fallen chairs and torn map-boards.

He reached the General just before Nettles, knelt beside him, gently touched his shoulder. 'Sir? Are you all right?'

The General raised his head very slowly, the small blue eyes rimmed with dust, lips caked. 'Not dead. Help Nettles there.'

Nettles was kneeling upright, swaying a little, hands to his head. 'I'm all right; winded.' He got unsteadily to his feet and together they pulled the General to his.

'Nothing broken, it's all right, don't fuss.' He was a heavy man, and once they had him leaning upright against his pillar they all stood, catching their breaths. 'Near thing,' said the General. 'Anyone in here hurt? Who was here? Can't remember . . .'

272

A white face appeared suddenly from behind a counter streaked with blood from a scalp wound, white with dust and plaster, hair like a hedgehog, hands shaking. 'There was me, Sir. Corporal Batt, Cypher Clerk.'

'You all right?' The General was starting to brush his shoulders slowly.

'Clobbered on the head, I think, Sir. Saw stars. Nothing broken, Sir. Guess we was lucky.'

'I reckon we bloody well were. Where's me cap?'

They found his cap, he thumped it hard against a thigh, crammed it on and clambered into the smoke-filled square. Rooke following unsteadily behind him.

It was littered with blocks of masonry, fallen cables, piles of shattered glass glistening like crushed ice, shreds of cloth, planks and shards of wood. The high-pitched screaming had stopped. Almost instantly Gaunt was there before them, cap askew, face pale through the swirling smoke. He saluted smartly.

' 'Morning, Sir.'

'What were they? Shells?'

'No, Sir. Bombs, I think. Delayed action probably.'

'Are we hard hit?'

'Two trucks gone up.'

'Casualties, I mean.'

'Collecting them now, Sir, trying to. They were queueing up for tea.'

'How many?'

'Hard to tell. Havildar Dozinga copped it. He was beside one of the trucks.'

'Badly?'

'Bits and pieces, I'm afraid, Sir.'

'Fuckers,' said the General. 'Where are they?'

Lying in rows on the black and white tiled floor of an empty shop, blood running in meandering streams, the crumpled, tattered bodies lay silently, patiently, in a triple row. The stink of blood, urine and excreta in the jammed place forced Rooke to the gaping doorway. His head was throbbing from the clout he must have received, and his legs were shaking; someone behind him shouted, 'Move yer arse, for fuck's sake,' and he turned to help ease a grey-faced huddle of uniform which had been half-dragged, half-carried by a capless blood-stained

Corporal onto a space at his feet. The General walked slowly down the ragged lines, stooping to speak to those who could, reaching for a hand when it was offered, squatting beside someone who could do neither but whose eyes mutely implored his attention. He stayed for a few moments, speaking softly, comforting the wide-eyed body whose thin brown hand was tightly clasped between his own, soothing, assuring, promising care, murmuring words of gratitude, applauding the frail courage.

This is the man, thought Rooke. This is My General. This is what he is all about. Not a foolish man at all. Sad, unhappy maybe. But not foolish; either as a man or as a soldier. This is his job and he knows it by heart and does it with his heart. This is a good man and a brave one. I have never felt proud about anyone else before: but I am proud today.

'So you should be,' said Nettles a few moments later, sorting through a spilled bundle of chinagraph pencils which he had retrieved from the ruins of his once orderly Ops. Room. 'So you should. He's a common man, you see. Who has retained the common touch. Very rare—far more valuable than any cultist General. God knows, we have had enough of those in our time . . . his intellect doesn't get in the way of his basic instincts, and even though they might be frightfully simple, as you say; like *The Warsaw Concerto*, Marmite sandwiches, that ghastly house, and only reading *Biggles*, they are at least true.' He stacked the pencils tidily into a box and wiped his sleeve over the top of his map-case. 'He knows about war and soldiers, and when you are dealing with both, and your life is at stake, it really does help. Quite apart from anything else, Rooke, he *cares*. Give that a thought next time you hear a ricochet.'

A little before midday 16th Indian Grenadiers signalled that they had linked up with the Dutch VI Brigade and that their area, except for a sniper here and there, was clear; and the General ordered that the whole of the south area should be now taken to avoid any further destruction by saboteurs and to relieve the refugee situation which was becoming acute, with hundreds of Chinese milling about the streets, cheering or weeping and all trying to make for the north which was already overwhelmed by their numbers. The operation was to continue until the entire city from north to south was secured: 'No more shilly-shally, get the buggers cleared out once and for all, we

274

have the initiative and the RAF . . . let's get on with it. Right, Bunny?'

'Bunny' Blackett screwed the top onto his hip flask, and slid it back into his pocket. 'Absolutely, Sir.' His eyes were red with dust and smoke, he reached for his cap.

'It's perfectly feasible,' said the General. 'Seem to remember you complained about casualties some time ago? Quite right, far too many. Thirty alone in the square this morning. Six of them gonners. Let's put a stop to it, eh? Anyway, I'm the ruddy piper so I call the tune — and that's it!'

'Perfectly feasible, Sir,' said 'Bunny' Blackett. 'Off we go then.' He clapped on his cap, saluted neatly, and clumped through fallen bricks and glass to his jeep. Swinging himself in beside his driver he started to whistle wearily. 'Come, follow! Follow! Follow! The merry, merry pipes of Pan!'

The sallow-faced Lady Communist eased an irregular piece of glass from the shattered window beside her and examined it carefully: two hands clasped in prayer thrusting from scarlet cuffs. She dropped it listlessly to the stone floor. 'Whatever belief people profess to have, they always clasp their hands to indicate appeal. The movement is beyond any religion, however; it is a basic human gesture and one which now I make to you. Look!' She clasped her hands tightly together and held them towards him.

'Come away now, please, with me. You are aware that I know all the ways to join Comrade Suka. We can avoid the big streets, come with me now. I am appealing to you, please.'

The boy shook his head and started to get out of his ill-fitting, home-made uniform. 'I cannot go with you, I have told you this.' He wrenched at a bright red cotton star stitched to each side of his collar, the highest award for zeal which his Cadre could command. He had been very proud to receive them and now that he was to discard the uniform he had no intention of discarding his stars.

She watched him pulling at the stitching, remembering how proudly he had watched her sew them on such a short time before. However hard she tried to eradicate the feeling within her heart, she knew, sadly, that it was not merely his bravery

275

and courage, his determination and dedication to the Cause which had made her stay behind with him when all the rest had either been killed or had fled. It was a deeper emotion and one she bitterly despised herself for recognizing. This was not in the Teachings, this was a bourgeois emotion, against all the force and endeavour which she had applied to her own. In the end, she reasoned wanly, he was man and she was woman and the common enemy and the savage situation had brought them close together. She admired his skill, his cunning, his willingness to take frightful risks, his aptitude with the Mk. 92 automatic which she had taken weeks to master, his bravery under fire, his disdain for safety, and above all the way in which he had brought back the information needed to fire the City and cause confusion and dismay among the enemy, allowing Comrade Suka and the other Company Commanders to alter plans rapidly and retreat to the hills where, well-entrenched and surrounded by their comrades in arms who had not yet been corrupted by the invaders, they could hold out and continue the fight. The splendour of last night and the devastation and delay they had caused today. were his triumph. And now he was leaving, slipping away among the hordes of fleeing Chinese under cover of night, so that he could continue his own fight in the north. But alone. Not with her, and not with the Commando Cadre. An uncontrollable despair overtook her and so distressed her body that she was forced to sit heavily on a wooden bench.

He had removed the stars from the jacket collar and now stepped out of his baggy uniform trousers, grey with dust and black with smoke and oil, reached for a pair of dirty cotton ones and, stuffing the two crumpled stars into the pockets, started to pull them on. He had legs as slender as a girl's, she thought, a gazelle. She turned and looked through the fragments of stained glass. In the wide street below the smoke still drifted heavily from their fires, lanced here and there by shafts of sunlight which spilled across the throngs of people struggling along with their bundles, carts, cycles, all heading, as the boy was soon to do, for the north. The sounds of shuffling feet, barking dogs, creaking wheels, urgent voices and the almost continuous rumble and rattle of tanks and tracked vehicles heading to the south came up to her in continuous waves which filled her

276

drained mind and threatened to burst her head. She started to weep, the tears running down her cheeks. The boy looked at her with a smile. 'You *weep* for a victory, Comrade?'

She shook her head. 'No. I weep for myself. I have lost.'

He had taken up a dirty blood-stained shirt which he had removed from the body of one of his comrades lying in a black pool of filth in the hall below and pulled it over his head. 'We have won. We have won what we set out to win. To cause dismay, to fill them with alarm, to send them into disarray, morally we have won, now we pull back to fight from our own territory.'

'Cannon shells,' she said. 'Against grenades and rifles; you speak like the little parrots. Disarray, dismay, alarm, morale! These are new words for you, you use them as a child who has found coloured stones upon the beach.'

He was tucking in the bloody shirt, fastening a cheap belt round his slender waist. 'You are doubting, Comrade?'

'I do not doubt. No. I do not doubt.' She wiped her face with the stubby, worn, fingers. 'I am weary only. You will not let me come with you? It is certain?'

'It is certain,' said the boy. 'I can move better on my own: I know where to cross, where to hide, I have friends there.'

She looked about the shadowy room, heavy with jumbled bits of ecclesiastical stuff which the Japanese had never bothered to remove. Carved gothic chairs, benches, a headless plaster Christ baring a blazing heart with stigmata'd hands, battered filing cabinets with Japanese markings, a tilted hat-stand made from animal horns, a splinter-torn photograph of Marx and Lenin, above which someone had painted a crude red star on the whitewashed wall.

'Once this room was full of hope,' she said. 'We had high courage, we saw such a future.' Suddenly she got to her feet and raised her arm in proud salute to the torn photograph before her. 'But we will survive! We will conquer! We have no need to fight with guns and tanks to bring our Faith to every corner of the earth; we need only the words and persuasion and it will come to be. We must exploit their weakness, be ever alert, we must infiltrate their sloth. We have a world to gain! A world of Liberty!'

The boy watched her curiously, a half-smile on his lips, and

277

slid a Japanese Mk. 14 pistol into the front of his shirt. 'You too speak as the little parrots,' he said.

She lowered her arm slowly, brushed her skirt with her hands. 'They will search you and they will find your gun.'

'They will not search me and they will not find the gun.' He emptied a small box of bullets into the palm of his hand and thrust them into his trouser pocket.

'I speak like this because it is the Teaching and I must repeat the words unless I lose heart.'

'You will go now to join Suka and the others?' he said.

'I will go now. Before the night, the streets are full, no one will notice me. I know the lanes and alleys.' She shrugged tiredly. 'After all, I am just a girl; who will notice me among so many others who are lost?'

The boy was in the centre of the room poking with his foot at a large heap of dead ashes. 'You will tell Suka that I have finished my duty here. Everything is destroyed as he said, they will find no names, all is ashes.'

'I will say.'

'And when I have done my other duties in the north I shall return. He must tell me where; leave the message at the barber's shop. You will remember this?'

She nodded and turned away to the window. 'It is still so light,' she said.

'I will wait here a little longer, and then I will walk in the streets to see what damage we have done.'

Her sudden stifled cry of alarm stopped him. She ran across the cluttered room, hands to her mouth, eyes wide with fright.

'What?'

'Soldiers. British: coming into the garden.'

'How many?'

'A jeep, a truck. Go! Go!'

Instead he crept across to the window and looked down into the ruined garden, screened by sagging fragments of coloured glass. A jeep had swung into the gateway followed by a truck. Two officers were standing on the steps, a score of Indian soldiers clambered stiffly from the back of the truck, with full packs, rifles slung, boots crunching on the broken glass and thick gravel. Someone gave orders and they shuffled into a double line. The boy turned into the room, the girl was standing by the door, a straw bag over her shoulder, in her hand a small packet of bullets which she threw to him as he came towards her. 'Come with me, there is a window at the back, we can get down onto the tennis courts . . . hurry.' He took her hand and she followed him into the long corridor.

'It's an odd time to come sight-seeing,' said Nettles. 'I should have thought you'd have had a bellyful today.'

'I told Emmie I'd check if it was still here, just curious,' said Rooke.

'Well, I only want to have a quick look around, get the chaps in and settled, then we can get to work tomorrow. I don't suppose there's anything to look at, but we can't risk looters: no electric light of course. They'll have to use torches or something. What a frightful place.' They walked up the chipped stone steps, pushed through the shattered doors into the echoing stone-pillared hall.

'My goodness,' said Nettles. 'The Catholics really do build their places to last, great belief in their Faith, I suppose.' He picked his way over fallen bricks, scattered papers, broken glass and tumbled books; at the foot of the wide stone staircase leading to the upper floor, a shirtless body sprawled in a spread of blood, sticky and dark as tar, flies buzzing, arms flung wide.

'Cannon shell through the front doors here: whammed into the pillar, y'see? Taken quite a chunk and this little chap caught the splinters. Oh! the frailty of mortal flesh, I *do* wonder how we ever survive. I always hoped that my particular war would be a gentle occupation. Vain hope. It never is. By the way, get your pop-gun out, one never knows who may be lurking about.'

'It is out,' said Rooke and raised it.

'I feel so utterly implausible with a gun. Really not my style at all. So awfully Tom Mixish. I crumple if anyone throws a streamer . . .'

On the floor above the boy had reached the far end of the corridor, lined on one side with tall barred windows, on both by rows of headless plaster saints, admonishing or blessing, from high oak plinths.

At the window he froze, then ducked swiftly into a corner dragging the girl with him. Her face was grey with fear.

'Soldiers. Armed, on the tennis courts.'

From below the English voices echoing lightly in the hall, doors shutting, metal-studded boots squealing on the stone steps, coming upwards slowly. The boy looked about him, alert as a stoat, he pushed the girl across the floor behind one of the saints. 'Get down, crouch low, they may turn right.' She pressed herself against the oak plinth, hugging the straw bag to her breast, the boy was flat against the opposite wall, pistol in his hand, the English voices growing clearer.

'Not a sign of life, cleared off last night.' The two men had got to the top of the staircase and stopped. Three corridors: one to the left, one ahead, one to the right. From below a vaguely anxious voice called.

'Major Nettles? Major Nettles, Sir?'

Nettles turned, a hand on the balustrade, shouted down comfortingly. 'Here, Corporal Batt, up here. Just swanning about.' He looked at Rooke. 'Dilemma. Left, right or centre?'

'There's an open door, on the left,' said Rooke uncertainly.

'All these headless people, got their names up, I notice. St Ulrich, St Thomas, St Hubert, never seen so many.'

The dark room. Headless Christ, tilted hat-stand, empty bottles fallen, jumbled chairs, the last of the sunlight sparkling through the shattered stained glass window.

'Pretty effect,' said Nettles. 'Like a jar of wine-gums.' He moved about the disordered room carefully, poked here and there with the barrel of his revolver, lightly raised the crumpled jacket the boy had discarded.

'Uniform, one could say? Ex-Japanese Infantry adapted to Mr Marx and Mr Lenin up there, note the little cloth hammer and sickle: rather badly stitched, I fear: left his pants behind too it would seem; what are you kicking at?'

'Ashes,' said Rooke sifting them with his boot. 'Burned papers and stuff.' He placed his hand on the drifting pile. 'Cold. Last night's effort, done before they lit the fuses.'

Nettles swung out a couple of drawers in the filing cabinets, rolled them shut. 'All Jap stuff. Sort it in the morning, get the experts along, nothing much to amuse us here: I gather that most of the activities took place in the cellars.'

'Oh God! Not this evening?' said Rooke.

'Not this evening.' Nettles crossed thoughtfully to the door. 'It's been a long day.'

280

In the corridor they paused for an instant looking down the long lines of beheaded dusty saints. 'Like the British Museum, isn't it? All those dreary Elgin Marble things — no other rooms along here.' He turned away and at the precise moment that he did the girl pulled a small grenade from the straw bag and bowled it expertly down the long corridor. Rooke saw it from the corner of his eye and with a harsh yell of warning grabbed Nettles and slammed him backwards into the room, they hit the floor together as the grenade trailed a gentle arc and exploded against the base of St Ulrich with a blinding roar of flame and smoke and the singing of spinning metal shards. A moment of complete silence. The hurried sound of boots on stone from far off and Corporal Batt's high voice.

'Sir? Major Nettles? All right then? You all right?'

They lay still, made no sound. Smoke drifted idly through the open door, a bullet whanged past suddenly from their left, they stared at each other in silent shock, hearing Corporal Batt's urgent boots clattering away. On his belly Rooke inched slowly to the threshold, hugging the floor. Using the bulk of St Ulrich's solid plinth as a cover he squinted through the gap made between it and the wall. Through the drifting smoke the crumpled figure of the girl on her face, one arm stretched before her, twitching like a dreaming dog, moaning softly. From the room behind the diffused rumble of traffic, from the hall the muffled sound of moving men, orders given, click of rifle bolts. He lay still, watching along the line of saints. Suddenly from the cover of the last one a movement as, with infinite caution, the boy inched out on his knees, gun in hand, staring with blazing eyes towards the staircase arch. He was kneeling upright facing unseeingly in Rooke's direction, edging himself inch by inch to the whimpering girl opposite. As if she had sensed him she raised the extended hand a fraction from the floor, and as the boy turned swiftly to her, Rooke fired.

In the deafening explosion which reverberated down the long room, the boy jerked violently backwards like a string-pulled toy, slamming against the far wall. Rooke pulled himself to his knees as the screaming started. High, harsh screams of agony drowning the sound of soldiers who had reached the top of the stairs. Nettles waved them back wildly as Rooke ran towards the bucking figure under the window.

281

The boy was on his back, arms thrown wide, an enormous red stain growing larger and larger in the white fork of his splayed-apart legs, twitching and heaving convulsively, hands clawing the air, lips dragged back tautly from the screaming mouth.

'You've got him low!' yelled Nettles. 'You got him in the balls! Finish him! Finish him! Finish him!'

Rooke stared at the widening stain on the white trousers, at the dreadful rivulets of brilliant red spilling across the stone floor, ebbing at his feet: he felt Nettles grab his arm violently, heard the harshness of his voice above the echoing screams.

'Kill him! Kill him! Finish him off: oh! for the love of Christ, man, come of age.'

Deliberately Rooke raised his revolver and fired into the wide open mouth.

CHAPTER ELEVEN

Minnie leant over the verandah rail and called anxiously towards the two boys at the far end of the garden; the blond one knelt up shielding his eyes from the sun; Pullen moved into the light and waved. The boy waved back and started running through the sere grasses. Minnie bowed nervously, thrust her hands into wide cuffs and hurried into the house.

'Nigel! Sir! I am so pleased.'

'Not interrupting, I hope? I was just passing, Wim. You have a friend there.'

'He's my friend from the camp, Bert, you do not interrupt; he cannot speak English, he is busy.'

'What are you doing?'

'Making a lizard trap. You know this? There is a big one down there, but we must have patience to catch him.'

'Of course. You've got fatter since I last saw you.'

'Thank you, I am very fine. My mother is today in the City.'

'Actually I came to see you. Brought you this: should have given it to you at Christmas-time, but we had a lot going on.'

'I know. The battle, was it? In the City?'

'The battle. Anyway, a delayed present, better late than never.'

'Oh yes! Than never! A present!' He ripped Muriel Pullen's carefully hoarded wrapping paper into strips at his feet. Holly and mistletoe curling into a dazzle of alien crimson flowers.

'*Treasure Island*!! You remembered! Oh Nigel.' He made a wide gesture with his open arms, corrected the movement swiftly. 'I mean, thank you, thank you.'

'All in English, as you said. Hope you can manage.'

'And pictures, you see? Oh ho! It is a fat book.' He pressed it open firmly. ' "The Landing On The Island." You see? I am reading well already.'

'It'll take you a time.'

'I read fast. Would you like some tea, also we have coffee?'

'No, I must be off, and Bert is waiting for you.'

Wim dismissed Bert with a shrug and sat in a deck-chair

clasping the book. 'Bert is very serious. He wears glasses and everything takes him a long time to do; he is funny, he puts out his tongue quite far when he is working. Shall I ask Minnie for some tea perhaps?' He was instantly on his feet and had run into the house before Pullen could properly reply, returning almost as soon. 'She is bringing it, anyway. So you will stay, yes? Beer.' He laughed and riffled through the book. 'She is silly. She is frightened still of uniforms.'

'I'll try not to frighten her.'

'You could not. You are too nice-looking.'

'Thank you. How is your Papa?'

Wim kept his eyes on a page, screwing them up to little slits, his lips silently mouthing words. 'My Papa? I have seen him, you know this?'

'I'm glad. Splendid. I hoped that you would.'

'Yes. I have seen him.' Eyes still on the page, one finger pulling at a fall of blond hair. 'Not at first. When he was better.'

'He is stronger by now, I am sure.'

'His face is broken up, you know this? His mouth is . . .' He hunted for the word and suddenly looking directly at Pullen pulled his upper lip high towards his nose, tilting his head back. 'Like this. Cut in two.'

'I am sorry.'

'So he speaks not well. He likes to see me, but he cannot smile much. But I know from his eyes, sometimes they do.'

'But they'll mend that, you know. Stitch it together or something.'

Wim shook his head with authority. 'No. It is not so. They say it.'

'Oh come! I'm sure they can, they do wonderful things for people now.'

'I go not often, sometimes he sits by the window in a chair. He does not care to walk very much.'

Minnie arrived with a clink of glasses, set the tray before them, called down to Bert who replied in a mumble, poured a tall glass of lime juice for him and flapped down the steps with it.

'He also is shy, this Bert. He will not come, you see. Shall I open the tin? The beer? Is funny in a tin, is American.'

'I can do it, don't you bother, you having a drink?'

284

'I will make it.'

'And your Mother. She is well? She must be very happy now?'

Wim lay back in the chair swinging one leg, his arms crossed over the top of his head; he looked down into the blinding light of the garden. 'Sometimes. Your beer is quite well cold?'

'Perfect, thank you.'

'From your refrigerator. Now it works so fine.'

'That's because we have the electricity plant now.'

'From the battle?'

'From the battle. And the RAF.'

Wim folded his hands across his chest. 'It was quite big, I think? We have heard all the noise. Whoom! Whoom! And the sky red and so many things in the night.'

'Were you frightened?'

Wim laughed shortly. 'At first. But my Mother said it was all right because it had been planned.'

'Some of it had,' said Pullen ruefully. 'They did a lot of damage, I'm afraid.'

'It was a big battle?'

'No, not a very big one. But not a very nice one.'

'But people were killed, is it?'

'Yes, people were killed. People often are in battles, you know.'

'I know. It was because of that there was no Christmas?'

'Because of that. Not, very, well, not a very happy time really. And there are still people locked in the camps like your Papa was. It is not fair to celebrate when so many people are still not free.'

'My Mother said this.' Wim picked up his book, opened the fly leaf, suddenly squinted hard at it, holding it close to his face. 'For Wim Doorne with Best Wishes for a Very Happy Christmas 1945, from Muriel Pullen.' He laid the book in his lap. 'But who is this?'

'My sister.'

'She knows my name?'

'I wrote and told her. She found it for you.'

Wim looked silently at the fly leaf, ran his hand across the tidy ink script. 'She is a very nice woman. If she is like you she must be very, very nice.'

Pullen flushed slightly and crossed his legs. 'Christmas comes but once a year, Wim!'

'It is a pity: I would like it to be once a week.' He was smiling but his eyes were grave. Suddenly he said: 'I think my Papa will not get well,' and put the book under his arm.

'Oh now, come!' said Pullen helplessly. 'That's a wild thing to say, he's had a very bad time, Wim, it'll take a lot of patience and a lot of care to make him well. But he will be, you'll see.'

'My Mother feels this too. I can tell.'

'I am sure that is not so, Wim.'

'She never sings now.'

'She is very busy: she has such a lot to do.'

'In the camp she sang. Even in the camp.' He rose quickly to his feet at the sound of voices from the house and, with a curt apologetic nod to Pullen, hurried into the shadowy hall. Pullen got up, set his glass on the table, took up his cap and cane.

'Look!' cried Wim. 'Look who is here! I told you a surprise!' He half-pulled, half-pushed Clair through the wide doors. 'He brought my book, he hadn't forgotten, for Christmas.'

'Awful just to barge in like this, but I was passing and thought if I left it any longer it'd be Easter.'

'How good of you, Nigel, I am so happy to see you. Such a long time!' She pulled a battered straw hat from her head, threw it on the table, and took his hands in both of hers. 'Wim looked after you? A drink? Ah, yes, forgive me, I am such a mess. David Gaunt brought me from the City, he drives like an idiot! But I was so grateful; Wim, tell Minnie to bring me a delicious drink, I am quite finished with dust and things. *You* get it. Go now.'

'Look. See, *Treasure Island*, with a message from his sister, see.'

'Go and get my drink, I die of thirst while you chatter.' She ran her hand lightly through his hair; he ducked away and went into the house leaving the book in her hands.

'Read what it says. She knew my name even,' he called.

There was a tight silence. Suddenly she laughed and touched Pullen with a finger.

'Oh sit! We stand like strangers. I am exhausted.'

'I really mustn't stay.'

'Well, finish your beer. I hate to drink alone, a bad habit.'

286

She put the book on the table. 'How good of you to remember. At a time like this with so many other things to worry about.'

'Oh, it's all slackening off a bit now. Was a bit of a rumble bumble, but all a bit calmer now.'

She smiled across at him, pulling her skirt across her knees. 'I have missed that word of yours so much.'

'What word?'

'Rumble bumble. It means so much.'

'Family joke, I suppose. A rumble bumble. Well it *has* been, I can tell you.'

'You look well.'

'And you.'

'I'm an old hag. Getting used to the Peace is something I never expected to be so exhausting. I looked forward to it so much I didn't really think it would be so much work.'

'You go to the hospital every day?'

'Every day, yes. Sometimes there are not such good days, so I stay away, but mostly every day.'

'And?'

'And it is slow. Slower than I thought, I suppose.'

'It's been barely six weeks, you know.'

'Oh I know. I do not expect miracles. He is physically so much better, stronger, he walks well, he has put on weight, really very good. Sister Pritchard, you know . . .'

'With the hair on her face.'

'Oh you are so unkind. Yes, only a little fluff, not hair. But she is like a saint, you know, this woman. So warm, she cares for them all so much, it is a real dedication, like being a nun, I imagine. I am humbled daily by her goodness and her patience.'

'So I have to take back all I said about her?'

She laughed. 'All! She is my friend, so be careful now!'

Wim returned with a can of beer which he opened, pouring it too quickly, it foamed up and spilled down over his hand.

'It is full of gas, this beer!'

'You poured it like milk. No, don't sit down again, take your gift and show it to Bert.'

'He can't read English.'

'Show him the book anyway.'

'I would like to stay with Nigel.'

287

Clair was firm and calm. 'So would I. Be off.'

Grinning he got up, took the book, made his formal little bow. 'You'll call me before you go, please?'

'I'll call you,' said Pullen.

Clair lay back in her low chair watching him go. 'The sooner I get him to a school the better.'

'I hear they are starting up again.'

'Not here,' she said, taking the half-empty glass. 'In Europe. Here is all over for us now. I must get Pieter back too; he will not stay.'

'To Europe? When?'

'When we can. When we are ready. It is difficult with the boats, so many people are leaving. We have no future in Indonesia any longer, it is ended for ever. And in any case,' she smiled slightly, 'Pieter wants to leave, he cannot find his confidence; I think he has lost courage; I think that for a man like him the humiliations, apart from the suffering, of the last three years, were too much. He cannot forget and everything here reminds him.'

'Perhaps when he gets here, home, you know? Perhaps he will feel differently.'

'He doesn't want to come here. Isn't that strange? He prefers the hospital, it is less responsibility for him. In Europe I think he will manage to start again, the mind will heal more quickly there. The camps, he remembers, he dreams, he weeps sometimes. Not outside weeping, do you understand? Inside. It is so much worse.'

'Oh my dear Clair. I'm so sorry, dreadfully sorry.'

'He was such a proud man. With proud men the fall is greater.'

'Of course it is. I know. I'm so sorry. You've tried so hard for so long, it all really is a bit of a . . .'

She finished his sentence for him, smiling wanly, 'Rumble bumble? Yes. Yes, it is. It will be strange after so many years away, and they have to settle down after their own war which was not so amusing, I think. We'll try; and Wim must write to . . . your sister, was it?'

'Muriel, yes.'

'Is she in London?'

'No. My house. The family house. Hampshire.'

288

She got up and walked over to the steps, stooped to pick up the shreds of bright wrapping paper. 'It was really so kind of her, of you both. With so many other things to worry you and give you trouble.'

'Oh, no trouble. Easy stuff. She loves all that sort of thing, knitting soldiers' socks, reading to the blind; she sends me little packets all the time. "Surprises": a bar of chocolate, cake of soap, ten hoarded cigarettes, and I don't smoke them; she hoards everything. Envelopes, string, elastic bands and so on. Busy as a magpie.' He looked at his watch and got up. 'Must run, late for lunch already, mustn't keep you chattering away.'

I'm chattering away, he thought, to keep my distance, to avoid direct contact, to avoid your eyes which I know have lost their light. The light I knew and loved. I must be a good loser.

She was standing with her back to him, wadding the torn scraps of paper abstractedly into a neat ball, looking out into the glittering light.

'Don't be late.'

'No. I'll give Wim a shout.'

'No hat on, of course. They'll both get sunstroke.'

'Wim! Off now! Lunch!' He waved. Wim looked up, shouted something, waved, turned away again.

Pullen smiled. 'The lizard trap. At least he's got his priorities right.' A butterfly, large as a hand, flapped past them like a piece of incandescent cloth.

'Butterflies,' she said. 'How much I resented them in the camp. So free, stupid things, flying through the wire at will. I really hate them, you know.' She shrugged and bowed her head.

'Hampshire is big, isn't it?'

'Quite big.'

'The address, you won't forget?'

'No. I'll drop it in one day.'

She turned slowly, pushing the ball of paper into her skirt pocket. 'David Gaunt just told me that we are to have a big celebration quite soon. Can you imagine? He and Sister Pritchard are organizing the race-course at Rozendaal; we shall have a day at the races! Horses, jockeys, prizes even. It may not be exactly like Longchamps or Ascot but it is a real sign of peace, don't you think? Of looking forward again to a

289

future. And that's good.' She led him across to the double doors and through the cool hall. 'And that's another sign of peace, you see? The front door wide open, a symbol of freedom? You know, sometimes we almost forget to lock it at night, and that is really not very sensible after the night of the fires, is it? We are becoming quite careless already. The human mind! How easily it recovers.' She stopped herself abruptly, hand to her throat nervously. 'I make my own error. It is not as simple as that.'

'Not simple, no, but it does. Perhaps the word "adapt" is better than "recover", do you think? The human mind adapts itself pretty quickly.'

'Yes. Perhaps he will find it easier in Europe? A clear future with no past to remind him. I don't know. But I do know that when I saw your jeep standing here just now my mind recovered. Instantly. In that split second. It did not adapt. It will have to do *that* when you drive away again, I think that there is a dreadful difference between the words. Does that make any sense?'

'Of course. You know that; I know the difference too. I was adapting to my new role, you see?'

'Wise uncle?'

'Exactly so.' He turned quickly and ran down the steps to the jeep. 'I'll bring you the address, shan't forget.'

When he looked up again she had gone inside and closed the door.

It was cool in the shade of the stand: flies droned, sunlight slattered across the warped wooden benches through gaps in the tin roof. Across the rails the track appeared to swarm with Jap prisoners mowing, digging, rolling, forking the scorched grass. Already, thought Sister Pritchard, moving carefully down the steep steps with her wicker basket, the place is almost coming to life again. The rails stood firm, the arch was buttressed into place, its large wooden letters, Rozendaal Stadium, sparkled in a coat of fresh blue paint. However, the rickety clock-tower still insisted that it was a quarter to twelve, and the air of deep melancholy which she constantly sensed in the place was just as strong as ever, in spite of the activity all around, the sounds of hammering, banging, sawing, and the high, light cries of the Japanese calling to each other like migrating birds. Nothing, she thought, would ever dissipate the atmosphere of grief, fear and despair which lingered about the place like an invisible vapour. Not even cheering crowds or thundering hoofs on the baked earth would do that. Not even the efforts of valiant Sappers and the industrious prisoners bashing some form of life back into the wretched place would be able to do that. But she kept her thoughts to herself as she reached Gaunt's side and set the basket down between them.

'There you are. Think I've brought enough, you're not starving, I hope?'

'I could eat.'

'And so you shall; wizzo! But not a terrific lot. There's Spam, some of that foul American cheese which sweats and tastes of Sunlight Soap, fruit and beer. And that's it.' She looked at him with a grin. 'Not frightfully exciting, but all I could get together in the time. Raided my own larder. Got a pot of chutney to help with the cheese.'

'Splendid. Let's have the beer.'

'No glasses. Too heavy. And the beer's warm; no ice or anything larky.'

'Warm beer is my passion.'

'Good thing too. Better for your bowels.'

'They're in good nick.'

'Cold beer gives you the runs.' She opened a bottle and handed it to him.

'You're a treat to have on a picnic, old dear.'

'It's coming along, your scheme, isn't it? Really wizard—it's all getting quite shipshape.'

'Not bad. The going will be bloody hard: ground's like rock.'

'Thing is not to fall off if you can help it.'

'I'll try to remember that.' He wiped his mouth with the back of his hand. 'What about one of your Spam things? I'll forego the cheese for the moment.'

They ate in silence, watching the men working, kites wheeling in the high blue sky, a man on a ladder some way down the course painting the winning post bright orange.

'Is the General going to give the prizes?'

'Said so.'

'Not cups and things, surely?'

'No. Money. Twenty-five quid, fifteen, and five. For the main event.'

'Not much.'

'Not much of a race. A start, that's all. Only for fun. The Provost Section is running the Tote, that ought to raise some cries of protest.'

'There will be cries of protest, from me, if they bring you up to First Aid with a broken neck, that I can tell you. Daft thing to do to yourself in the first year of peace.'

'That what it is?'

'Nineteen forty-six. Sounds very futuristic, doesn't it? I was much more comfortable with the Thirties.'

'I quite liked the war,' he said with a full mouth. 'Had some good times as well as bloody awful. But that's the job.'

'Well, it's still going on, isn't it? I mean here?'

'Just little skirmishes now: nothing serious. Dutch are taking over slowly; we'll soon all be on our way out.'

'Handing over? Everyone going?'

'In time. Get the last of the internees away, then the job's done.'

She sat looking into the sunlight beyond the ant-like Japanese. 'I can't bear the idea really. It all being over, I mean; dreadful thing to say, but I shall hate it.'

'What'll you do? Back to UK?'

She spread some chutney over the greasy cheese, slapped the dry bread slices together. 'Tastes much better with this. Want some? Go back to UK? A Socialist Government, nationalizing everything: you know they've nationalized the Bank of England already? I mean to say! No, thanks ever so. Equality for the people, free medicine coming next. Good grief! Equality always leads to totalitarianism, and I'm too old a bird for that.'

'Where then? India?'

'Calcutta probably. I don't know. Somewhere I'm needed really.'

'Won't be there long, old girl. They'll chuck you out in a year or two. Congress and all the rest of it, "Quit India". They'll have us all out.'

'What about you? Been there all your life, haven't you?'

'All.' He tore off a bit of dry crust and threw it to a bicker of sparrows at his feet. 'Born and bred there.'

'Seems funny. You're so English, and you've never even been there.'

'I'd quite like to see it one day. Windsor, London. I'd like to see Runnymede too, Magna Carta, all that.'

'It's just a field,' she said, wiping her fingers.

'I'll go back to India. Of course. Where else? They'll probably need us for a while after Independence, much as they may dislike the idea. Someone's got to train the silly bastards, remind them to uphold the law, keep them from hacking each other to pieces. Any more Spam ones left? I don't know if you realize it but we've been a kind of bung in a barrel of blood.'

She handed him his sandwich. 'Barrel of blood! Corks, bungs, I mean!' she laughed suddenly. 'You think it'll be bloody when it comes: Independence?'

'Work it out for yourself. You'll have your work cut out for you running about with smelling salts and tourniquets. Blood! Half Hindu, the other half Muslim, all busting to settle old scores. As soon as we're out they'll be at each other with knives and hatchets; that's what I mean by "bung". We go; it spills. Whew!'

'Seems a bit far-fetched to me.'

'Seems a bit far-fetched to that old ninny in his nighty.'

'Gandhi, you mean?'

'The very one. Turn away wrath with a bunch of marigolds, brother to brother, love one another, peace not violence. Balls.' He lifted his beer and took a long swig, rolled the empty bottle between his hands thoughtfully. 'No. I'll go back to the Regiment for as long as it lasts, when it packs up I'll head for Africa, Rhodesia, Kenya, somewhere like that, join the Army or the Police, help keep the nig-nogs in their place.'

'You don't like them much do you? Black people?' She took his empty bottle and placed it tidily back in the basket.

'Despise them. Nothing to do with liking them.'

'And your Regiment? Born and bred in it, you said.'

He looked at her with suddenly narrowed eyes. 'They're different. Frontier people, different breed, different race. Bloody marvellous fighters, proud, tough; they aren't spineless; they're not black.' Fishing about in his jacket pocket he suddenly produced a mouth organ, blew through it a couple of times, knocked it hard against his leg. 'Fluff. Bits of dust and stuff.'

'You are a funny fellow,' she said mildly, peeling herself a banana. 'You don't like that Kalik chap, do you, and he's one of your lot, isn't he? The brave and proud and tough?'

'He's a bolshie sod. Just needs a bit of pulling down, that's all.' He blew a few tuneless phrases, ran up and down the scale, wiped his lips.

'Just because of that business with a statue months ago? Goodness.'

'Badness. Not goodness. He's got a funny kink. Not just the statue, old dear; there was a girl before. Just after we landed in the first days, Chinese, about twelve, refugee or something, damn nearly killed her, got away with it because no one could prove anything and all she could say was that the man was dark and wore cloth on his head. It could have been one of hundreds.'

'And how do you know it was him then?'

'In her pocket they found three fruit-drops.'

'So?' She dropped the banana skin into the basket.

'They were mine. Red, a green, a yellow. I'd given them to him that morning. We both like sticky sweets—instant energy or something.' He rubbed his face, grinned at her. 'It's a silly thing; I said they were like traffic lights, Stop, Caution, Go . . . you know?' He blew a long sustained note which startled the sparrows. 'That's why I suddenly remembered. It was him all right. No question. Got it?'

She nodded slowly and began to clear up the picnic, folding the remaining sandwiches into a cloth, collecting up the fruit, to the mournful and uncertain strains of 'We'll Gather Lilacs' which filled her with a strange melancholy, quite dispersing the feeling of pleasure and contentment she had been enjoying on the hard wooden bench. He sat half-turned away from her, legs apart, elbows on his knees, sucking and blowing with intense concentration, and when he came to the end, looked over his shoulder at her with a shy grin, shaking the spittle into the dust at his feet.

'Not too bad? By heart. Only know the chorus, I'm afraid.'

'Don't be,' she said. 'You should have reported him, or something, surely? I mean, if you knew.'

294

His grey eyes were flat. 'We had a ruddy war on our hands the day we got here, report him to whom? Half the damned Regiment was raping someone somewhere, I should think. All hell had broken loose. I just took my own action, thanks for the advice all the same; dealt with him my way, stuck him on Perimeter Duty, kept him out of temptation.'

'Apart from a statue, poor man.'

'Poor man, be buggered.' He slid the mouth organ into his pocket and buttoned the flap. 'I said that time, "The only thing you're fit for fucking is a concrete cunt".' He looked at her for a moment. She held his look unflinchingly. 'Shock you?'

'Not at all. Not you saying it to me. But you saying it to him does. Terribly.'

'Yes. He didn't like it much. Didn't like it much that he wasn't on the bif-bang business clearing the City, either. Destroys his sense of manhood. That'll teach him; he knows I know about the Chinese child, so he knows what I'm up to.'

'How does he know?'

He suddenly got up in exasperation. 'Oh! For Pete's sake, woman. You're like a bloody judge. He knows because I gave him back the three ruddy sweeties, that's how he knows.' He reached down and pulled her to her feet. 'Honestly, you're so full of curiosity, old thing. Know what it did to the cat, don't you?'

She slung the basket over her arm, and started up the wide steps. 'Yes,' she said over her shoulder. 'I know. Killed it.'

Nettles' office at HQ was as spartan as his bedroom in 'A' Mess. A large desk, filing cabinets, the normal paraphernalia of map boards, folding chairs, stacks of Army pamphlets, in one corner the Roneo machine, in another Corporal Batt's table supporting the radios and coils of wire, behind the desk, hanging large like an arras, covered with brilliant lines, circles, squares, a blow-up of the City area stuck about with little paper flags and coloured pins.

Nanni Singh stood smartly to attention before the desk, his eyes fixed hypnotically on the City map before him, his boots shining like ebony, the thin parting in his hair drawn as if by ruler, arms close to his sides.

'Do stand easy, Nanni Singh, this is not a parade, I asked you

295

to come so that we could have a private chat, quite informal, no one will disturb us, and you make me frightfully uncomfortable standing there like a nine-pin: there is a chair. Sit on it, for Heaven's sake.'

'It will make it more convenient, Sahib?'

'Much easier. Sit.'

He sat with the stiff elegance of a jack-knife. Nettles took up a pencil, tapped a little tattoo on the desk top.

'Now,' he said carefully. 'Some time ago, you remember, I promised to tell you if I ever discovered news of . . . of the boy? That is so?'

'It is so, Sahib.'

'I have this news. The boy is dead.'

Nanni Singh did not flick a muscle.

'I have seen him with my own eyes, in the City during the fighting.'

'I knew, this I already knew,' said Nanni Singh quietly. 'My heart has told me this long since.'

'He was found in the Headquarters of the Group which he joined, and who trained him to fight against us. I am very sorry. I'm sorry too, that I have taken so long to tell you, but . . .'

'He was dead easily? He was not . . .?'

'He was dead easily: by that I presume you mean he was not ugly in death?'

'That is so?'

'No. Easily. A bullet, in the heart possibly, or even a fragment of cannon shell, but he was not disfigured, you may rest easy on that.'

'Thank you, Sahib, for this news you give me; he was a burning and shining light for me.'

'I know that. And I also know your grief is deep. But you know, don't you, that it is entirely due to that idiotic letter of yours?'

'What I have written, I have written.'

'I know that! Don't keep on quoting chunks of the Bible to ease your silly soul, you exasperate me! You write a mean, spiteful, nasty little letter like a village spinster and set off a chain of reactions which explode in your own silly, hypocritical face. It serves you bloody well right.'

296

Nanni Singh suddenly gave a great cry and covered his hands over his face, his body slumped into the chair. 'Oh! Lord! Oh! Lord!' he cried. 'If it is possible, let this cup pass from me, let it pass!'

'Oh do shut up, Singh! For the love of God pull yourself together, you have done quite enough harm in the last few months. You can't pass the blasted cup; it is, and should be, brimming with bitterness and I hope you drink it deep. None of this was your business, *none* of it was your affair. You behaved like a cheap and vulgar old gossip.'

Nanni Singh sat broken in his seat, hands now between his knees, head low on his chest, fighting a silent battle to contain his grief. 'Oh, wretched man that I am,' he sobbed. 'Who will deliver me from the body of this death?'

'No one,' snapped Nettles. 'You're stuck with it, dear.'

'What I wrote, I wrote in truth and honour. For my master, for the good of the Division to which I swore my allegiance! The woman is wicked, all knew this, the boy knew well for he worked many years in the restaurant of the Oshima father, and *he* was a traitor, the Japanese sent him to this place many years since to tell them of the secret places on the Island, of the docks, the ships, the military installations, even the telephones and the radio things. All things this Oshima sent back to his land, all this the boy knew because the Oshima girl worked for the woman and told the secrets from the men who soiled her body in the house of this woman! This he tells me! And when the Japanese came to the City all was ready for them here! They knew every thing of the Island, they did not even fight but came ashore at night like to go for a simple walk. Maybe this you do not know, Nettles Sahib? It is possible? Girls this woman had in her house to find the secrets from the Navy men and the soldiers who went there in their wickedness. This woman is therefore not fit to be with my General? To share his bed? To share his house? To see his papers, to be in this building, free and not touched? It was my holy duty to write my letter to you, for you are the powerful one, you can discover the truth and drive her away. But you scorn me! Shame upon you, Sahib! Scorn you pour on my honour and my loyalty!' Spittle had made a white crust at the corners of his mouth.

Nettles snapped his pencil in two, dropped it into the basket

297

at his side, ran his hands wearily through auburn curls. 'I do not *scorn* you, Singh, I do not scorn your honour: I know that you did what you did to protect your master; but this is tittle-tattle, you know? How can you trust children to know what is fact? The boy was only a child at the time, they are fanciful creatures, Nanni Singh; you have children of your own, it is so? And thus you know. What the Oshimas did is one thing, what the woman did is another, we cannot be sure, on the memory of a child, that they were linked.'

Nanni Singh had more or less composed himself, his outburst of fury having to some extent assuaged his grief, and also his own intense sense of guilt which, since the night of the fire, had burned within him like sulphuric acid. In accepting guilt for himself he wished, not unnaturally, to spread it elsewhere, in the frail hope that it might possibly ease the unbearable burden which he carried in silence. He was well aware of his own hand in the burning of the City and the resulting death and mutilation which it accompanied, and no amount of Mr Bishop's teaching now could ease his pain. Only a dogged determination to continue his personal fight against Miss Foto gave him courage and blunted the edge of his shame. Quietly he took a neatly folded handkerchief from his immaculate trouser pocket and blew his nose discreetly.

'The Oshima girl was this evil woman's slave and her servant, but she loved her very well and when the Japanese came she protected her mistress with all her might and main. She even told them where the Australians were hiding. It was a grave offence to hide Allied soldiers, but the woman was not punished because the Oshima girl and her father told the Japanese of the many secret things which they had learned from the woman's house and of the help which she had given them to aid the cause of Nippon. When the liberation came many of these wicked people were killed, in wrath and righteous indignation by the people, but the woman was safe in the European Camp, and now, Nettles Sahib, she is in the house of my master. Where is honour?'

'All this may be so,' said Nettles patiently. 'But there was no reason for you to set yourself up as the angel of vengeance. If these things are true they will all come to light one day, probably when we have gone from here, when the Dutch have taken full control. It is not our business to arrest War Criminals, we have not the facilities; there are special investigators for that who will come, you will see.' He got up and walked thoughtfully across to the wide window which looked out over the scarlet branches of the flame-of-the-forest. When he turned back Nanni Singh was on his feet, putting away his handkerchief. 'I asked you here, Nanni Singh, because I promised that if I had news for you I should tell you. Which I have. And that is that. I do not want any more inaccurate accusations from you. The boy is dead, that is all that concerns you at the moment.'

'And he was not ugly in his death?'

'No,' said Nettles evenly. 'He was not ugly. It was quick, he would not have known.'

Nanni Singh carefully removed the folded cap from his epaulette, ran a finger over the shining badge. 'He would not have known. That is good. I am permitted to say one more thing from my Book, Sahib?' He smiled a sudden twisted little smile.

'What does your Book say?'

'All flesh is as grass, Sahib, and all the glory of man as the flower of grass, the grass withereth, and the flower thereof falleth away.'

'Very apt,' said Nettles, coming back to the desk and sitting into his chair. 'Very apt. I hope that it gives you comfort.'

'Thank you, Sahib. You are most gracious. But Hell is before me and I will surely perish in the fire,' said Nanni Singh, and quietly left the room.

Nettles buried his face in his hands. 'All strange and terrible events are welcome, but comforts we despise,' he murmured, and then, pulling himself together, reached for the hand-set and asked to speak to Captain Rooke.

The small electric fan in the corner whirred softly, rhythmically, moving slowly from right to left in a limited arc, troubling the air only so that it lightly fluttered the red silk scarf draped over the lamp on one side, and nodded the dried grasses and paper poppies in a Lalique jar on the other. However, the sickening scent of joss-sticks was not dispersed, and clung to every piece of heavy fabric in the stifling room with an intensity which made Rooke's eyes glaze. There was no air, and he looked longingly at the shaded verandah beyond but, since he had been shown into the room and placed in his chair and told to wait, he felt it wiser to remain where he was and await the arrival of his hostess who would, he had been assured in a reverent whisper, be down directly. So he sat and perspired gently, holding his slender file of photographs lightly on his knees, much as if he were in a dentist's waiting-room with a difficult extraction ahead and not even a back number of *The National Geographic* to flip through.

Miss Foto always managed her entrances extremely well: it was something which she had been brought up to do from a very early age. A good entrance gave you the advantage over the client, of whatever kind, and set the scene for the performance which might follow. It therefore had to be considered very carefully, and since the telephone call from Rooke had suggested that the meeting was to be both intimate and extremely personal, she had taken particular trouble. And since, too, the meeting was requested at very short notice and appeared to have an air of unease about it, she discarded anything too floating or light or clinging, or even, for that matter, overtly feminine, and changed into a trim tailored little suit in navy blue shantung with white cuffs and no jewellery; taking a long blue chiffon scarf in one hand, for she found that she could use a scarf to good advantage during conversations of a slightly uneasy kind, she descended the stairs with calm deliberation and arrived in the archway of her suffocating sitting-room with quiet, elegant grace.

Rooke rose swiftly to his feet, tucking his file under one arm. He took the offered ringless hand, brought it almost to his lips.

'My dear Captain Rooke! How tall you are! I am always forgetting that time when we danced together, you remember? The big party so long ago, what a tall young man, I thought, and I am such a shrimp of a thing; just before we made you the ADC, do you recall? "I am not the ADC yet," you said to me. "Ah ha!" I replied, "not *yet*, but who can tell?" You recall this? I told you that I had a "nose", I believe, and so I had. Now.' She took his hand and led him across the cluttered room to the verandah. 'Now, shall we sit here in the shade, or do you

300

prefer to sit in the house? If we are to speak very personally, I believe you said, we shall be quite safe in either place. My maid speaks only poor Dutch or Malay.'

Attack, she thought, is the best method of defence.

'Perhaps the verandah would be cooler,' he said. 'If you don't mind?'

'As you will, as you will. I am a most adaptable creature, and the air is very pleasant. Sit there, it is a comfortable chair, and here is a cushion. I shall sit here, and thus we are so and so. Now.' She sat very upright in a high-backed Bangkok chair, her elbows resting lightly on the arms, the scarf flowing from one pale hand; she crossed her ankles, looked suddenly up at the hanging macaw on its brass ring above Rooke's head. 'Oh!' she said, with a gentle laugh, 'do not worry about my polly-parrot, Captain Rooke, she is, I am afraid, only full of cotton-wool and so on, she cannot speak and cannot hear. I keep her there only because a dear friend gave her to me. Do you remember little Yoko Oshima? A sweet girl. Smoke if you wish, but please don't throw a match into my garden! It is so dry we would have another terrible fire; the ash tray is there.'

'First of all,' said Rooke lowering himself into the chair opposite her, 'I'd better explain, as simply as I can, why I am here. It'll take a bit of time, I ask your patience.'

'I am most intrigued. Also I am a patient woman, please.' She indicated with a slight flick of the scarf that she was ready, and did not move once during his long, detailed but succinct report. When he had finished she lightly clasped her hands together in her lap and smiled at him pleasantly.

'And that is why you are here?'

'That is why.'

'Are you from the Gestapo perhaps?'

'No. I beg your pardon if I have been offensive.'

'Offensive!' she laughed lightly. 'What a strange word to use. You speak of some letter to this Major Nettles which says that I was the keeper of a brothel, that I corrupted the innocent, betrayed four soldiers to the Japanese and could be, you suggest, therefore considered as a, what is the phrase?'

'War Criminal.'

'Just so. Offensive? Captain Rooke, not at all. You offer me a nosegay of mignonette.'

'I know that it is extremely unpleasant. But so are the suggestions made.'

'They are vile and disgusting.'

'Exactly. I am here to tell you these things; I ask only so that you may refute them.'

'Refute! How can I refute slander?'

'You may have to do so to an Investigation Committee, Miss Foto.'

'But why? Who will investigate, as you call it, such rubbish?'

'The British Military Police already are in possession of these suggestions, they will very likely hand them all over to the Dutch Administration, if they do not proceed themselves.'

'And you are giving me a chance to "save myself", is that it, noble Captain?'

'Giving you a chance to do that, if you like, but mostly it is our concern to save the reputation of General Cutts.'

She rested her chin carefully in her cupped hand. 'How does this concern General Cutts, pray?'

'Deeply. He has brought this Division through a long, bloody and bitter war, he is much respected by us all, he is not a young man, in a short time he will reach the age of retirement, it would be a cruel and vicious blow if he were to be involved in any kind of scandal through no real fault of his own.'

'Scandal! There is no scandal!'

'The betrayal of prisoners of war to the enemy is a scandal. If it is true.'

'Of course it is not true.'

'There is a witness to the executions.'

'Ah yes! The anonymous creature you call the Boy. The letter is also quite anonymous, I understand, since you mention no brave name.'

'We have the names.'

'So you keep them secret? I am to be accused by two vile gossip-mongers.'

'And Miss Oshima.'

For a moment she almost lost the disdainful composure which shrouded her like a veil. 'Miss Oshima? Yoko? It is impossible.'

'She spoke at great length with Major Nettles, she did her best to defend you for she also had seen the letter.'

'Yoko chick,' said Miss Foto to the stuffed macaw, and

deciding to change track. 'A silly chatterbox! That is all, you know, she was like a little parrot bird.'

'She had a rather larger vocabulary than the usual parrot.'

'Captain Rooke, I am not a stranger to these stories. I imagine you know the words jealousy, envy, spite and avarice, no? Well, let me try to refute, as you say, these things, you would like that?' She started to fold the scarf into a neat rectangle. 'First I did not run a brothel. Ever. I had a very pleasant and fashionable dress shop here, and it was greatly successful. My little house was a centre of all that was amusing, delightful, and attractive in this city. It was well-known as a place for stimulating conversation, excellent food, and pleasing company. I am not a married lady, as you know; naturally I had many friends, for a woman does not thrive well in business if she lives like a nun? That is sense, is it not? I had many contacts for my business; this is a Port City; there were people who came from all over the world to this busy, pretty Island, from the Navy, from the Army too. Of course I was younger then, I had many admirers you could say, and why not? Is that so wrong? We would play cards, mah-jong, we would discuss the world, life, politics, and love, of course! Naturally in my shop I employed the prettiest girls in the city; it is good business to do this, even in a shop where only women come; sometimes, to be sure, they would be present at my little evenings. That too is natural, is it not? A man enjoys his wine and his cards the more if there is a pretty girl at hand to refill his glass and encourage him to win! What is so *wicked* about that?'

'And Miss Oshima was one of them.'

'Of course! She was not the prettiest, I know, but she was a warm child, kind and willing and very industrious, she took the greatest pains to be decorative, useful and delightful.' She placed the neatly folded rectangle carefully on the arm of the chair. 'But there was jealousy, naturally. Of course there was. I was very successful, my little salon was well-known, it was not hidden in some dark street, you know! But colonial life is very narrow, very snobbish and the Dutch are very like their cheeses; heavy, solid, covered tightly in the wax of the self-righteous. I was never really accepted here socially; for one thing I am a foreigner, French from Nice, this you are aware of since you know so much about me.'

'I did not know that, no.'

'Ah! Then perhaps you do not know that also I am a Jewess?'

'No.'

'Yes, my beloved Mamma called herself Lucienne but in truth she was Leah; and my Papa . . .' She spread her small white hands and smiled at him in a sweet complicity. 'Well, I am sure you know. A girl can make many a mistake when her heart is in flight, and she made one. Me. But my Papa was a member of a very, very important Jewish banking family, you would know their name extremely well, and he was instantly recalled home, cruelly deserting my poor little mother who was of modest bourgeois stock, all humble musicians. So you see I was not exactly considered *comme il faut*: the women, particularly, were resentful. A woman in business is considered to be very vulgar. Even if her designs are original.'

'Tell me about Miss Oshima's father?'

'Nonnie Oshima? A good man, he ran a charming restaurant, and provided delicious suppers for my little salon very often.'

'And that is all?'

'What else? They killed him on the Liberation Day because he was Japanese! And he had lived quietly and diligently among them for many years; oh this cruel war.' She fanned herself slowly with the pale blue rectangle of chiffon.

'And the Australians?'

'Australians? Ah, well, there were so *many* soldiers here after Singapore. Poor boys, all trying to get away to Ceylon, to Java, even to India, trying to buy a boat; many of us tried to help them in those terrible days, but what could one do? We were trapped ourselves. One, very charming, asked me to help him to get away, he had the idea to go to Timor, I think, and then to Australia. It was so silly, but what do you do? I gave him money: to try and buy a boat. The peasants were selling all their fishing boats, rowing boats, anything which would go to sea, and many, Captain Rooke, which would *not*! They were so cruel, so avaricious!'

'But he didn't get away?'

'No. No. When the Japanese landed there was great confusion, where to go?'

'What happened?'

304

'Some of them hid in the forests, you know. To try and escape later.'

'And did you help them then?'

She shrugged sadly. 'Where it was possible. We would leave some food for them at the house of a woman I trusted, who made beautiful batik for me in the days before . . . She lived in a kampong outside the City. They would steal in at night to her chicken-house where it was hidden; this we arranged.'

'You were very brave.'

'Everyone had to be brave in those terrible days. But worse was to come. The Japanese arrested all civilians quite suddenly. With no warning. We heard rumours, but of course we could not believe them. What harm could we do, isolated from the world? But to the camps we were sent. Oh God! The terror, the fear, you cannot imagine.'

'And your friend in the forest?'

'I begged him to surrender, what could I do to help him from in the camp? He was trapped; I begged him to remember the Geneva Convention. He was a soldier. He would be a prisoner of war, of course, but that was better than perishing alone in the forest, with no food, no boat, nothing to help him. But he was most determined. "No!" he said.'

'And?'

'The night before we had to go to the camp I admit my courage left me: I broke down and confessed to Miss Oshima, she was so warm, so kind, so understanding, in those days she had become most friendly with a charming Japanese who was the City Engineer, or some such thing, I really forget the military terms, he was most kind to her, I think he was also a friend of her father's, she promised that she would try, very discreetly, to get his assistance to help anyone who was "lost" in that manner safely into a camp for prisoners of war, and one day in my dreadful camp I received a little message from her to say that I should be happy because all was now well finally. So I knew that she had found a way to help these poor soldiers. That is what happened, that is how it was. I betrayed no one.'

'He was one of many?'

'Oh, I suppose. I don't even know his name, he was good-looking, but very rash and daring, young, like you. There were

305

so many like him at that time, all so brave and patriotic. Headstrong.'

'And when you heard, as you must have done, what they did to these brave young patriotic soldiers, you were not shocked?'

Suddenly, and with alarming speed, Miss Foto lost her temper, clenched her fists into tight white balls and thumped the arm of her chair until it shook. 'I never heard! I never heard anything! I never heard again!' The white fists relaxed, she rearranged a white cuff carefully.

'Oh, there were rumours that the Japanese were killing many Chinese and people who had worked for the Europeans; they were terrible times. We heard this; in a camp full of women shut away together there is nothing else to do but gossip and talk and spread rumours.' She leant forward and fixed him with a cold, hard eye. 'If anything so terrible had ever happened Yoko would have told me, *this* I know. And it was not so.'

'The boy was a witness to the executions, Miss Foto, we have detailed information from him.'

'This boy! This wicked anonymous boy! Bring him to me! I will talk with him and you will listen. Then you will see.'

Rooke crossed his legs deliberately, adjusting the crease in his trouser with care.

'The boy is dead.'

There was a long silence. Crickets sang: from far away the sound of bicycle bells in a distant street. When she moved in her chair the cane creaked like a rifle shot.

'So. Now we have it. So! He is dead! Yoko is dead! You bring to me terrible tales of evil, you say wicked and vile things to me, you trick me into speaking to you because of some cruel, false, letter. You do not behave as a man, even as a gentleman, you do not even have the manners of a common soldier, but those of a sniggering little schoolboy, which is after all what you are, finally. I am a defenceless woman, alone, and you dare to come and slander me! With no proof, no evidence at all!'

'There is this,' said Rooke civilly, and handed her the file. 'Perhaps while you look at it I may take a walk in your garden, stretch my legs a bit, stiff after sitting; you know?'

She stared at the file on her lap, placed a hand upon it, looked
306

up at him with wide, clear eyes. 'Please do. But if you smoke,' she looked back at the file, ran her hand across the shiny buff cardboard, 'do not throw matches.'

It had not been a garden for many years. A giant eucalyptus threw dappled shade across a wilderness of trailing creeper and rampant banana. In one corner a sagging wrought-iron gazebo buried in vines; in the centre of the rough, dry, grass a ragged path led down to a gap in the bamboo thicket beyond which lay the garden of what had been the General's house. A convenient line of access which had overcome the confining curfew of those days. Lying in her teeth, of course, he thought, French instead of Belgian, a rich banker for a father, God knows what he was but banker he was not, and how many soldiers *were* there? Soldiers plural as often as she could manage it, a careful vagueness: cards and mah-jong and sparkling conversation, my backside. She'd have your balls in three seconds flat from first meeting. I shouldn't think she had one real grain of feeling in her whole plump, venal, little body. And she is so bloody obvious! How do you get away with that kind of performance, for God's sake? Terrific in bed is the answer; just depends who you land there. Poor sodding General with a saintly wife, poor ruddy Australian in need of cash for a boat, all those gentle-manly soldiers and sailors and businessmen from all over the world hiking off to her hospitable little drawing room awash with gin and ladies. I suppose she'd call herself a survivor. All that Jewish business, hated by the world but I'll spit in your eyes. 'I'll get even, my dears, I'll win in the end: I have the Emperor of Japan's private telephone number.' What a shitty bitch. 'Sniggering little schoolboy', 'defenceless woman alone'. Christ! And really means it, what's more. 'You come to slander me with no evidence!' Well. He stripped a leaf from the eucalyptus, looked back towards the house. She's got a bit now. There she sits in her high-backed chair, the Cleopatra of South-East Asia, picking her way delicately through photographs of a dead Australian's wallet. From the corner of his eye he saw her slowly close the buff file, place it on the table before her, and as she lay back in the cane chair he started back towards the house, crushing a fragment of leaf in his fingers, inhaling the pungent, cough-drop scent.

'You are eating something, Captain Rooke?'

'No. Smelling something. Eucalyptus, memories of child-hood. Cold and coughs and Vick's Vapour Rub.'

'Which is?'

'An ointment. Rub it on your chest.'

'Where did you get this. Not from Miss Oshima?'

He told her, standing with one knee bent, on the lowest step of the verandah.

'Ah. Mr Wizzersby. He also took that? As well as her life.'

'I think that she took her own life, don't you?'

'Because of him. He tortured her, you know. To find all the imagined riches she had.'

'But it was not imagined, I understand. He got quite a lot. Shipped it out.'

'Not very far.'

'No, not so far. Another little letter saw to that. Yours?'

She watched him calmly, lying back in the chair, eyes half-closed. She nodded. 'Mine. Yes. Why not? It seems to be a fashionable occupation these days. I am glad that he is dead, he was a truly evil man to my chick.'

'And the photographs? You know what they are?'

She looked briefly at the file, took up her blue scarf, ran it through white fingers. Eyes like agates. 'Yes. It is him. Mel. What a silly, silly girl. Why did she keep it? She was *so* senti-mental. Oh Yoko chick.' She said softly, looking up at the motionless macaw above her head. 'What a silly scatterbrain you were. So kind, so stupid!'

'So he was not just a name, as you said.'

She looked at him directly, her eyes perfectly steady, very gentle. 'No. Not just a name. A man, a real man.' She indicated the file casually with a nod. 'You have the original of these pictures, I suppose? And Yoko's little note to me? Locked away with the Crown Jewels.'

'We have.'

'It proves nothing, you know, Captain Rooke; only that I had his wallet, his most treasured possession, you could say. That, in there is a picture of Nancy, his wife, and the cinema ticket from the last show they saw together on his last leave, but I imagine you know all that too?'

'Not that. And it's not full proof, I know, but it is damaging.'

'To me or to your General?'

'To you both.'

'I did not betray him.'

'You told Miss Oshima where he was, it comes to much the same thing.'

'Much the same thing! Not at all, Yoko was the only person I knew, or trusted, to help him. I was destroyed finally; I did all I could to help him get away, I did all I could. You do not know the times then, finally you cannot judge the fear and the terror.'

'There were three others with him, I believe. Four altogether.'

'Which made it more difficult: one was ill, he was trapped, he would not leave them.'

'And so Miss Oshima told where they all were.'

'It was the only way! The only way! I thought he would be safe.'

'And when you knew?'

She folded her hands in her lap, looking at them curiously as if for the first time, flexing the fingers to see if they could move, and finding that they did she looked up at him, her eyes rimmed with unexpected tears. 'You have a sword, Captain Rooke, and you twist it I think with pleasure? It is so?'

'No pleasure.'

'Yes, I knew. Yoko told me in a message. They had executed four European soldiers. One had red hair.' She raised her head slightly to contain the tear which threatened to slip from her eye. 'They said he was very brave.' The tear slid slowly down her pale cheek. 'He was singing, you know this?' She managed it all quite beautifully.

Rooke turned away and looked out into the garden.

'Don't look away, Captain Rooke, I am quite composed. You know my Mamma always said to me when I was quite small, three hundred years ago, that every time one told a lie one made a hole in one's shroud, but that before you died you must mend them all otherwise you could not be buried and go to your Maker in a presentable manner. He would know that you had been untruthful all your life.' She laughed suddenly, a soft, pleasant sound. 'I think that when I go, finally, I will be dressed in lace, isn't it?' She wiped her cheek with a small finger. 'And now what must I do?'

'We want you to go away. To leave the Island.'

309

She looked at him in true astonishment. 'To leave? To go away?'

'Leave before they start any enquiries, before it is too late.'

'And where would I go? How?'

'To Europe, anywhere. Clear out.'

'And if I do not? This is my home here.'

'If you do not we hand over the wallet.'

'Which is not any proof.'

'But which is very ugly evidence. If you get out now it is possible that we could avoid any scandal for the General, unless the War Crimes Investigators get here first, which is possible. And the Dutch will not be lenient, I think; you would be very wise.'

She slid the scarf gently round her neck, tied it into a full bow with expert fingers. 'I am very fond of General Cutts you know: he has been so very kind to me, so wonderfully kind.'

'I know. A house, this furniture, a car even, everything you wanted.'

'But I too have helped him. I have paid my debts you know. My advice was most useful to him in the early days, and now you wish me to take my leave of him. He will be very, very distressed.'

'More distressed if he knows what I know.'

She looked at him sharply. 'He does not, I think?'

'He does not.'

'Nor would he believe such nonsense. He was always so deeply concerned for my personal happiness, that is what is so generous about him, you see? And I think that when I tell him that I will be very happy indeed to be in . . . Japan,' she let the word hang in the still, hot air, 'then perhaps his distress will be less: I could not be happy again in Europe, although he sweetly insists that I should, but I have lived in the East too long, I am used to its way, its culture, its life. I could not go back to the cold, grey north light, to a flat in London, for example! I would be suffocated, I would die of unhappiness: even with someone as warm and generous as he is. So, I have had time to make up my mind, he asked me to do this, not to hurry, to think it over. "I am not a bully, you know," he said so sweetly, so now I can tell him that I cannot accept this generous invitation, but I will move on again, as you say, it surely must be wiser, no? And there is no future now in the Island, after the Dutch, the Indonesians and a Republic, and there will be no place for a pretty dress shop in a People's Republic, I think? So I will go. Yes, I will go. You have my word.'

'To Japan?'

'The Japanese are not all monsters, Captain Rooke. Not at all. Also they have learned a very big lesson, I think, and now that the Americans occupy that land they will bring true Democracy to these feudal people. It will be a very exciting change, very stimulating, the birth of a New People. That is what Mr Novak says; he says to me that it is a land which is full of promise. Those were his words. Like in the old days with California. We shall open the East, he says, we have already opened the West! I think that very interesting, don't you?'

'Very,' said Rooke. 'Do I take it that Mr Novak has interests in . . . he will go to Japan?'

'Very soon, I think. You see, so much of the City here was destroyed in the big battle, you remember? He was very depressed when he went there to see. "Nothing for me here," he said. And it is so uncertain, life here, don't you think? He feels it is wiser to leave. He says that Japan will one day become another State of America. And that is a *most* exciting prospect, I think, finally.'

Rooke crossed over to the little table, picked up the buff file. He held it in his hand for a second, as if weighing it. 'Does Mr Novak think that you'll be happy, shall we say, in Japan?'

Miss Foto suddenly looked rather small in her large chair; she combed her fringe with not over-steady fingers, thoughtfully. 'He is sure,' she said presently. 'And Mr Walter Smedley, you know him of course, the American Vice-Consul who came last week, most pleasing and polite, from New England; Mr Smedley feels that my comprehension, he calls it, of the Asian mind will be of great use to Mr Novak. There is so much to reconstruct in Japan, you see, the firm will be very occupied, and Mr Novak is not so good socially, if you know what I mean. He is a shy man. I feel in my heart, and he persuades me, that I could help him. But of course,' she sighed softly, 'it is a difficult decision to take.'

'I think that we have taken it, haven't we?' said Rooke pleasantly, thumbing casually through the glossy photographs.

311

She inclined her head gently in reply. ' "What Buzz wants, Buzz gets." That is what Mr Smedley said, they have great belief in him, the Americans.' She picked an invisible speck from her sleeve. 'Dark blue is so difficult. It shows every mark you know. You will go to the big race at the Stadium, I suppose? Mr Novak and Mr Smedley have sweetly asked me but I think—' She looked out across the ochre grass, the ragged little path, the scissoring crickets. 'I think that perhaps it would be . . . unwise.'

'Not easy.'

'So I shall not. But if you should see them,' she picked at another piece of invisible fluff on her dress, 'if you see them . . .'

'I think it unlikely. We have very little in common, and nothing to say to each other.'

She smiled up at him suddenly, a bleak smile. 'The General will give the prizes, I am told? He should perhaps give you one also; for valour?'

'I have no valour, Miss Foto.'

'Then for achievement perhaps?'

'What particular thing have you in mind?'

'Two things.' She opened her palms like small flowers to the sun. 'You have made me cry and also to lose my temper. That is a great achievement, Captain Rooke.'

He slid an elastic band round the file and put it under his arm. She watched him in silence.

'And the original of all that under your manly arm?'

He took up his cap. 'I shall destroy it: as soon as you sail. End of the story.'

She rested her head against the wide cane arc of her chair. 'Such a little story, Captain Rooke. When you go home to your grey English skies and tell them all your brave histories, you will realize that mine was just a very little one, not even worth the telling.'

'I doubt that I shall even remember it,' said Rooke.

CHAPTER TWELVE

She had heard his whistle all along the corridor and knew that she was smiling as she unrolled the small red and black lettered poster which she had found in the In tray of her desk. He stopped outside the wire-grilled door and stood to attention.

'Permission to come in? That was a *full* tune I whistled, you know. Not "mindless". A full chorus of "Some Day My Prince Will Come".'

'I know. I heard. I was very relieved.'

'And I've come.' He pushed the door open and crossed to the desk. 'What have you got there?'

She held the poster before him, half-curled. 'It just arrived; I don't know. What is ENSA?'

'Oh Lord! They here already? The war *must* be over then. Entertainment for the Forces. It is popularly known as Every Night Shit Again. Who's coming?'

She shook her head. 'It doesn't say who. Just "A Rollicking Feast of Fun and Girls" it is called, I think, "Peaches and Screams".'

'I see,' said Rooke and sat in the chair opposite her.

'At the Harmonie Hall, Amsterdamse Weg. On Friday and Saturday, there is a matinée on the Saturday.'

'I've come to tell you something. I want to share it with you. Very confidential.' He looked across at the cubicle where Pearl normally sat; it was empty.

'Pearl is away; she has a migraine.'

'I've got a mention.' He grinned shyly, fiddled with his lanyard.

'You are unwell too?' A flick of anxiety.

'Mentioned in Despatches. A sort of award-thing.'

'Like a medal you mean?'

'No, not a medal, only a mention: the Old Man told me.'

'But that's very good, isn't it?'

'It's very nice. I had to tell you.'

She rolled the poster into a tight tube, 'For the time at the Convent?'

'For that. Yes. Nettles again, I'm afraid.'

'Don't be afraid.'

'Well, you'll be waspish or something.'

'Which is?'

'Sarcastic. He insists I saved his life, and Corporal Batt's; all bunk really. I just chucked him on the floor when I saw the grenade, and then the chap up the corridor. I didn't think I had the guts.'

'I think you were very brave. You know that.'

'You were wonderfully sweet and loving and kind. Thank you.'

'It sounds most romantic, doesn't it? A mention in despatches. You think of some gallant horseman riding through the night from the battlefield to tell the King.'

'Don't suppose the King will know much about it. I've written to Nanny J. of course.'

'She'll be very pleased.'

'She'll think it not enough but tell me not to show off about it, so I won't. Yes, she'll be pleased.' He fished for a cigarette, lit it, snapped his lighter shut, blew a ring of smoke towards Pearl's empty chair. 'Wish my father could have known before he died, that's all. He was very upset about the acting part; never quite got over that. "Not a man's job," he said.'

'But this would have been? In the Convent? That would have been a man's job?'

'He would have thought so. Yes. Redemption. It really wasn't very nice. I hope I never have to do it again.'

'But the General is happy, it proves so.'

'He doesn't know who it was, you know. Nanni Singh's boy; we just said a man and left it at that—a terrorist.'

'It was true.'

'It was true. Yes. But I am doubly guilty; for the killing and for the concealing.'

'You must conceal. It would cause greater grief not to.'

He knocked ash onto the floor and crushed it with his boot. 'And the other thing? Miss Foto? I must conceal that too? It's like going behind his back, I hate the feeling.'

'You have to go behind his back. It's for him you have done all this thing.'

He stubbed out the cigarette, reached for a copy of *The Daily Cobra* on her desk, folded it carefully. 'I'll take this up to the house. Show him the Churchill bit. Might interest him. Then off to the damned races. You quite sure you don't want to go?'

She shook her head slowly. 'I'm very, very sure. Anyway, I'm going with Clair to see Pieter. I promised. A new face, the first one; me, I mean. He said he'd like to see me: so I go.'

'Poor old you.'

'Well, he has to get used to people now; they're leaving, you know? For Europe. I think Nigel managed to get them a passage; isn't it strange, sad I mean, for him and Clair? That *he* should be the one to arrange for her to leave him after all.'

'When do they go?'

'I don't know. Soon, quite soon. I shall miss her very much.'

Rooke tapped the folded paper thoughtfully on his knee. 'Isn't it strange? It all seems to be sliding away, doesn't it?'

'What does?'

'Oh. Everything. The Dutch coming in, Clair going, Weathersby, the Oshima girl, with any luck, Miss Foto.'

'We can't be sure about that.'

'And the Old Man hasn't an idea. Not a clue. Nothing. The boy, Nanni Singh, the Australians, Nigel and Clair. He doesn't know that anything has happened at all.'

'Well,' she said and pulled the cover briskly over her typewriter, 'nothing very much did after all. Just ordinary things, human errors. And he will never know about Miss Foto, will he? He doesn't have to know anything.'

Rooke got up slowly adjusting his belt, patted his revolver holster thoughtfully. 'Funny; this thing feels quite different now. In six years of a war I never used it until that day, feels much heavier somehow.' He crossed to the door and stood for a moment looking out through the rusty grillwork at the dusty window across the corridor. 'Got to be getting up to the house. Early lunch today because of the blasted races. No, you're quite right. He doesn't have to know anything: she'll flit off one day. Probably give him some wonderfully invented reason, she has a big fat packet of those.' He turned back into the tidy little cubicle. Emmie was sitting motionless, arms on her desk, slim fingers lightly curled.

'Tonight then? All right?' He was looking very serious, bit the edge of his thumb nail, the folded newspaper half-covering his face. 'I'll come down to your place, if you wouldn't mind?'

She nodded, smiling softly. 'I wouldn't mind. You might though.'

'Why?'

'Narrow bed. You fell out . . .'

He laughed suddenly at the memory. 'Terrific thump. No. I want to talk to you. Just that. You've got two chairs, I remember them.'

'I've got two chairs.'

'That's it. I'll bring some tins of something, and a bottle.'

'Don't lose all your money at the races.'

He thrust his fingers carefully through the grille and pushed open the door. 'Not me. I never gamble,' he said. 'Well, not any more. I'm going out for a secure old age, you know? No more chances or risks; everything neat, safe and tidy.'

'A monk?'

He grinned cheerfully, 'Oh no! Not a monk. That's not my idea at all.' With a brief nod he turned into the corridor and closed the door.

Rough stone steps zig-zagged down the face of the high cliff between clumps of thorny scrub, ferns and trailing vine, to the smooth marble terrace below jutting out over the plain like the stern of a ship, its centre glittering with the turquoise waters of a heart-shaped pool, the sides surrounded by a low wall, the end nearest the cliff-face flanked by the two small pagoda-like pavilions, their glazed, green, tiled roofs rising to sharp points like stacked piles of limpet shells. Over one louvred door a faded red apple; over the other a fig-leaf. The changing-rooms. Between them, under a sagging bamboo-pole roof, shelves had been cut into the cliff fronted by a long, chipped, marble counter which had obviously been a bar but now contained nothing more than a scatter of empty snail shells and spatters of bird droppings.

If there were any faint echoes of long-ago laughter, splashing water, bare feet slapping on hot marble, glasses clinking in the shade, the General, sitting in a sagging cane chair in the barred sunlight didn't hear them: he was not a man of great imagination and on this still, hot morning he had other things to occupy his mind. The first was a confidential Signal summoning him to GHQ Delhi in five days' time which interested him, and the second a letter from Pegs which distressed him. Nanni Singh had brought it down in a slim packet of mail from UK which had just arrived, together with a bucket containing ice, three bottles of Tiger beer, and a thick glass mug. He knew the hand-writing instantly, and slid it into his pocket to keep for the last, aware that a couple of beers would be the wisest course to take before trying to read the precise looped script which reminded him sourly of all the little notes she used to leave about the place telling him where she would be playing bridge, who was dining that evening, who should be demoted and who could be promoted. He had slit the pale blue envelope with the blade of his pen-knife, smoothed out the densely written sheets and read them on his knee.

'Dear Old Boy:
Sorry there has been a bit of a delay in replying to your letter, but to tell the truth I've really been up to my eyes. It's no joke here with rationing, fuel shortages, bitter, bitter cold. This wretched Socialist Government isn't cheering things up, I must say, and people of our class are in for a hard time with awful Mr Attlee, who is v. middle-class, if not lower, and appears quite vindictive . . .'

Wearily, he skipped her political problems, jumped into the domestic ones . . .

'. . . has not been at all well this winter: bronchitis which worried me a good deal for she is, *like us all*, not getting any younger, however still game. Last week we managed a matinée of *The Winslow Boy* although she found it difficult to hear the actors, and I found it all a bit theatrical for my tastes. Daphne off for a week to the Goughs in Aberdovey, so I'm coping here on my own . . .'

He took a strong pull at his beer, skipped again, finding, at last, the heart of the matter.

'Now. About this extraordinary proposition which you made about a separation or a divorce. You were right, I *was* shocked, not to say gravely hurt. I have never considered you to be a plaster saint, as you well know. The business with Winnie Scanlon in Srinagar in '35 made that *quite* clear. But in this instance I can only think that you have taken leave of your senses, old boy. You may as well realize

317

right away that I am your wife, I stick to my vows, and will do so until the grave. There can be no question of either a separation or a divorce as far as I am concerned, even if you do, as you so quaintly put it, give me grounds! But it is against my beliefs and against my Faith. And you can't take *those* away from me however hard you try. There is also the question of money. I suppose you have given this some thought? Your salary didn't afford us the little luxuries we managed in the past . . . my inheritance, dwindling as it is under this wretched Government, did that. Just remember! Retirement for you is not so far-off, I imagine, and with India determined on self-rule you'll probably be on your way out within a year or so . . . if not less. Your pension won't go very far in England today, and Heaven knows what you'll find to do here. Not easy to get a job with no qualifications at your age. Also, which you might just think about, there is always the possibility, on your retirement, that after so many loyal years' service, in which I admit I have played no small part, you might be offered some form of recognition by HM's Government which would be very handy if you ever applied for a seat on a Board of Directors etc. This of course would not happen if there was any degree of *scandal* on your part. Mark my words. We may be going Socialist or even Communist, but the British still have their standards, especially in our class. So I should pull yourself together, old chap, and get things sorted out.'

There wasn't much more, thankfully, and he had got the gist of things, and also heard Rooke's tuneless whistle coming down the zig-zag path behind him, so he folded it neatly and put it in a pocket, taking another drink of his beer to moisten a suddenly dry-with-anger mouth. 'Get things sorted out!' That's exactly what he had been trying to do, for God's sake. Silly, bigoted, selfish bitch. The sudden vista before him of a retired life hanging about Moscow Mansions, trapped until he or she died, filled him with such misery and frustration that he snapped at Rooke the moment he came into sight round the side of one of the idiotic changing-rooms.

'That bloody whistle! Mindless noise.'

'Sorry, Sir. Wasn't thinking.'

318

'Never bloody well do. Think! Wouldn't mind if it was a tune: it's just a jingle-jangle. Goes through my head like a red hot knife.'

Rooke looked at the scatter of envelopes, the two empty beer bottles, the sulking lump in its sagging chair. Had some bad news, I expect. Getting it off his chest. Just ignore it, that's what you're here for, whipping boy from time to time, better get him cheered up or we'll all have a bloody awful afternoon.

'Came down to tell you that lunch will be ready in half an hour . . .'

The small blue eyes looked up at him balefully. 'Half an hour? Why the ruddy rush, it's only noon, for God's sake?'

'You told Brigadier Blackett and Colonel Nicholls to be here sharp at twelve-thirty, Sir. The races start at three o'clock, it'll take us about twenty minutes to the Stadium.'

'That bloody race. Gaunt's off his head.'

'So I thought I'd give you good warning.'

'Nanni Singh still mute, I see?'

'Pretty silent, Sir. Yes.'

'Don't know what's come over the silly sod. Sulking about something, I suppose. Won't say; I've got some news for him. Taking him up to Delhi shortly.'

'Delhi, Sir!'

'Yes. Not you, Ben, shan't need you there, take Singh along, he can cope for me, only a couple of days. You hang on here, have a rest from your "demanding" duties.'

'I'd like to come, Sir. If I could.'

'Sure you would. No room for ADCs, anyway it's all confidential. GHQ, you'd only get in the way.' He opened the third bottle, poured himself half a mug, offered the other half to Rooke. 'Want this? Wet your *whistle*, what? This damned race meeting: just what I want today. What do I have to do then?' Knowing perfectly well.

'Oh, just be there, Sir. You know. Give the prizes for the Cobra Stakes, the main event, three, prizes, I mean.'

'Won't have to stay the whole time? I'd go stark raving mad, all those idiots tearing round on ruddy ponies.'

'No, Sir. Slip away after the main event, I should say. The rest is all just for fun so to speak, for the Division.'

'Your girl going to be there, I suppose?'

'No, Sir. No, she won't be there.'

'Who's going to write it all up for the *Cobra* then? You?'

'Got three experts, Sir, it'll be well-covered; even got a couple of tame photographers lined up with their Brownies.'

'She doesn't like races, is that it?'

Rooke finished the beer, placed the empty bottle back in the tin bucket. 'Doesn't like the Stadium, frankly, Sir. Too many memories, I rather think.'

'Was she there then? During the Jap business?'

'No. She wasn't. But she knew a few who were, and still are.'

The General looked vaguely about him. 'Still are?'

'In the graves at the back on the football pitch. Mass graves, Sir. You remember? Behind the stands.'

'Yes, yes, I know all about them. Brim full of jolly cheer and mirth this morning eh? Damned bad taste in my opinion, careering about on horses with all that just behind the stands . . .'

Rooke placed *The Daily Cobra* on top of the scattered envelopes by the General's side. 'Well you know how it is, Sir. "In the Midst of Life" etcetera, etcetera. I brought this along, thought you might like to see the bit about Mr Churchill.'

'What's he been up to *now*? They've chucked him out, haven't they?'

'Still had something he wanted to say, I gather. Rather good speech in America, some University. Thought it was worth front-paging.'

'Cheerful?'

'Not very, no.'

'Christ! What a Jeremiah! You won't get a mention for this morning's work, I can tell you.' The mood was easing off, his eyes were glinting knowingly, warm, wry.

Rooke grinned back. 'Don't think I could handle a second, Sir.'

'Couldn't?'

'Go to my head in a flash.'

'Plenty of holes up there left to plug, I'll wager.' He skimmed quickly across the fresh inky page. Grunted a couple of times, dropped the paper lightly onto the table. 'Iron Curtain, eh? More warnings. Good grief, we're hardly through with this lot.' He looked up at Rooke squinting into the sunlight sliding through the bamboo slats above his head. 'Your number's coming up soon, I gather? Repat?'

'Yes, Sir. June.'

'Three months left. Suppose you're pleased?'

'Not very. Not as much as I had thought I'd be.'

'Well, I'm bloody sure you haven't fallen in love with the Division all of a sudden! I suppose it's woman-trouble, that it?'

'In a way. The Division too, strangely enough.'

The General looked out across his turquoise pool as Naik Kalik and two of his patrol came up the steps from behind the wall, rifles slung, talking among themselves. Seeing the General sitting under his canopy they sprang to attention, saluted, about turned neatly and went back out of sight in silence.

'Took 'em by surprise! Good lot. Yes, it's a good lot, been through bloody hell together, made us strong, united. This girl, what's her name, Emily or something? You serious, Ben?'

'*I* am.'

'Oh, we all are. At the time. What about her?'

'Not absolutely sure. She hasn't said.'

'No. They keep you guessing a bit.' The General crossed his legs, ran a finger over his knee. When he spoke he was almost shy. 'Sure you know what you're doing?'

'I am, Sir.'

'Quite . . . wise, do you think?'

'I think so.'

'Your family approve?'

'I'm an orphan as a matter of fact.'

'Oh. Oh, I see. No one?'

'Nanny Jarvis, remember?'

'Ah yes. You said so. Nanny. Your father?'

'A V-2 near Charing Cross.'

'Sorry. Wasn't prying.'

'No, Sir. And she's an orphan too, oddly enough. Babes in the wood, you might say.'

'You might,' said the General uncrossing his legs. 'You want to marry her?'

'Yes. I think she'll refuse.'

'Refuse you? Why, in God's name?'

'She's afraid, I think; mixed blood.'

'Ah. Yes. Difficult. Something you'd have to face. Not so easy in this world.'

321

'But I don't quite know how I'd manage without her, if you know what I mean, Sir.'

The General leant forward and started to collect up his scattered envelopes; he left the pale blue one with the South Kensington post-mark and Peg's looping script isolated on the table. He stared at it for a long moment and then deliberately crushed it into a ball in his fist. 'Yes. I know what you mean,' he said and threw it into the shadows behind the chipped marble bar among the snail shells.

Rooke looked at his watch. 'I think we ought to be making a move, Sir.'

'Yes. Yes, I'm coming along.' The General got to his feet slowly, pulling down his jacket, staring out into the midday sun sparkling on the water. 'Dangerous thing to do though, marrying out here. Lots of chaps doing it, all carting their wives back to Blighty. It's one thing in the sun, all the ruddy palm trees, this blue sky, a bit different in a council house in Stoke on Trent. But you can't tell 'em. Can't tell you, can I? Can't even tell meself, come to that.' He started across the marble floor towards the zig-zag path. At the first step he stopped and turned to Rooke, fiddling with his crimson lanyard.

'After I slip away from the races, Ben, I'll be at Miss Foto's place. See? You might as well know, if anything urgent, you know, crops up. But keep mum, right?'

'Right, Sir.'

'Nothing to worry about.' He stared up the steps. 'What a bloody climb, I'm getting old. It just might be the last time, you understand?'

'Yes, Sir.'

'You don't; but never mind, not your business, mine.' He started up the steps slowly. When they reached the first bend among the ferns and vines, he stopped again, hand on the iron rail, looking down to the heart-shaped pool below. 'No one much uses it, you know. All that water, when I'm up in Delhi, have a bit of a party one afternoon. I know you will behind my back so I'm giving you my permission now, get it? Very romantic and all that.'

'Thank you, Sir. I'd like to.'

They started up the second flight.

'And if she says "yes" I might come in useful, you know.'

'Useful, Sir? I'm sorry, I . . .'

'Orphan, too, isn't she? Got to have someone to give her away, what? Done it a couple of times before. I know the drill.'

Rooke followed him up in silence.

It was not at all like Longchamps or Ascot as Mrs Doorne had suggested it might be. Not by a long chalk. More like the Donkey Derby at Wivelsfield, thought Sister Pritchard wryly, sitting in comfortable splendour in the shade of the General's enclosure among an assortment of what she would call the Top Brass: Brigadiers, Colonels, Consular Officials, Dutch politicians, and a flurry of white-suited Americans flocking like mewing seagulls around a pale Mr Smedley seated on the General's right. However, Donkey Derby or not, it all appeared to be great fun and everyone seemed jolly and to be enjoying themselves. There were a number of people she recognized and many more she did not, and some familiar faces were not in the hallowed precincts as she might have expected. No Miss Foto, she noticed with satisfaction, but no Major Pullen either and no Mrs Doorne. However, that was very understandable under the circumstances. She sat among a carefully chosen group of her own nurses, bright and pretty, she thought, in little cotton frocks; she was wearing a wide-brimmed straw hat which she had selected for the occasion the moment that she was told that she'd be sitting in a place of such honour. Apart from a feeling of intense satisfaction at this, she was also aware of a deep sense of achievement, for although she had done nothing physically to make this day an event to remember, she had encouraged, suggested, pushed and advised David Gaunt to help make his dream come true and in so doing bring tremendous pleasure to the Division to which she now felt, after even so short a time, she truly belonged. And belonging, she reckoned, was just about the most important feeling that there was in the world. Anyway for her. Of course, she reasoned to herself, it was not absolutely true to say that she had done *nothing* physically to assist the day . . . for it was she who had designed the splendid new Divisional flag, the red and yellow silk banner with its proudly coiled cobra in the centre, surmounted by an enormous, only slightly crooked, 95 in golden sequins, which six diligent Chinese girls at the

323

hospital had worked at for hours and hours. Her heart had almost split with pride when it had appeared in the opening procession, borne aloft by two gigantic turbanned figures, glittering in the blazing sun: and the great cheer which went up from the massed ranks of white, khaki and green shirts across the track in the open stands brought a discreet tear to her eye. She had felt quite dizzy with emotion: I belong here! She thought, they are mine and I am theirs, we have been through some tough times together, and some good times. Oh! Please! Let it never end! Let it go on for ever!

Naturally the absolute highlight of the afternoon was when Gaunt had won the main event, the Cobra Stakes, by half a length. Tremendously exciting, longed for, and achieved. How splendid he had looked on his perfectly groomed mount. Not a *horse*, one would say in all truth, rather a wonderfully elegant pony almost. Small, but swift, and Gaunt, with his sleek golden hair, his white shirt rippling in the wind of his speed, was almost God-like; he made all the others look like a ragged band of scallywags straight out of Jorrocks, lumbering along on their shaggy beasts. However, a couple of magnificent Punjabi's gave him a terrific run and jolly nearly overtook him. But he won. He won! And she had found it extremely difficult to remain seated, which she did determinedly, as he flashed past the winning post. To have stood and screamed, as her silly young nurses did, would simply not have done. But her restraint contained a bursting pride which found its outlet in two severely bruised hands, so fiercely and excitedly did she applaud.

But then the prize-giving was a bit sad. There had been an interval after the race, and everyone had clambered happily up to the charming little bar at the top of the stand for refreshment, while the excellent Captain Rooke arranged the prizes on the Union Jack-draped table before the General's seat. She and Gaunt had decided, long before, that money, in the form of a cheque or even in notes, was vulgar and to be avoided. A Symbol was what was needed. Gaunt chose a small silver bowl for the first prize, a silver cigarette lighter for the second, and a silver pencil for the third. These they had found in and around the market in the City and polished them up till they hurt the eye with their brilliance and there they stood winking in the sun. Bells rang, and the interval was over, the band started up with

'Hail the Conquering Hero!' and Gaunt arrived briskly at the dais, his head a cap of burnished gold, boots and spurs glittering, cream breeches unmarked, white shirt freshly starched (he had obviously changed in the interval), a figure of radiant splendour; cool, erect, unsmiling. Oh! she had thought, but let him *smile* just once! Let him move a hand if only to acknowledge the tremendous cheers of pleasure which he must hear! Why this graven face, the cold eyes, why turn his back, as he did literally, on all the delight which he had worked so hard to give. *Smile!* she pleaded silently, make some gesture to show that you are alive, that you care, that you are aware, it's only a silly little sugar bowl you are receiving, not a death sentence. But he had merely moved one pace backwards, dropped his golden head in a brief, silent salute to his General and marched briskly away. She felt a sense of great despair sweep her in the middle of the gaiety, for no one else, but she, had seemed to notice the icy desolation of his soul.

Shortly afterwards the General eased himself out of his chair, made some polite remarks to Mr Smedley, and followed by the attentive Captain Rooke had made his way out of the enclosure hardly noticed by the chattering, laughing gathering. After that, she thought, the day is really over, a little cloud has passed over my sun, and looking at her programme with suddenly blurred eyes, she felt very sure that the next event, a Fancy-Dress Race between the 24th Field Ambulance and Divisional Signals, would do nothing to help disperse it. I never liked this place, never, she thought, staring through the capering horsemen dressed in top-hats and poke-bonnets trailing coloured balloons in the dusty light; it has never made me happy to be here, and that hideous football pitch just behind this stand, surrounded by barbed wire, scabbed with mounds of weed-ridden tortured soil, just puts the kibosh on the whole afternoon. I'm miserable. I want to leave. I hate it all suddenly, I really could have a jolly good old blub.

She took it damned well, thought the General, staring unseeingly at the back of his driver's neck, damned well. Not a tear, not a whimper. Helped me no end. Bloody good effort. So understanding: *that's* behaviour for you. Just read through the letter without a mumur, gave it back with such a sweet smile.

325

God! She must have felt unhappy, but you'd never have known it. Not a murmur. Just said, very sadly, 'Well, Leo, that's that, I suppose?' Not a word of criticism against Peggy, not a word. 'Faith and Belief,' she said, 'those are the important things, we cannot take those away from her and she will not allow it. We cannot fight her, Leo, she is a strong woman, and a good woman, and she has won. You cannot destroy such faith, it would be impossible, and we cannot betray a union which she feels is a bond for life. I will always cherish the wonderful things which you have said to me, the kindness and the love you have shown me, the generosity of your heart will always be with me here, in mine.' That's what she said. I shall remember those words for the rest of my life. Behaviour! And when I said to her that I loved her she was so bloody marvellous. You might have thought a tear or two . . . Nothing. So pale, so calm, so wise. 'You do not have the right to love me, Leo, that is all there is to be said. You are not free to love. You *are* loved.' 'You came into my life like the sun, Dora,' I said, didn't I? Like the sun, and what did she say? She said very softly, 'The sun must give way to the evening and the evening to the night, and so like the sun I must just fade into your evening, Leo. We are powerless, we cannot consider only ourselves, and you have a brave future ahead, a brilliant past behind you, if I have brought you just a little comfort, I am content. It is a wonderful thing for a woman to know that she has been loved just once. *Really* loved. We are not children, Leo, we have known life. I am content. I accept. Be brave and accept too, you will find great strength, as I am finding now,' I think she said, and I remember that she got up and walked away from me so that I wouldn't see her face, I suppose, I remember that she said, 'It would be better now if we did not meet again, it is a terrible thing which I say, but now that I know you belong to someone else, my feeling of guilt would destroy me, and destroy all our love and all that we have had; before, when I was not sure, I dared to believe that we could perhaps be happy, and that what we were doing was not wickedness, but now that we both know. Finish! Finish! I shall slip away just as I slipped into your life that wonderful day so long ago. Everyone is leaving now; we no longer belong here, so I will go also. I shall not be alone, there are many like me: all in the same boat, you might say.' That little laugh! So soft

326

and so gentle, nearly broke my heart. My Dora! Driving away
from you . . . 'If we meet again in public,' she said, 'we must
behave correctly, a smile, a hand, nothing more, but nothing
less; let us take our parting with the dignity our love deserves!'
Now *that's* bloody behaviour for you! My God it is. But my God,
it hurts.

Nettles looked about the shadowy room with deep satisfaction: an embarrassment of red and black lacquer, tassled
lanterns, white table-cloths, fluted jars of paper flowers. On a
tankful of shouldering carp, a full-breasted Hoti, stuck about
with joss-sticks, whose broadly smiling face was reflected by
Nettles' own. He peeled a coral prawn with relish and dipped it
into its sauce.

'I simply couldn't like it more. Came here ages ago, in the
first days, only place open then.' He ate his prawn thoughtfully.
'With Sydney Grout. Sweet lad. Frightful name and *frightfully*
common but everything in the right place and plenty of it.' He
smiled across at Emmie apologetically. 'I brag of course; it was
null and void. I was a sort of uncle at half-term, if you know
what I mean. Desolating business.'

'No score?' said Rooke sympathetically.

'No score. Had a child-bride in Middlesborough. Kept
dragging out the wedding snapshots each time I laid a finger on
him. Maddening.' He reached for a second prawn and started
to peel it carefully. 'He was also in the Merchant Navy and
that's simply not on.'

'I thought that was rather ... productive; isn't it?' said Rooke.

'Well, the trouble with me is that I am always searching for a
permanent relationship, you see? Idiotic, but that's my bad
luck. And trying to have a permanent relationship with someone in the Merchant Navy is like trying to have a permanent
relationship with a revolving door.'

Emmie laughed and placed her hand lightly on his sleeve.
'You are a very shameful man, I think, shameful.'

'Shame*less*, you mean, but as I said, I brag most fearfully.
But I do think this is all very jolly. Our first evening out. Ever.
While the cat's away the mice will play. Nothing truer.'

Rooke ran a finger round the rim of his rice bowl. 'It was all

327

quite splendid this morning, wasn't it? When he left. Everyone lined up glittering in the sun, the flags, you'd have thought he was leaving for the UK instead of five days in Delhi. All most touching.'

'Do we know what it's all about?' said Nettles. 'The Delhi trip? Promotion? I ask myself . . .'

'I don't know. Never said. Something urgent. Probably to do with the India business, reshuffle and handing over, all that. If it's a Staff Job he'll cut his throat.'

Emmie reached for the chicken and helped herself deftly with her chopsticks. 'He's a fighting General, Rooke says, and now there is nearly nothing left here to fight. Maybe in India, do you think?'

'Maybe,' said Nettles. 'But that won't concern you, Rooke? Will it? A free man in June I gather, back to Blighty. I hear they give one a cotton tweed suit, a pork pie hat, or trilby if preferred, cardboard shoes and the fare to your Next of Kin. For helping to save Democracy.'

Rooke slowly poured himself another glass of wine. 'That's the rub, leaving.'

'Rub! Aren't you ecstatic?'

'Not really. Odd, isn't it? I'm rather like you at the moment, trying to establish a permanent relationship, no go.'

Nettles raised polite eyebrows. 'With whom?'

'This one.' Rooke indicated Emmie with a jerk of his head. 'I want her to come with me. She won't.'

Nettles pushed the prawns away from him, folded his arms on the table. 'Are you out of your pretty little mind, girl?'

Emmie looked at him levelly. 'No. Not at all. I am quite in my mind.'

'To turn down this golden Apollo! Madness . . .'

'It's complicated,' said Emmie awkwardly. 'Don't talk about it, not tonight, please Rooke? Please not.'

'Spent a whole night on a very hard chair in her foul little parlour just begging. She was as stubborn as hell. That's why I asked you to join us tonight. Another voice, another reasoning.'

'I wish you would be silent,' said Emmie.

'I'm to be a sort of Auntie Agony, is that it?' said Nettles. 'Advice to the Lovelorn?'

328

'That's about it. You're cleverer than me. You ask her.'

'Propose to her for you, do you mean? Dear God—really not my sort of thing!'

'Shut up!' said Emmie. 'Now be silent both of you. I stay until Rooke leaves, I have promised. For that silly paper if he wants, after that I will go to school.'

'To school?' Nettles was smiling.

'To help them start up again. I will teach English. I am not so bad at it.'

'To whom? Dutch or Indonesians?' asked Nettles.

Emmie shrugged. 'To either. I am both.'

'And that,' said Rooke, lifting his glass, 'is the whole bloody trouble.'

'But what trouble?' said Nettles.

'I have mixed blood,' said Emmie prodding a chopstick into the tablecloth.

'Absolutely splendid!'

'Not for children,' said Emmie. 'I know. I know the English.'

'Oh shit!' said Rooke in irritation. 'Eastbourne . . .'

'Not Eastbourne. I knew them here, the British from India, Malaya; there was a woman in the camp, she was so cruel.'

'Oh my God!' said Nettles. 'The mem-sahibs! You've been got at by the mem-sahibs, I do believe: what a dire misfortune.'

'A Mrs Bethell-Wood; she was quite old, you know. But some were young too.'

Nettles swung a prawn head gently by its whiskers: a black-eyed pendulum.

'You know, my dear Emmie, it is not syphilis, drink, cholera or even the midday sun which is the curse of the East. It is they. Those grim creatures struggling desperately through the lower reaches of the British Middle Classes like homing elvers determined to attain the upper stratas and die with an OBE. The spawn of countless domestic servants, clerks, shopkeepers and shabby gentry all hell-bent on saving the Empire from the Natives, spreading the word of their own particular God and making, ultimately, a curtsey at the Viceroy's house.'

Emmie laughed shortly. 'Oh dear. I am confused so. Something like that perhaps.'

'Oh! The insularity of them, the narrowness. Do you know that at this very moment on the main doors of Raffles Hotel in

329

Singapore there is a sign which says: "If You Are In HM Uniform You Are Unwelcome." In Singapore! Which we all liberated not so long ago. That is the mem-sahib mentality for you. It is not only you who have suffered from their inverted form of ridiculous snobbery, gentility and ignorance.'

'I did not suffer, you know,' said Emmie quietly. 'But in England, you see, I had never met this kind of people, so it was a surprise.'

'Of course you wouldn't meet them. I very much doubt that you'll ever meet a mem-sahib unless you have the grave misfortune to wander into Camberley, Frimley, Bagshot or Fleet! They are a singular breed and flourish in small coveys, like quail.'

Emmie folded her arms, pushed her bracelets up to the elbow.

'Perhaps they are silly, but perhaps, too, they mean well; only Nigel Pullen told me a long time ago that this was a very bad thing to do. It is so?'

'They *believe* that they mean well. Quite a different thing. And in so doing they have caused more harm to this declining Indian Empire which they so revere than almost any other single factor. They speak proudly of themselves as the backbone, whereas they are nothing but torn cartilage. Gristle!'

Rooke burst out laughing and shook his head happily. 'My goodness, Geoffrey! Such spleen! Such wrath, no longer the weary philosopher!'

'Well, it makes me so wild!' said Nettles and spun the prawn head into a dish. 'That they should distress this glowing creature before us. However, their sun is sinking, their shadows grow long. It is almost time for them to go, one hundred million Moslems and three hundred million Hindus seething for a Holy War will very shortly see to that, not to mention a bankrupt Socialist Government in the UK which can't afford them either. I promise you, Emmie, that within a year or two Frimley and Bagshot, which I implore you to avoid, will be awash, literally awash, with tiger skins, Benares brass and dinner gongs to which no-one will pay heed while the mulligatawny soup chills in the tureens for lack of a servile Indian.'

'Oh bravo!' laughed Rooke with delight. 'Take notice of what he says. The tiger of wrath is wiser than the horses of instruction!'

Nettles shrugged, rubbed his face quickly, grinned suddenly.

330

'I'm carrying on again, aren't I? Well, you know me. Too awful. It's all better now. I think you asked me to propose to the child? Not paralyse her with rhetoric. But you see, I'm a liberal creature truthfully. I don't give a tinker's gob for anyone's colour, race or creed. I care only that they shall be . . . dare I say it? Why ever not? I care only that they are pretty. There! I *like* pretty people, I make no bones about it. And I admit that I am not as generous as I should be to the plain and the dull, and I detest the ugly in heart, mind and matter. I've had my fair share of them during my wandering life, they comprise more than half of mankind.'

Emmie unfolded her arms, extended an open palm towards him across the littered table.

'You must tell me how I can be brave enough against so many, please?' She took up a chop-stick and scored a deep question mark into the tablecloth.

Nettles leaned across the table very carefully, his face extremely serious, only a slight shadow of amusement in his eyes. 'Now look here, Emmie, I'm going to have to talk to you very frankly, otherwise we will sit here all night picking about at things. Tell me one quite, quite simple thing, will you? In perfect honesty?'

'What?'

'Do you love this chap, this Rooke?'

Emmie prodded the tablecloth harder, her head down, her lips firm.

'Do you?'

'Yes,' she said almost reluctantly.

'With all your heart? Can you possibly say it aloud?'

The prodding went on angrily, she turned her head away swiftly to conceal rapidly brimming eyes. 'With all my heart,' she said finally.

Rooke shifted uncomfortably in his chair, pushed his wine glass in a small circle, looked up at Nettles who was smiling.

'And you, Rooke? Same thing, I take it? Do you want to actually say it to her?'

'With all my heart,' said Rooke and snapped the stem of his wine glass.

'Now see what you've done!' said Nettles. 'Oh God! All this suppressed emotion is too exhausting. It is all utterly simple.

You both adore each other and you both seem to lack sufficient courage to face a perfectly simple fact.'

'I don't lack the courage!' said Rooke hotly. 'It's her. She's got this bee in her bonnet about having black babies . . .'

'I have *not* got a bee in my bonnet! It's true. It is a terrible thing to haunt me.'

Nettles stroked his fine nose thoughtfully.

'I very much doubt that you have a whole tribe of wild Sudanese waiting in the shadows to blight your life, Emmie.'

'My grandmother was Moluccan.'

'And a very nice job she has made of things, if I may say so. Moluccan! Emmie! Black is black, Moluccans . . .'

'Are coloured people. They are dark,' said Emmie with force.

'Well, don't let's *have* any blasted children. I don't know if Moluccans are blue, green, or beige!' said Rooke. 'I told you: I don't want them if you don't.'

'But I do. I would . . .'

'Oh for God's sake. We're back to square one again.' Rooke stacked his broken glass in a bowl, and reached across for Emmie's which he drained desperately.

'And you see!' said Emmie accusingly, pointing her chopstick directly at the calm-eyed Nettles. 'You see! You who are so liberal, even you start to make distinctions. Black, Sudanese, Moluccans, you differentiate, but it is still a matter of colour.'

Nettles leaned back in his chair and shook his head. 'No, Emmie, not colour, courage. Now look here, both of you. Neither of you lack courage. You have both had to prove that. You, Emmie, in your little cupboard all that time. Hiding the cars in the forests, smuggling petrol and spare parts under the noses of the Japs, that was courage. Joining us, when you did, was courage.'

Emmie suddenly sat up very straight and roughly pulled her hair behind her neck. 'I saw him. You know that?'

Nettles looked startled for a moment at her change of course. 'Who?'

'The Australian. The four Australians. When we took some things to the forest they were there. Hiding. I have never said.'

Rooke looked at her in sudden shock. 'But you never told me!'

'I know. It was not proof of anything. I just saw them, that's all. We did not even speak. I tell you now.'

'I knew anyway,' said Nettles gently. 'The Ruby girl told me, Oshima. But it was not important, it is not important now. That's over.'

Emmie put her hand on Rooke's and pressed it firmly. 'You see? I had no courage for that. To tell you. I didn't want to be involved in anything, I wanted just that we would not be anything to do with those things. I have little courage.'

'You have great courage, both of you. Rooke managed pretty well one wretched day not so long ago, he didn't fail himself or me, for that matter. Life is all testing and proving, you know, it never stops cropping up.' Nettles smiled across at Rooke. 'You could almost say, in an actor's parlance, that you have both got through the rehearsals pretty well, you know all your "words", your "places" on this strange stage of life, the "moves" you will make and the love which you both have for this odd play which you are about to perform together; now go ahead and play it. Go out now, before the common mass, the plankton, Rooke, remember? Go out and dazzle them, this audience of the mundane, of the ordinary, the whale soup! Show them your beauty, show them your love, prove to them that from the wreckage of this savaged, shabby little Island, you have taken one tiny grain which will grow into some splendid tree from which you will take the shelter, the strength, and the harvest, of whatever colour, Emmie dear, to secure you for the rest of your lives. Blaze with your glory, defy them with your courage and your love! Oh dear, how deeply I envy you both.' He turned swiftly to a bobbing waiter who hurried eagerly to his side. 'My dear fellow, I would rather like champagne. You have some?'

The waiter nodded brightly. 'Have champagne. Very good. From Germally.'

'The provenance is of no importance; as long as it sparkles.'

'Thank you,' said Rooke after a silence. 'Not for the champagne, for the other part.'

'Well, you know how I go on, don't you? Verbal diarrhoea, I often think, and of course I am assuming that we have reached a conclusion. Conceited me. Have we? I mean, before he uncorks his alien brew.'

Rooke looked anxiously at Emmie who was sitting quite still staring at the carp in their tank beyond Nettles.

'Have we? Reached a conclusion, I mean?'

333

She nodded slowly and he took her hand. 'You know: I am too weary to fight you both—but if you will help me. Always. Be patient, I am a foolish person . . .'

'I'll help you always. We have to help each other. Orphans, remember?'

'I feel quite strange. Light. Floating.'

'A not unusual phenomenon I believe,' said Nettles, 'although I confess that I have never, alas, experienced it myself. Yet. Perhaps one day, who can tell? One goes on searching. However, it didn't take a great deal of persuasion to get you into this condition, delicious as it is, it must be quite a strong attack?'

'Attack?'

'Of love.'

Emmie twisted a piece of hair into a knot. 'Yes, it is. And he was bullying to me, so much, now you, and Clair Doorne, she also.'

'What did Mrs Doorne have to say?' asked Nettles lifting the champagne from its bucket.

'Not bullying really. Not so. She just said that the worst thing in life was to live with regret. So that is why I have said yes, I suppose, because I would have lived like that for the rest of mine.' She smiled suddenly at Nettles and put her hand across the table. 'Will you take my hand? Will you hold it while I thank you for reminding me of courage? It is such a simple word, and very beautiful, I lost it. Thank you, for giving it back to me.'

Nettles looked at her with rather bright eyes. 'You are a very remarkable pair, I drink to you both. To a wonderfully happy long run; your kindness, Emmie, has reduced me to banality.'

Rooke raised his glass. 'No. This is my toast, I think. So let me offer it. This is to Clair who said "Regret" and Geoffrey who said "Courage", that we may, together, never know the former and always have the latter.'

They drank in solemn silence as the bobbing waiter started to clear the dishes.

'God knows where this wine came from,' said Nettles, placing his glass carefully on the table. 'It's like hot Ribena. But I do think that this is the nicest supper I have been to for years, it is not the wine but the company, we ought really to have an enormous party.'

334

'Oh no!' said Emmie with wide eyes. 'Not a party, no one, please, Rooke, not a party or anything so awful.'

'One on Sunday,' said Rooke.

'Sunday? Where, you did not say?' Emmie clasped her hands in anguish.

'Not really a party. At the swimming-pool. Nothing to do with us: the Old Man suggested that I ask some people up while he was away, for a swim, a drink. Just that, not a party.'

'But who?'

Rooke searched busily for his cigarettes, accepted one from Nettles' proffered case. 'Well, first of all Sister Pritchard, then David Gaunt.' He caught Emmie's wild eye and laughed nervously. 'Because of the races, you see. He thought they ought to be sort of, I don't know, thanked, I suppose. And because he can't stand poor old Pritchard and doesn't go a bundle on Gaunt, even though he admires him, he suggested they came up and so on, while he was away. A coward, you see? No real courage after all!'

Nettles lit his cigarette and leant across to Rooke with the match. 'And who else is asked for this Bacchanal? Medea and Dr Crippen?'

'You're being bloody. She's just bringing a couple of her nurses down, that's all; it's a sort of thanks-for-the-races-and-morale-business. That's all. You'll come?'

'Detest cold water, loathe swimming-pools: athlete's foot and stale pee. Anyway I'm going to the ENSA thing at the Harmonie.'

'But that's on Saturday!'

'And who knows,' said Nettles moving his glass aside, 'what Sunday may bring? There's a lissom creature dancing "The Bolero" in a bunch of grapes. How's that for culture? Mad to miss him. Seen the piccies.'

Emmie found her purse and took out lipstick and mirror. 'I'm going to Clair's in the morning, to help with the packing, they leave soon, you know. And the inventory is difficult. All she took she must replace to the Dumps. I shall help.'

'You are both a couple of shits,' said Rooke helplessly.

'And you are the ADC. Your job. Not ours,' said Nettles with a grin.

'It's just so that they can look over the house while he's not

there, have a bit of a swim, kindness only. Emmie. Please? I'll
pick you up at Clair's about two-ish. It won't last long.
Pritchard's on duty again at six, she said so.'

Emmie put away the lipstick and mirror, closed the purse.
'Very well. Two. Not one moment before. I will pour the tea, I
will be very gracious, the perfect English lady, I will talk of
horses to Gaunt and hospitals to Pritchard and show them all
the Coromandel Room. Is that it? But you will not say a word
about us? You swear?'

'I swear,' said Rooke with relief. 'Cross my heart and hope
to die.'

'I do declare,' said Nettles, 'that the girl has a mind of her
own, she's going to get her own way, Rooke, I warn you, no
fading little flower here. Are you absolutely sure you are right?'

'Absolutely! I am perfectly contented, I assure you.'

'So there we are.'

> 'How pleasant it is at the end of the day,
> No follies to have to repent;
> But reflect on the past, and be able to say,
> That my time has been properly spent!'

He raised his arms high, spread slender hands in a kind of
blessing. 'It's been a simply delicious evening, I do thank you
both. I really couldn't have liked it more!'

Kim placed the coffee tray beside him, lifted the dirty plates.
'Is Gaunt Sahib, coming in jeep. I bring other cup?'

Rooke sighed, closed his letter-pad, put the top on his
fountain-pen. 'Bring other cup. Where is Gaunt Sahib?'

'Soon come,' said Kim and crunched into the house. Rooke
rubbed his eyes, reached out for the coffee pot as Gaunt
arrived at the verandah steps.

'I'm early, I know. Terribly sorry. Hope I'm not disturbing
you.'

'No. No . . . not a bit. Want anything to eat? Sit down.'

'Eaten thanks. Wouldn't mind a coffee if it's going.'

'It's going; cup's just coming.'

Gaunt removed his cap, sat opposite Rooke, placed a large
green envelope on the table beside him. 'Writing letters home?
That it? I *did* disturb you.'

336

'No, no. Really; writing to my old Nanny, actually, weekly chore. It can wait, I'll have more news for her at the end of today, I reckon, swimming parties and all that.'

'All that. Yes. I'm a bit early, but I was in the area, checking the Perimeter Guard; they get a bit slack on Sundays, especially with the Old Man away, and I brought these up.' He indicated the green envelope with his thumb. 'Photos of the races last week. Some pretty good ones. He's back tomorrow, isn't he? Thought he'd like to have a shufti at them.'

Kim came back with a cup and saucer smiling brightly at Gaunt. 'Good day, Sahib. Good race, most splendid, I am thanking you sincerely.'

'Win much?' said Gaunt, taking the cup and starting to pour his coffee.

'Win twenty-five rupees with Gaunt Sahib. Is most excellent.'

'Good show,' said Gaunt indifferently. 'Got any sugar?'

'Will find, Sahib. Excuse me.' Kim hastened back to the house.

'A bit of sugar for energy.' He raised his cup and looked about him. 'Must say, you're very well set up here, what? Tidy little property, nice and snug: you'll miss it, I reckon, when you leave.'

'Miss a lot of things, the sun especially.'

Kim arrived back with a bowl of sugar. 'One piece, two piece, Sahib?'

Gaunt flicked a look at him. 'Just leave it there, will you, that's fine.' He took a piece of sugar, put it in his mouth, sipped his coffee, grinned at Rooke. 'That's how I like it, instant energy. When do the girls get here? Old Deidre-drear and company.'

'Who's that?'

'Sister Pritchard. Old Pritchard-Britchard. *Her* name for herself, not mine.'

'I'm going up at two, collecting Emmie.'

'In your beautiful pea-green Buick?'

'That's it. You be all right? We won't be long. Half an hour. Have a swim.'

'Wouldn't mind. If I'm not intruding, your letter, I mean.'

'That can wait. Honestly.'

Gaunt put another lump of sugar in his mouth, took a swig of coffee. 'Truth is, it's a bit dull, Sunday, good of you to have us all up.'

337

'The Old Man's idea really, you got his note? All this water going to waste, he said, pity not to share it. He was very chuffed about the races; all the morale stuff, you know how keen he is on that.'

'Worked out well, I must say, think it was successful. Your girl coming down too this afternoon?'

'Yes. She's stuck at the Doornes this morning, packing or something.'

'She's not leaving too?'

'No. No, the Doornes, they're old friends. Helping out.'

'Going out on *The Amsterdam*, I suppose. End of next week.'

'Don't honestly know.'

'Expect so.' Gaunt placed his cup on the table, took another lump of sugar and crunched it loudly. 'Quite a lot shipping out, I hear. Full load. Everyone getting away while they can, can't say I blame them, bloody awful place, and with the old Dutch in charge, practically, and another ruddy civil war ahead for certain, well, sensible thing to do.'

'Hope it doesn't start before I get away. June.'

'Rice planting starts in June. Don't think they'll try anything really big until they've got the bloody harvest in, you might just make it.'

'Well,' Rooke got up and stretched, looked at his watch. 'One-ten. Want a swim? Before they all descend.'

'What about you?'

'Yes. All right. Freshen me up.'

'Fact is, I haven't got a swimming-suit, packed for a war not a holiday.'

'I've got something. Emmie got some stuff from the Dumps, I'll look something out.'

Gaunt followed him into the house, stood for a time in the cool sitting-room. 'This is bloody good,' he said. 'Very stylish. All looted stuff, I take it?'

Rooke's voice was muffled from the bedroom. 'Well, I didn't actually cart it down from Calcutta with me.' He came into the room with a towel and trunks which he threw across to Gaunt. 'Not exactly loot. *Requisitioned*, like all the rest of the house. It all goes back when we pull out, listed. Those do?'

Gaunt held up a small pair of bright yellow briefs. 'These for swimming? Look like girls' knickers.'

338

'All I've got. Latest fashion.'

'Better have the swim before they arrive, Deidre-drear'll have a stroke if she sees these.'

'Don't see why. She's a nurse, seen it all.'

'Maybe. Repressed. They all are. That's why they ruddy joined up. See the fellers close to. They don't know it but it's all sex really. Rearing its ugly head.'

'Come on,' said Rooke, hiding sudden irritation, 'let's go down, I'll lead.'

'The Sappers did all this, I suppose: in their free time, so to speak?' said Gaunt standing by the sparkling pool, hands on hips, legs apart, looking around him with a sarcastic smile.

'Cleaned it out and fixed it up. Yes,' said Rooke going over to one of the green-tiled pagodas. 'The Old Man has them down to swim twice a week, did you know? Perhaps not. You can change over there, I think there are hooks and so on.' He changed quickly and went out into the sun, feeling the marble tiles hot to his feet, the sun burning on his back, and dived into the crystal water in the hope that the sudden shock of the cold would douse his mounting anger. Which it did, and as he surfaced and saw Gaunt coming out of his pagoda looking like a gold and ivory God he called out cheerfully that it was glorious, and thrashed about in the water like a child at the seaside. Gaunt seemed to catch his mood and with a sudden whoop of idiot delight leapt high in the air and crashed into the water in a gigantic spume of flying spray, emerging beside Rooke moments later in a huge flurry of foam and bubbles shaking his golden head like a dog.

'God! But it's so good,' he gasped. 'Gets all the stress and strain out.' He submerged and sped deeply into the green and silver depths with the elegance and grace of a fish. Rooke hauled himself out and sat at the edge. First time he's seemed human, he thought with amusement, perhaps he ought to do it more often, he's far more agreeable in water than on dry land. Almost human. No, not that even, a sort of merman, brainless, cold, of the sea. A cold fish. He got up and padded round the wide pool as Gaunt climbed out on the far side. 'You off then?' he called, a nearly fretful sound.

'Yes. Go up and get the others; but you hang on, shan't be long.'

Gaunt ran his hands through his hair. 'Well, give me a shout from the top when you get back. Don't want to be caught like this, these damn things are transparent. You give me a yell?'

'Do that,' called Rooke. 'You needn't fret. Perfectly decent. Some beer over here, in the bar if you want a drink; no ice but it's cool. It's in a bucket.'

He changed quickly, combed his hair in a piece of speckled mirror, went into the sun buckling on his belt.

Gaunt had found a beer and was sitting with his legs in the water splashing idly. He held up the bottle by the neck. 'Only one. That all right?'

'Blasted Kim's a nitwit, I said half-a-dozen. That do for the moment?'

Gaunt flashed his little cat's grin. Neat white teeth. 'Fine. I'm a humble soldier-boy, not used to such luxury.'

Rooke patted the revolver on his hip. 'Got this? Handy, I mean? Wise.'

Gaunt took a long drink from the bottle, wiped his mouth with his fist. ' 'Course. Always have. Soldier's friend. Over in the thingummetight there: but the Patrols are about, or should be, unless they're all kipping down under a tree somewhere, which wouldn't bloody well astonish me.'

'About the Patrols, by the way,' said Rooke, putting on his cap. 'The Old Man has given permission that they can wash-up and so on, bathe, if they want to in the over-flow fountain just below the wall there.' He smiled politely. 'So don't go and bawl anyone out if you see him washing his hair, or something. It's okay, just so that you know.'

'Tikh-hai,' said Gaunt. 'Understood, will do, Wilco, Roger and out. Not my pool.'

'Just so,' said Rooke pleasantly. 'I'm off. Won't be long.'

'You'll yell, won't you?' said Gaunt.

'Do that,' called Rooke and started up the steps briskly swinging his damp towel.

Gaunt watched him go, then he got to his feet and wandered with his beer to the low tiled-wall surrounding the terrace, sat down, elbows on his knees, looked about him with a faint smile of mixed amusement and envy. Not bad for a snotty little ADC. Better than anything Timmy Roberts ever got, class stuff, I suppose. Nannies and all that shit. Really! Car, house, damned great swimming pool to loll about in. No pride of course, no tradition, discipline, no sense of respect for the Army. Civilians. Conscript soldiers. Get all sorts now, quite pleasant, rides well, but no real toughness, a weak strata somewhere, nothing like Robin at all. My old Robin. Superficial resemblance. Nothing more, just that, oh well. He finished his beer, took it over to the empty bar, wandered into his pagoda, got his towel, spread it carefully on the hot marble tiles and stretched out, arms behind his head, tilting his face to the sun. Somewhere at the top of the cliff he heard the Buick start up. He closed contented eyes against the brilliant glare.

A shadow slid across the sun. He looked up hazily from a semi-doze.

Standing astride him the towering naked body of Kalik, a coiled webbing belt in his fist. He opened his eyes wider with shock, made a sudden and violent move to sit, but Kalik was swifter and crashed down on him, straddling his body, crushing his chest, grabbing his head in both hands; other hands scrabbled about and took his legs, and as he tore and struggled, trying to yell out, Kalik lifted his head and cracked it viciously twice against the tiles. In a daze of pain and shock he felt himself rolled onto his belly, hands securing his wrists tightly with cord behind his back; he was grabbed by the hair, his head wrenched backwards, choking him, a wiry hand pinched his nostrils so that he could not breathe, forcing him to open his gasping mouth into which a tight ball of cloth was rammed between his wide-stretched lips.

Half-dragged, half-carried, he was slung face downwards over the low surrounding wall, head and shoulders hanging helplessly into space, his legs pulled wide apart. Kalik moved deliberately towards the spreadeagled body, webbing belt raised, brass buckle winking in the light.

As the first monstrous blow ripped across his buttocks, Gaunt's entire body jerked into a bucking arc of searing pain, he snorted and snuffled through his nose, mucus ran, but he was securely held and did not lose consciousness until the fourth or fifth savage lash ripped across the back of his thighs, when, quite suddenly, his writhing body went limp and sagged brokenly.

Kalik dropped the belt and stood away from Gaunt, the three others who had been holding him down got to their feet unsteadily, stood swaying uneasily, huddled by the wall, eyes bloodshot, breath heavy with drink. One of them pointed to the blood marbling the splayed white thighs and giggled. Kalik struck him savagely across the mouth, the man whimpered and crouched behind his companions, staring with wide eyes as Kalik stooped down and deliberately stripped the thin briefs from the body before him, revealing the broad welts criss-crossing the pale waxen flesh, the red droplets trickling from the wounds torn by the brass buckle, and then with a harsh grunting cry, but almost tenderly, he folded himself over Gaunt's inert form.

'Oh! Do look! Brenda! Stella, look at the waterlilies, the little fountain . . . all these heavenly figures, isn't it fairy-land?' Sister Pritchard hurried across the upper terrace briskly, her straw hat flapping, skirt billowing, picnic basket banging her shins.

'Oh it's too, too beautiful for words. The view! The air up here! I had no idea, really no idea. Breathe it all in, fill your lungs and eyes.' She stopped at the carved balustrade and looked down to the pool sparkling far below.

'Captain Rooke, it's paradise, paradise. *How* you must love it all. We go down this way, do we, down this cliff-thing?'

'Be careful,' said Rooke. 'It's steep, hang onto the rail on your left.'

'It is steep! My goodness, yes, steep as anything. However did they cut all these steps out, one wonders? Brenda, mind the steps, dear, your glasses, you know.' She hurried happily on ahead and when she got to the first bend in the path she stopped, her hand to her breast. 'Oh the joy of it! Such joy, and there it is, the heart-shaped pool! You're quite right, Captain Rooke, it *is* heart-shaped, quite like a heart . . .' Suddenly her voice trailed away into the afternoon. She stood perfectly still staring down. When she spoke again her voice was flat and harsh.

'Stop!' she said. 'All of you stop. Stay where you are. Captain Rooke, Captain Rooke, something terrible has happened!'

342

CHAPTER THIRTEEN

In the Coromandel Room the General lightly ran a liver-spotted hand across a nugget of uncut amethyst in one of the luxuriant floral wall-panels.

'You see? *Dust?* The whole place is filthy. Go off for a few days, turn my back and what happens? Negligence. Negligence. God knows, he's got a fleet of ruddy women and girls to give him a hand, what does he do?'

'Two girls, Sir, not a fleet,' said Rooke politely.

'Well, even so, can't take them all week to just dust one ruddy room.'

'If you'll excuse me, Sir, you took Nanni Singh with you, the house was closed, bolted up.'

'This dust has been here for months,' said the General flatly. 'Months.'

'I'll speak to him today, Sir.'

'Can't turn my blasted back. Not for a moment.' He sat down heavily in a carved chair and cracked his elbow. 'Hell take it!' He rubbed his arm angrily. 'Just not my day. Upsetting morning. Get me a drink, Ben, or has he forgotten that too?'

Rooke turned the assorted bottles on the brass tray. 'No, Sir. What would you like?'

'Whisky. No water. I need a strengthener.'

'I imagine, Sir, he was pretty pleased to see you?'

The General took the glass and stared up at Rooke. 'Pleased? How should I know? Didn't say, silly bloody question.' He sipped his drink gratefully, pursed his lips, licked them, set the glass on the table by his chair.

'But he knew who you were, Sir? I mean . . .'

'Not bloody gaga, if that's what you mean. Dopy, concussed, but not daft, kept on trying to salute. I told him not to bother. Anyway,' he reached for his glass again, 'can't wear a cap in bed. Frightful business, absolutely frightful.'

'And I feel terribly to blame, my fault.' Rooke went over to the piano and sat heavily on the ornate stool.

The General watched him through half-closed eyes, sipped his drink. 'Bloody negligence on your part; what a damned

343

idiotic thing to do, leave a bucket of bloody beer down there. Damned stupid. You knew the Patrols were about? *Know* the rules.'

'Totally forgot, Sir. They were all coming after lunch; I told Kim to get things set up. I thought Pathans, Muslims . . . you know, forbidden to drink alcohol.'

'You've got a hell of a lot to learn about men, Muslim, Hindu or Christian, never been tempted yourself, for God's sake? No one around, ruddy great bucket of beer bottles begging to be swigged? Middle of the day?'

Rooke leaned on the piano lid, stared through the windows at the hazy hills. 'I'm dreadfully sorry: I simply didn't think.'

'Never do,' said the General with a shrug of hopelessness. 'You'll have to come up with all that at the court-martial. I suppose you'll plead ignorance, something. Unused to dealing with Indian Troops. European. White knees.'

Rooke shook his head. 'I won't plead anything, Sir. My fault. God, I'm sorry.'

The General cleared his throat, softened his tone fractionally. 'Well. There it is. Negligence, not the first time it's happened, human error, I suppose, and there's no need for you to wallow in self-pity, not all your fault by a very long chalk. I rather think, from what I've heard recently, that David Gaunt and this Naik have been running a sort of private feud for months now. Know anything about that?'

'I was up here on "Operation Palace", that morning. He was fooling about in the gardens with one of the statues. Nothing much, just ragging really, Gaunt was furious, tore him off a strip, but it wasn't much. Not enough for this to happen.'

The General stuck out his glass. 'Fill me up again, it's doing the trick, not too much, couple of fingers.' He fumbled for a handkerchief, wiped his brow. 'Well, whatever went wrong, it'll all come out in the wash; bloody nasty business.'

'When'll that be, Sir?'

'God knows, takes its time, witnesses, so on; evidence. Thank God they got the lot of them.'

'And David?' asked Rooke handing him his two-finger drink.

'Sending him up to Singapore soon as they can. I don't think we'll be seeing him back here with 2nd Brigade one way and another, until the court-martial, if he's fit, that is.' He picked up

344

the green envelope of photographs which Gaunt had brought on the Sunday morning, flipped through them in silence, looked briefly at one or two, stuck them back. 'Bloody good chap. Knew his job. Loved it. Lived for it you could say. Born soldier. We'll miss him. But there we are, damned bad show.' He waved the envelope across at Rooke. 'Better hang onto these, put them with his effects, will you? I suppose someone's arranging to bundle them all up, are they? You know?'

'No, Sir. But I'll find out.'

'Stick those with them. Know anything about a mouth organ?'

Rooke looked blank. 'A mouth organ?'

'Harmonica. Thing you blow.'

'No, Sir. Nothing.'

'Well he's fussing about that. Wants his mouth organ. The Sister told me.'

'I'll try and find out, Sir.'

'Said he was frightened he'd lost it; lost a mouth organ! God!' He got up suddenly and wandered down the long shadowy room to the wide bay windows. 'If that was all he'd lost.'

He stood for a little in silence, one hand in his trouser pocket, the other holding his glass against his chest. No fountain playing, today, in the lily-pool, the terrace blinding white in the sun, far below the swimming-pool, misted in haze; from where he stood he could only see the stern-like end sticking out over the valley. He laughed suddenly, a dry bark.

'Wasn't very romantic after all, was it? Sunday at the pool?'

'No. Not at all romantic, Sir.'

'And your young woman, Emily or whatever . . .'

'Oh. That. All right, Sir. I think; we had a long talk about things before, cleared the air. She's said she'll give it a try.'

'Give it a try?' said the General with a wry smile. 'Christ Almighty, sounds as if she was going to take up sailing, or something, not take up on a marriage.'

'Very much the same thing, Sir, isn't it?'

The General snorted. 'Don't start one of your "intellectual conversations", Ben not in the mood this morning. Just hope you know what you're doing, hope she knows too, for your sake. It won't be a joke, marriage never is. Know the saying? Marry in haste, repent in leisure; damned right.'

'Except this is not in haste, Sir. I think we'll manage. Together. We'll do it together.'

'And jolly good luck to you.'

Rooke suddenly picked up the brass frog from the desk beside him and examined it carefully, as if he had never seen it before.

'There is another thing, Sir, could I speak to you about it?'

'If you must,' said the General, indifferently. 'What's wrong?'

'Nothing wrong, Sir. Really. But about the court-martial?'

'What about it?'

'My negligence, the beer thing. Would that prejudice my chances of staying on in the Army, I mean?'

The General turned swiftly and stared at him with surprise. 'Staying on?'

'Yes, Sir.'

'The Army?' He came across the room slowly. 'Don't think I follow you. You haven't broken King's Regulations or anything, it was just a sort of House rule, if you like. Damned careless and thoughtless. Can't be blamed for what happened down there, it was going to happen one day, that seems clear, Gaunt was in for the chop. Not your fault. But you'll get a bloody good wigging, shouldn't wonder.'

'But it wouldn't prevent me from signing on?'

'Don't think so. No. But what the hell is all this? Your number's up, June, you said?'

'Yes, Sir. But I'd like to stay on, if that was possible.' He replaced the frog carefully in the long silence, folded his arms tightly behind his back. The General scratched his head worriedly.

'Now look here, Ben, this is all a bit sudden. Change of pace, isn't it? You got some damned silly romantic notion about the Army suddenly, that it?'

'No, Sir. Not romantic. I'd just like to stay on—with you. Quite simply it's the first time in my life that I have ever been really happy.'

'Been happy!' The General's eyes were wide. 'You got a touch of the sun, man?'

'No. When I first got here, to the Island, I was in a panic; like most of the others, all I could think of was to save my skin, after five years of war, and get the hell home out of someone else's mess, I didn't want any part of it. I felt I'd done my fair

346

share in Europe. Conscript mentality. I didn't give a damn who got the place, the Dutch or the terrorists. All I wanted was my rightful place on a troopship home all in one piece.'

'Conscript mentality all right. What's changed it?'

'A lot of things, Sir. The Division, joining you, growing up, belonging to something I became proud of . . . just things. It happens.'

'Take your word for it. Now look here. Confidentially, and mark that word, I'm moving on shortly. Delhi. GHQ Staff. Won't be with the Division much longer. Bloody awful blow after so long together, but there you are. Got to go where I'm most needed, what? And in any case they're pulling us *all* out by the end of the year, expect you know that? Gossip.'

'Yes, Sir. Rumours. October, November.'

'Near enough. Handing over the whole sheebang to the Dutch.' He finished his drink, looked at his watch. 'Just a small one, with soda. Drown it.' He watched Rooke narrowly as he crossed to the drink tray. 'So I don't quite see where you'd fit in, if you follow me?'

'In Delhi, Sir?' Rooke lifted the soda syphon, filled the glass to the brim. 'Perhaps I'm not really soldier material, is that it, Sir?'

The General took the glass with care. 'Balls,' he said tersely. 'Balls. I never said that and don't think it either. You'd be a damn fine soldier if you put your mind to it. I'd be glad to have you with me, very glad indeed: got my word for that. Need a kick up the arse from time to time, but you'd make it.' He took a long sip of his drink, wiped his lips. 'You just said that you are taking a wife, this Emily, that's correct?'

'Correct, Sir.'

'She know anything about this sudden whim of yours?'

'No, Sir. Not a whim either. Or sudden. I made up my mind some time ago; didn't want to say anything until I'd asked you. And then this Gaunt business and court-martial rather forced me, so I'm asking you now, Sir.'

'Bit too hasty. Cards on the table, right? Down to brass tacks? Look: even if it were possible for you to stay on, even if I pulled a few strings to get you up to India with me, *supposing* that I could, it couldn't possibly work out.'

'Because I'd be married, Sir?'

'Because she's a Eurasian, Ben.'

The dust motes spilling through the bars of sunlight whispered as they fell into the worn Persian rugs.

'It matters that much, Sir?'

'That much. Sorry. There it is. Fact. I know, I damned well know. Seen it all before. Can't change the rules, can't break the code. Especially there. Delhi. GHQ. Staff life, social life, that sort of thing. Not a hope.'

'But, Sir . . .'

'Don't "but" me! I bloody know!' The General sat heavily on the arm of his chair. He looked up at Rooke for a moment in silence and when he spoke again his voice was gruff.

'Sorry, damned sorry. Not my rules, not my regulations, not my damned code. It's been going on for over a hundred years and you won't change them. Ever. Oh, I know, I know she doesn't, well,' he searched about his boots with worried eyes 'she doesn't look like it. I know that. She's a damned pretty woman, a fine girl, hasn't got that God-awful accent, the give away, doesn't look, you know, "muddy"; none of that whining chip-on-the-shoulder business. But *they'd* know, you mark my words, and you wouldn't stand a snowball's chance in hell. That's flat. Flat as I can make it. Neither of you. Want to put her through all that? Want her to start a married life with that before her? Think it fair to the girl? Anyway . . .' He took another sip of his drink, stared at his boots again. 'Anyway, no shilly shally, very nice of you to say what you did, appreciate it. Very much. Thank you. I think we had a good time. As you say, you've learned a few things, done damned well, pulled yourself together splendidly, but this idea won't do. Still got stars in your eyes, eh?' He looked up, smiling slightly. 'Well, you keep 'em. What's wrong with a few stars, I'd like to know? But they're not for her. Take her back home, it won't be easy for you both, but I reckon you'll get through. But not here. That's out; impossible. No more to be said. Got it? Message clear?'

'Clear, Sir. Thank you.'

'Didn't like saying all that, you know. Understand each other, don't we?'

'Perfectly.'

'And what I said just now about marrying in haste and repenting at leisure, it's only what *I* did, Ben. Not what you'll do, so strike that off the record, will you?'

348

'Yes, Sir.'

'And now,' said the General rising heavily to his feet, 'let's get back to the normal routine, eh? Back to business, shall we?' He looked at his watch, finished off his drink. 'Eleven-thirty. Started a bit early on my burra peg today. What time is Smedley coming up? Now, isn't it?'

'Yes, Sir, about now.'

'Well, I'll see him alone. Show him in and then clear off, it's a personal matter. See there's ice, they live on ice, the Yanks, and tell Nanni Singh about the dust. Bloody disgraceful, can't turn my ruddy back.'

Walter Arthur Smedley, Wally A. to his close friends, none of whom were on this side of the ocean, had the appearance of a cautious evangelist. Everything about him was neat, compact and tidy. Small head, small hands, small feet, astonishing in an American, and an extremely small smile which glimmered, occasionally, in a long pale face through rectangular lips. His eyes, thought the General, were rather like two black grapes in the pallor, gleaming with suppressed zeal. He was spendidly composed, accepting his glass of tomato juice with grace, and looking about the monstrous room with well-feigned pleasure.

'I am awed, General Cutts. Awed. It is all greatly impressive.'

'Would you like to sit here,' asked the General genially. 'Or here? One soft, one hard. Some people like a hard seat, I know; I'm all for a bit of comfort myself, but take your pick.'

Mr Smedley selected a black lacquer 'Chippendale' chair, straight-backed, garlanded all about with little golden dragons. 'This will be just fine. In the heat I find it cooler. Back home I have a personal chair, you might say, which is very, very fine, carved from oak, very simple, about seventeen-twenty-five they think, and I am very contented in that. However, our winters in New England can be exceptionally harsh, and then, well then I fear the flesh becomes a little weak and I am forced to use a cushion. For the seat, you know.' He smiled eagerly. Happy to share his private, and intimate, life-style.

'Now,' said the General, pouring himself a large glass of soda water and sitting in his over-cushioned ebony chair. 'Mr Smedley,' he raised his glass, 'your health, I hope you have enough ice in your glass?'

'This is just fine,' said Mr Smedley affably. 'Just perfect.'

'Now, what can I do for you? Your note suggested that this was a personal business.'

'That is so. Quite so,' said Mr Smedley putting down his glass and removing his glasses which he polished furiously with a white handkerchief. 'It is quite personal.' He slipped the glasses on again, put his handkerchief away and folded his hands tidily in his barren lap.

'And it is something which I can help you with, is that it?'

'Precisely so. You could be greatly helpful, because I understand that you are very well-acquainted with the person in question.'

'Who is?'

'A Miss Dora Foto, a perfectly charming lady, as I well know. Perfectly charming.'

'Yes,' said the General shortly. 'She is.'

'And I believe, that you are acquainted with our Mr Novak, Bernard, but you will probably remember him best as just "Buzz". A comical name I always think. Buzz, Buzz, Buzz . . .' He waved a small, thin-boned hand about the room airily. 'Buzz, busy as a bee.'

'Yes. Mr Novak: he has been a guest here, pleasant man. Been to Newfoundland, I remember, in a canoe.'

'That could be Buzz. Very industrious, very curious to learn about other countries, a great pioneer spirit, which of course is inherent in every true American.'

'Quite,' said the General. 'How can I assist you in the matter of Miss Foto?'

'Well,' Mr Smedley folded his hands together again, moth's wings closing, 'Mr Novak is extremely fond of the lady, it is not difficult to see why of course, a more enchanting person would be hard to find. Even on this Island of many delights. Now he is off to another assignment shortly. To Tokyo, Japan. It is a very important move for him,' he smiled through the rectangular lips, 'as you will appreciate? Japan offers, we feel, far more opportunities for a man of his great capabilities than this delightful, but small it must be admitted, Island, and the situation, as you know only too well, General, is not what one might call really stable yet, is it? That is to say, not for a thriving new business venture. So much has to be done here

350

before we could risk a heavy investment; you will sympathize with that, I have no doubt at all. When one sows a field of corn one hopes to have the pleasure of the harvest, that is so, I think? And we in America really do not see that possibility here right now. As of this moment. It'll come, it'll *come*. In time. But we are a vigorous nation, we are a flourishing nation, we wish to share our bounty with our Asian brothers, but just perhaps this place is not *quite* ready, so we move on, we move, always we move, to pastures new.'

'Like locusts,' said the General and drained his soda water.

Mr Smedley's grape eyes did not flick. 'It is a quaint analogy, coming as it does with harvests and pastures. I see your point, I do indeed, but I confess that I prefer bee to locust; the one pollinates and spreads plenty, the other is not such a happy choice! However, that is bringing us back to Mr Novak, Buzz.'

'Let us by all means do that,' said the General. 'Do I take it that Miss Foto wishes to go with Mr Novak to Japan?'

'She is most anxious to go, he to take her, I to bless, if you will forgive the paternal phraseology, them. But, and this is the point, just what is your candid opinion of Miss Foto from the point of view of managing?'

The General raised his small red eyebrows. 'Managing?' he echoed dully.

'I am given to understand that she has assisted you from the moment that you all arrived in this Island, that she has arranged housing, organized gatherings etcetera, that she has, in fact, been a kind of Woman Friday, if you will forgive the vulgarity.'

'I'll forgive it,' said the General. 'Doubt very much if she would, however. Yes, in principle what you say is so; she was of very great assistance to us when we arrived here, loyal, kind, willing, nothing too much trouble . . . you can take it from me, a great comfort to this Division. She was, is, clearly devoted to it, to its responsibilities, and all that it represents.'

Mr Smedley clapped his mothy little hands together in delight. 'I am just so very thrilled to hear all these words, General. Loyalty, kindness, willingness, devotion to her responsibilities. Words which are so very, very important to a potential servant of a great country.'

The General rose from his chair as if struck by a charge of electricity. 'Servant!' he bellowed. 'Servant! You come here, Mr Smiddley, on a personal mission and behave as if you were seeking references for a bloody cook! Do you know who I am? Do you even know who Miss Foto is? No, obviously not, otherwise I would not be under the burden of your company! Miss Foto is a remarkable, exceptional woman. I find your enquiries damned distasteful and offensive.' Beside himself with anger and tiredness, he poured himself four fingers of whisky and sat down at the far end of the room on the piano stool staring through the tall windows.

'I had not the slightest intention of being offensive, indeed I am truly shattered that you consider me to have been so: I came only to ask you, General, as the Military Governor of this Island, for your personal opinion of someone of whose capabilities you are aware, and whose respectability you can endorse.'

'Respectability?' said the General from the far end of the room, using the word as if he had just discovered it in a neglected pocket. 'Respectability? What has that to do with anything? Miss Foto is an honourable woman. She is a *close personal friend*. That is all I have to say.'

Mr Smedley left his Chippendale chair carefully. Folding both moth-like hands he moved, uncertainly, into the middle of the room and looked earnestly at the angry back which the piano stool presented to him.

'I know that I am a newcomer, Sir, no one knows better than I that fact, and I don't know all the facts and figures, but there are tiny, weeny, little rumours floating about . . .'

The General's face was scarlet with anger. 'Rumours? What rumours?' He turned slowly on the stool.

Mr Smedley spread his fingers like wings, they trembled gently in the warm air. 'Of no consequence, General, gossip, idle gossip, no more. I am certain.'

'I should bloody well think so. Miss Foto spent the last four years in a prison camp. Ever seen one? Been near one? Smelled one, Mr Smaddly? How can you ask a woman, after that, if she is a good, normal, honourable, gentle woman fit for your blasted country! Tell me that, sir!'

'We have to be so very careful now, General, in this terrible state of flux in the world, after this really terrifying war, just

352

whom we let in. An American passport, even a paper with a consular stamp upon it, is worth more today than all the gold in the Klondike.'

The General left his stool and walked deliberately across the frightful room to Mr Smedley's wincing side. 'Respectability? Eh? Capabilities? Devotion to cause, loyalty? Those the words she needs to get one of your ruddy little stamps? To trot off to Japan with your Mr Novak? Well, she's got 'em all. I endorse that statement. She's got 'em all and more besides: how many stamps does that entitle her to? How many?'

Mr Smedley smiled slightly, inclined his head like a neat bird. 'I think only one, General, one will be sufficient: at this point. Mr Novak will be very, very happy. If Miss Foto will ease his burdens, help him with his duties, make life more tolerable under very, very difficult conditions, then, why . . .' The moth-hands spread delicately again, transparent almost in a shaft of sunlight. 'Why, she should go with him. Just for a time.'

The double doors at the far end of the room opened silently and Nanni Singh stole on slippered feet through the room with a high-held tray.

'What do you want, what is it?' said the General in irritation.

'Is midday, Burra Sahib, you said midday bring extra ice. I bring.' He rattled the glass jug, set it on the brass tray, spun round and went away.

'I must go,' said Mr Smedley in relief at the interruption. 'Midday! My saints, I had no idea the time had sped so fast.' He offered the light hand. 'So good of you to spare me so long. I apologize if I have caused you any anger, General. It's just that we all have to be so ultra-careful now. We are facing another exodus here you see, South-East Asia will be in ferment for generations to come, General. It's a big responsibility for us both. I serve my country just as you serve yours, with pride and diligence, it is a heavy burden and a proud duty.'

'From what I gather you're thinking of fixing her papers to go to Japan, is that it, Mr Smuddley?'

'That is so. In simple terms.'

'Not to America?'

Mr Smedley shook his head regretfully. 'Oh, dear me, no. My word, no. Not America. That is strictly not my department. But you know, General, Mr Novak, that is Buzz, has his

353

sights set very, very high. Ambitious fellow! I do believe that there is a little gleam in his eye, you know that? And what can you do, Sir, when two hearts beat as one together. Eh? We are helpless in the hands of romance I always say.'

'Romance?' said the General tiredly.

'Well, you know something? I'll tell you this, *entre nous*.' Mr Smedley wagged a slim white finger at the defeated red face glowering before him. 'A middle-aged Polish–American in love is no way different from any callow youth in High School! Not a whit!' He patted his thin hips, looked briskly about the room. 'Now then. Did I bring anything with me? No, in the car. It was so good of you to spare me the time and to support our, or should I say Buzz Novak's? hopes. And this room. My! If Miss Foto did all this, well? What can I say? A really great job. I can see you are losing a real treasure.'

The General's heart made a slight swerve, almost stopped for a second, continued on its sluggish way. 'When does all this arrangement, so to speak, take place, may I ask?'

'Leaving here, you mean? For Japan?'

'That is what I meant.'

'The twentieth I think. *The Amsterdam*. Full ship but I managed to obtain two berths. It'll be uncomfortable, but that isn't the main priority. Anyway, Singapore first stop next morning.'

The General swung wide the double doors, called loudly for Rooke who was instantly at his side. 'Mr Smiddle is leaving.'

'Perhaps I shall see you at the ship, Sir? Evening sailing, I'm told.'

The General looked at him for a second with tired eyes. 'I have never found severance particularly pleasurable,' he said.

As Rooke swung the jeep through the main dock yard gates he saw the funnel of *The Amsterdam* rising high above the battered godown roofs. A thread of thin vapour spiralled into the late afternoon sky. Nothing much, he thought, has changed here. The same smell of jute-sacks, coffee, rubber and oil. The Rotterdam Lloyd sign still hung brokenly like a fallen brooch. Crates, bales, boxes, scurrying Indonesians in flapping shorts, rickshaws, cycles, trucks and jeeps, tall cranes marching against the skyline, skeleton fingers.

He parked the jeep alongside a Staff Humber, pushed his way through the crowds. There were more civilians now than before, returning internees, worried women holding fretful children, Military Police, RAPWI personnel bare-headed in sweaty shirts and arm-bands, hurrying Dutch officials clutching sheaves of papers; at the far end of the dock a neat rectangle of British troops in full marching order, kit bags on their shoulders waiting to embark, laughing, joking, pushing each other lightly, shouting obscenities at the pedlars besieging them with trays of cold drinks and cheap, carved wooden toys. Coming towards him, little swagger-stick gently tapping people out of his path, crimson lanyard swinging, Pullen: just as he had arrived so many months before.

'Spot you a mile off! Stand out in a crowd like this even.' He was smiling tightly under his neat moustache. 'Down here to say farewell to the Foto, that it? Do I guess correctly?'

'Guess correctly. Old Man's idea. Sort of courtesy, if you like. Brought her a note. Final duties.'

'She's aboard. Went on quite early, with Novak and a couple of Yankees; you want to go on?'

'Can I?'

Pullen looked about, then towards the British troops who had started to sing good-naturedly, 'Why Are We Waiting?' He shrugged. 'Well, a bit of a rumble bumble at the moment, let them all get up and then go on. Get the chaps sorted out; all mixed up with the internees at present, it's pretty chaotic, I doubt if you'd find her.' He stared up at the serried row of decks above him. 'She was up there a little time ago. Leaning over the rail. Promenade Deck, aft. Difficult to see with so many faces. Ship's busting.' He laughed shortly. 'All a bit wistful, isn't it? A sailing?' His eyes were dull.

'Wistful. Yes. Funny feeling. The Old Man said the other day it was a severance.'

'Damned right. What else?' He rubbed his nose. 'Clair's aboard.'

'You saw her?'

'Saw. Her. All the family. Seemed to have managed very well. She always will, of course. Didn't see me. Didn't want to butt in, you know. Kept my distance. The boy, Wim, you remember? Think he saw me, waved at someone. I didn't wave

355

back. Think he saw me. Pretended not to notice, wiser really.'

'Yes.'

'I mean what's the use, eh?' He looked vaguely about the bustling crowd, stroked his moustache. 'Actually, I suppose, I really came down because old "Cash and Carry" has just come in: remember? The LST? Think it was the one you came on originally. Shuttle service. Frightfully good fellow aboard brings me bits and pieces from time to time, most welcome. I think I've possibly got a case of White Horse and, most important, a couple of tins of baccy. Balkan Sobranie. He said four ounces! Think of that! Haven't had a pipe for ages, reduced to chewing that filthy gum stuff. Can you imagine? Awful habit, no wonder I've got an ulcer.'

Rooke was looking up at the scabby white side of the ship, the decks a blur of pink and brown faces, waving arms. Someone dropped a can of beer onto the dock, in a burst of laughter and shouts of 'Silly fart! Booze below there!'

Pullen tapped him on the arm with his little stick. 'Look here, try and get aboard as soon as that lot are all on. There go the last of the women and children. Odd isn't it? The last of European rule, women and kids scrambling up a gangplank. Well. There we are. The sunset, I suppose. I'm off to see old "Cash and Carry", we've got about half an hour till sailing. Meet you back here?'

'Fine,' said Rooke. 'Here.' Poor Pullen, he thought, the Englishman in love. Mustn't show your feelings. Bury them in your tobacco-pouch. He fanned himself slowly with the slim buff file which he had decided to bring down with him. Empty of photographs, but easy to spot, even from the boat-deck. If she saw him. If he saw her. She might not. Probably have to give Novak the note. He had to deliver it, no getting away from that. As soon as they had embarked the troops he'd go aboard.

A soft plucking at his sleeve, he turned quickly, looked down into a smiling, round, face under a wide-brimmed cotton hat bright with daisies. 'You remember me, Sir. Is Pearl?'

He took her offered hand. 'Goodness me! Pearl! Of course, *Daily Cobra*. What are you doing here? You left us, didn't you, a couple of weeks ago?'

'That's right. I left. Most sad. Miss Emmie not say to you about me?'

356

'Yes, yes, perhaps she did: I'm not sure. You were ill, I think?'

Pearl gave a little shriek of laughter, covered her mouth apologetically with her hand, her eyes danced with pleasure. 'Not ill. I am not ill. I am married, Sir!'

'Oh gosh, I'd no idea. Or if I had, I forgot. How marvellous. Miss Emmie didn't say.'

'Oh yes. Married. I am most happy girl. I am Mrs Dennis Batt, you know this?'

'Batt?' said Rooke blankly.

'You know Mr Batt. You had big trouble with him in the City, he is with Major Nettles, you know, and you were very brave to him. He tells me. He tells everyone.'

'Oh,' said Rooke. 'Corporal *Batt* . . . Signals?'

'Is so. Is so. Is Corporal. Now we are going together on this ship to London. You know this place? Is very lovely, I think?'

'Yes. Lovely. Of course I remember. Is he over there?'

Pearl nodded happily, the cotton daisies bobbing. 'Is there, you can see.' She pointed towards the troops, kit-bags swinging, brasses gleaming. Put her hands to her mouth suddenly and screamed, 'Coooeee! Dennis!'

Corporal Batt turned suddenly, shifted his kit-bag, waved back.

'I must say goodbye, Pearl, excuse me.'

'He will be most happy, Sir. Is still waving to you.'

Rooke hurried across the cobbles to the slow-moving group at the foot of the gangplank. 'Corporal Batt, I'd no idea, you and Pearl.'

'Good to see you, Sir. Yes, me and Pearl. Who said never the twain shall meet, eh?'

'Splendid news. I am glad. I didn't put two and two together.'

'No, Sir. I did that in a manner of speaking.'

'No worse for the bang on your head, I gather?'

'Can't be too sure, Sir. Must have gone a bit do-lally-tap, I reckon, otherwise why this? Married man. Lumbered myself with old Pearl girl, what do you know?'

'Well, the very best of luck.'

'I'll need that, Sir. A rum old day that was, Sir, in the Convent, not nice really. Owe you a lot, Sir, thought I'd never see today.'

'Nonsense.'

'Well, it's all nonsense, in a way, Sir, isn't it? Not keen on war, Sir, are you? I mean, what does it ever prove Sir, bugger bloody all, if you'll pardon the expression. No one wins.'

There was a sudden shouting, soldiers shoved and hustled up the steep gangplank.

'You'll miss your place, Corporal, off you go. Good luck.'

Corporal Batt hoisted his kit-bag back onto his shoulder. 'Well, Sir, any time you're near Clissold Park just drop in, cup of char, glass of beer. We'll be there, Lordship Road, near the cemetery, can't miss it. Proud to have known you, Sir.'

'Was happy, isn't it? Dennis?' Pearl was pulling on a pair of white crochet gloves.

'Yes. He was happy. I was too. Pearl, tell me, I believe Miss Foto is sailing with you, that right?'

Pearl clapped delighted cotton hands. 'Miss Foto! Yes! Is on the ship, I saw her, she spoke with me, was very kind when I say about Dennis and me; she had tears, you know this thing?'

'Would you do me a very big favour, Pearl?' He produced the General's letter and held it towards her clasped hands. 'Would you take this to her, when you see her, as soon as you are settled down. It is from General Cutts. Just to say thank you. It will make her very happy. Could you do that?'

'Oh Sir, yes. Could.' She took the letter and put it carefully in her cheap crocodile bag. 'I am honoured to do this, Sir. Look! Dennis! He is waving!'

They turned and waved together as Corporal Batt shuffled out of sight.

'Now we will perhaps go. The wives. I am so frightening that they will forget.'

'They won't forget,' said Rooke. 'Look, here comes the chap you need, off you go.'

A sweating Military Police Sergeant came hurrying across to the little group of Army wives, a clipboard of papers in his hand. 'Now then! Come along, my ladies. All NCOs and OR wives follow me, come along girls, don't waddle about like ducks, get your backsides up, your wedding lines ready, got your things together? That's the ticket, learned the ruddy National Anthem? Off we go then: left, right, left, right, left . . .'

358

Pearl feverishly grabbed a small straw basket, slung the crocodile bag on her elbow, reached up and took Rooke's face in her hands and kissed him firmly on the mouth. Her eyes were swimming with tears. 'I cannot speak . . . you say for me to Miss Emmie?' Without waiting for his reply she turned and scurried after her little group, wiping her face with a white gloved hand.

Rooke wandered slowly back to the jeep. Kim looked at him anxiously, put his tooth-pick away and reached for a tin of cigarettes. 'You wanting cigarettes, Sahib? I have. Most plenty . . .'

He took the cigarette, lit it, spun the match away. The crowds were thinning out, or gathering in tight groups nearer the ship. Movement became a little more urgent, people hurried, last-minute orders were yelled. The sky was fading. At the sudden harsh blast from the ship's siren, Kim ducked and stuffed his fingers into his ears, bowing his head low in pain. The shadows had grown longer, a lint-pink light began to suffuse the hazy sky, an ambulance rumbled past them, lurching over the rusty tracks and shell-pocked cobbles and suddenly he looked up and saw her. At the far end of the Promenade Deck. A slight figure in the blue suit with white cuffs which he remembered so well, bandeau round her head. She was quite alone, standing very still, hands on the rail looking out over the godown roofs towards the City through an enormous pair of round sun-glasses. He left the jeep and walked deliberately towards the ship, holding the buff file closely to his body; when he was immediately below her, beside a rope-lashed bollard, he raised the file high in the air waving it slowly back and forth like a heavy banner. For a moment she did not see him, and then quite suddenly looked down. He stilled the file above his head for a count of two. Lowered it gently to his side. She nodded very slightly, raised one small hand, opened her fingers like a tiny fan. She looked very small, very distant so far above him. He thought she might have smiled, then she turned and went away.

Gulls cried and swung about the stern, ropes coiled down, splashing into the greasy swell. Someone shouted down at Rooke and he jumped away from the bollard as the ropes fell from the ship like strings cut from a parcel: the siren went

359

again, three sharp warning blasts. He walked slowly through the small groups of people standing close together, women in batik sarongs and cheap sandals, girls in cotton frocks, handkerchiefs fluttering like wilting petals, men in crumpled whites, soldiers in trim jungle-green. No cheering, an occasional name called suddenly in loud regret, a truck back-firing, the rumble and squeal of iron wheels as the gangplank rattled down onto the quayside. The gulls wheeled about in the fading day. He leant against the jeep, arms folded, file still in his hand. *The Amsterdam* looked very big from this distance. A tall white cliff. Somewhere on the lower deck the sound of singing, at first two or three voices only, then the volume grew as others joined and courage mounted. The words floating clear and crisp through the soft, still, air.

> 'Oh! I don't want to be a soldier,
> I don't want to go to war,
> I'd rather hang around Piccadilly Underground,
> Living on the earnings
> Of a High-born Lady . . .'

'Done your errands? Everything all right, shipshape?' said Pullen, coming towards him with a large canvas bag.

'Yes. Errands done. Mission completed. Didn't go aboard. Someone she knows took her the note. Better really.'

'Much. Much better. I must say "Cash and Carry" turned up trumps. Almost.' His voice trailed away huskily. They stood in silence. Lights sprang up in the distant portholes. The siren gave one long, last shuddering cry.

'Four ounces of Balkan Sobranie. Now that *is* a luxury. It'll keep me going jolly comfortably. Until the next time.' He patted the canvas bag gently, looked up. 'She's going, Rooke.'

The white cliff was inching slowly away from the quay. The gulls swung high in the darkening sky, then swooped down in a tumbling flock to skim, scream and bicker in the swirling waters astern. Far out at the end of the jetty the lighthouse blinked urgently. A star was up.

Pullen cleared his throat very softly. 'Well,' he said. 'Well, that's that. I rather think that this is where we came in, isn't it?'

A Note on the Type

This book was set on the Monotype in Baskerville No. 353, a recutting of a typeface originally designed by John Baskerville (1706–75). Baskerville, a writing master in Birmingham, England, began experimenting about 1750 with type design and punch cutting. His first book, set throughout in his new types, was a Virgil in royal quatro, published in 1757, and it was followed by other famous editions from his press. Baskerville's types, which are distinctive and elegant in design, were a forerunner of what we know today as the "modern" group of typefaces.

Composed by Ebenezer Baylis, Worcester, England, and printed and bound by American Book–Stratford Press, Saddle Brook, New Jersey.